YOU'RE READING THE WRONG WAY!

This book has been printed in the original Japanese format in order to preserve the orientation of the original artwork. Have fun with it!

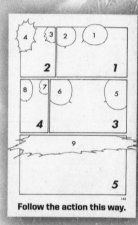

Follow the action this way.

THE STORY CONCLUDES IN VOLUME 2!

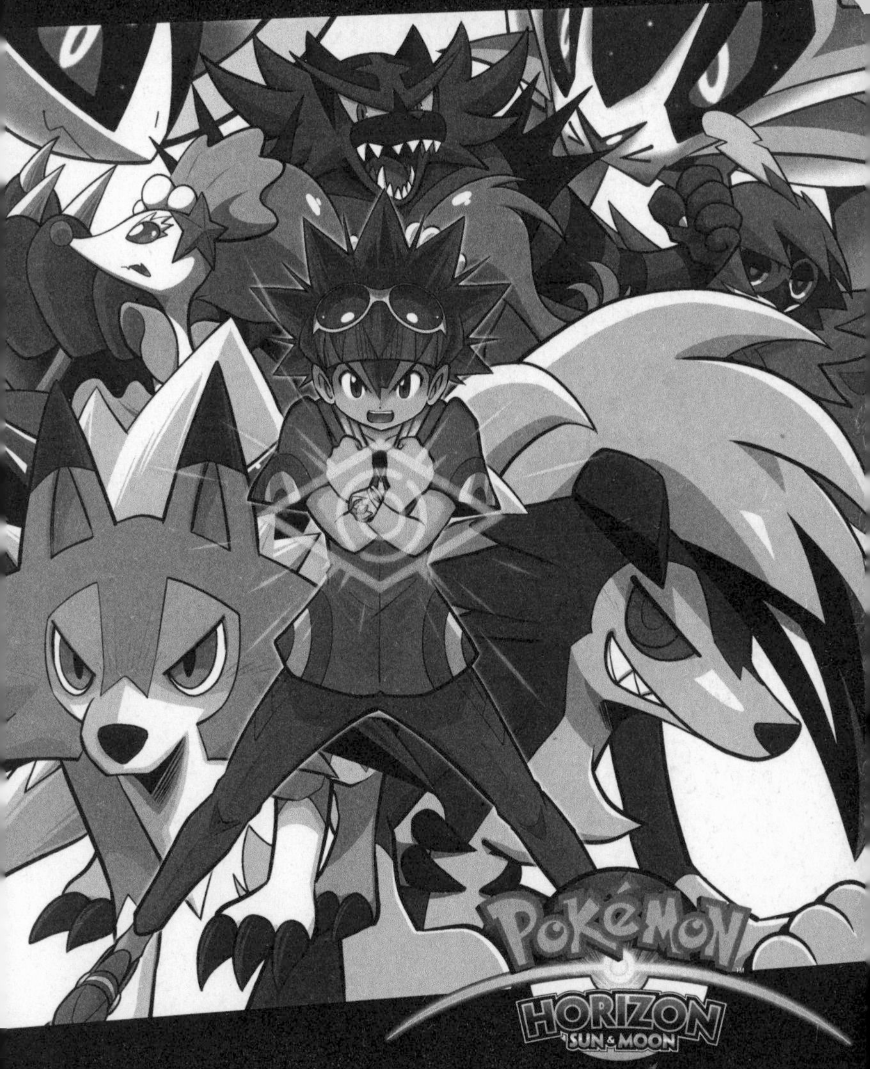
Pokémon
HORIZON
SUN & MOON

Akira's Rockruff evolves into Lycanroc but won't stay in its evolved form or follow orders! And a lot is at stake with Team Kings trying to take over the world and all. Is Akira's new acquaintance Tokio, with his charismatic Trainer talent, friend or foe? And what role will Legendary Pokémon Lunala and Solgaleo play in this epic showdown between night and day...?!

Pokémon Horizon: Sun & Moon
Volume 1
VIZ Media Edition

Story and Art by TENYA YABUNO

©2018 The Pokémon Company International.
©1995–2017 Nintendo / Creatures Inc. / GAME FREAK inc.
TM, ®, and character names are trademarks of Nintendo.
POKÉMON HORIZON Vol. 1
by Tenya YABUNO
© 2017 Tenya YABUNO
All rights reserved.
Original Japanese edition published by SHOGAKUKAN.
English translation rights in the United States of America, Canada,
the United Kingdom, Ireland, Australia and New Zealand arranged
with SHOGAKUKAN.

Original Cover Design/Takuya KUROSAWA

Translation/Tetsuichiro Miyaki
English Adaptation/Annette Roman
Touch-Up & Lettering/Susan Daigle-Leach
Design/Julian [JR] Robinson
Editor/Annette Roman

Printed in the U.S.A.

Published by VIZ Media, LLC
P.O. Box 77010
San Francisco, CA 94107

10 9 8 7 6 5 4 3 2 1
First printing, July 2018

viz.com

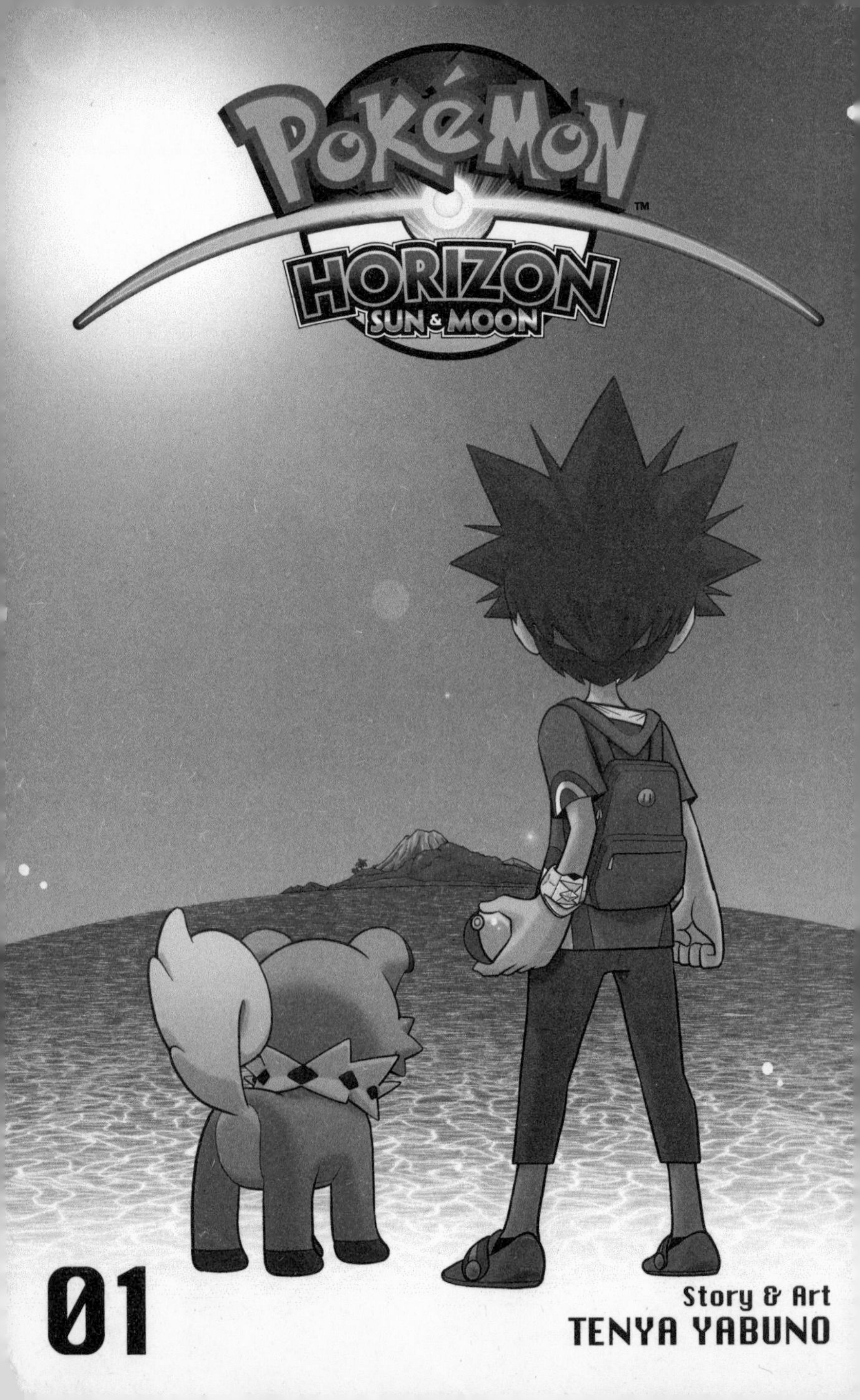
POKéMON™
HORIZON
SUN & MOON
01
Story & Art
TENYA YABUNO

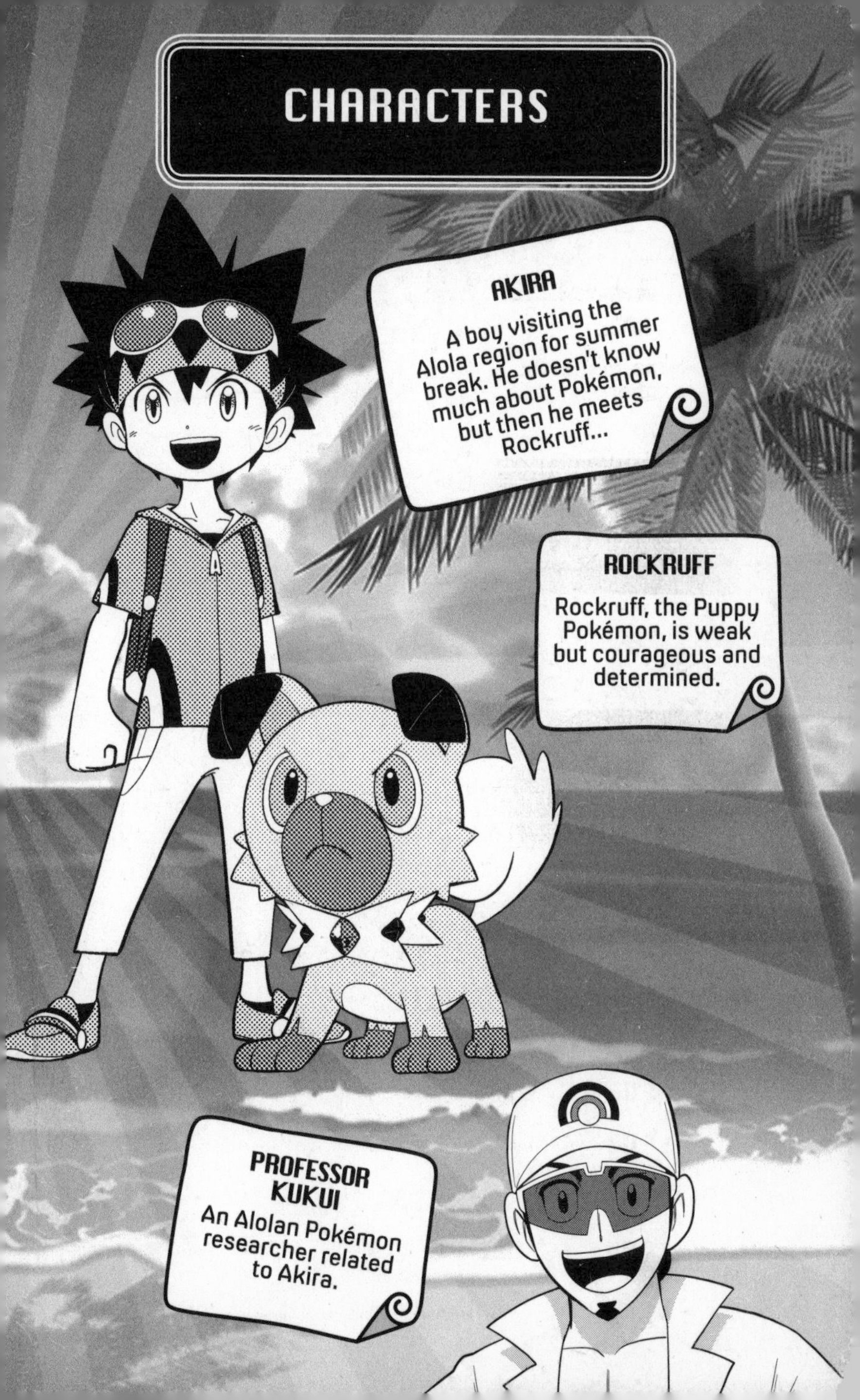
CHARACTERS
AKIRA
A boy visiting the Alola region for summer break. He doesn't know much about Pokémon, but then he meets Rockruff...
ROCKRUFF
Rockruff, the Puppy Pokémon, is weak but courageous and determined.
PROFESSOR KUKUI
An Alolan Pokémon researcher related to Akira.

HALA

A kahuna, or master, who teaches Z-Moves.

MANA

A girl striving to become the best Pokémon Trainer she can be.

DULIO

A member of Team Kings, an evil organization that seeks world domination.

TOKIO

A very powerful itinerant Pokémon Trainer. What is his true identity...?

EVENT HORIZON

EVENT 01	JOURNEY TO A NEW HORIZON	6
EVENT 02	THE POWER OF TEAMWORK	46
EVENT 03	TRAVELING TRAINER TOKIO	79
EVENT 04	MASTERING THE Z-MOVE!	115
EVENT 05	ROCKRUFF'S SECRET	149

Event 1: Journey to a New Horizon

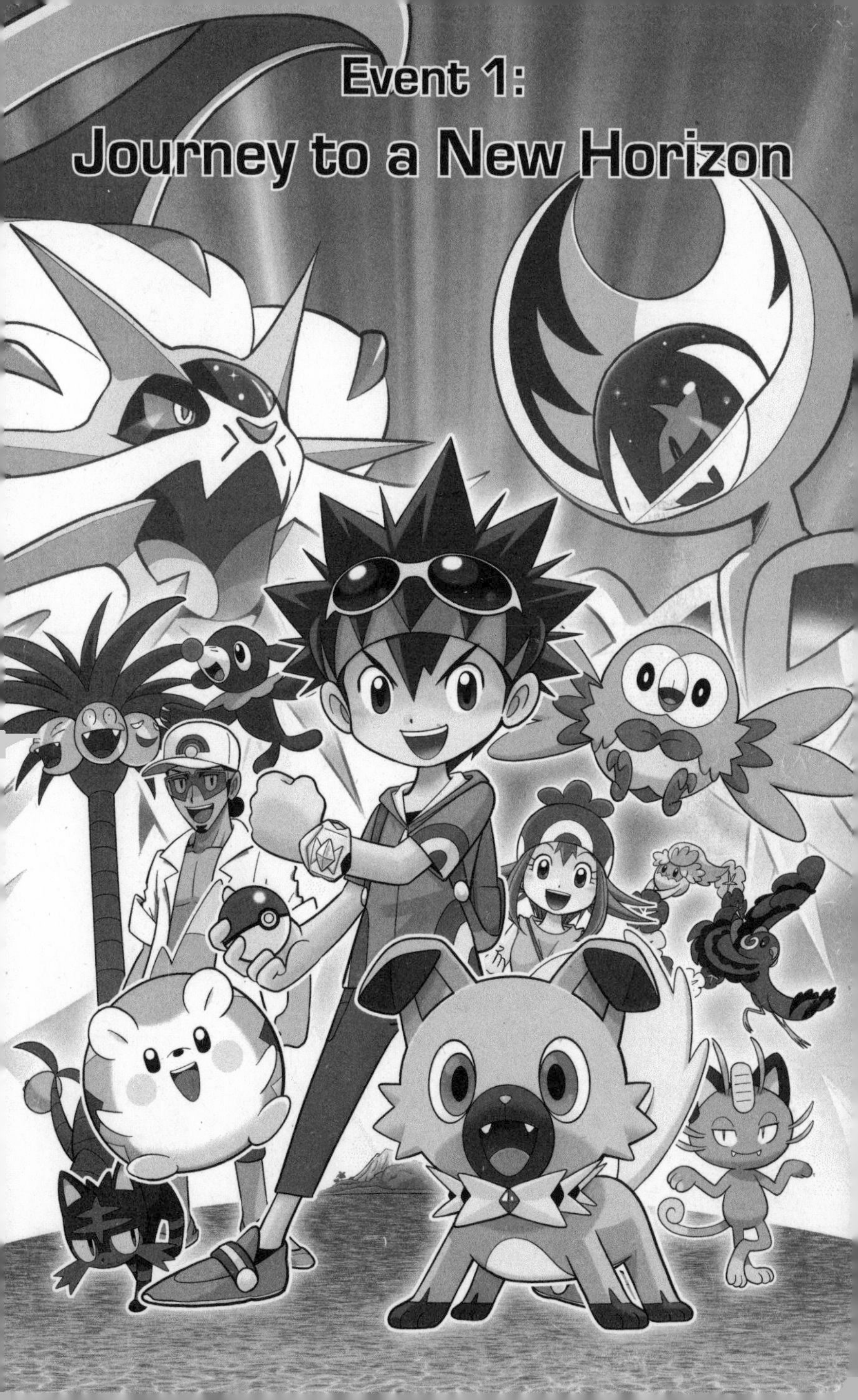

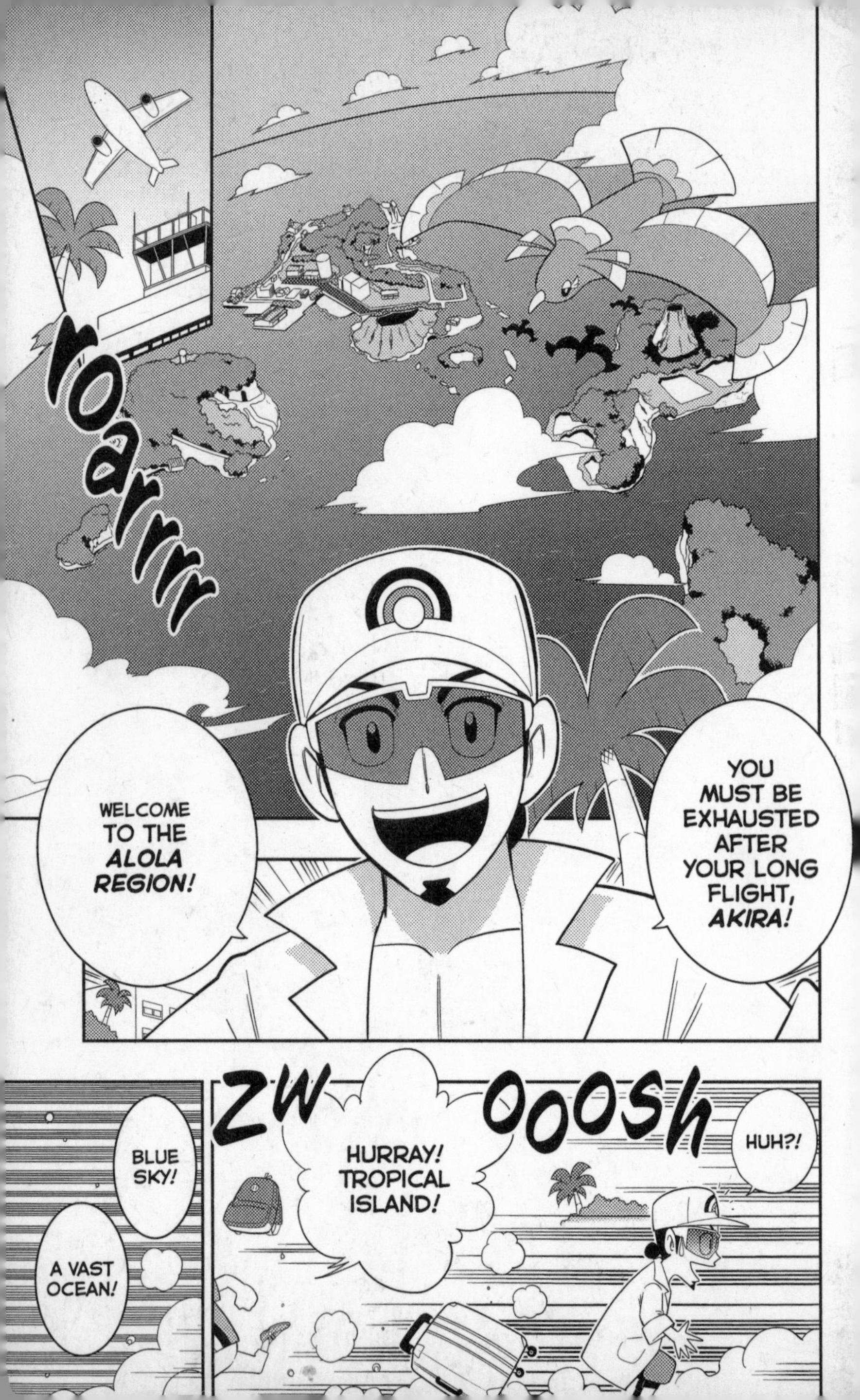
ROARRRR
YOU MUST BE EXHAUSTED AFTER YOUR LONG FLIGHT, AKIRA!
WELCOME TO THE ALOLA REGION!
HUH?!
ZW OOOSH
HURRAY! TROPICAL ISLAND!
BLUE SKY!
A VAST OCEAN!

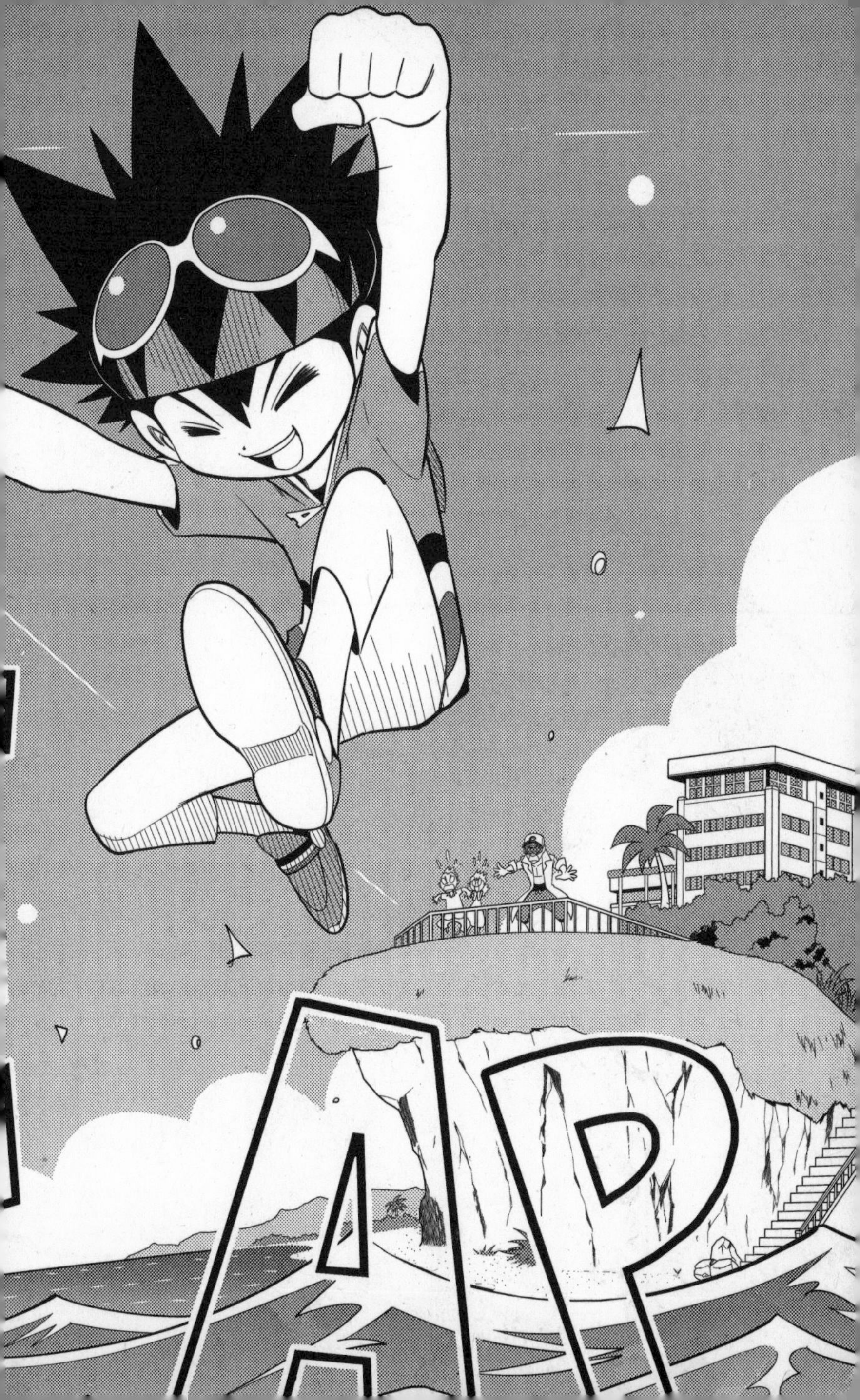
AP

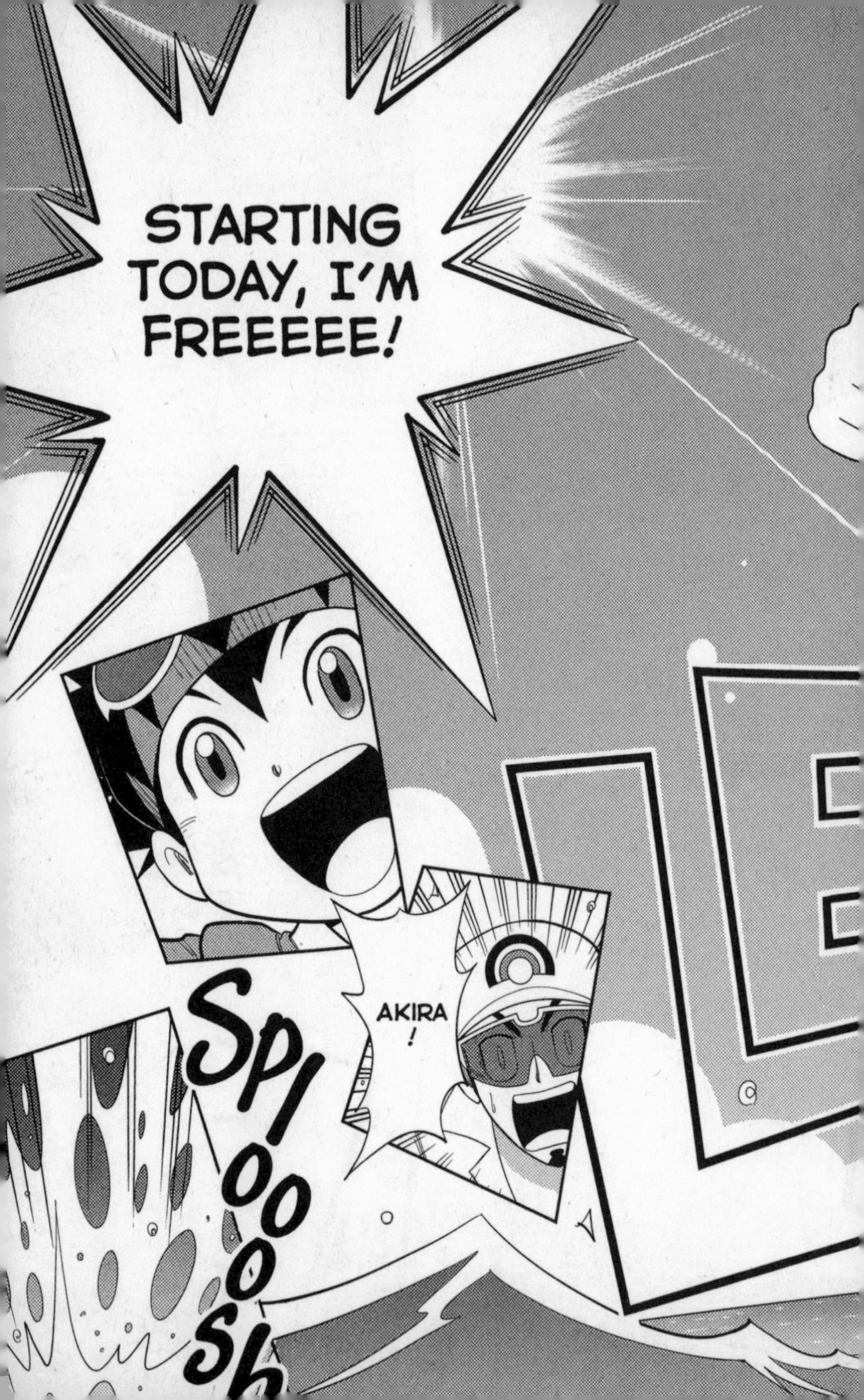
STARTING TODAY, I'M FREEEEEE!
AKIRA!
SPlOOOOSh

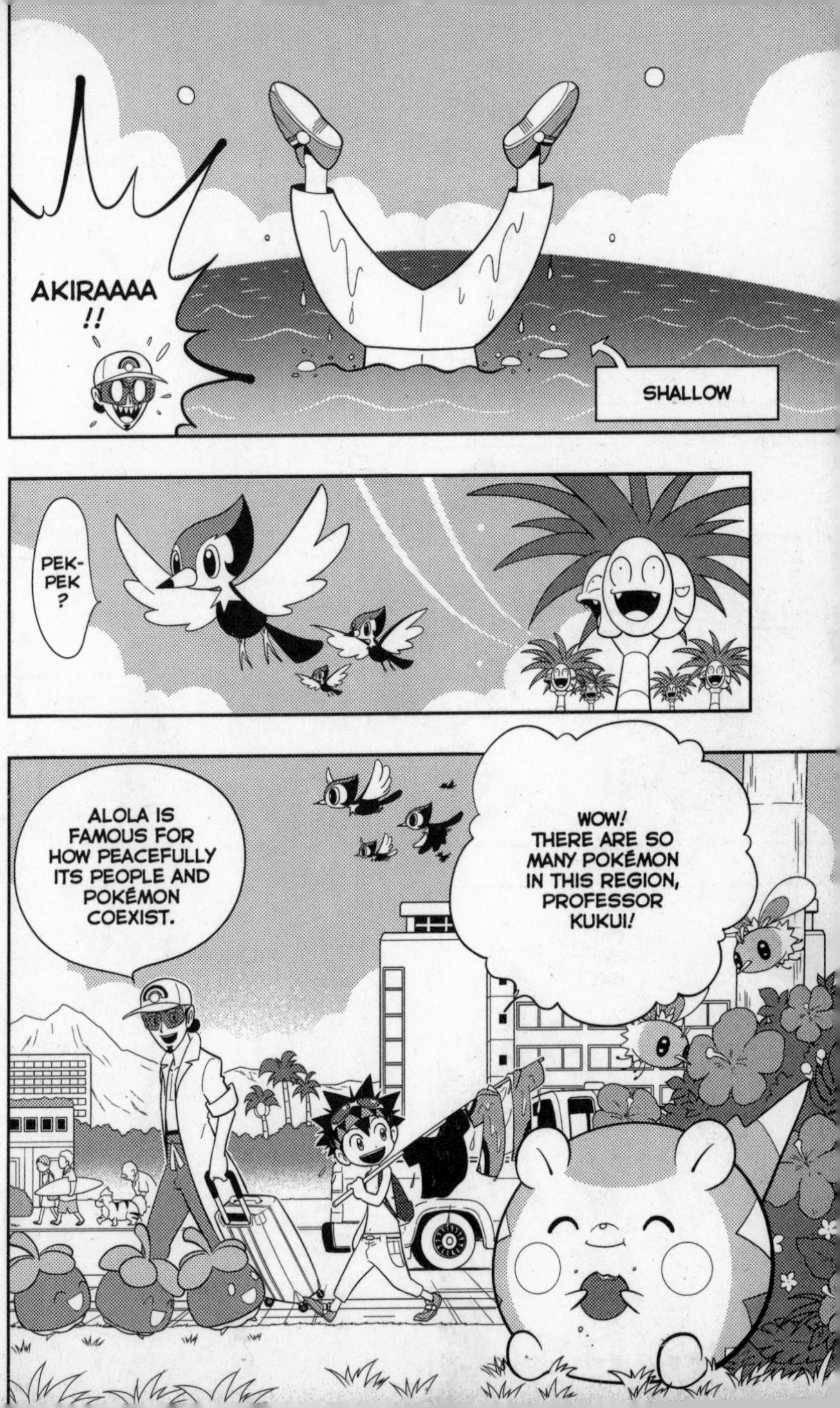
AKIRAAAA !!
SHALLOW
PEK-PEK ?
WOW! THERE ARE SO MANY POKÉMON IN THIS REGION, PROFESSOR KUKUI!
ALOLA IS FAMOUS FOR HOW PEACEFULLY ITS PEOPLE AND POKÉMON COEXIST.

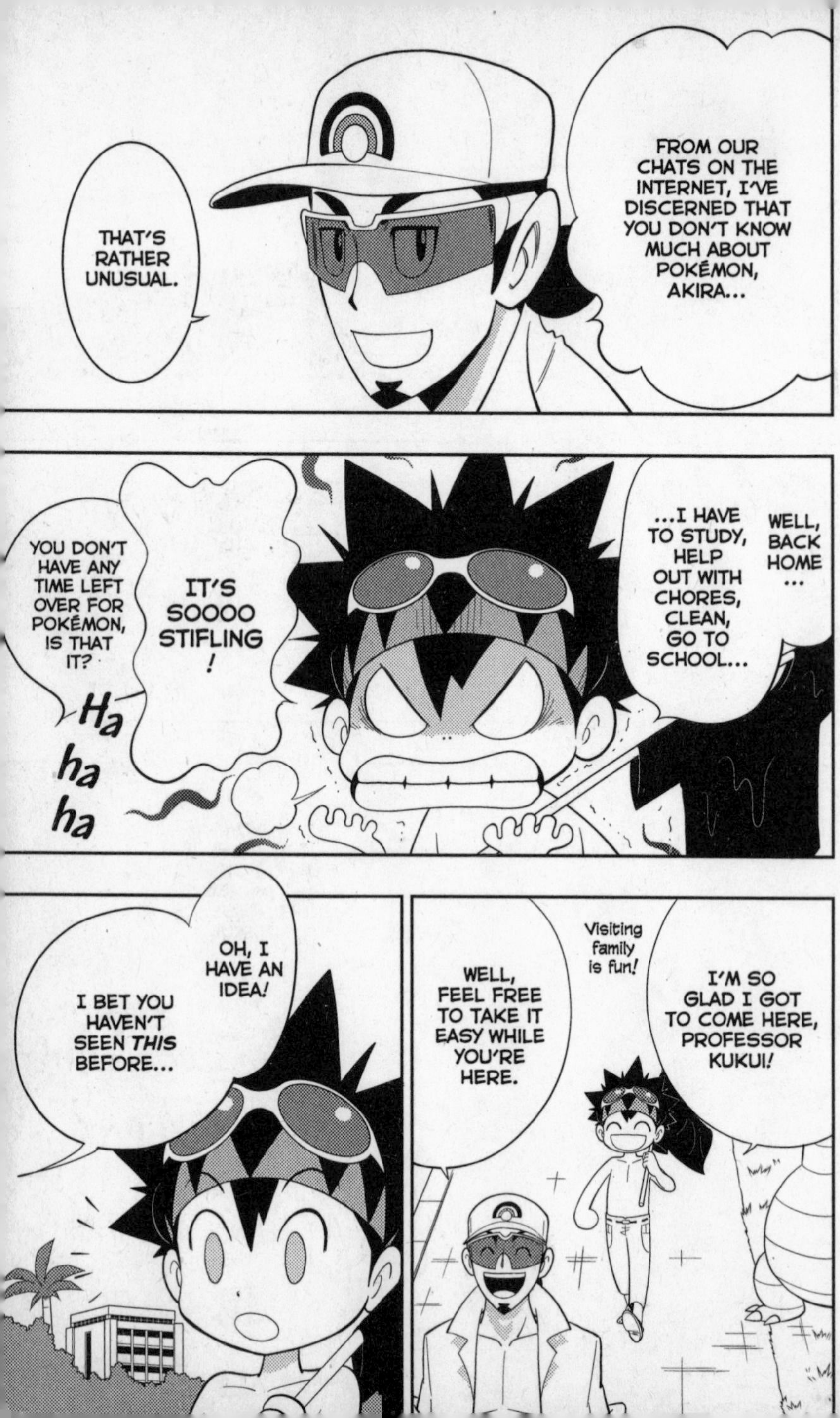
FROM OUR CHATS ON THE INTERNET, I'VE DISCERNED THAT YOU DON'T KNOW MUCH ABOUT POKÉMON, AKIRA...
THAT'S RATHER UNUSUAL.
WELL, BACK HOME...
...I HAVE TO STUDY, HELP OUT WITH CHORES, CLEAN, GO TO SCHOOL...
IT'S SOOOO STIFLING!
YOU DON'T HAVE ANY TIME LEFT OVER FOR POKÉMON, IS THAT IT?
Ha ha ha
I'M SO GLAD I GOT TO COME HERE, PROFESSOR KUKUI!
Visiting family is fun!
WELL, FEEL FREE TO TAKE IT EASY WHILE YOU'RE HERE.
OH, I HAVE AN IDEA!
I BET YOU HAVEN'T SEEN *THIS* BEFORE...

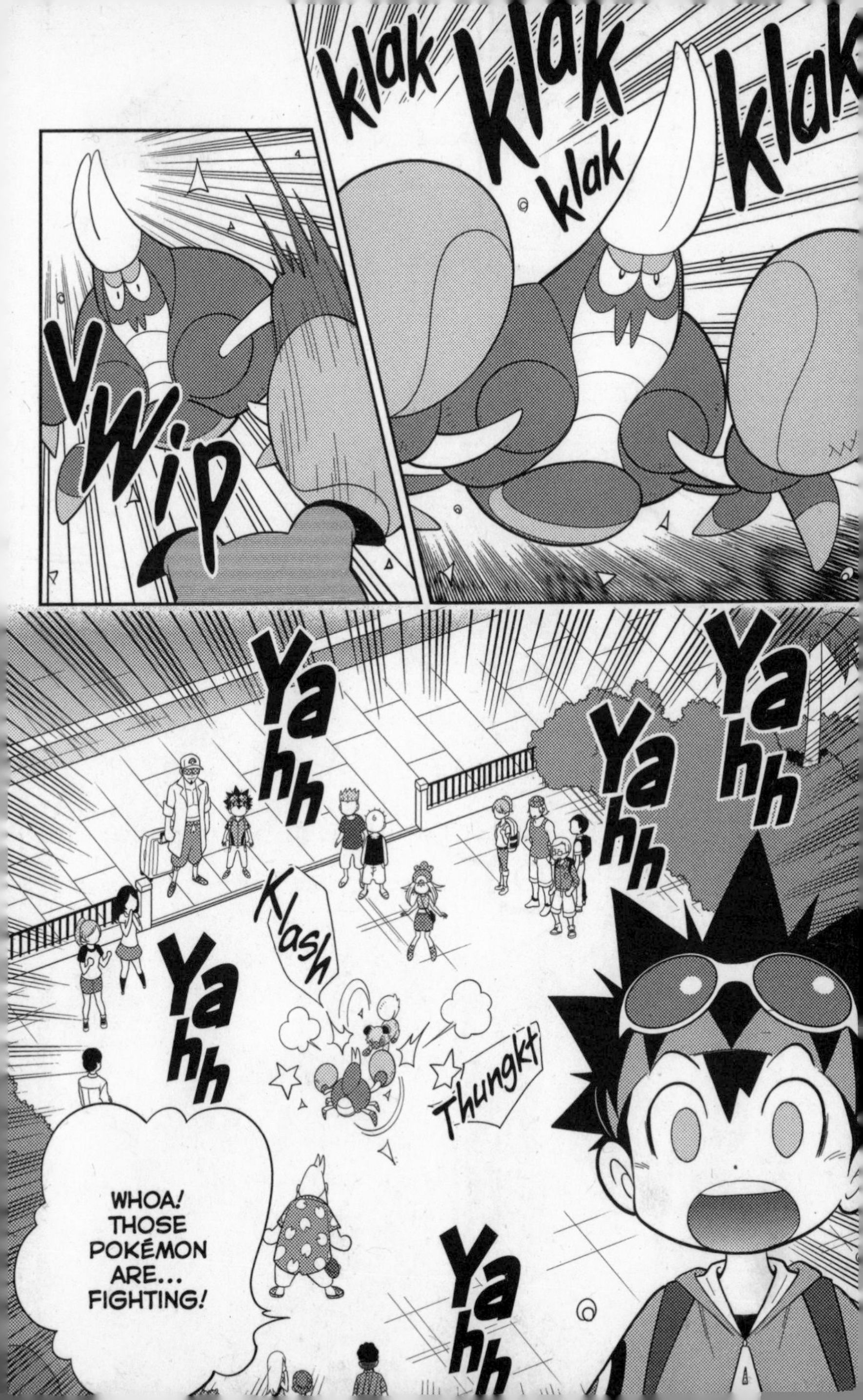
klak
klak
klak
klak
Vwip
Yahh
Yahh
Yahh
Klash
Thungkt
Yahh
Yahh
WHOA! THOSE POKÉMON ARE... FIGHTING!

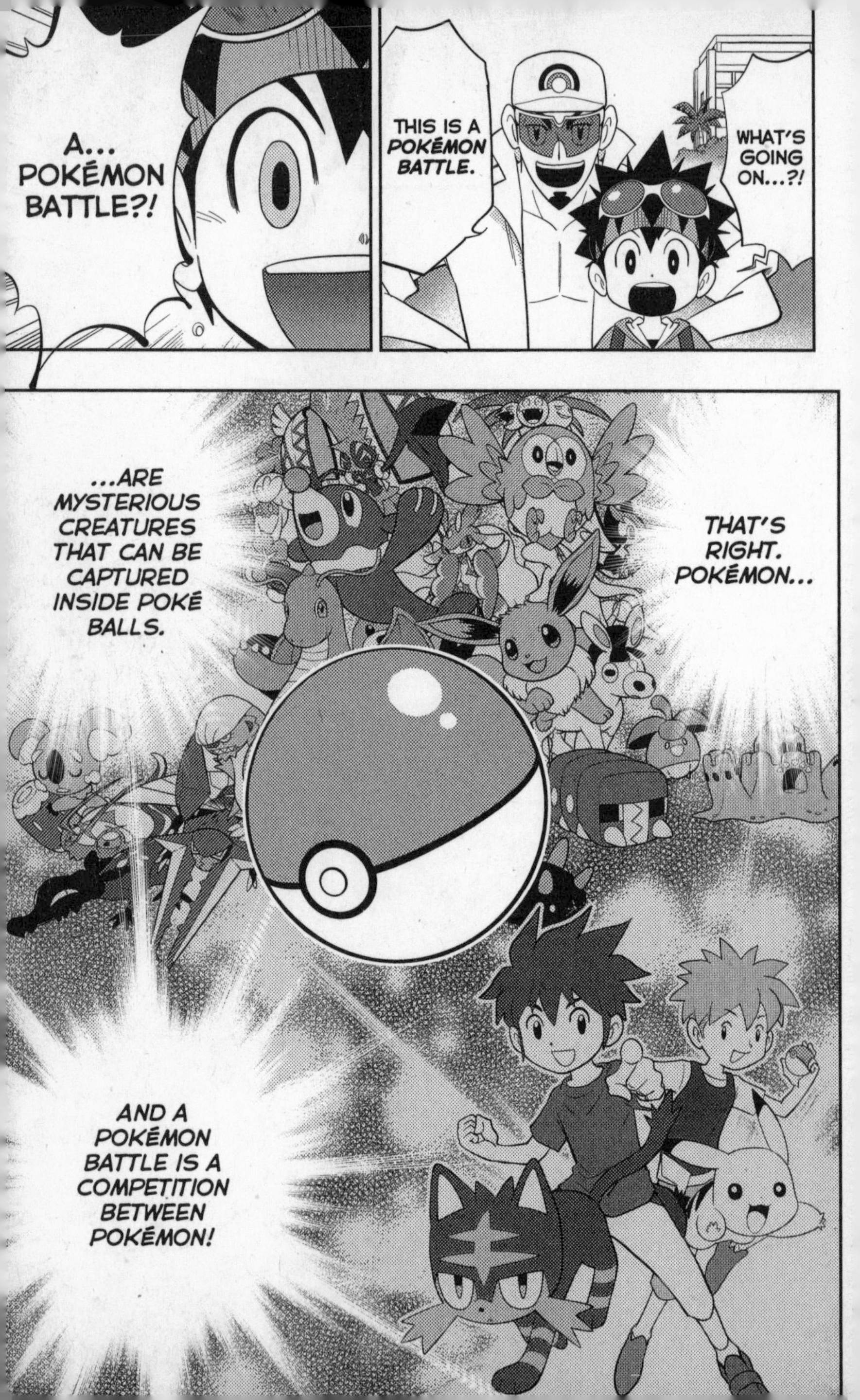
WHAT'S GOING ON...?!
THIS IS A POKÉMON BATTLE.
A... POKÉMON BATTLE?!
THAT'S RIGHT. POKÉMON...
...ARE MYSTERIOUS CREATURES THAT CAN BE CAPTURED INSIDE POKÉ BALLS.
AND A POKÉMON BATTLE IS A COMPETITION BETWEEN POKÉMON!

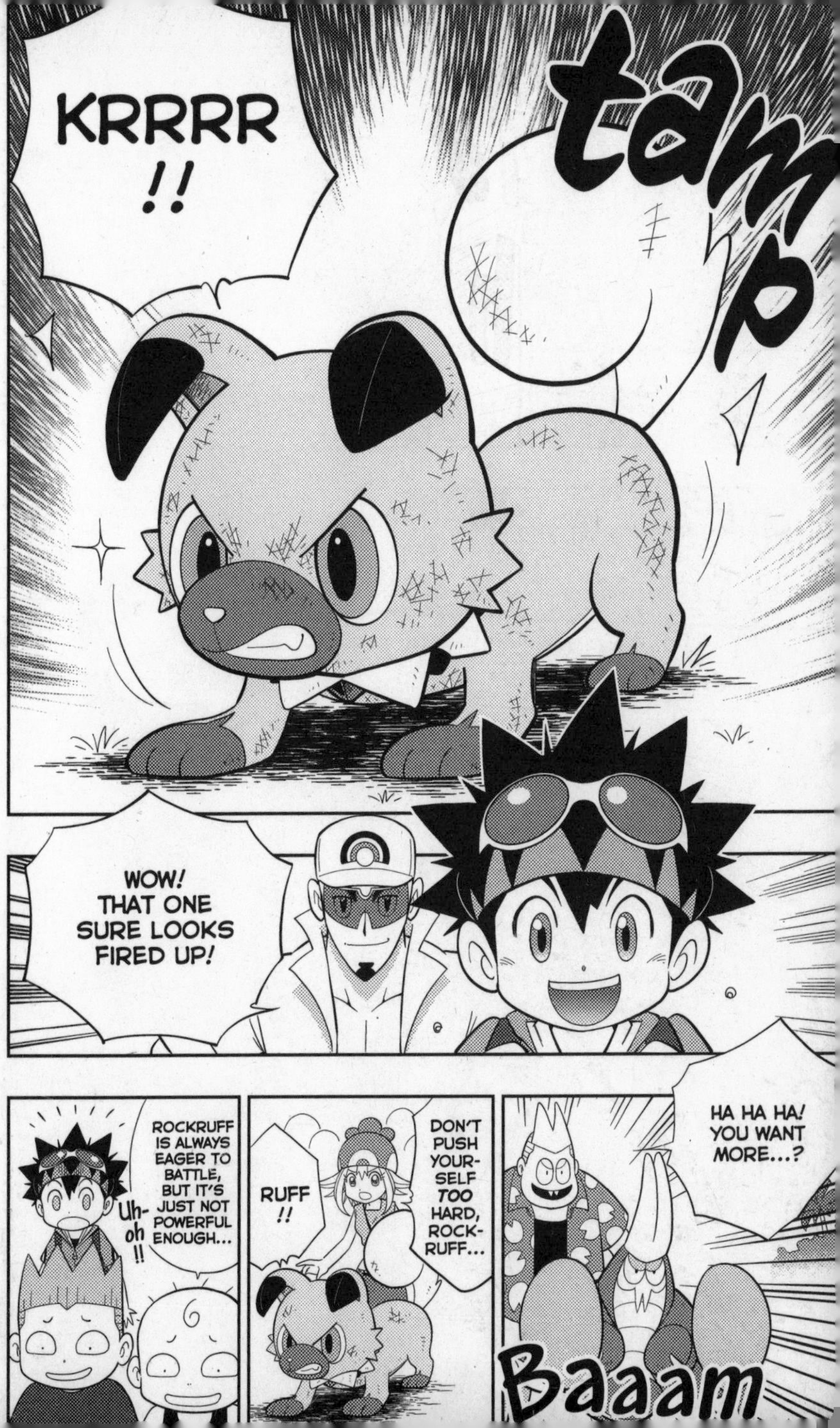
tamp
KRRRR!!
WOW! THAT ONE SURE LOOKS FIRED UP!
HA HA HA! YOU WANT MORE...?
Baaam
DON'T PUSH YOURSELF TOO HARD, ROCKRUFF...
RUFF!!
ROCKRUFF IS ALWAYS EAGER TO BATTLE, BUT IT'S JUST NOT POWERFUL ENOUGH...
Uh-oh!!

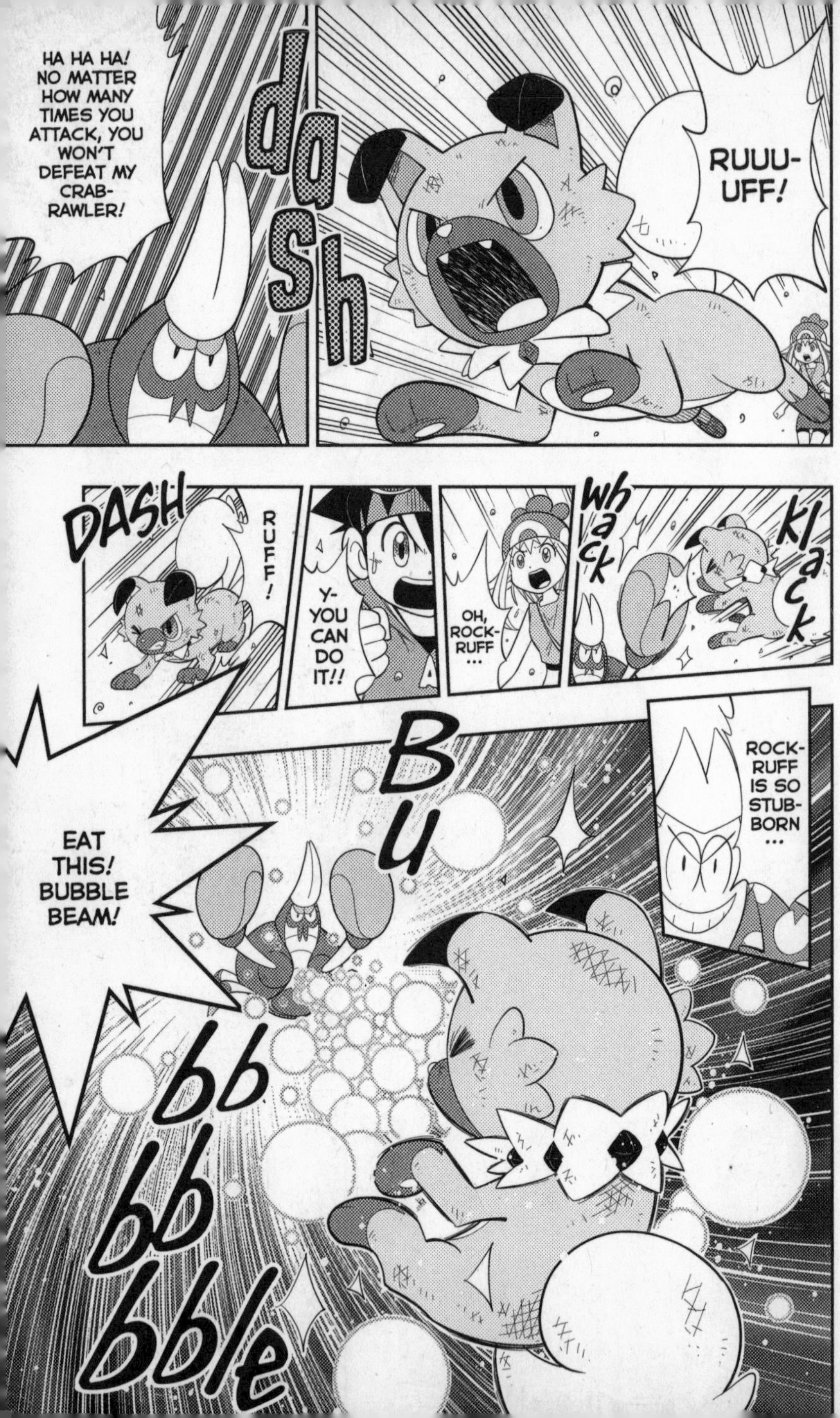
RUUU-UFF!
dash
HA HA HA! NO MATTER HOW MANY TIMES YOU ATTACK, YOU WON'T DEFEAT MY CRAB-RAWLER!
whack
klack
OH, ROCK-RUFF...
Y-YOU CAN DO IT!!
DASH
RUFF!
ROCK-RUFF IS SO STUB-BORN...
EAT THIS! BUBBLE BEAM!
Bubbbbbbble

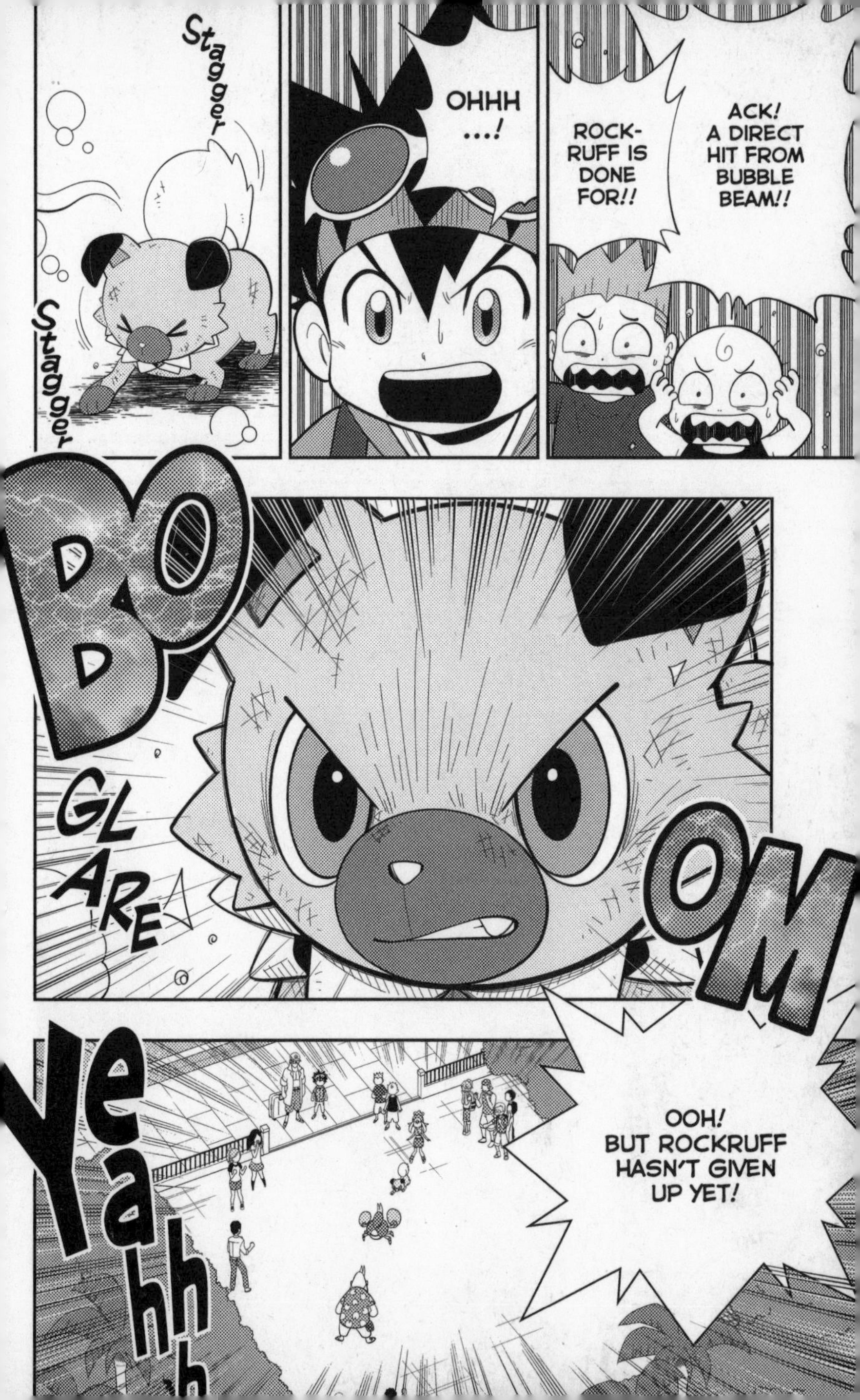
ACK! A DIRECT HIT FROM BUBBLE BEAM!!
ROCK-RUFF IS DONE FOR!!
OHHH ...!
Stagger
Stagger
BOOM
GLARE
OOH! BUT ROCKRUFF HASN'T GIVEN UP YET!
Yeahhh

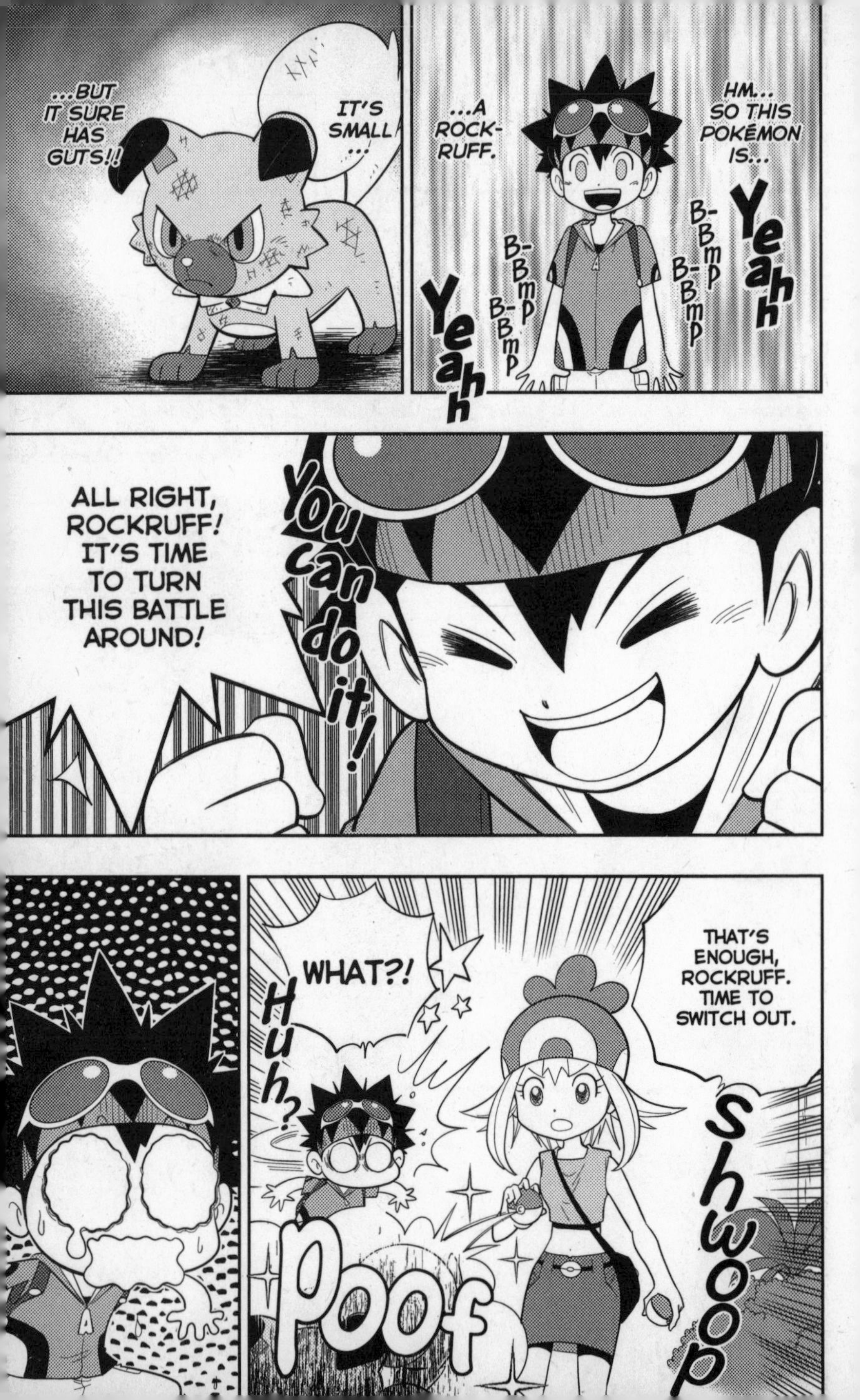
HM... SO THIS POKÉMON IS...
Yeahh
B-Bmp
B-Bmp
B-Bmp
B-Bmp
...A ROCK-RUFF.
Yeahh
IT'S SMALL...
...BUT IT SURE HAS GUTS!!
You can do it!!
ALL RIGHT, ROCKRUFF! IT'S TIME TO TURN THIS BATTLE AROUND!
THAT'S ENOUGH, ROCKRUFF. TIME TO SWITCH OUT.
Shwoop
WHAT?!
Huh?
Poof

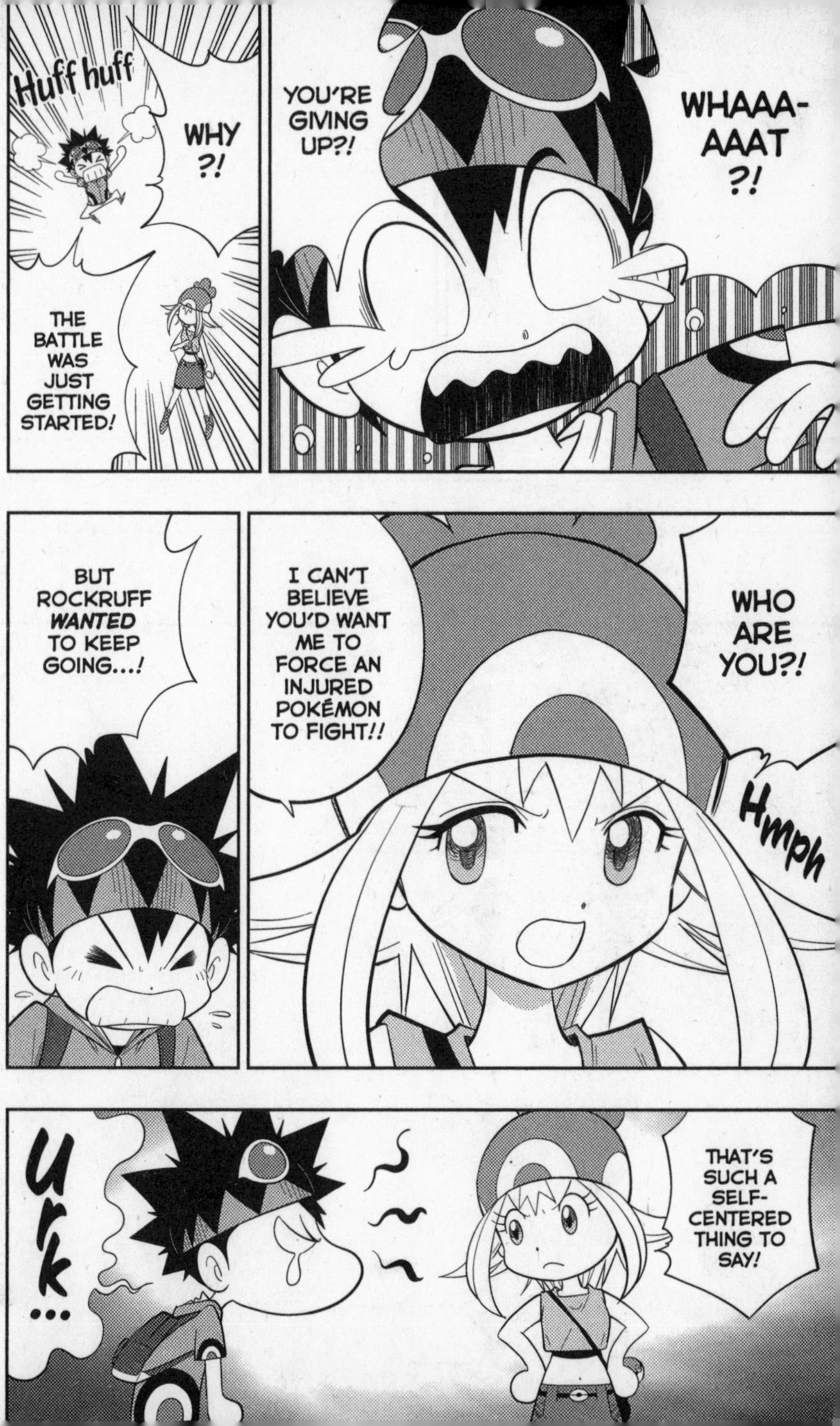
WHAAAA-AAAT ?!
YOU'RE GIVING UP?!
Huff huff
WHY ?!
THE BATTLE WAS JUST GETTING STARTED!
WHO ARE YOU?!
I CAN'T BELIEVE YOU'D WANT ME TO FORCE AN INJURED POKÉMON TO FIGHT!!
Hmph
BUT ROCKRUFF *WANTED* TO KEEP GOING...!
THAT'S SUCH A SELF-CENTERED THING TO SAY!
Urk...

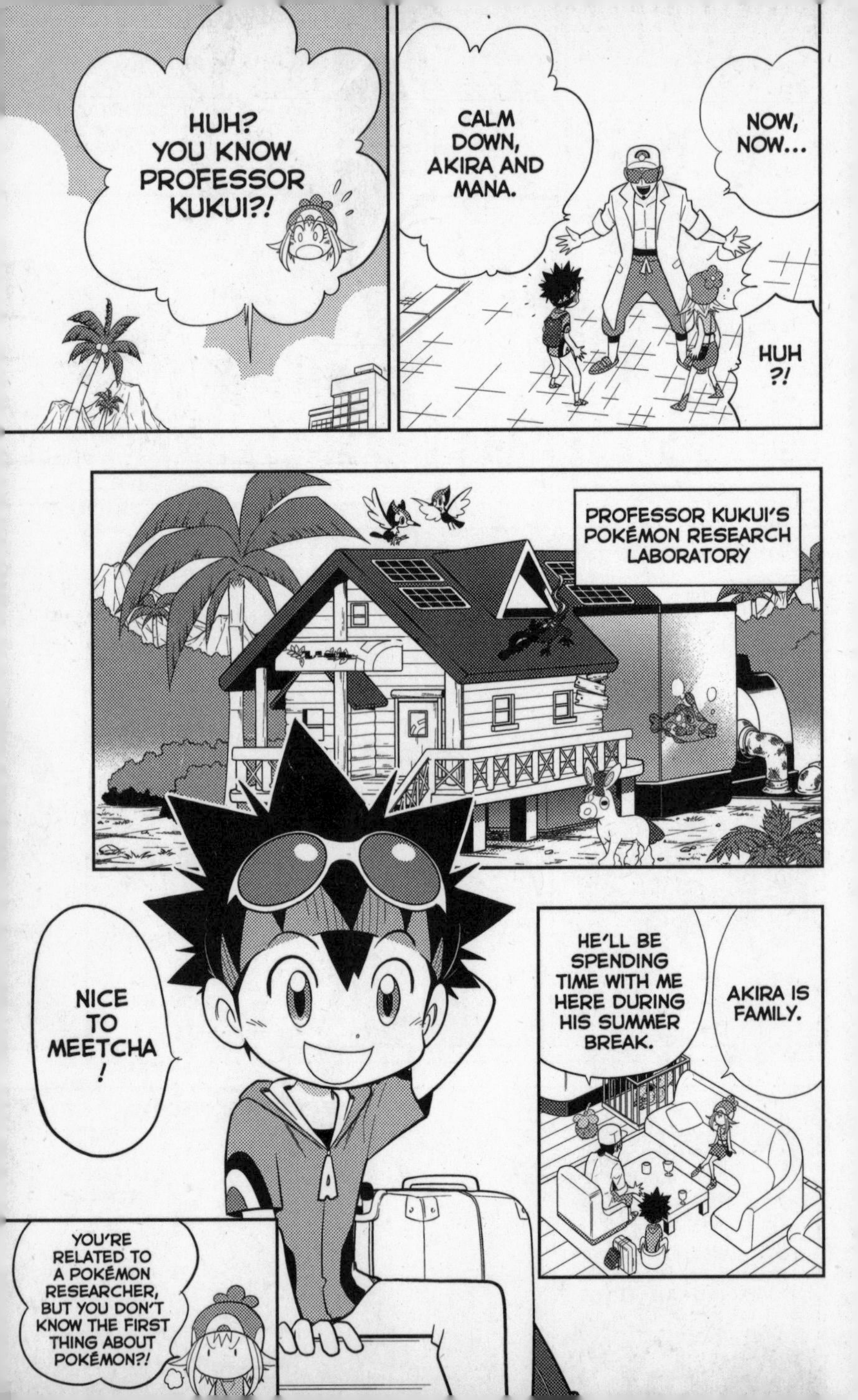
NOW, NOW...
CALM DOWN, AKIRA AND MANA.
HUH ?!
HUH? YOU KNOW PROFESSOR KUKUI?!
PROFESSOR KUKUI'S POKÉMON RESEARCH LABORATORY
AKIRA IS FAMILY.
HE'LL BE SPENDING TIME WITH ME HERE DURING HIS SUMMER BREAK.
NICE TO MEETCHA!
YOU'RE RELATED TO A POKÉMON RESEARCHER, BUT YOU DON'T KNOW THE FIRST THING ABOUT POKÉMON?!

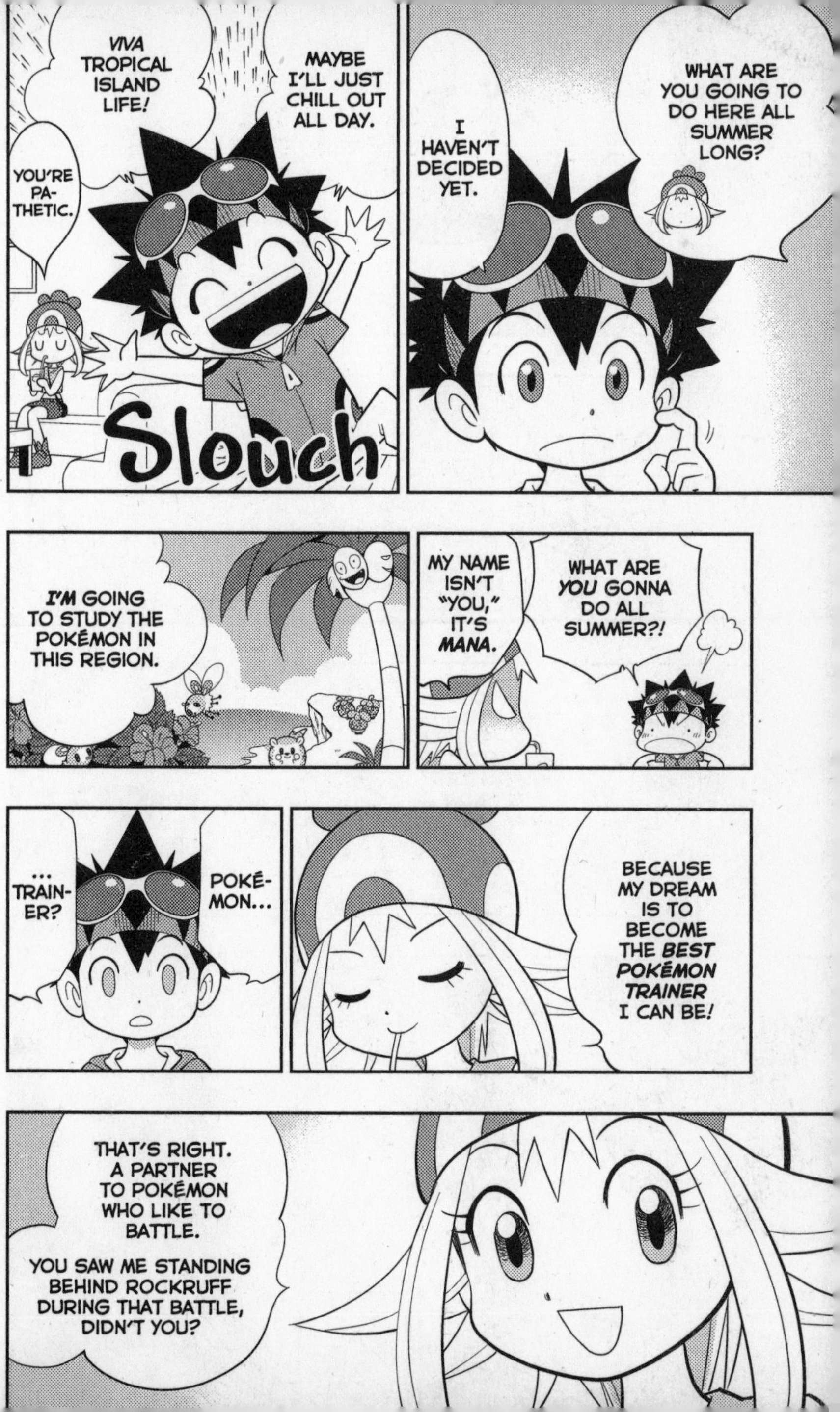
WHAT ARE YOU GOING TO DO HERE ALL SUMMER LONG?
I HAVEN'T DECIDED YET.
MAYBE I'LL JUST CHILL OUT ALL DAY.
VIVA TROPICAL ISLAND LIFE!
YOU'RE PATHETIC.
Slouch
WHAT ARE YOU GONNA DO ALL SUMMER?!
MY NAME ISN'T "YOU," IT'S MANA.
I'M GOING TO STUDY THE POKéMON IN THIS REGION.
BECAUSE MY DREAM IS TO BECOME THE BEST POKéMON TRAINER I CAN BE!
POKé-MON...
... TRAIN-ER?
THAT'S RIGHT. A PARTNER TO POKéMON WHO LIKE TO BATTLE.
YOU SAW ME STANDING BEHIND ROCKRUFF DURING THAT BATTLE, DIDN'T YOU?

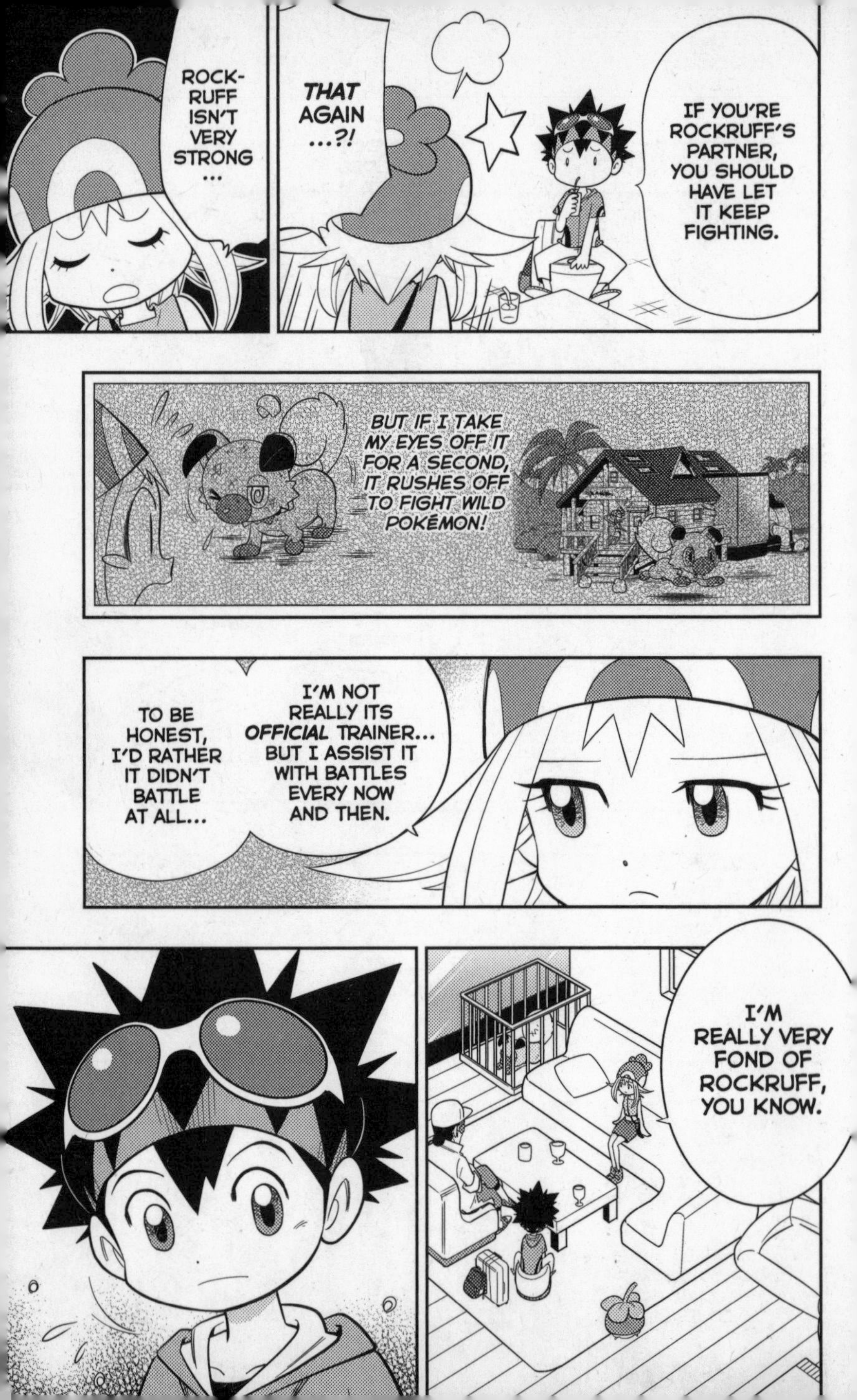
IF YOU'RE ROCKRUFF'S PARTNER, YOU SHOULD HAVE LET IT KEEP FIGHTING.
THAT AGAIN...?!
ROCK-RUFF ISN'T VERY STRONG...
BUT IF I TAKE MY EYES OFF IT FOR A SECOND, IT RUSHES OFF TO FIGHT WILD POKÉMON!
I'M NOT REALLY ITS *OFFICIAL* TRAINER... BUT I ASSIST IT WITH BATTLES EVERY NOW AND THEN.
TO BE HONEST, I'D RATHER IT DIDN'T BATTLE AT ALL...
I'M REALLY VERY FOND OF ROCKRUFF, YOU KNOW.

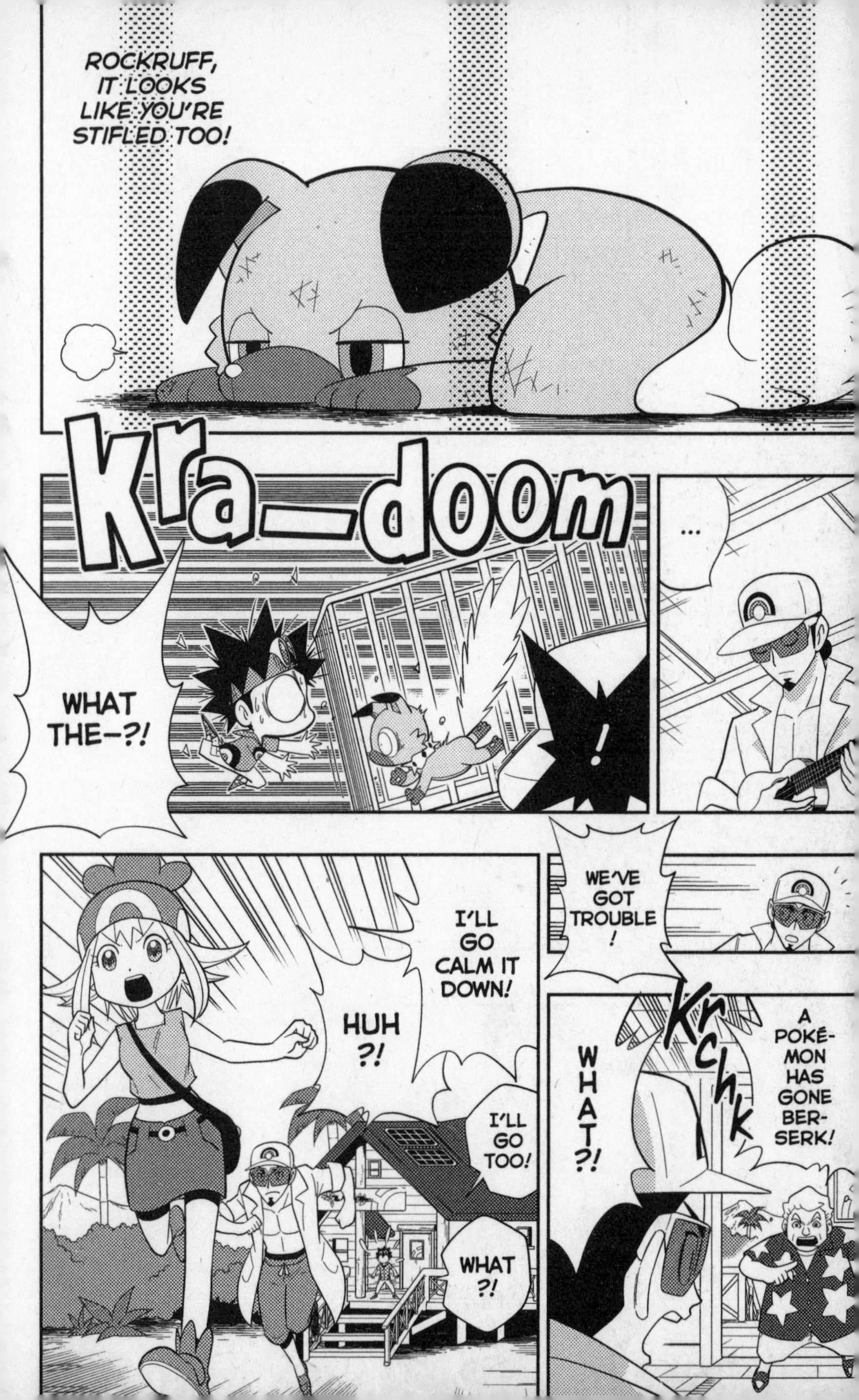
ROCKRUFF, IT LOOKS LIKE YOU'RE STIFLED TOO!
...
Kra-doom
WHAT THE-?!
!
WE'VE GOT TROUBLE!
Krchk
A POKÉ-MON HAS GONE BER-SERK!
WHAT?!
I'LL GO CALM IT DOWN!
HUH?!
I'LL GO TOO!
WHAT?!

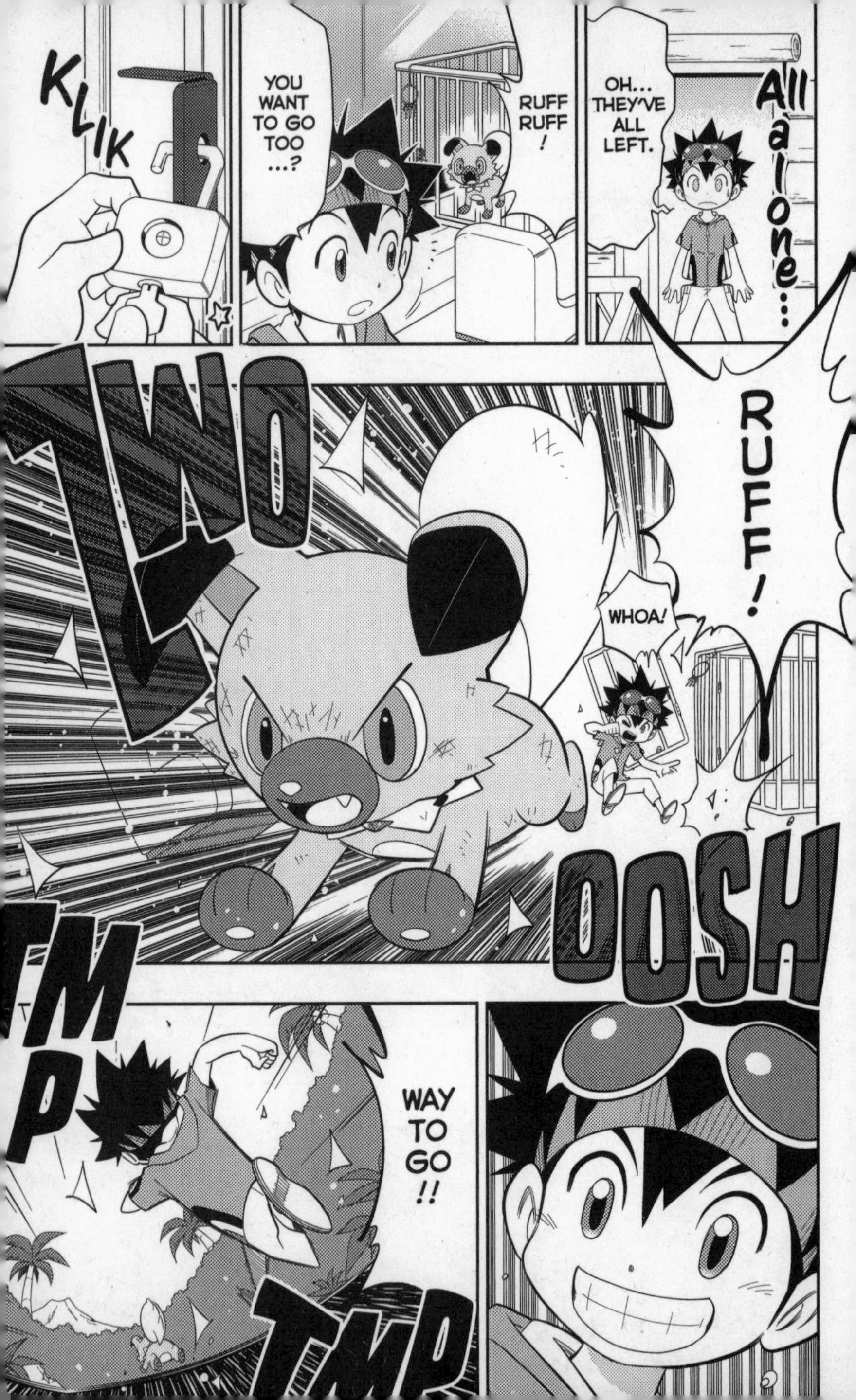
OH... THEY'VE ALL LEFT.
All alone...
RUFF RUFF!
YOU WANT TO GO TOO ...?
KLIK
RUFF!
WHOA!
TWO
OOSH
WAY TO GO!!
TMP
TMP

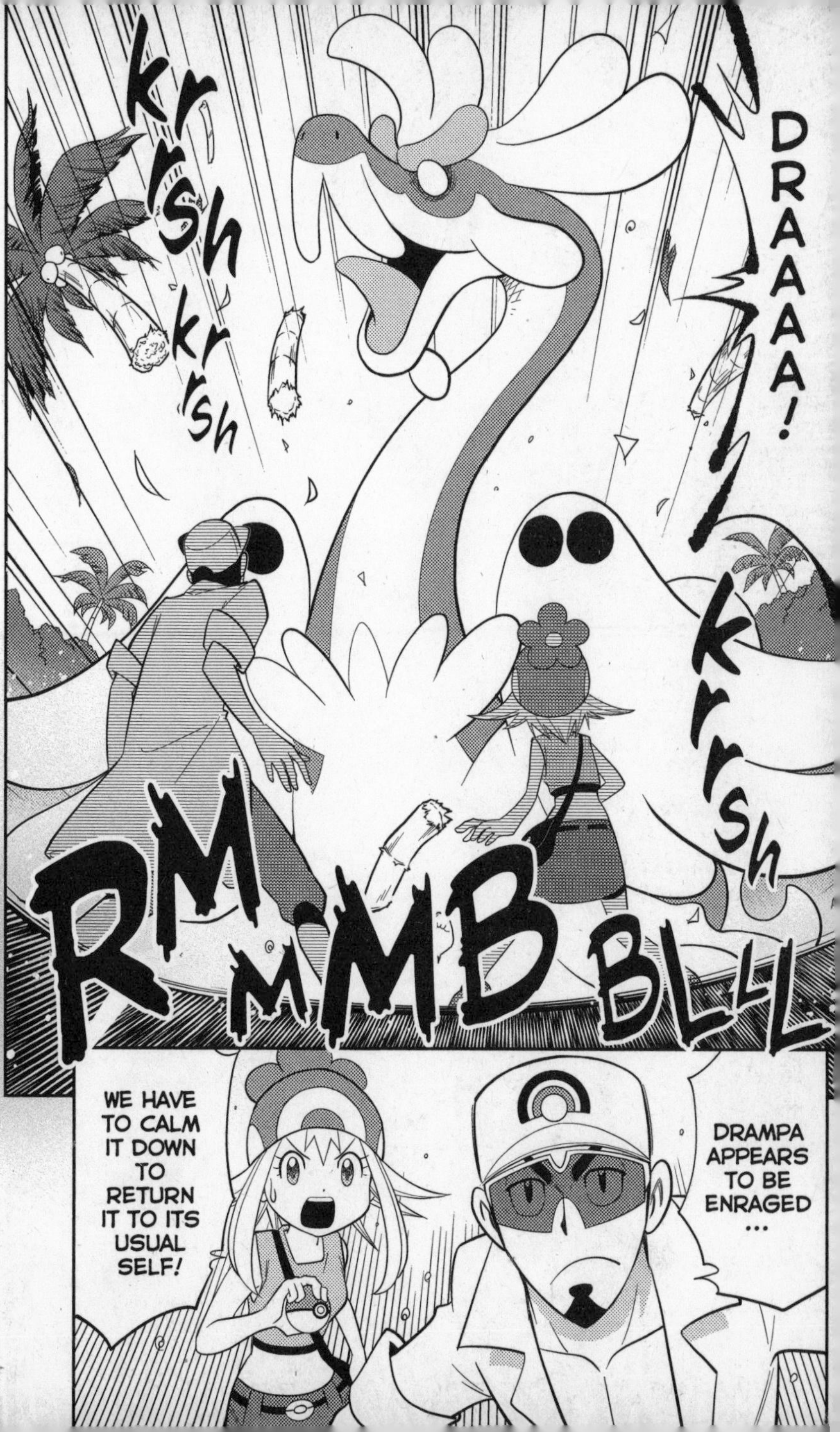
DRAAAA!
krrsh
krrsh krrsh krrsh
RMMMB BLLL
DRAMPA APPEARS TO BE ENRAGED...
WE HAVE TO CALM IT DOWN TO RETURN IT TO ITS USUAL SELF!

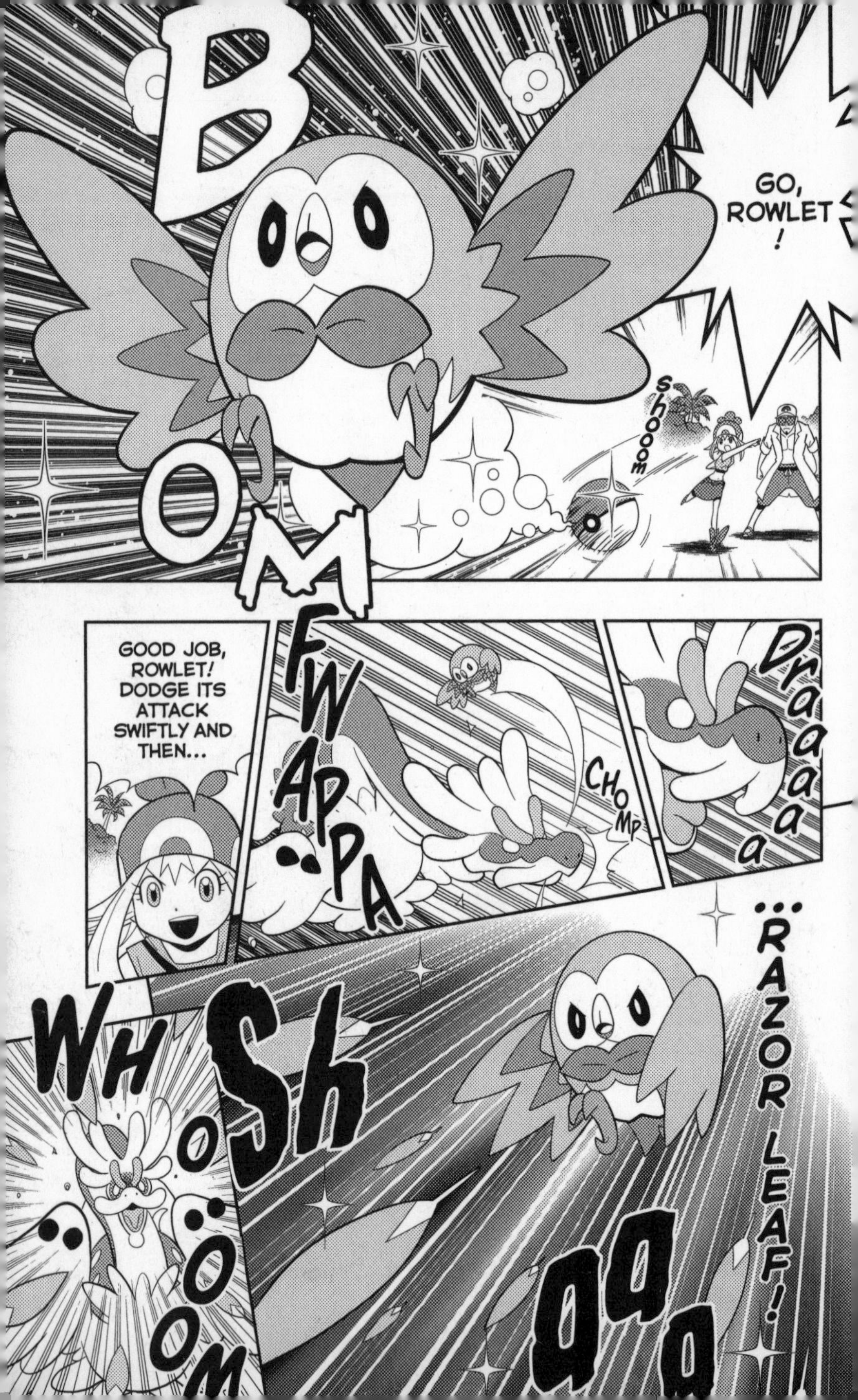
GO, ROWLET!
BOOM
shoooom
Draaaaaaa
FWAPPA
CHOMP
GOOD JOB, ROWLET! DODGE ITS ATTACK SWIFTLY AND THEN...
...RAZOR LEAF!
aaa
WHOSH
OOOM

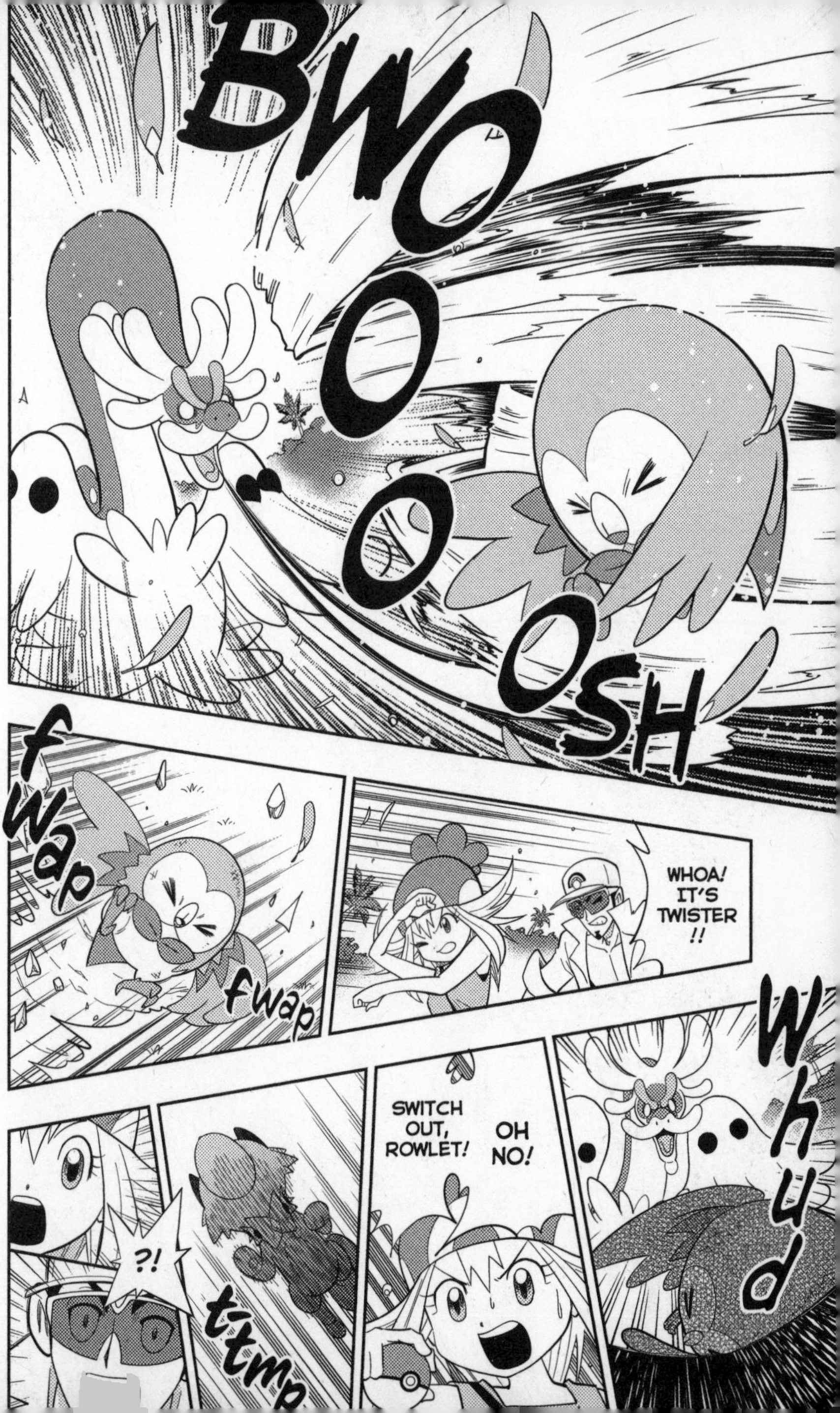
BWOOOOOSH
WHOA! IT'S TWISTER !!
fwap
fwap
Whud
OH NO!
SWITCH OUT, ROWLET!
ttmp
?!

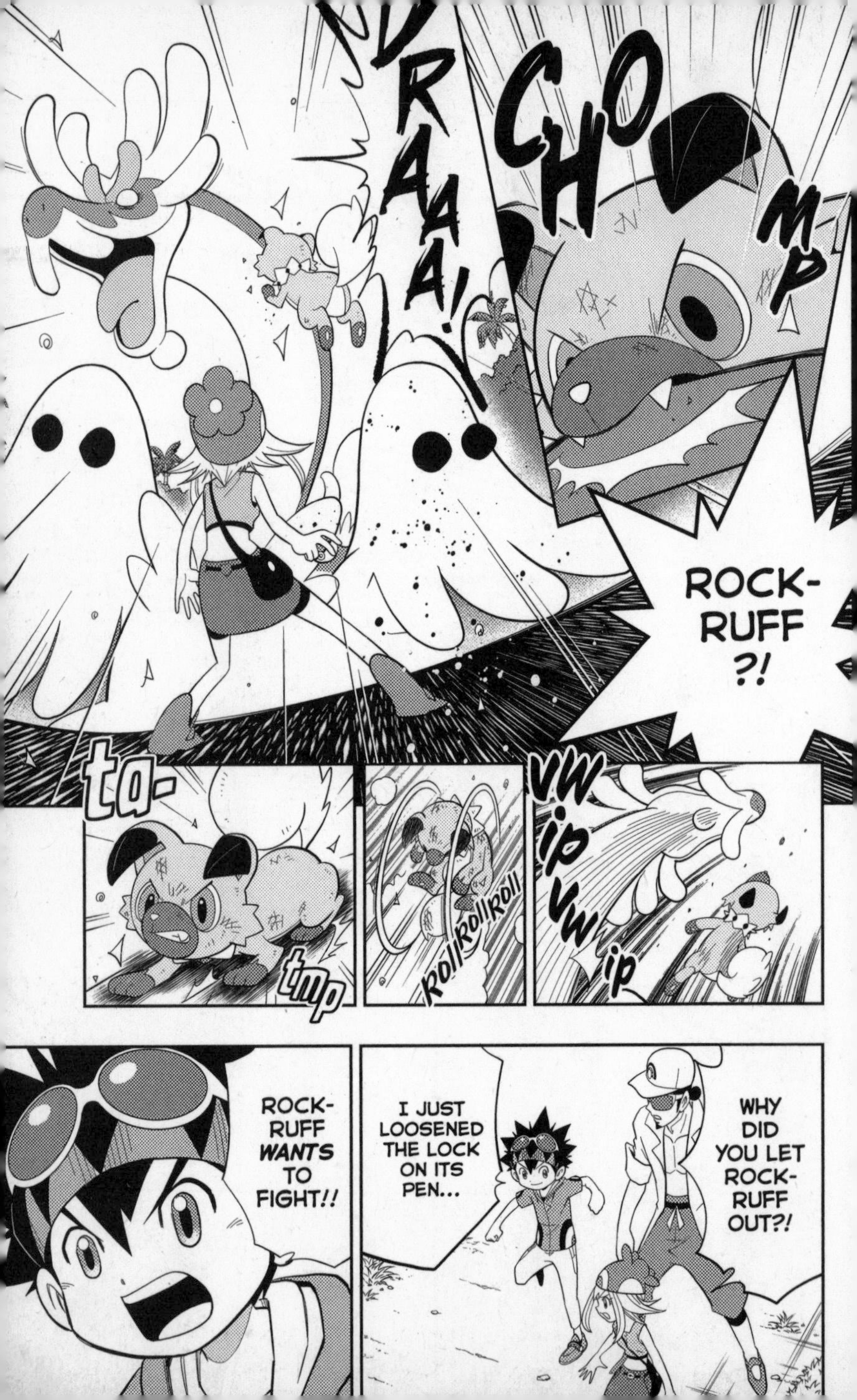
CHOMP
ROCK-RUFF?!
VRAAAA!
vwip vwip
Roll Roll Roll
ta-
tmp
WHY DID YOU LET ROCK-RUFF OUT?!
I JUST LOOSENED THE LOCK ON ITS PEN...
ROCK-RUFF *WANTS* TO FIGHT!!

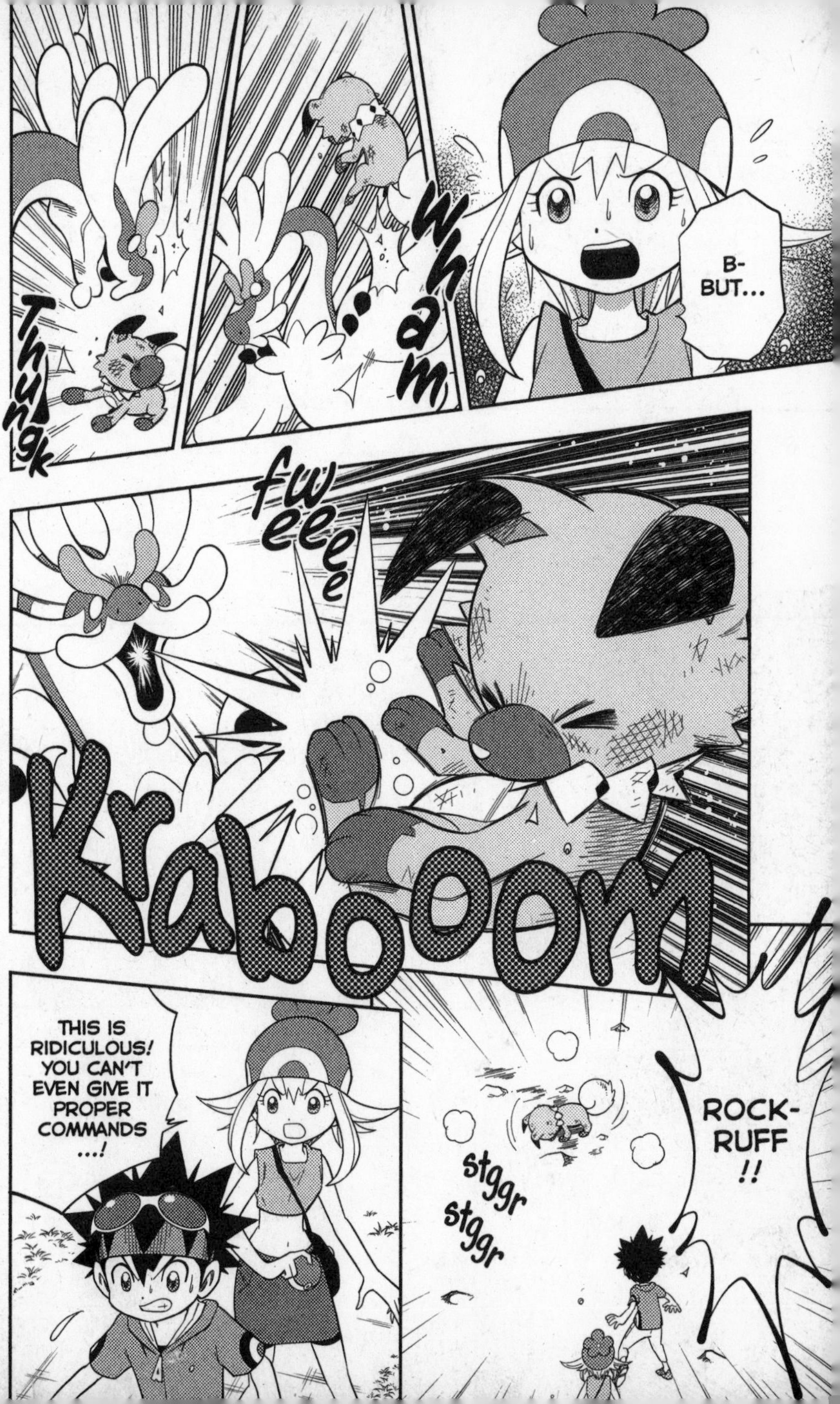
B- BUT...
Wham
Thungk
fweeee
Kraboooom
ROCK-RUFF!!
stggr stggr
THIS IS RIDICULOUS! YOU CAN'T EVEN GIVE IT PROPER COMMANDS ...!

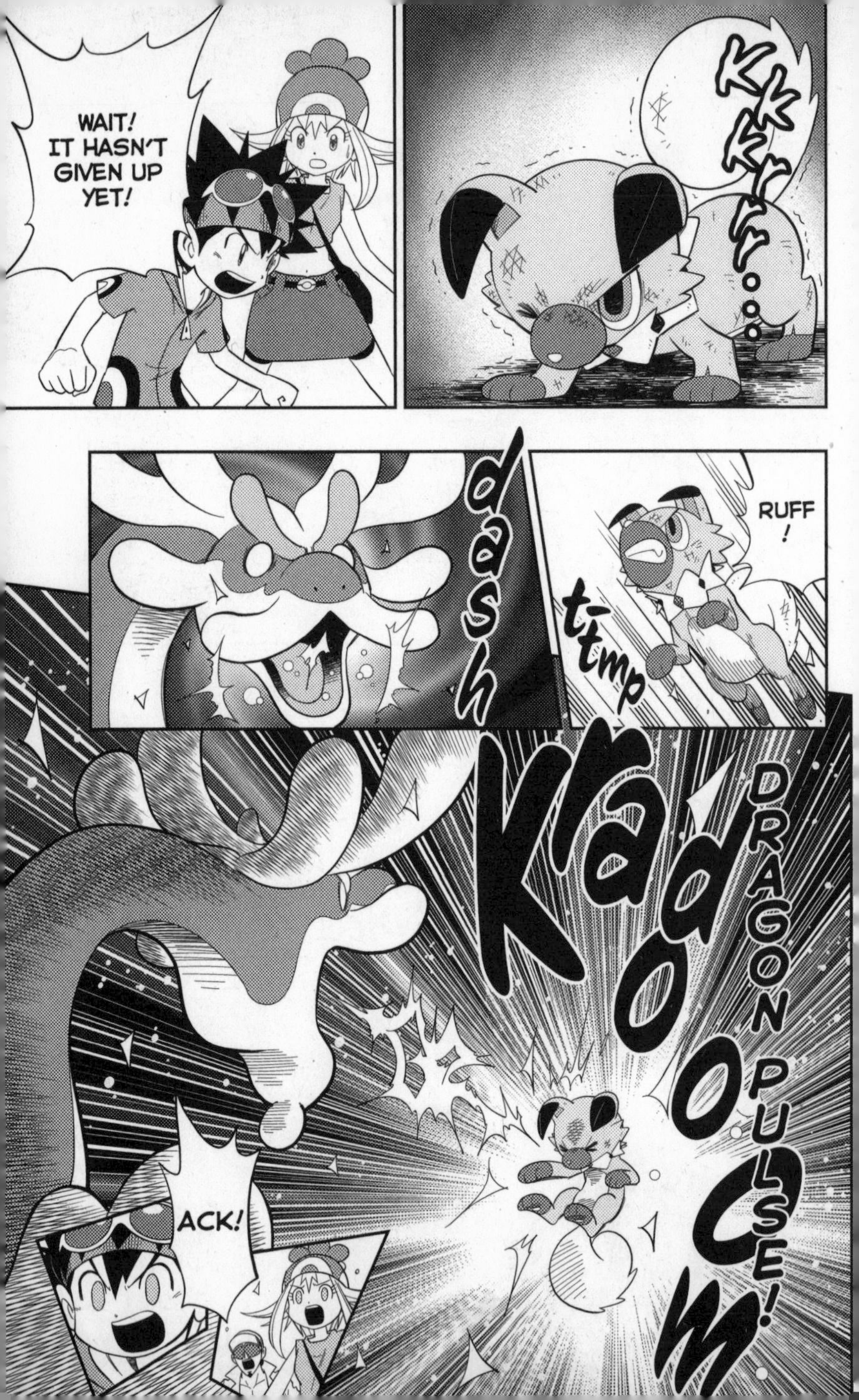

Kkkrr...
WAIT! IT HASN'T GIVEN UP YET!
RUFF!
ttmp
dash
Kladooom
DRAGON PULSE!
ACK!

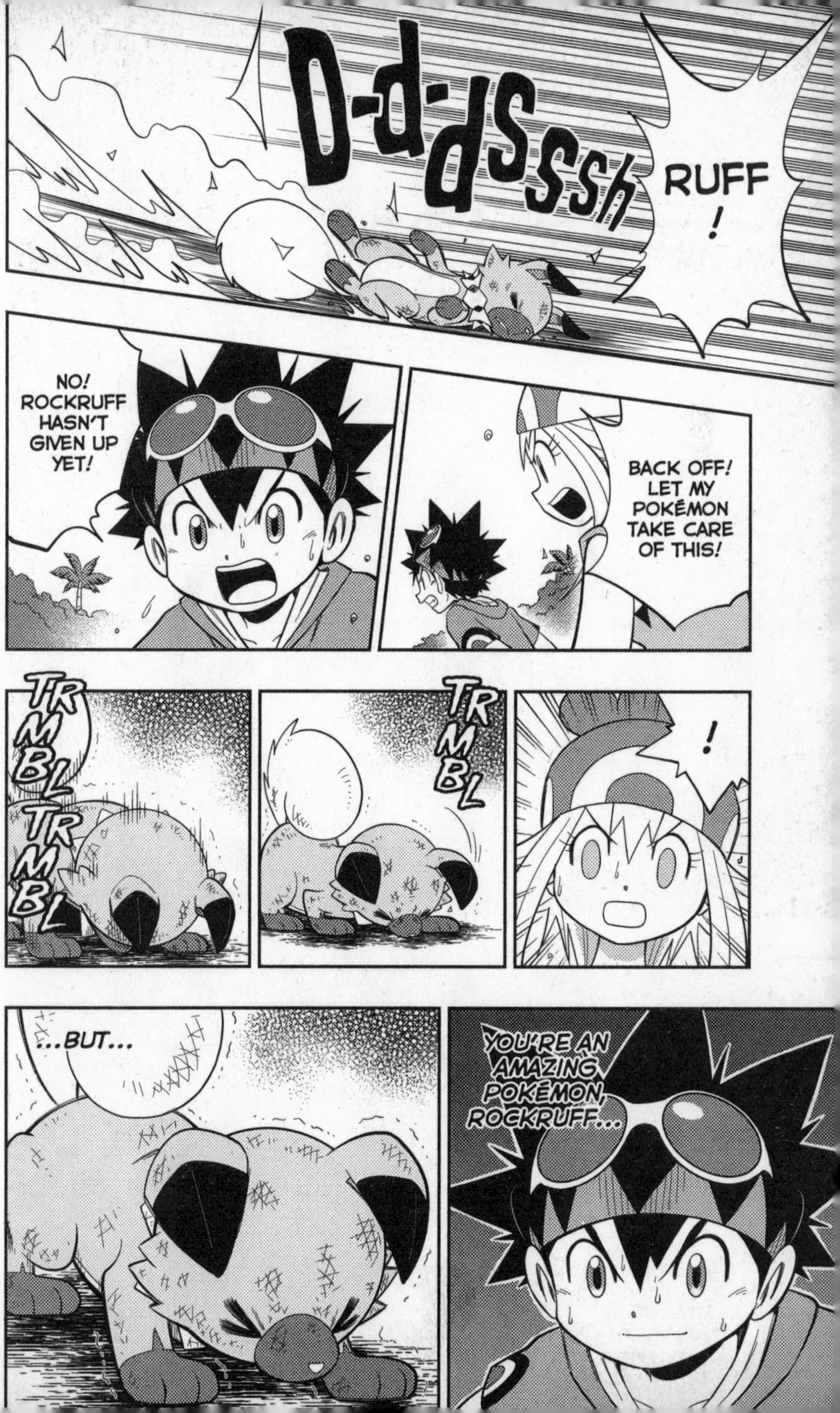
D-d-dSSSh
RUFF!
BACK OFF! LET MY POKÉMON TAKE CARE OF THIS!
NO! ROCKRUFF HASN'T GIVEN UP YET!
!
TRMBL
TRMBL TRMBL
YOU'RE AN AMAZING POKÉMON, ROCKRUFF...
...BUT...

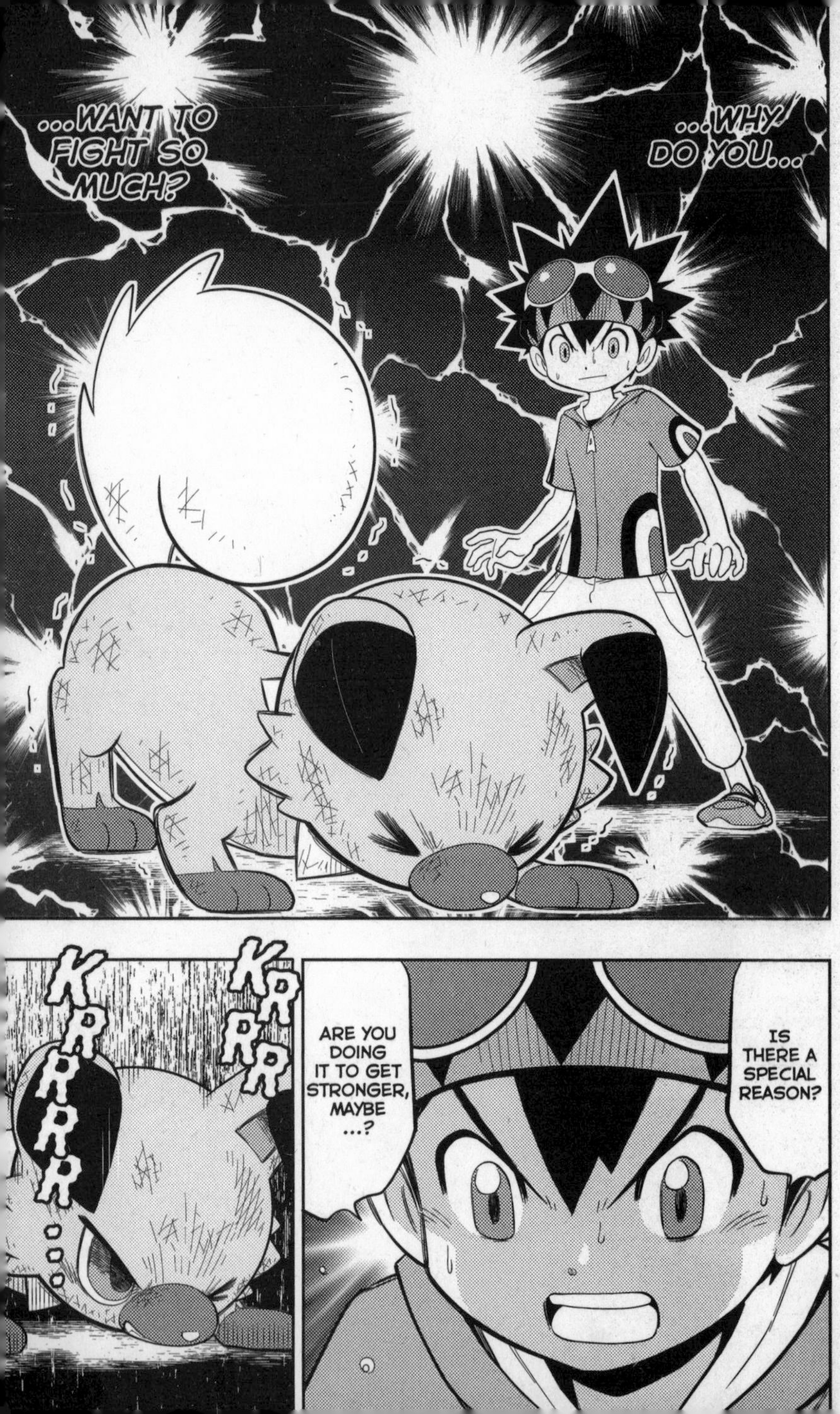
...WHY DO YOU...
...WANT TO FIGHT SO MUCH?
IS THERE A SPECIAL REASON?
ARE YOU DOING IT TO GET STRONGER, MAYBE ...?
KRRR
KRRRR...

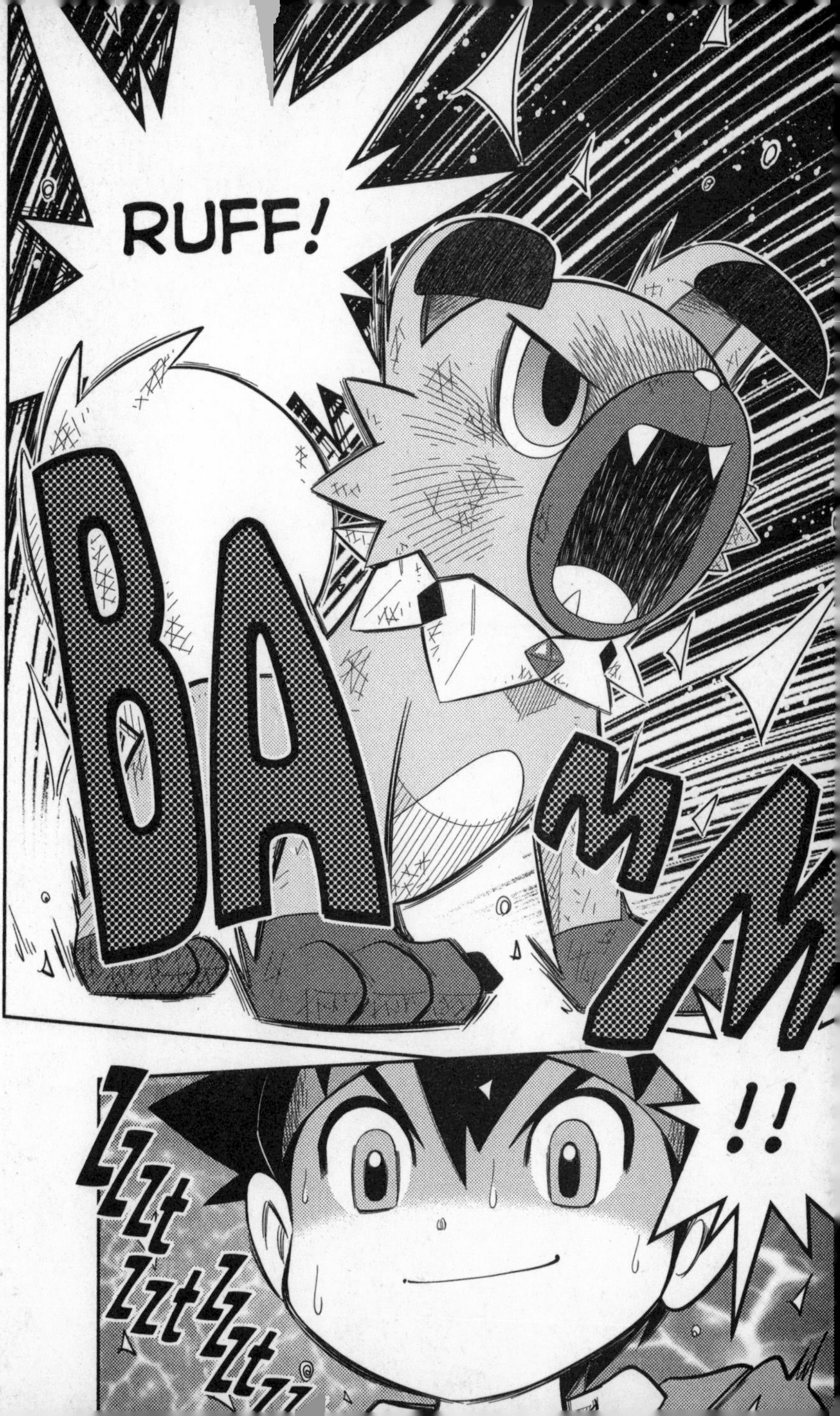
RUFF!
BAMM
!!
Zzzt Zzzt Zzzt

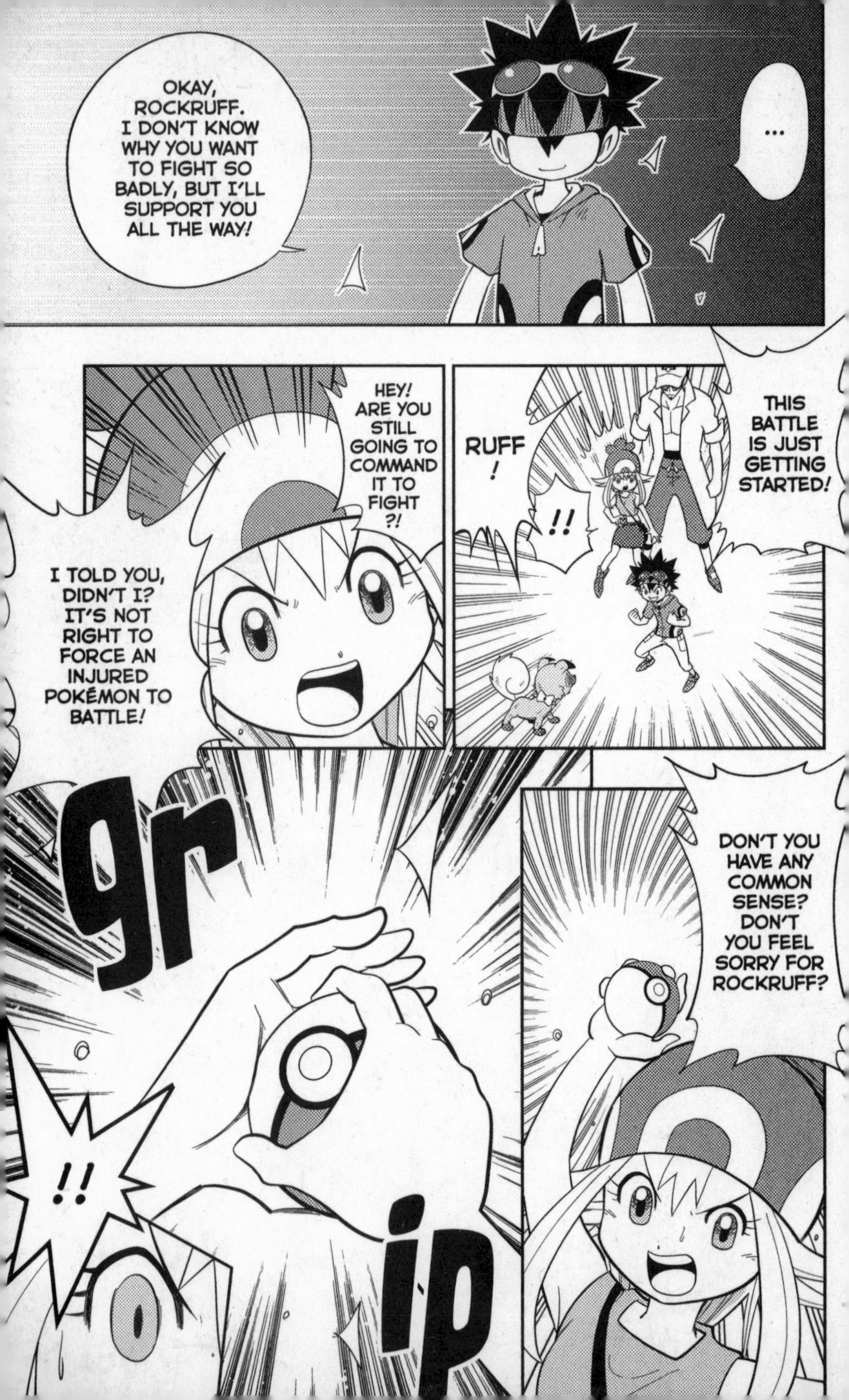
...
OKAY, ROCKRUFF. I DON'T KNOW WHY YOU WANT TO FIGHT SO BADLY, BUT I'LL SUPPORT YOU ALL THE WAY!
THIS BATTLE IS JUST GETTING STARTED!
RUFF!
!!
HEY! ARE YOU STILL GOING TO COMMAND IT TO FIGHT?!
I TOLD YOU, DIDN'T I? IT'S NOT RIGHT TO FORCE AN INJURED POKÉMON TO BATTLE!
DON'T YOU HAVE ANY COMMON SENSE? DON'T YOU FEEL SORRY FOR ROCKRUFF?
gr
!!
ip

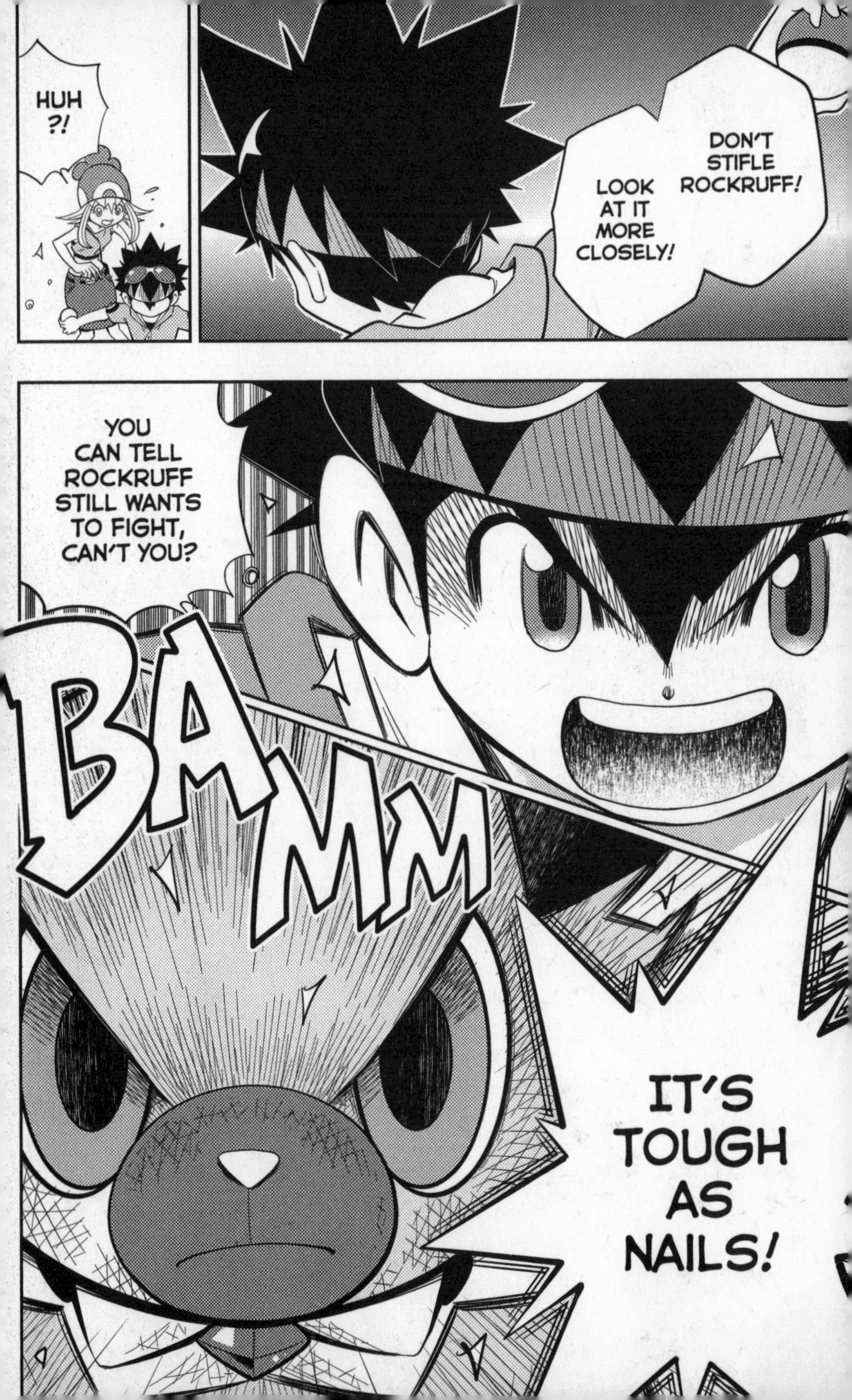
DON'T STIFLE ROCKRUFF!
LOOK AT IT MORE CLOSELY!
HUH ?!
YOU CAN TELL ROCKRUFF STILL WANTS TO FIGHT, CAN'T YOU?
BAMM
IT'S TOUGH AS NAILS!

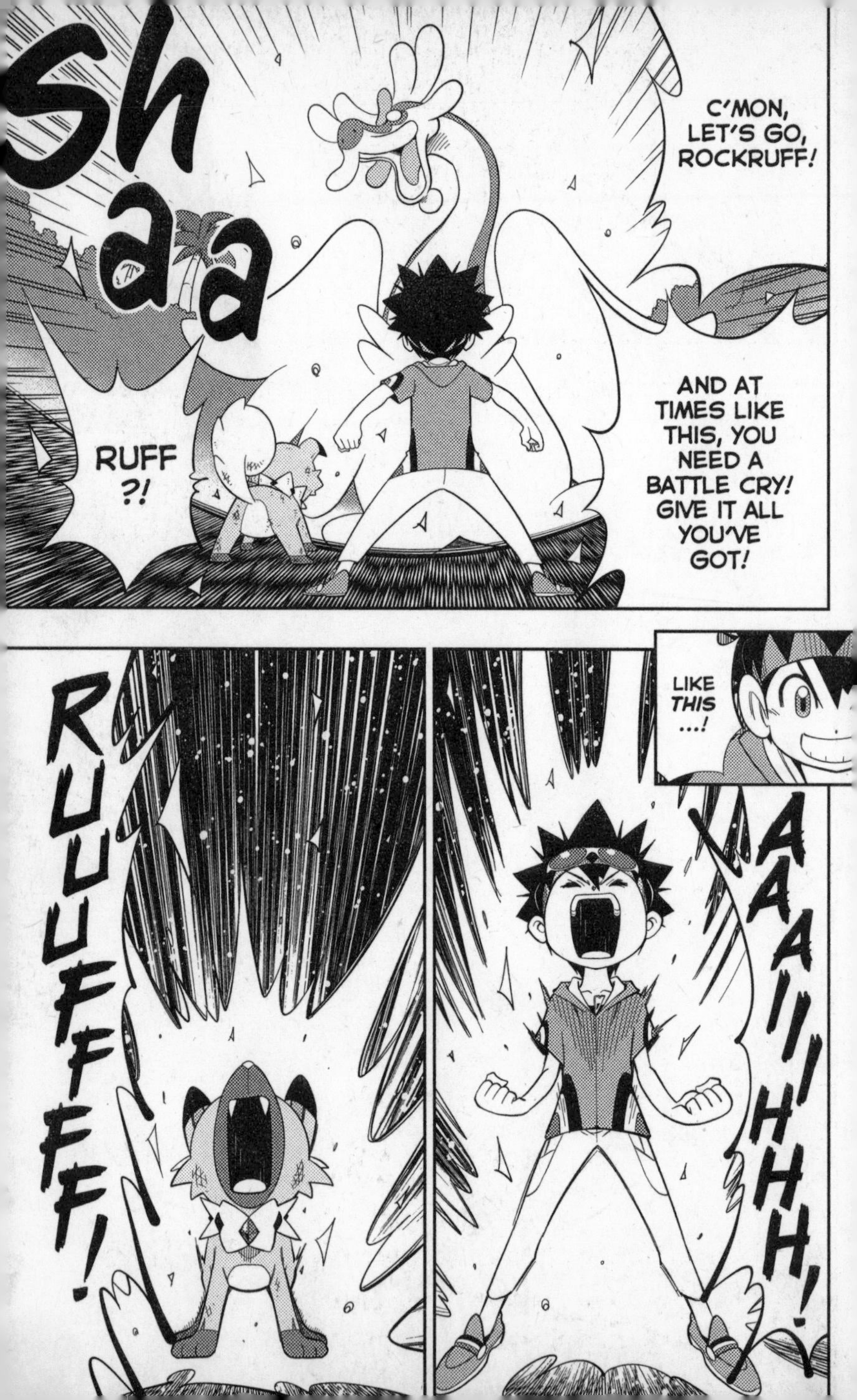
C'MON, LET'S GO, ROCKRUFF!
AND AT TIMES LIKE THIS, YOU NEED A BATTLE CRY! GIVE IT ALL YOU'VE GOT!
Shaa
RUFF ?!
LIKE THIS ...!
AAAIIIIHHHH!
RUUUFFFF!

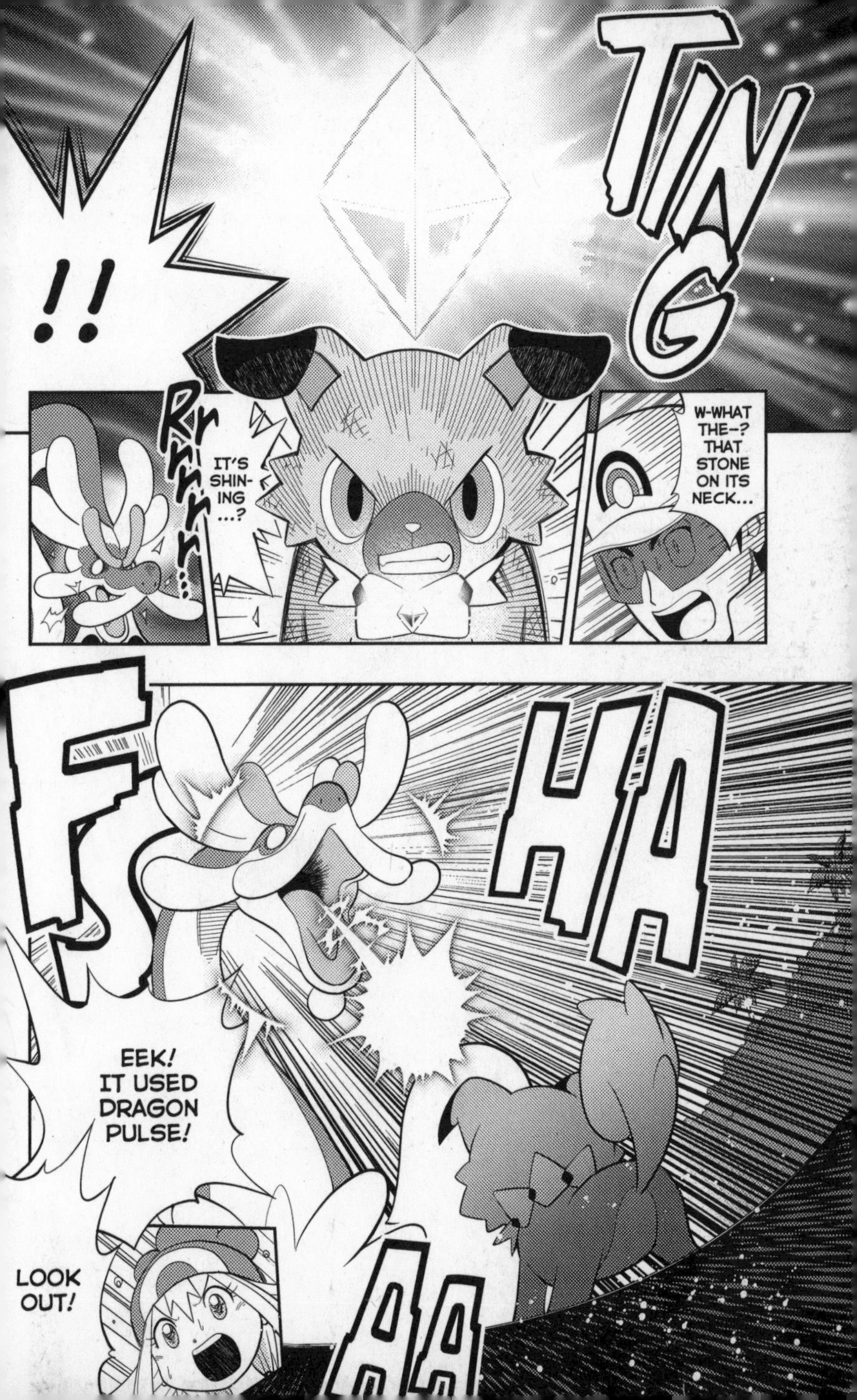
TING
W
!!
W-WHAT THE--? THAT STONE ON ITS NECK...
IT'S SHINING...?
Rrrrrr...
FHAAA
EEK! IT USED DRAGON PULSE!
LOOK OUT!

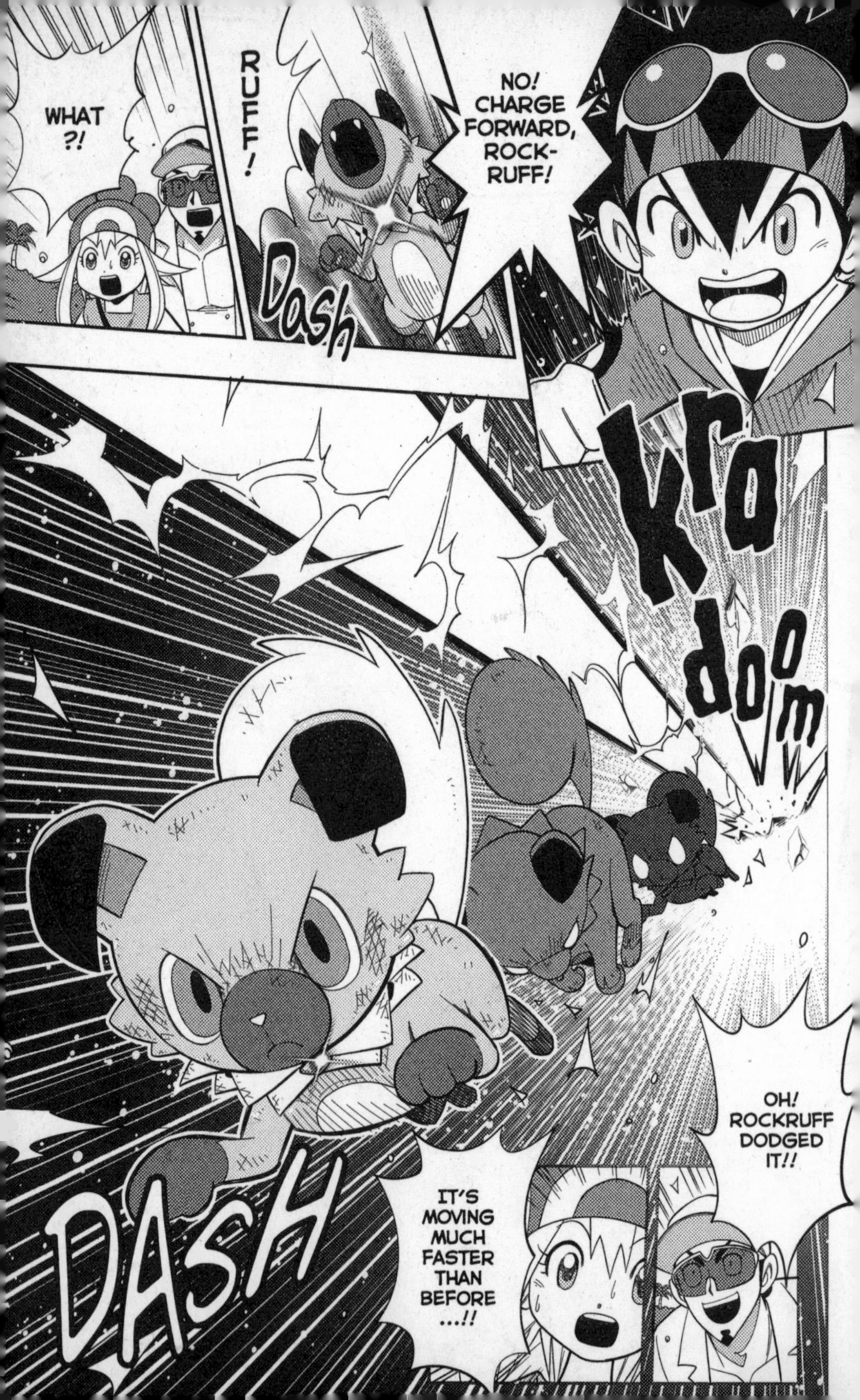
NO! CHARGE FORWARD, ROCK-RUFF!
RUFF!
Dash
WHAT ?!
Kradooom
DASH
OH! ROCKRUFF DODGED IT!!
IT'S MOVING MUCH FASTER THAN BEFORE ...!!

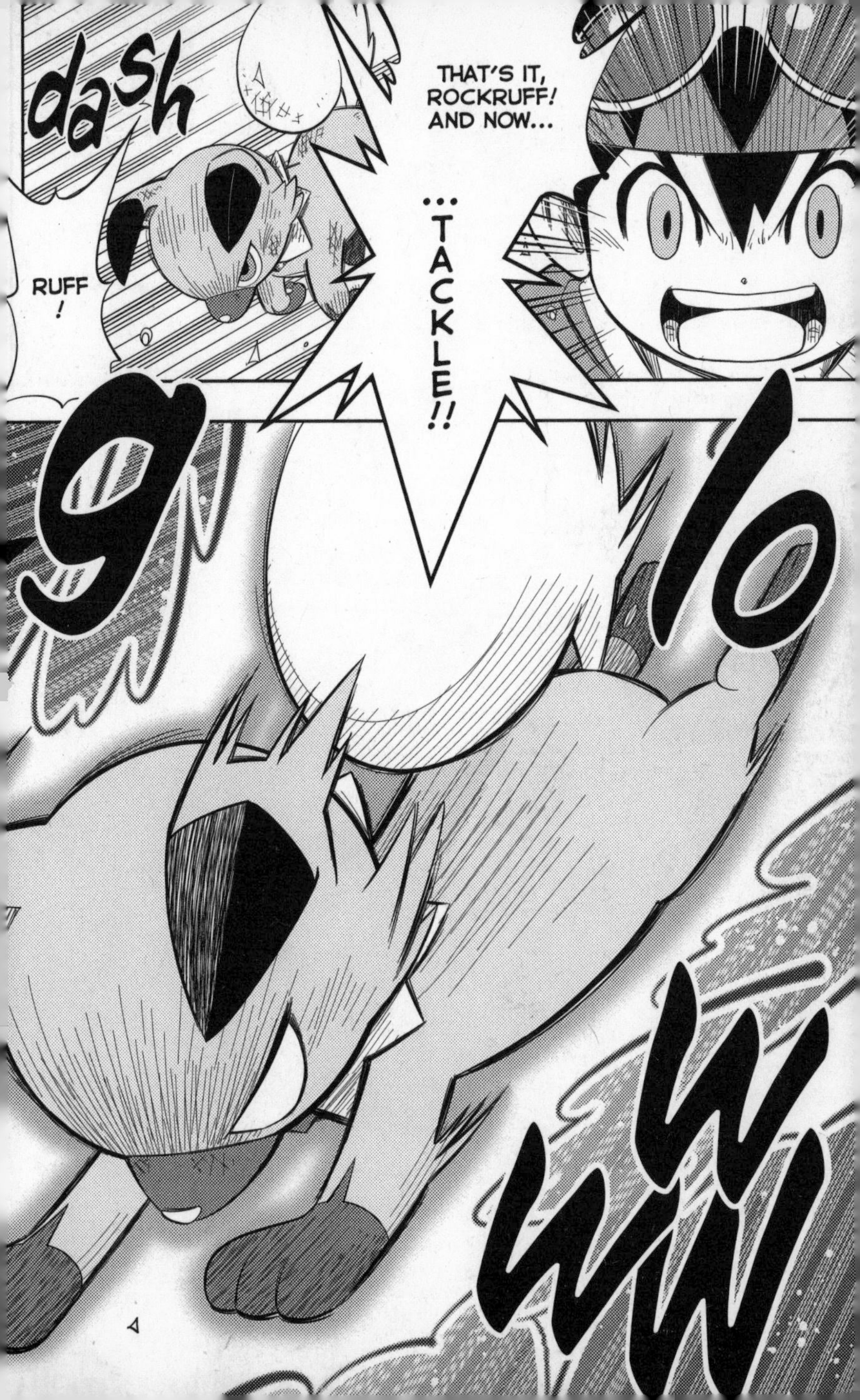
THAT'S IT, ROCKRUFF! AND NOW...
...TACKLE!!
dash
RUFF!

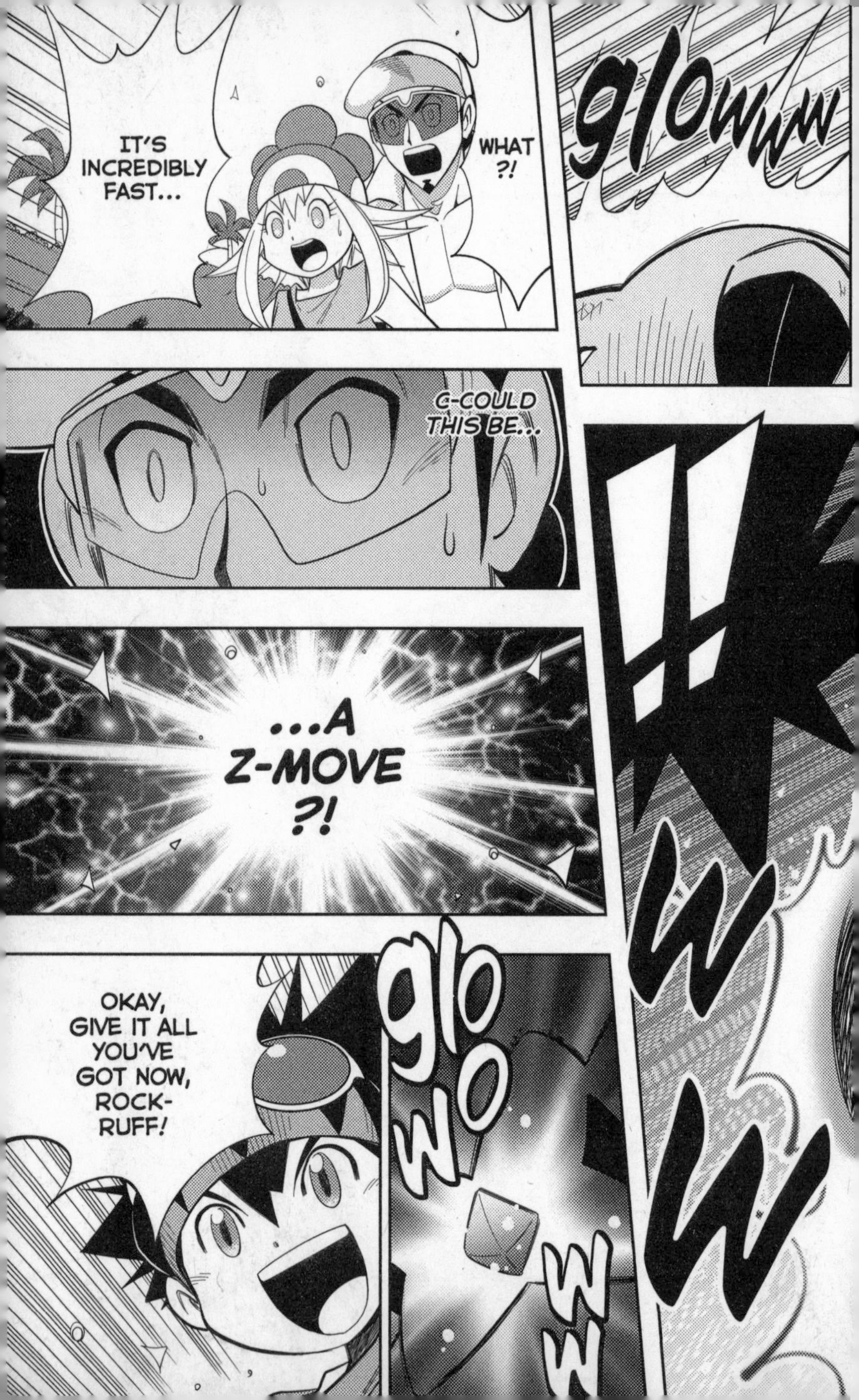
glowww
WHAT ?!
IT'S INCREDIBLY FAST...
!!
C-COULD THIS BE...
...A Z-MOVE ?!
glowww
OKAY, GIVE IT ALL YOU'VE GOT NOW, ROCK-RUFF!

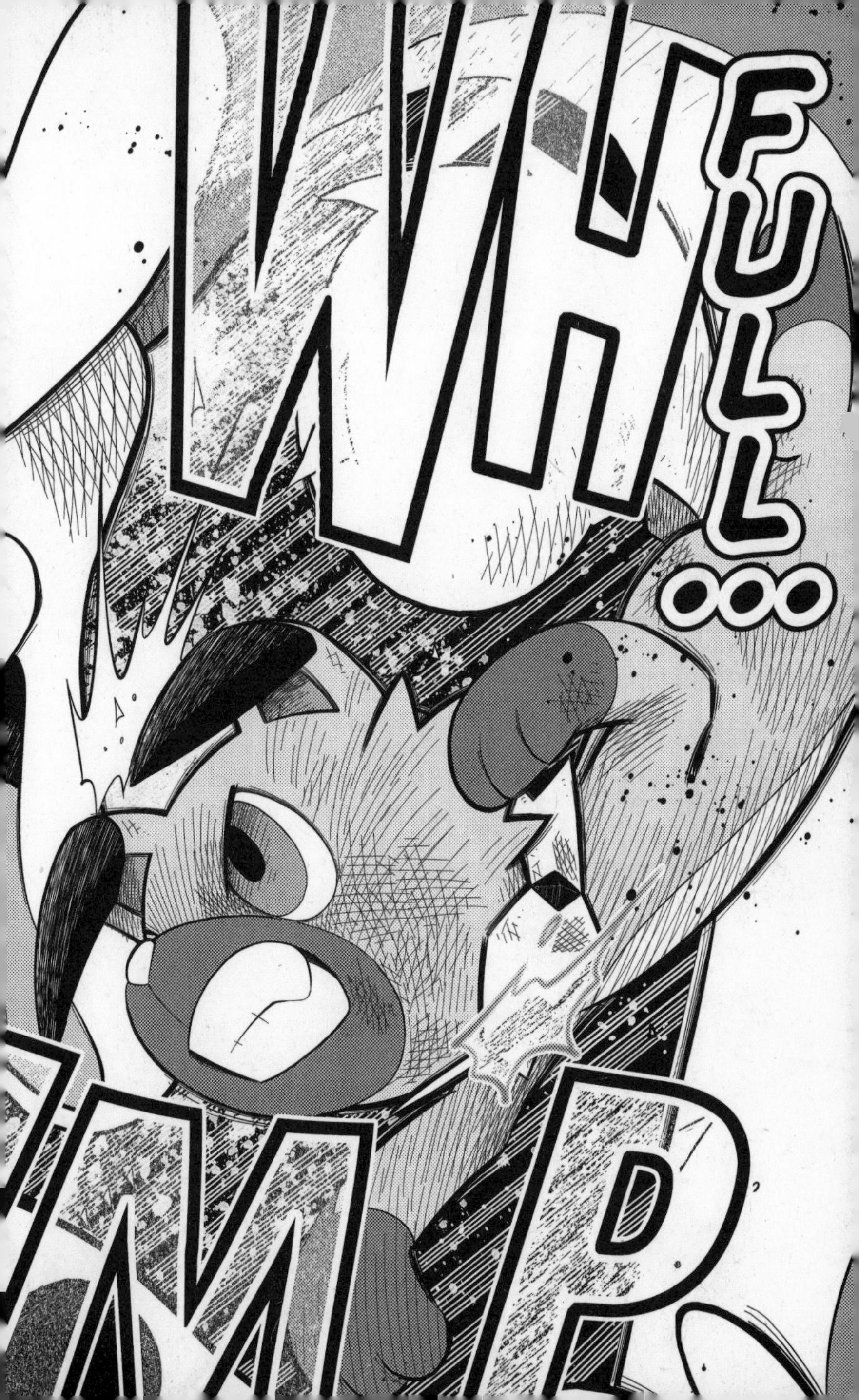
FULL...
WH
MP

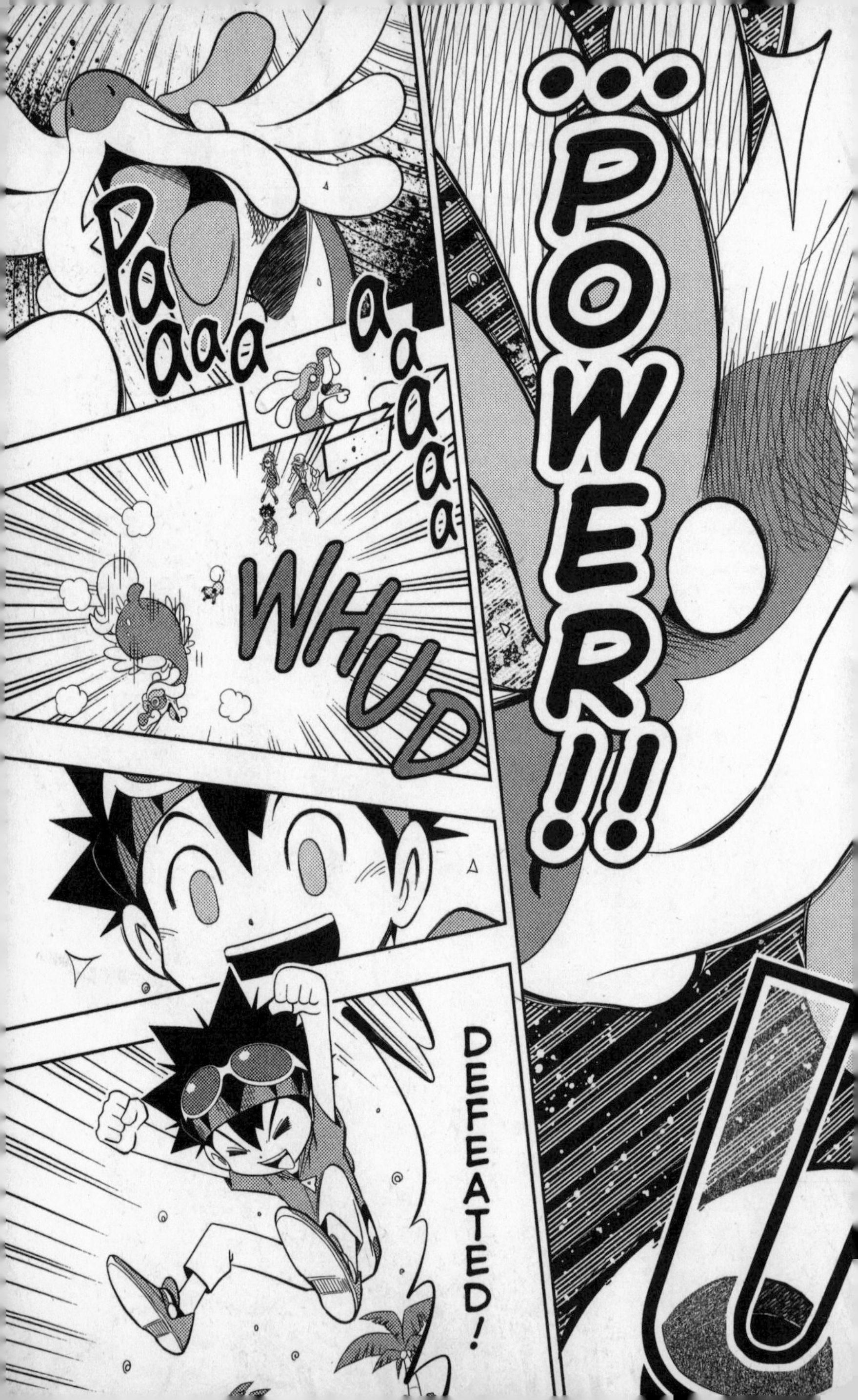

...POWER!!
!
Paaaaaaaaaa
WHUD
DEFEATED!

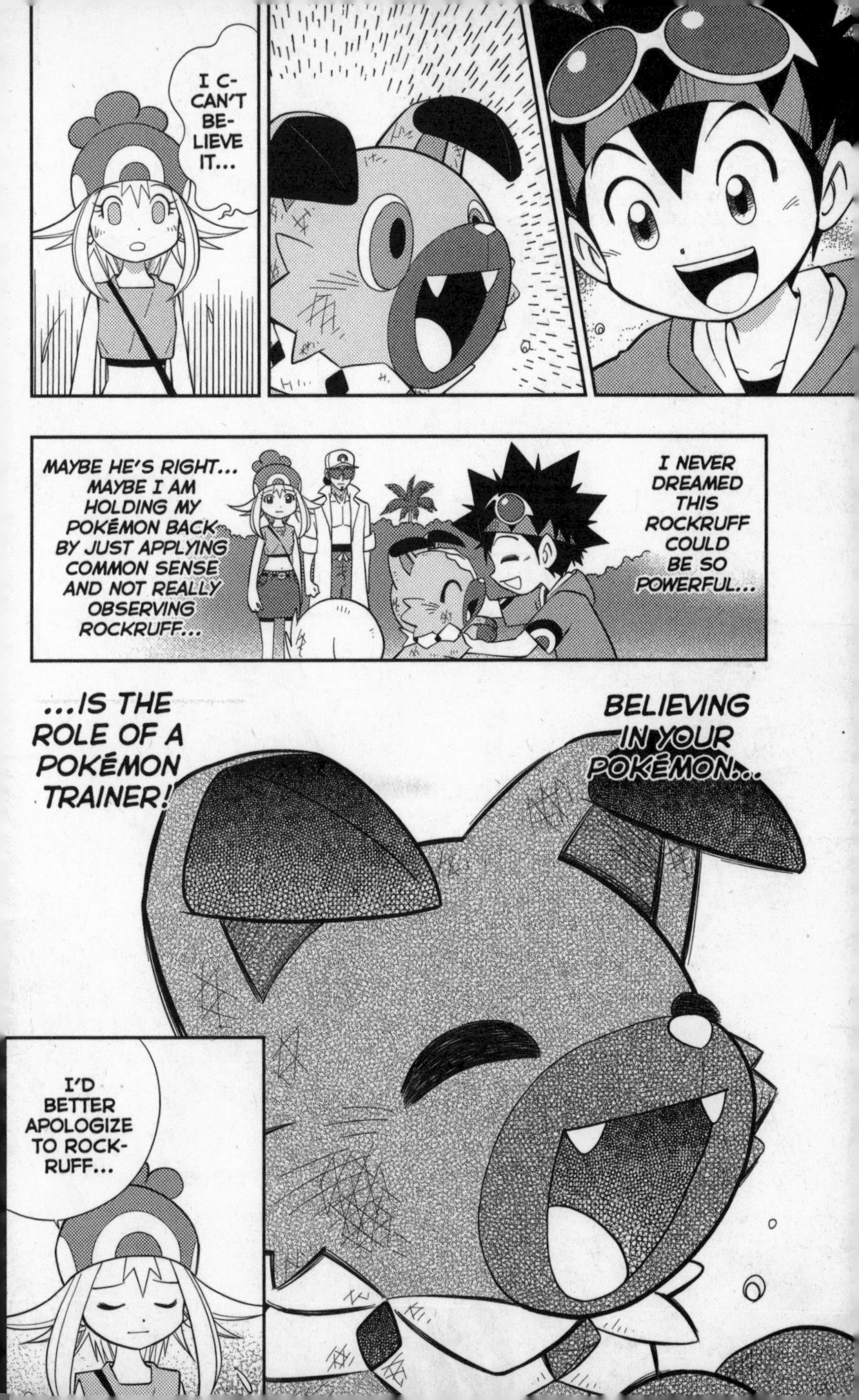
I C-CAN'T BE-LIEVE IT...
I NEVER DREAMED THIS ROCKRUFF COULD BE SO POWERFUL...
MAYBE HE'S RIGHT... MAYBE I AM HOLDING MY POKÉMON BACK BY JUST APPLYING COMMON SENSE AND NOT REALLY OBSERVING ROCKRUFF...
BELIEVING IN YOUR POKÉMON...
...IS THE ROLE OF A POKÉMON TRAINER!
I'D BETTER APOLOGIZE TO ROCK-RUFF...

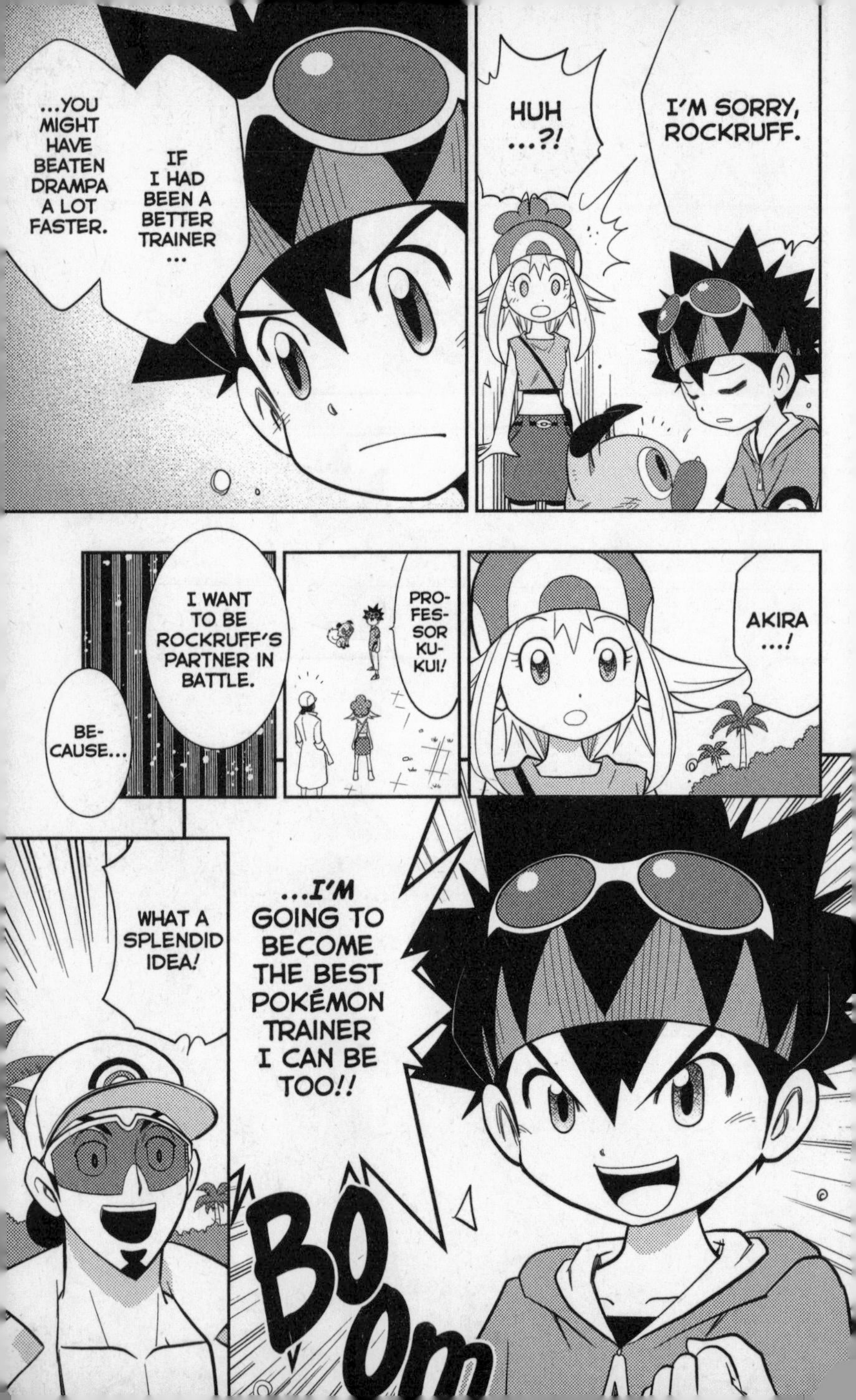
I'M SORRY, ROCKRUFF.
HUH ...?!
IF I HAD BEEN A BETTER TRAINER ...
...YOU MIGHT HAVE BEATEN DRAMPA A LOT FASTER.
AKIRA ...!
PRO-FES-SOR KU-KUI!
I WANT TO BE ROCKRUFF'S PARTNER IN BATTLE.
BE-CAUSE...
...I'M GOING TO BECOME THE BEST POKÉMON TRAINER I CAN BE TOO!!
BOOM
WHAT A SPLENDID IDEA!

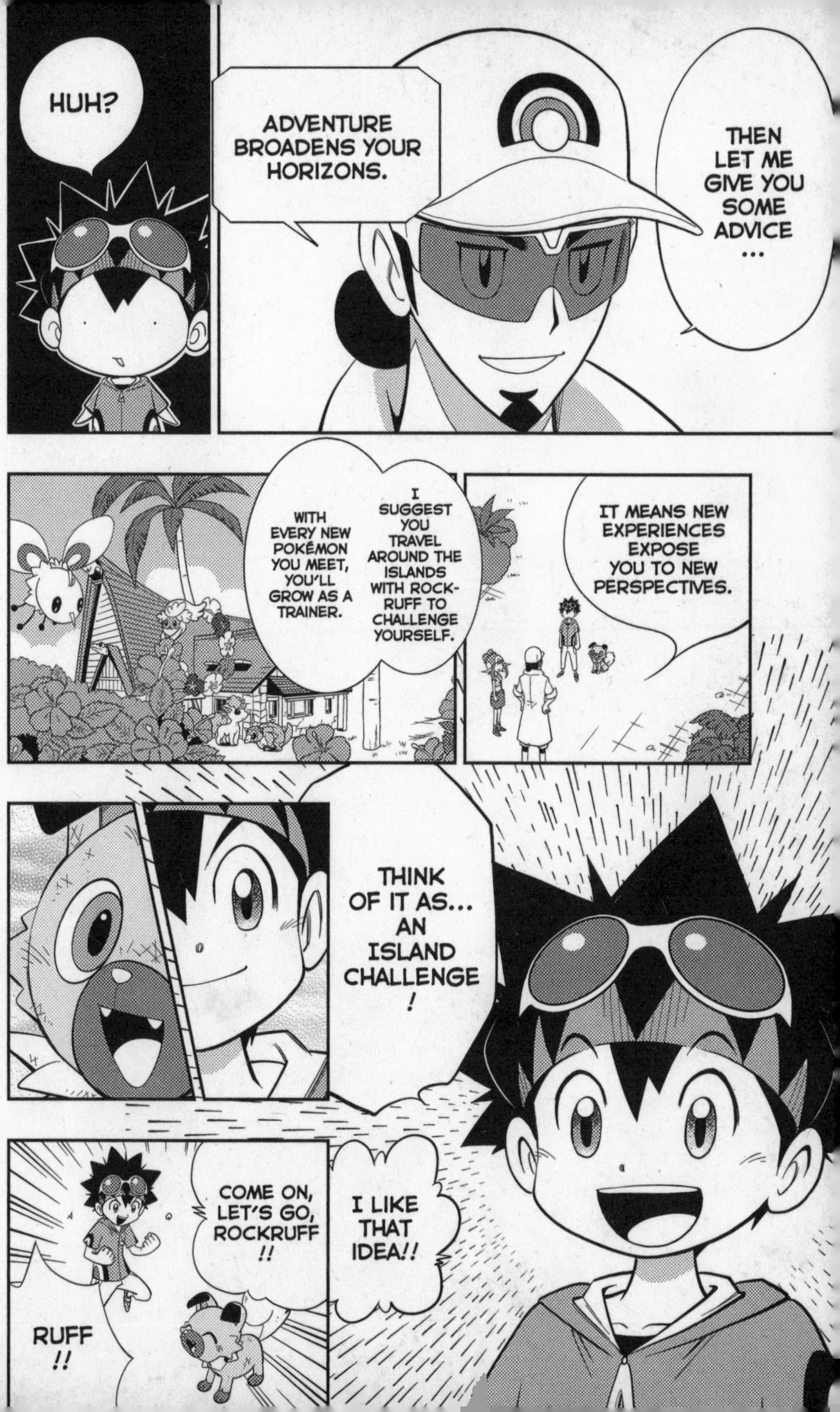
THEN LET ME GIVE YOU SOME ADVICE ...
ADVENTURE BROADENS YOUR HORIZONS.
HUH?
IT MEANS NEW EXPERIENCES EXPOSE YOU TO NEW PERSPECTIVES.
I SUGGEST YOU TRAVEL AROUND THE ISLANDS WITH ROCK-RUFF TO CHALLENGE YOURSELF.
WITH EVERY NEW POKÉMON YOU MEET, YOU'LL GROW AS A TRAINER.
THINK OF IT AS... AN ISLAND CHALLENGE!
I LIKE THAT IDEA!!
COME ON, LET'S GO, ROCKRUFF!!
RUFF!!

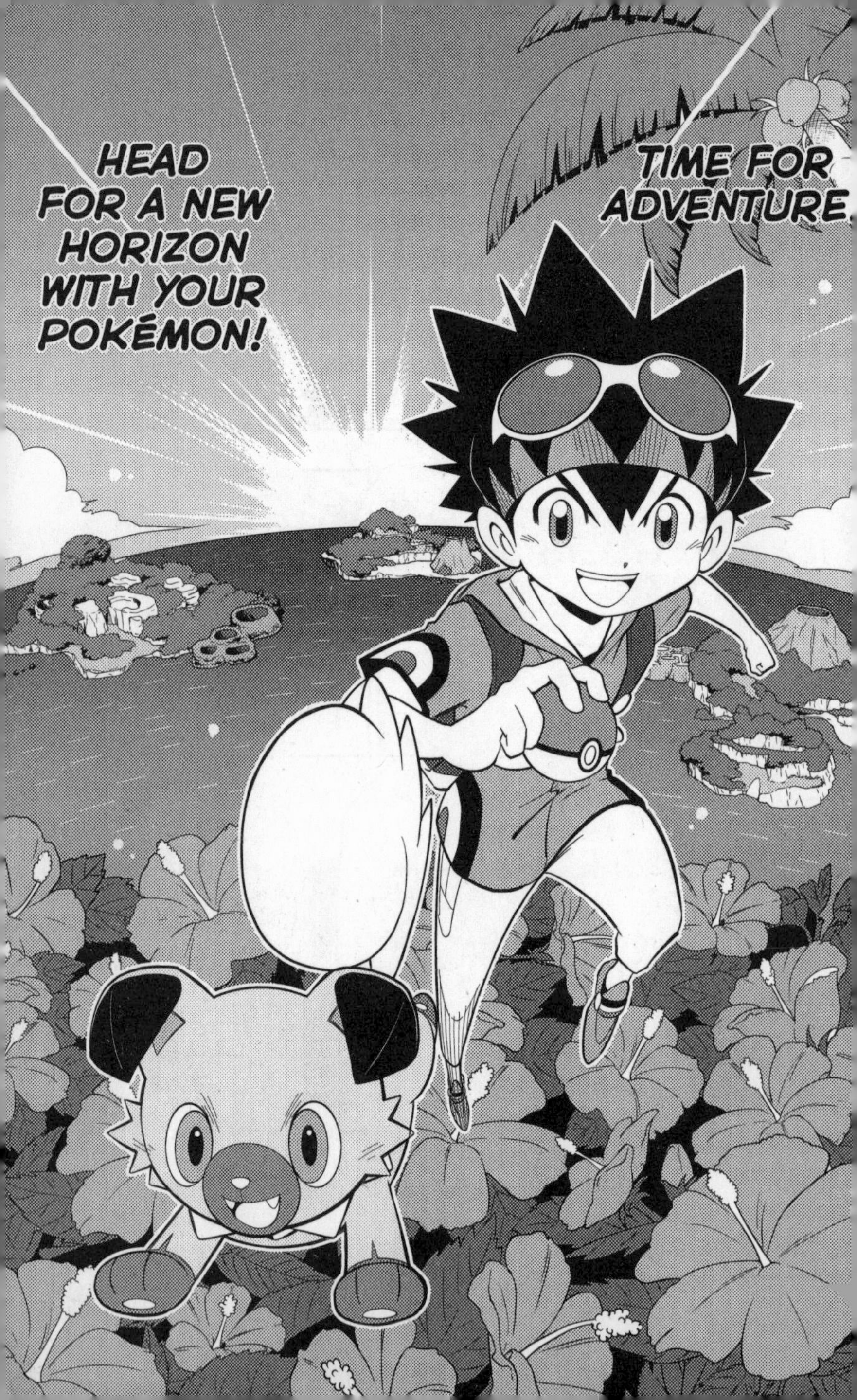
TIME FOR ADVENTURE
HEAD FOR A NEW HORIZON WITH YOUR POKÉMON!

Event 2:
The Power of Teamwork

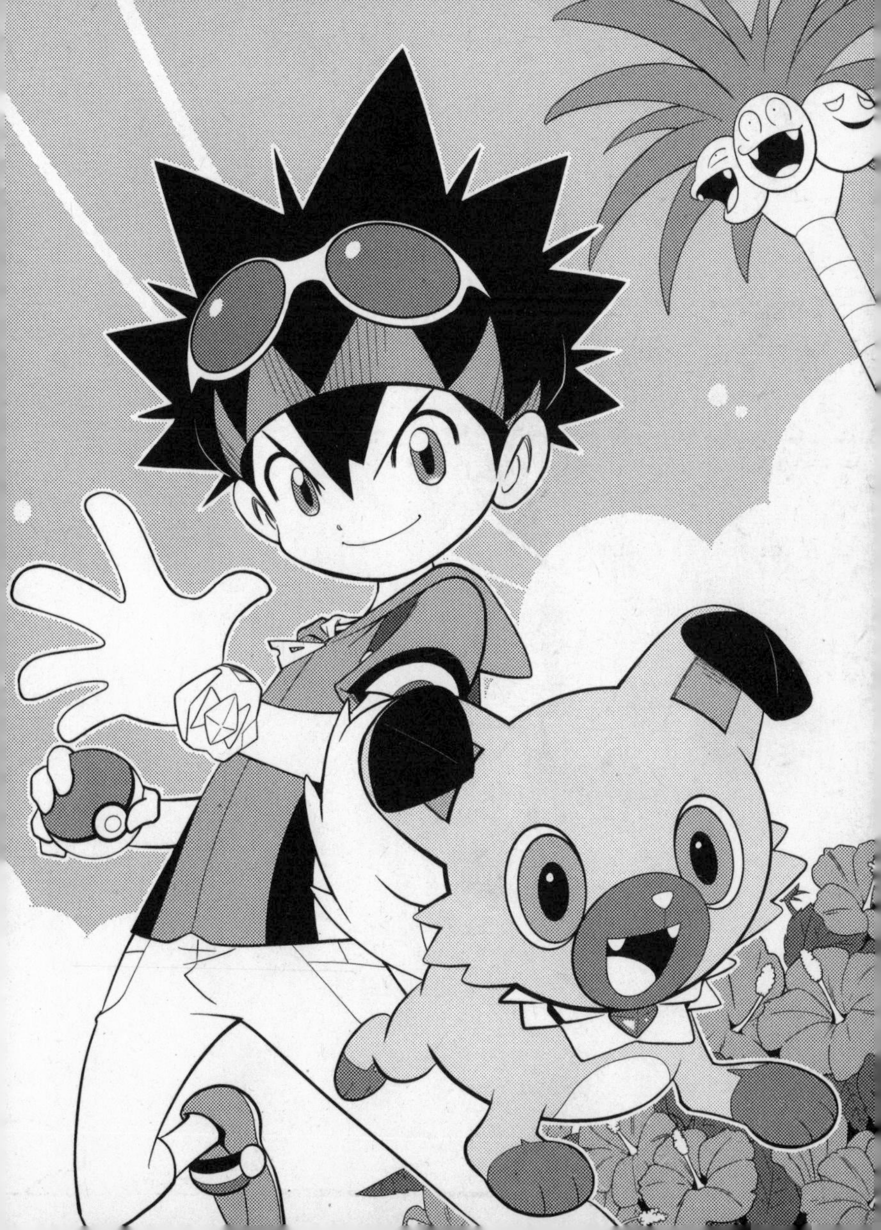

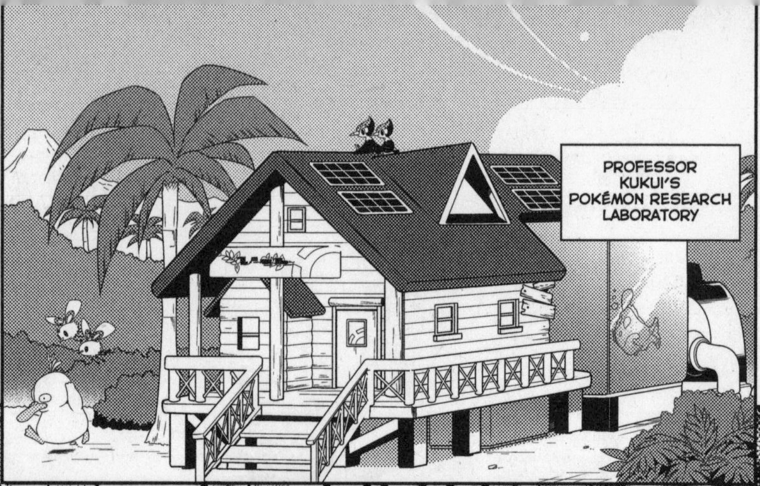
PROFESSOR KUKUI'S POKÉMON RESEARCH LABORATORY

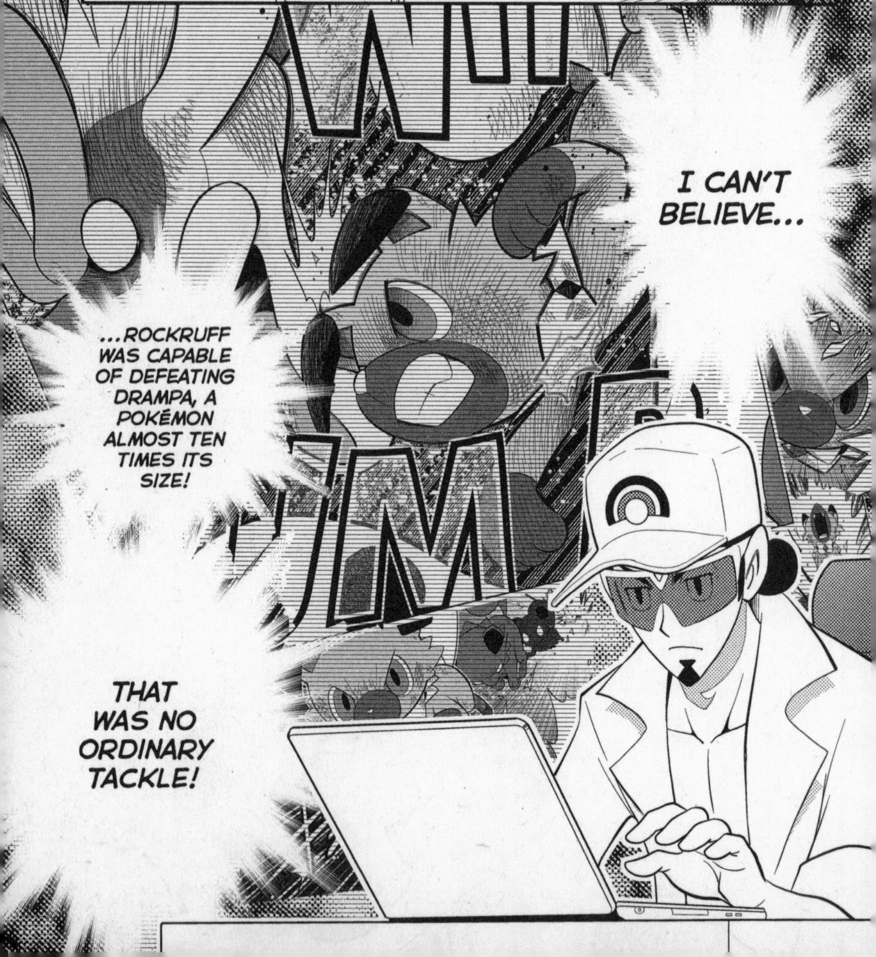
I CAN'T BELIEVE...
...ROCKRUFF WAS CAPABLE OF DEFEATING DRAMPA, A POKÉMON ALMOST TEN TIMES ITS SIZE!
THAT WAS NO ORDINARY TACKLE!

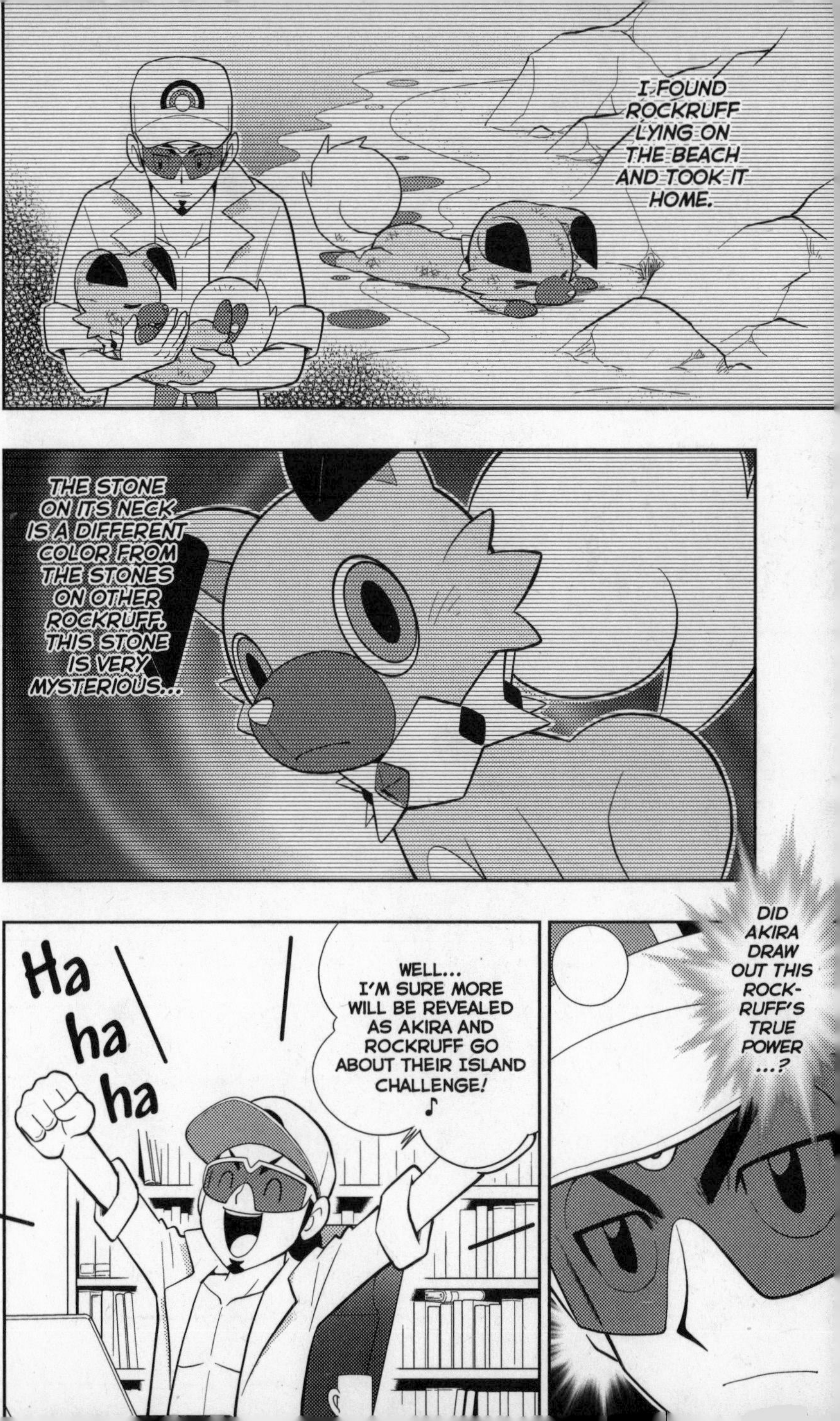
I FOUND ROCKRUFF LYING ON THE BEACH AND TOOK IT HOME.
THE STONE ON ITS NECK IS A DIFFERENT COLOR FROM THE STONES ON OTHER ROCKRUFF. THIS STONE IS VERY MYSTERIOUS...
DID AKIRA DRAW OUT THIS ROCK-RUFF'S TRUE POWER ...?
WELL... I'M SURE MORE WILL BE REVEALED AS AKIRA AND ROCKRUFF GO ABOUT THEIR ISLAND CHALLENGE! ♪
Ha ha ha

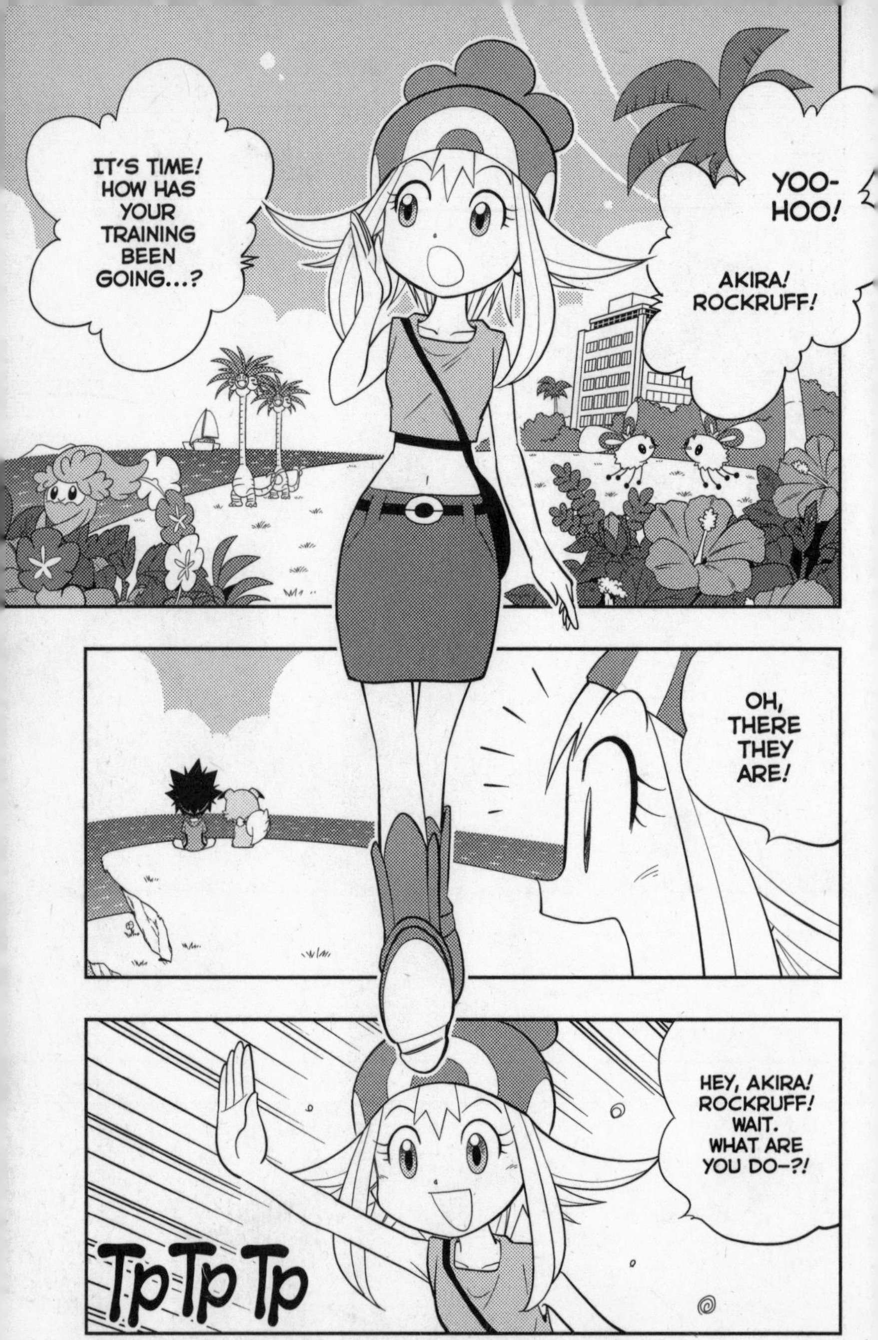
YOO-HOO!
AKIRA! ROCKRUFF!
IT'S TIME! HOW HAS YOUR TRAINING BEEN GOING...?
OH, THERE THEY ARE!
HEY, AKIRA! ROCKRUFF! WAIT. WHAT ARE YOU DO-?!
Tp Tp Tp

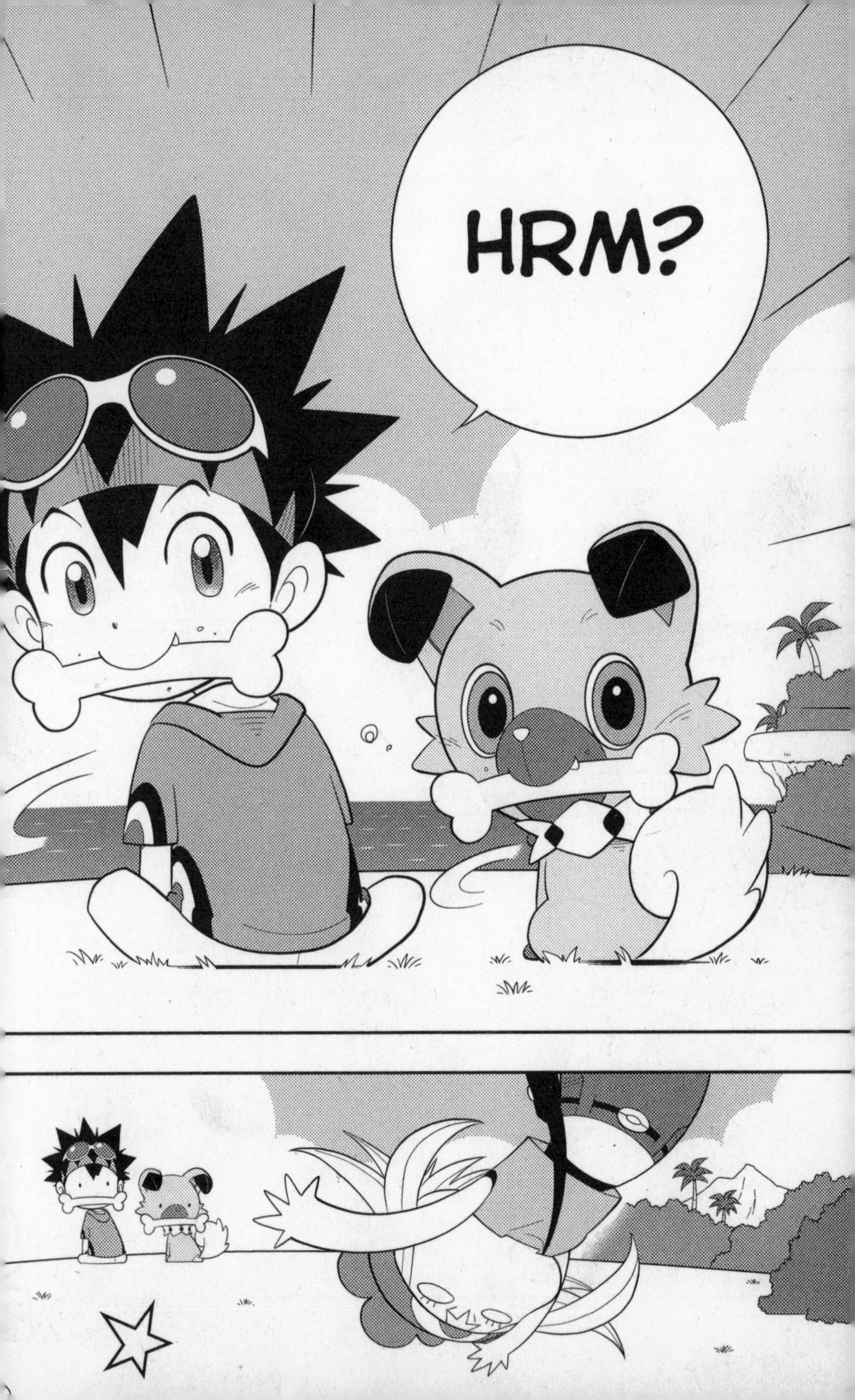
HRM?

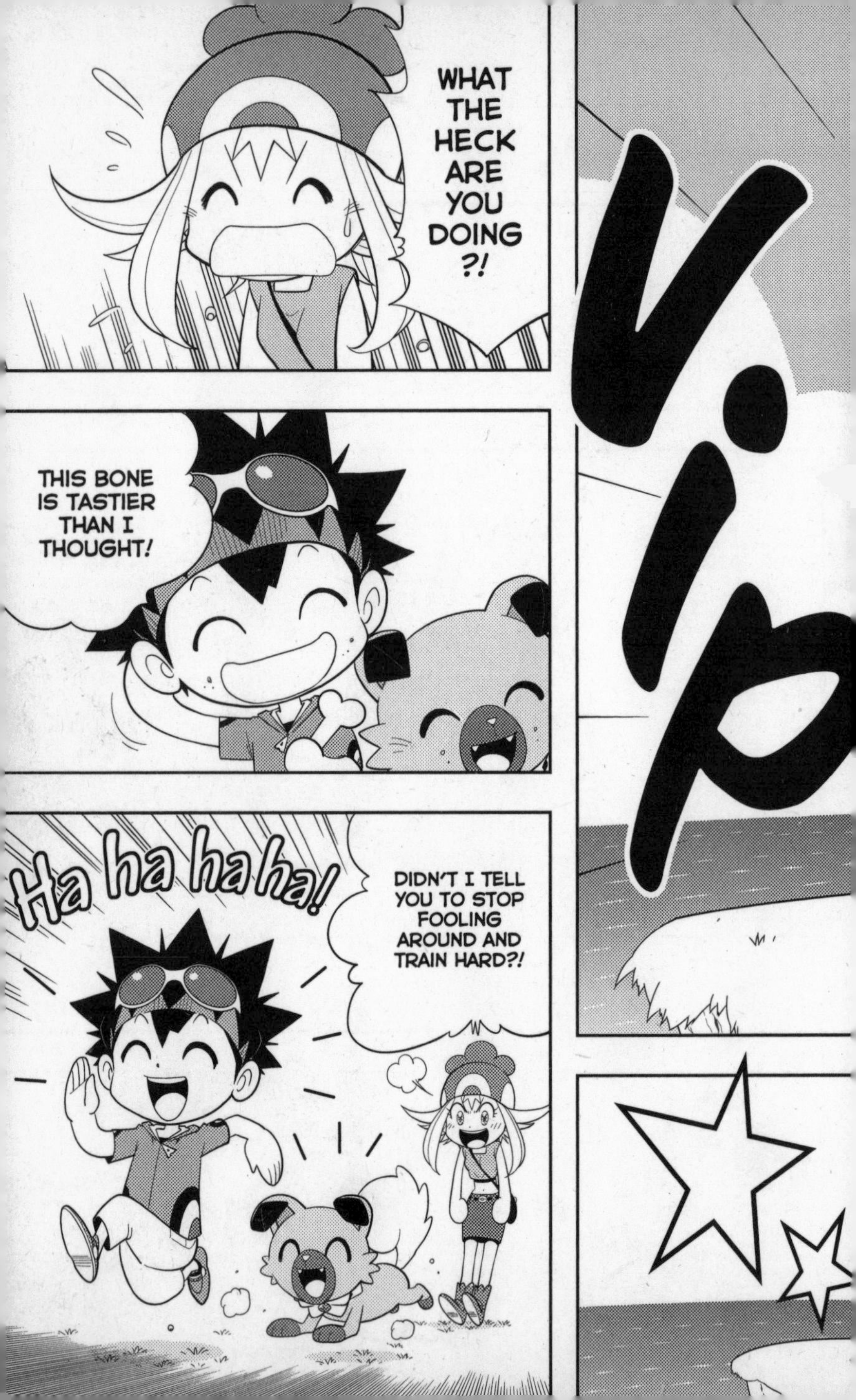
WHAT THE HECK ARE YOU DOING ?!
THIS BONE IS TASTIER THAN I THOUGHT!
DIDN'T I TELL YOU TO STOP FOOLING AROUND AND TRAIN HARD?!
Ha ha ha ha!

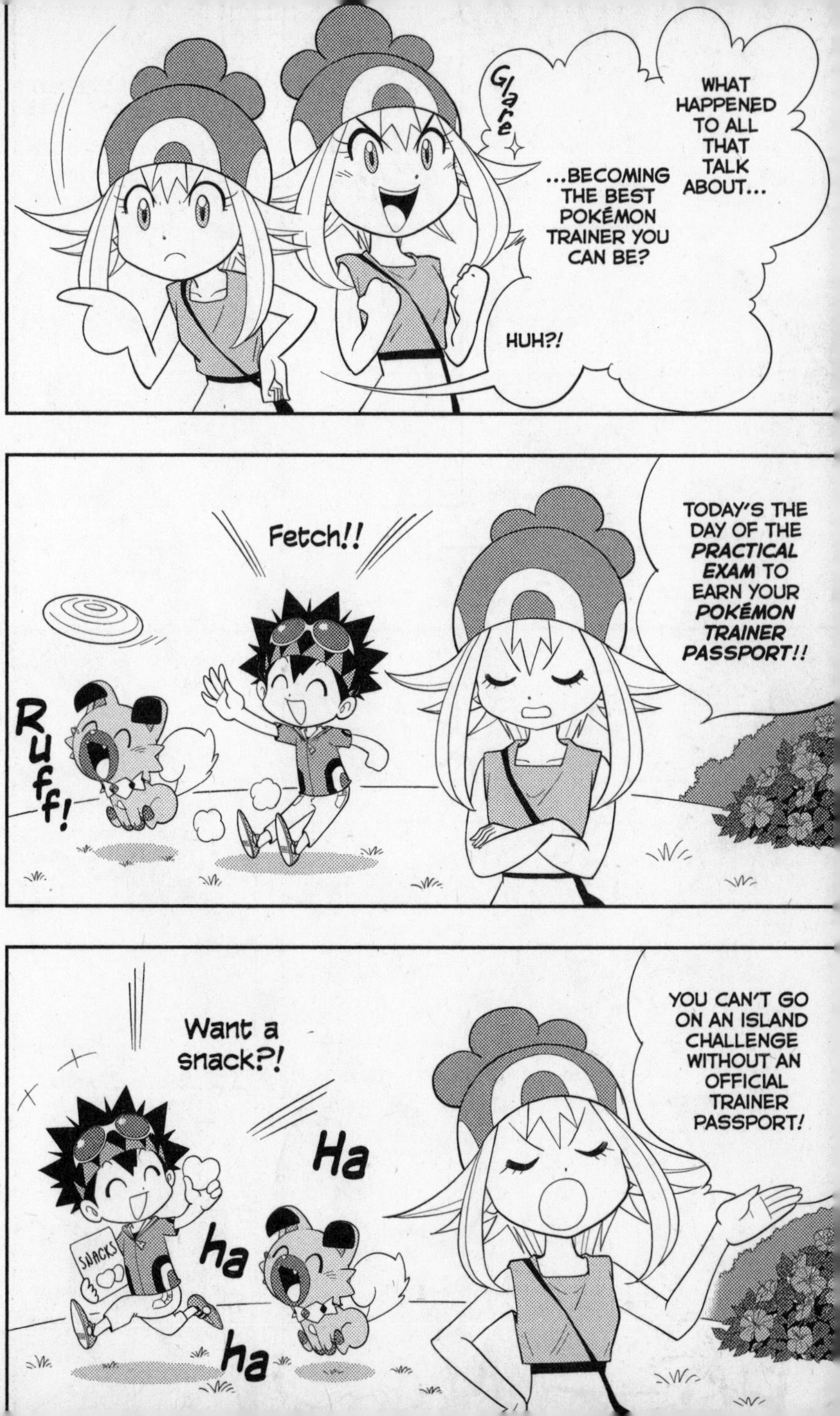
WHAT HAPPENED TO ALL THAT TALK ABOUT...
Glare
...BECOMING THE BEST POKéMON TRAINER YOU CAN BE?
HUH?!
TODAY'S THE DAY OF THE *PRACTICAL EXAM* TO EARN YOUR *POKéMON TRAINER PASSPORT!!*
Fetch!!
Ruff!
YOU CAN'T GO ON AN ISLAND CHALLENGE WITHOUT AN OFFICIAL TRAINER PASSPORT!
Want a snack?!
Ha
ha
ha
SNACKS

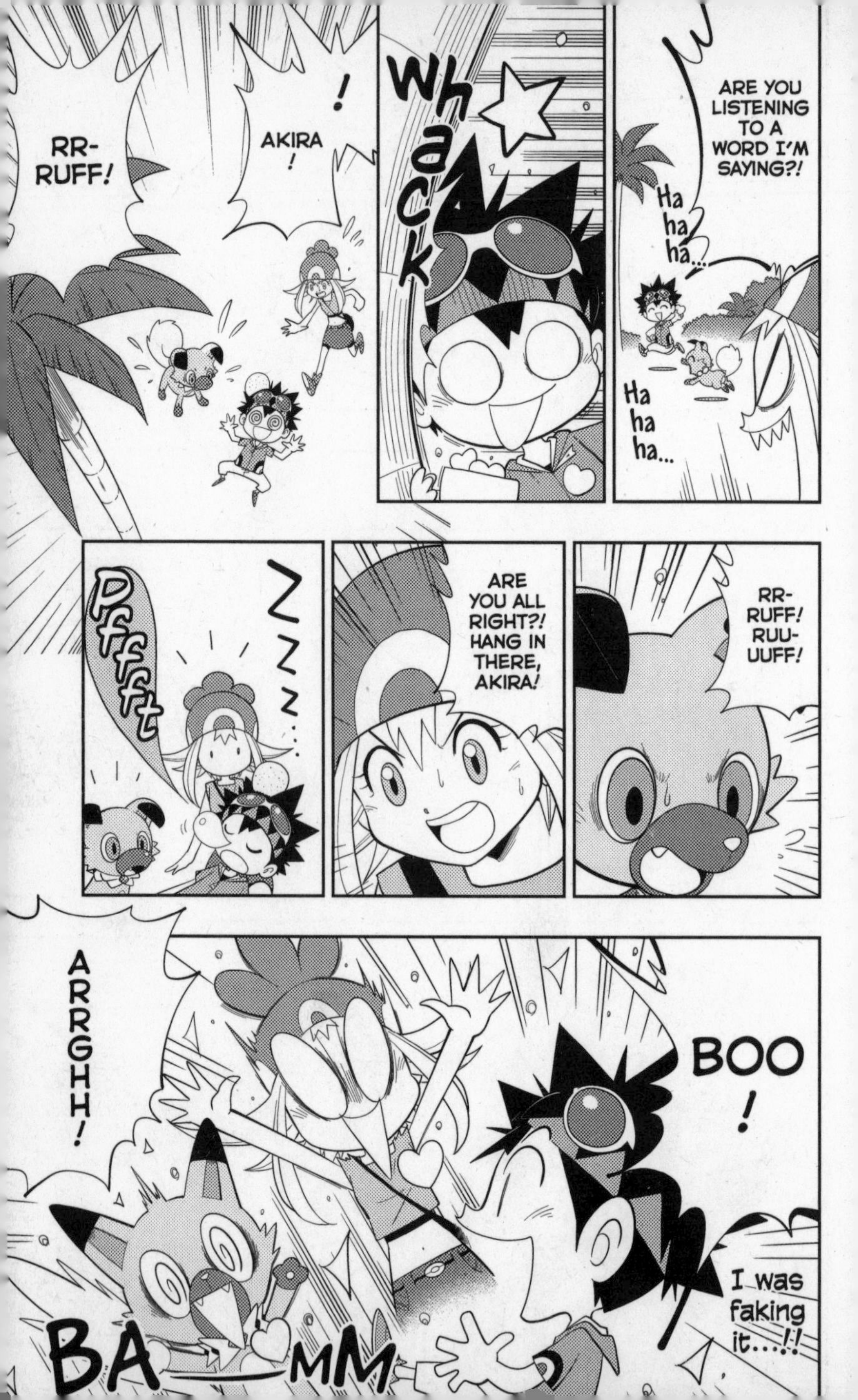
ARE YOU LISTENING TO A WORD I'M SAYING?!
Ha ha ha...
Ha ha ha...
Whack
!
AKIRA!
RR-RUFF!
RR-RUFF! RUU-UUFF!
ARE YOU ALL RIGHT?! HANG IN THERE, AKIRA!
Zzz...
Pffft
BOO!
ARRGHH!
I was faking it...!!
BA—MM

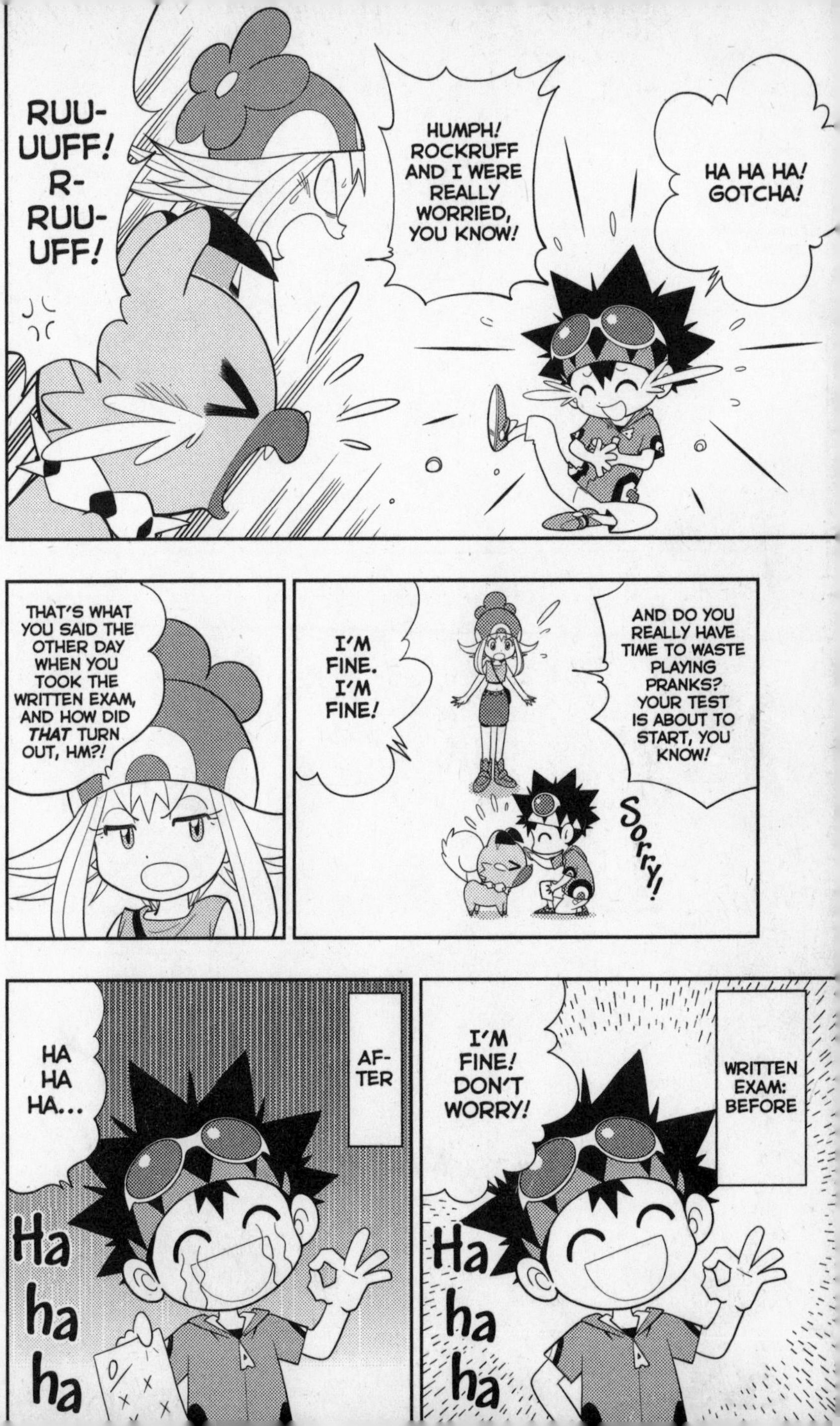
HA HA HA! GOTCHA!
HUMPH! ROCKRUFF AND I WERE REALLY WORRIED, YOU KNOW!
RUU-UUFF! R-RUU-UFF!
AND DO YOU REALLY HAVE TIME TO WASTE PLAYING PRANKS? YOUR TEST IS ABOUT TO START, YOU KNOW!
I'M FINE. I'M FINE!
Sorry!
THAT'S WHAT YOU SAID THE OTHER DAY WHEN YOU TOOK THE WRITTEN EXAM, AND HOW DID *THAT* TURN OUT, HM?!
WRITTEN EXAM: BEFORE
I'M FINE! DON'T WORRY!
Ha ha ha ha
AF-TER
HA HA HA...
Ha ha ha ha

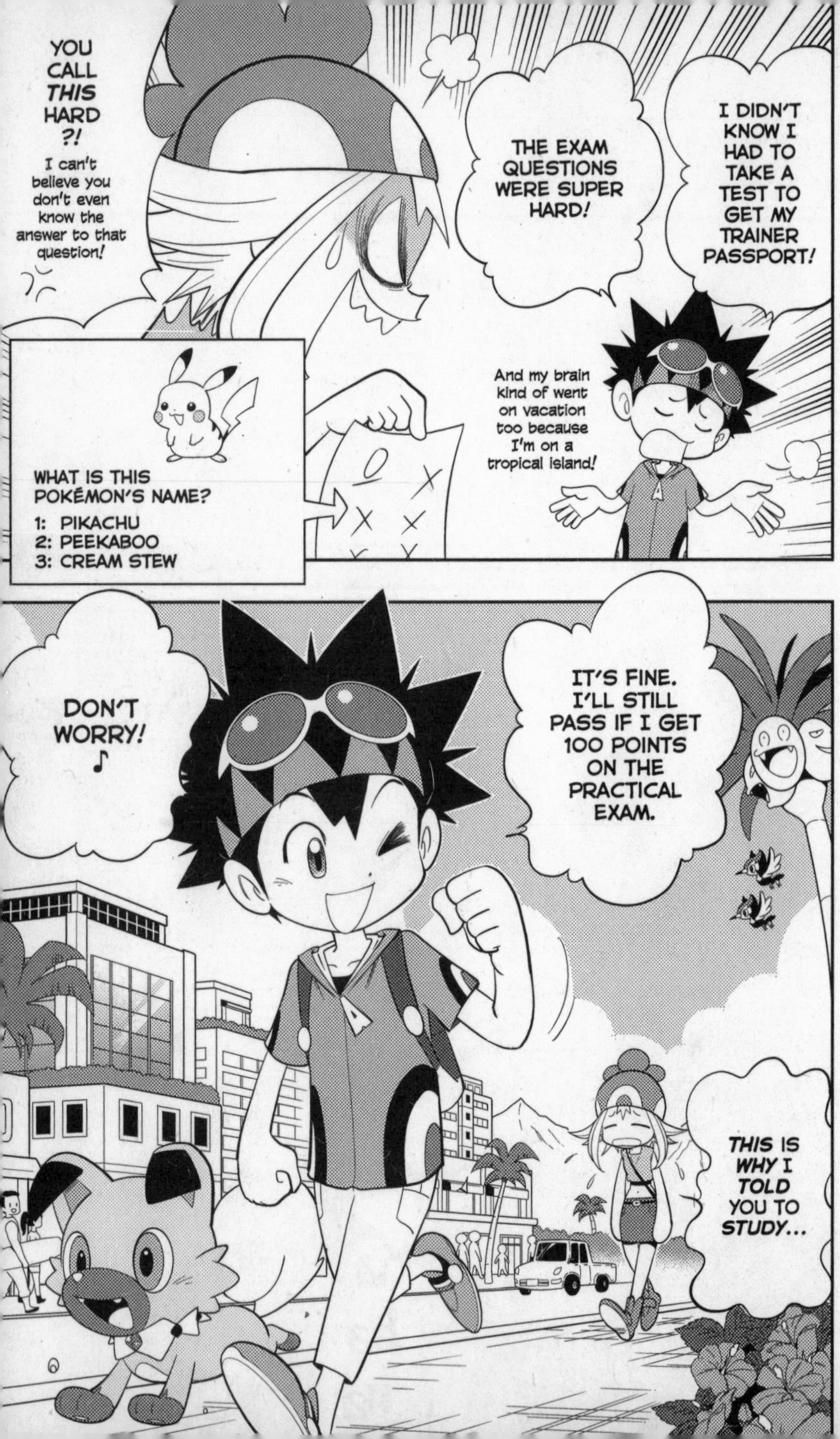
I DIDN'T KNOW I HAD TO TAKE A TEST TO GET MY TRAINER PASSPORT!
THE EXAM QUESTIONS WERE SUPER HARD!
And my brain kind of went on vacation too because I'm on a tropical island!
YOU CALL *THIS* HARD?!
I can't believe you don't even know the answer to that question!
WHAT IS THIS POKÉMON'S NAME?
1: PIKACHU
2: PEEKABOO
3: CREAM STEW
IT'S FINE. I'LL STILL PASS IF I GET 100 POINTS ON THE PRACTICAL EXAM.
DON'T WORRY! ♪
THIS IS *WHY* I *TOLD* YOU TO *STUDY*...

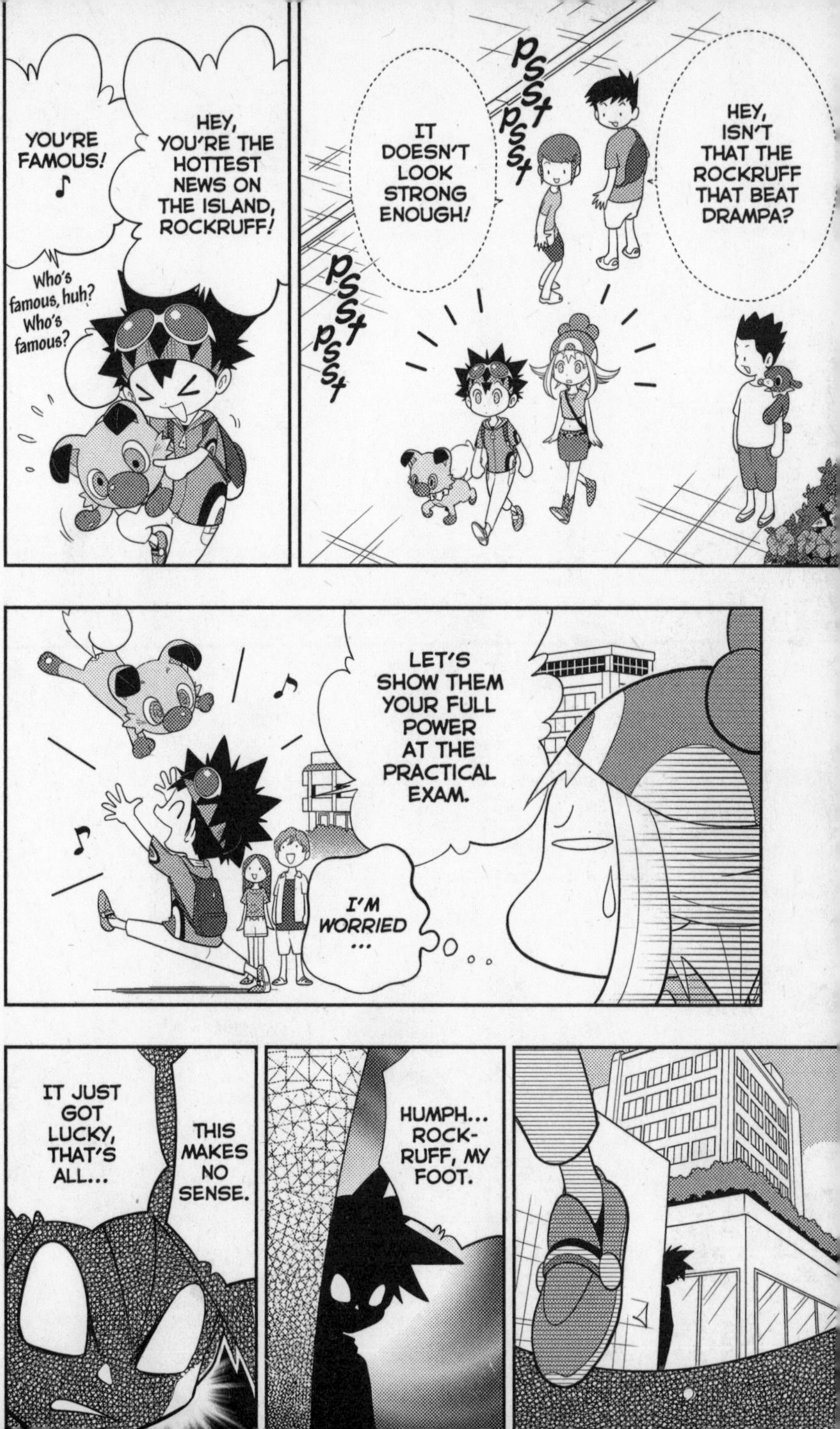
HEY, ISN'T THAT THE ROCKRUFF THAT BEAT DRAMPA?
PSST PSST
IT DOESN'T LOOK STRONG ENOUGH!
PSST PSST
HEY, YOU'RE THE HOTTEST NEWS ON THE ISLAND, ROCKRUFF!
YOU'RE FAMOUS! ♪
Who's famous, huh? Who's famous?
LET'S SHOW THEM YOUR FULL POWER AT THE PRACTICAL EXAM.
I'M WORRIED...
HUMPH... ROCK-RUFF, MY FOOT.
THIS MAKES NO SENSE.
IT JUST GOT LUCKY, THAT'S ALL...

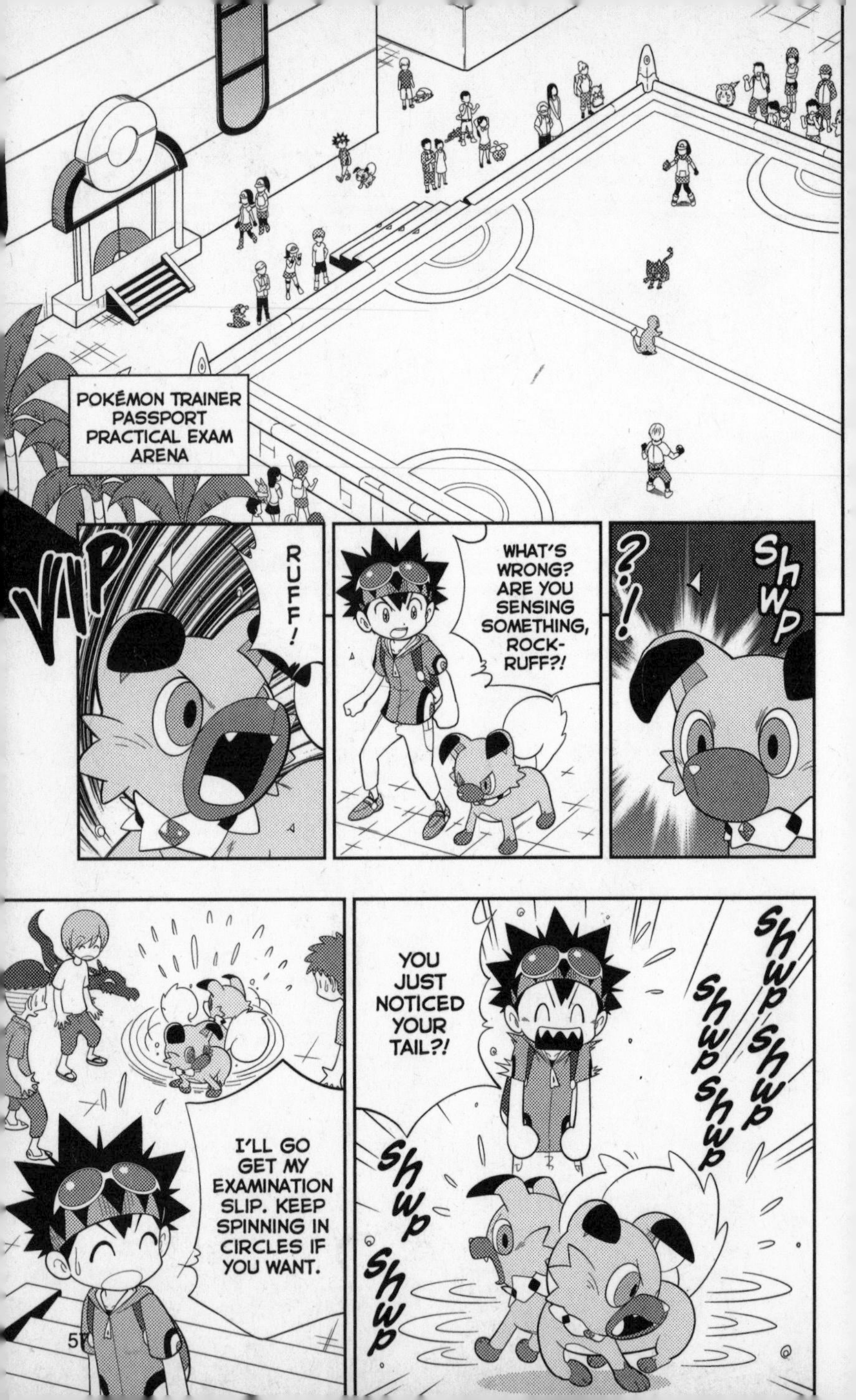
POKÉMON TRAINER PASSPORT PRACTICAL EXAM ARENA
SHWP
?!
WHAT'S WRONG? ARE YOU SENSING SOMETHING, ROCK-RUFF?!
RUFF!
YIP
YOU JUST NOTICED YOUR TAIL?!
SHWP SHWP SHWP SHWP SHWP SHWP SHWP
I'LL GO GET MY EXAMINATION SLIP. KEEP SPINNING IN CIRCLES IF YOU WANT.

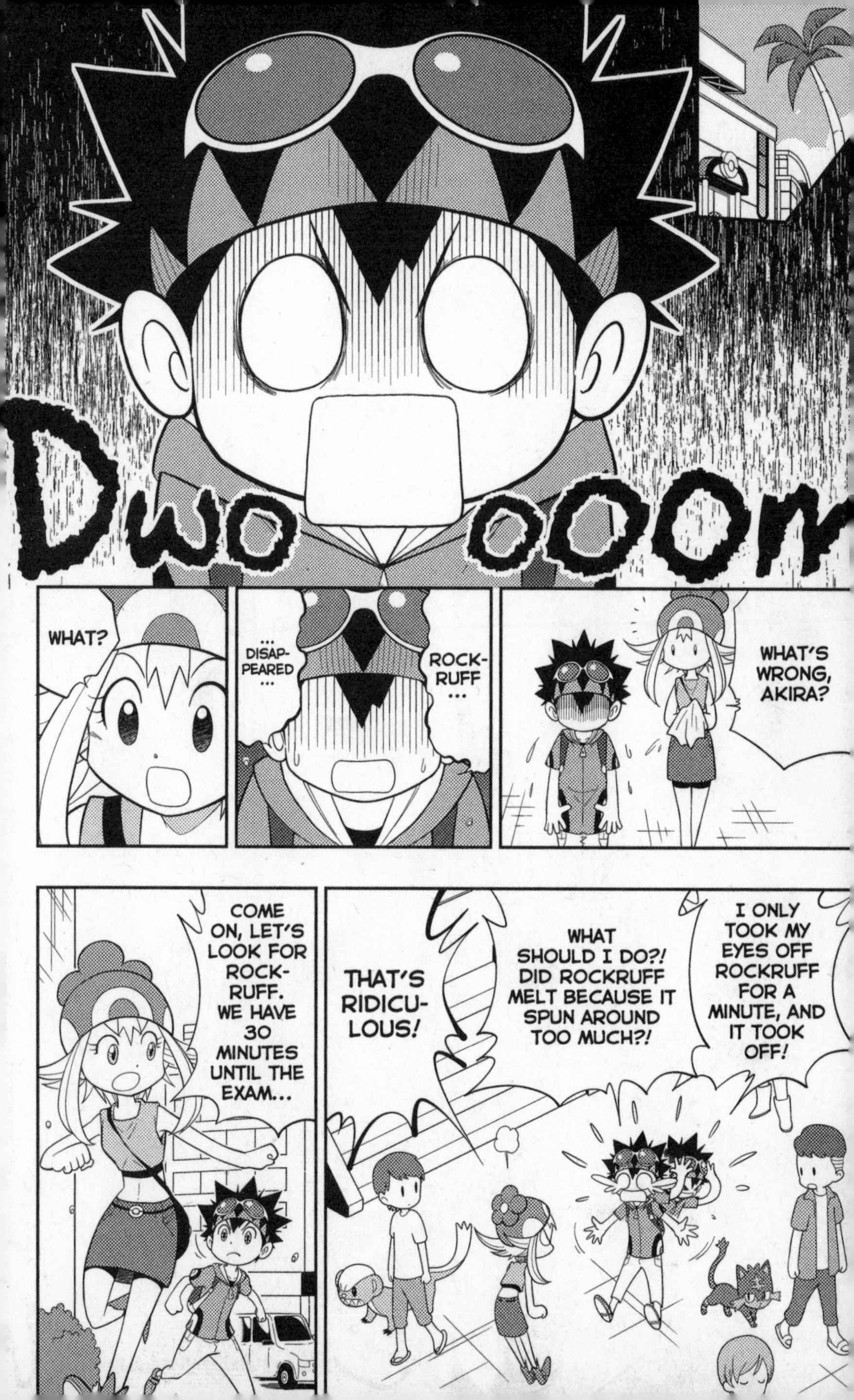

DWOOOOOM
WHAT'S WRONG, AKIRA?
ROCK-RUFF...
...DISAP-PEARED...
WHAT?
I ONLY TOOK MY EYES OFF ROCKRUFF FOR A MINUTE, AND IT TOOK OFF!
WHAT SHOULD I DO?! DID ROCKRUFF MELT BECAUSE IT SPUN AROUND TOO MUCH?!
THAT'S RIDICULOUS!
COME ON, LET'S LOOK FOR ROCK-RUFF. WE HAVE 30 MINUTES UNTIL THE EXAM...

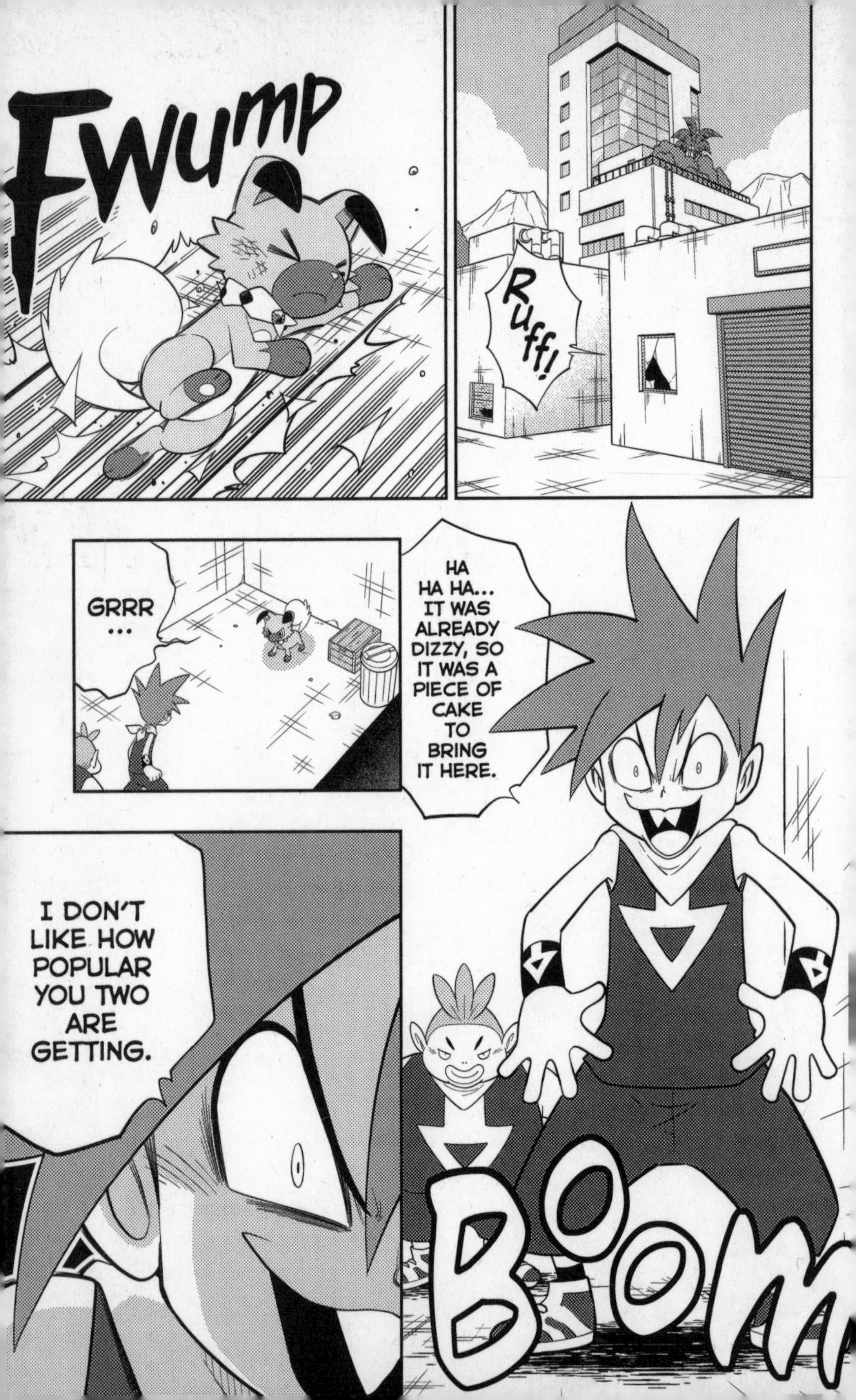
RUFF!
FWUMP
HA HA HA... IT WAS ALREADY DIZZY, SO IT WAS A PIECE OF CAKE TO BRING IT HERE.
BOOM
GRRR...
I DON'T LIKE HOW POPULAR YOU TWO ARE GETTING.

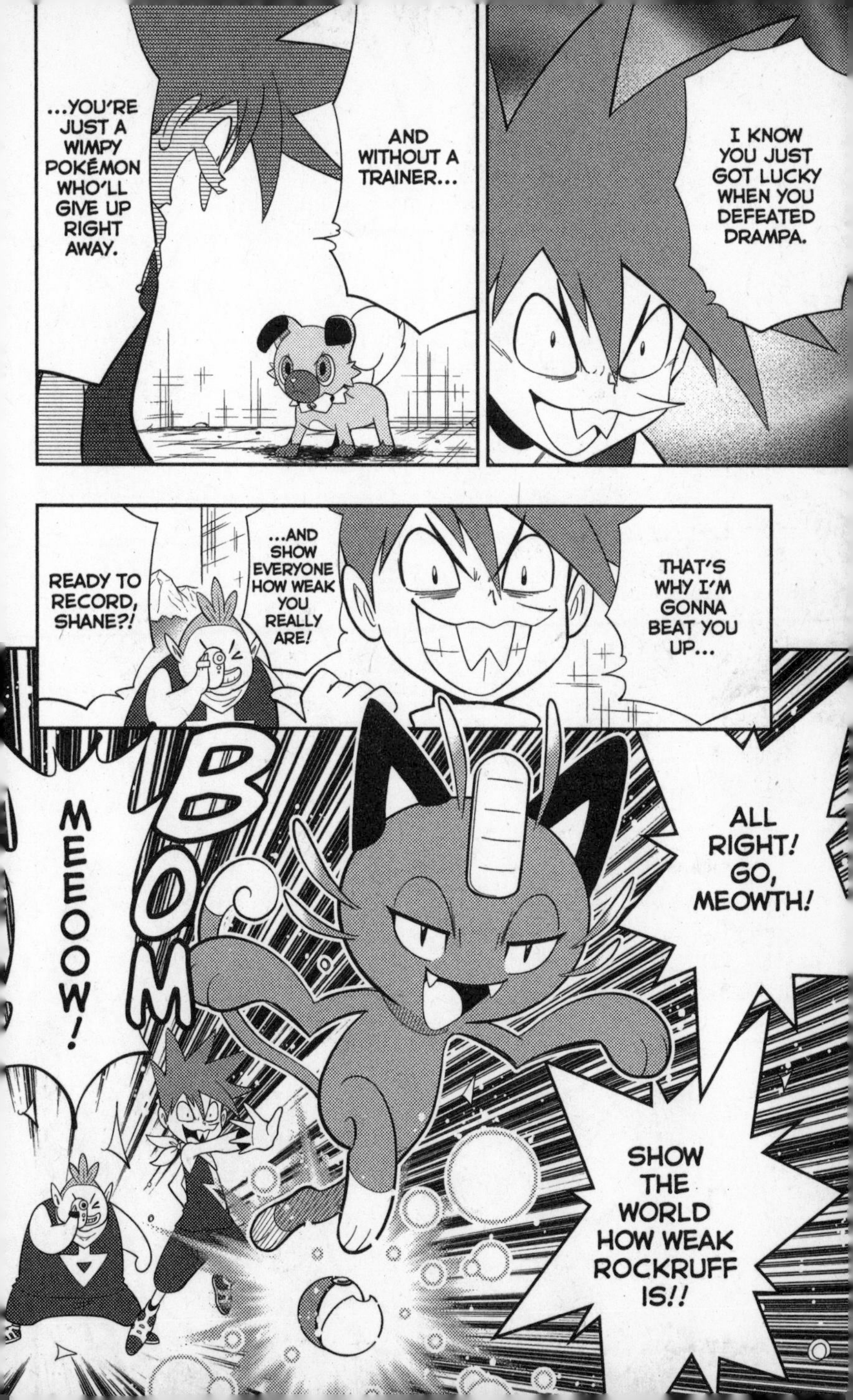
I KNOW YOU JUST GOT LUCKY WHEN YOU DEFEATED DRAMPA.
AND WITHOUT A TRAINER...
...YOU'RE JUST A WIMPY POKÉMON WHO'LL GIVE UP RIGHT AWAY.
THAT'S WHY I'M GONNA BEAT YOU UP...
...AND SHOW EVERYONE HOW WEAK YOU REALLY ARE!
READY TO RECORD, SHANE?!
ALL RIGHT! GO, MEOWTH!
BOOM
MEEOOW!
SHOW THE WORLD HOW WEAK ROCKRUFF IS!!

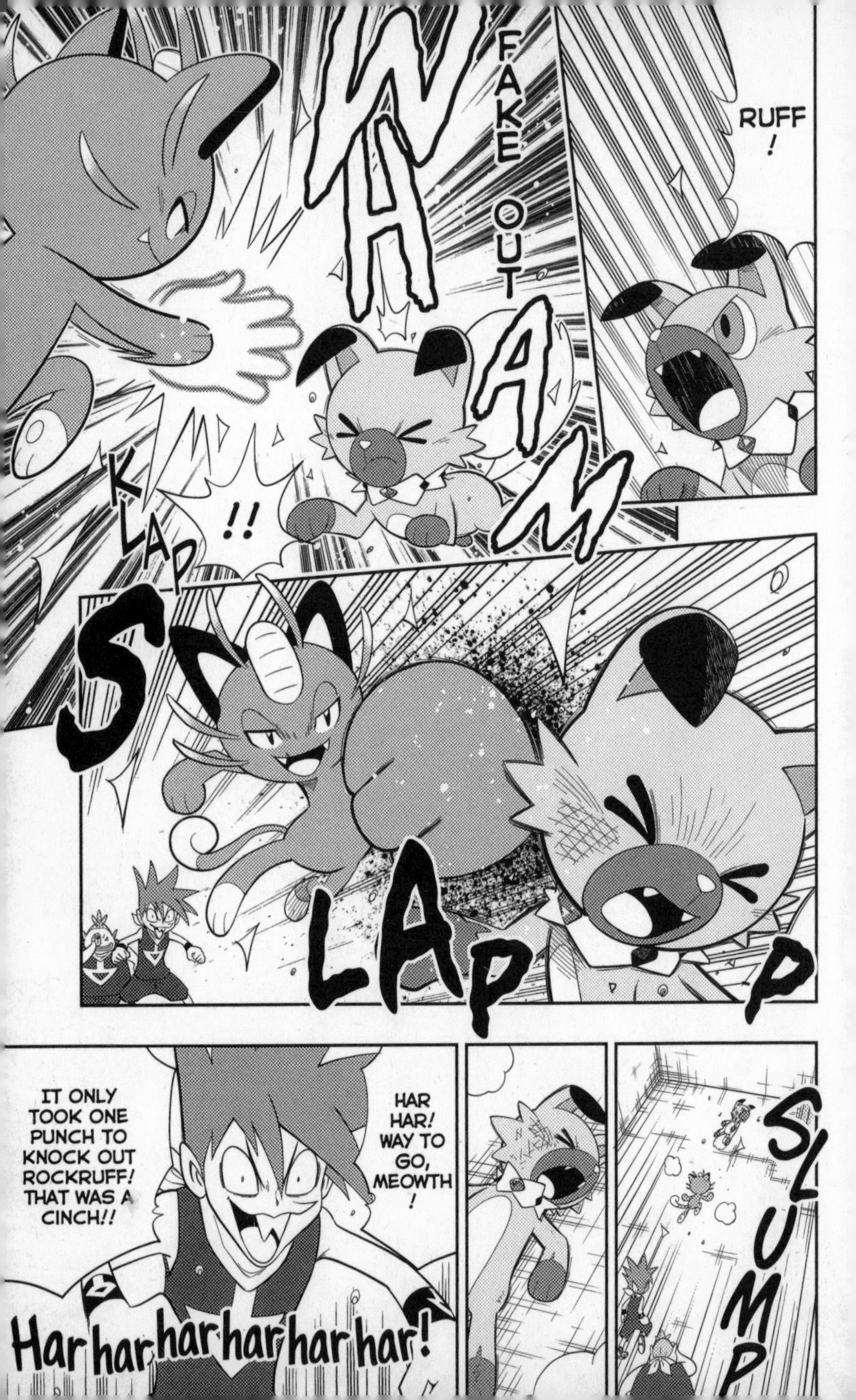
RUFF!
WHAM
FAKE OUT
KLAP!!
SMLAPP
SLUMP
HAR HAR! WAY TO GO, MEOWTH!
IT ONLY TOOK ONE PUNCH TO KNOCK OUT ROCKRUFF! THAT WAS A CINCH!!
Har har har har har har!

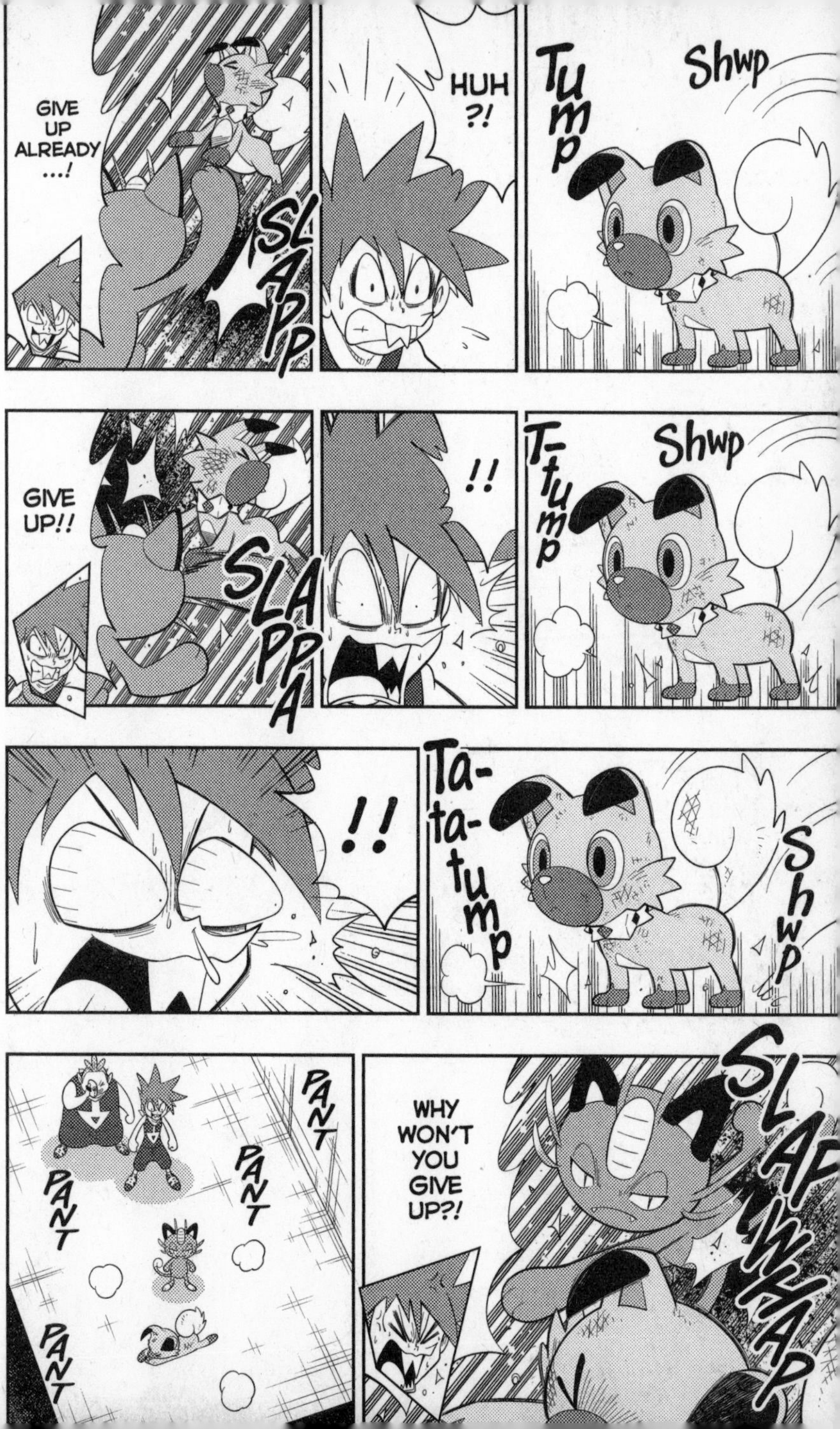
Shwp
Tump
HUH ?!
GIVE UP ALREADY ...!
SLAPP
Shwp
T-tump
!!
GIVE UP!!
SLAPPA
Shwp
Ta-ta-tump
!!
SLAPWHAP
WHY WON'T YOU GIVE UP?!
PANT
PANT
PANT
PANT
PANT

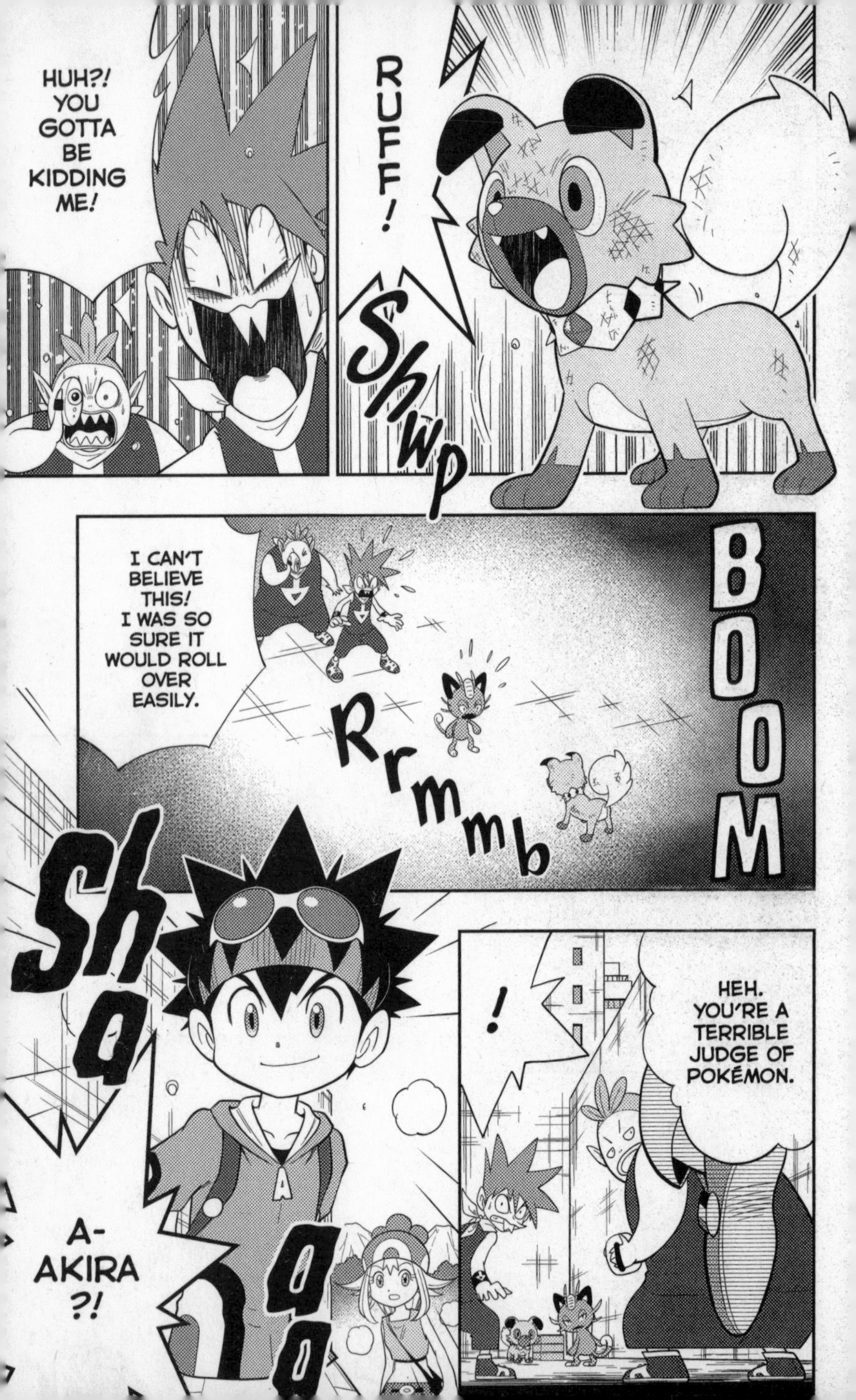
RUFF!
Shwp
HUH?! YOU GOTTA BE KIDDING ME!
BOOM
Rrmmb
I CAN'T BELIEVE THIS! I WAS SO SURE IT WOULD ROLL OVER EASILY.
HEH. YOU'RE A TERRIBLE JUDGE OF POKÉMON.
!
Shaaa
A-AKIRA?!

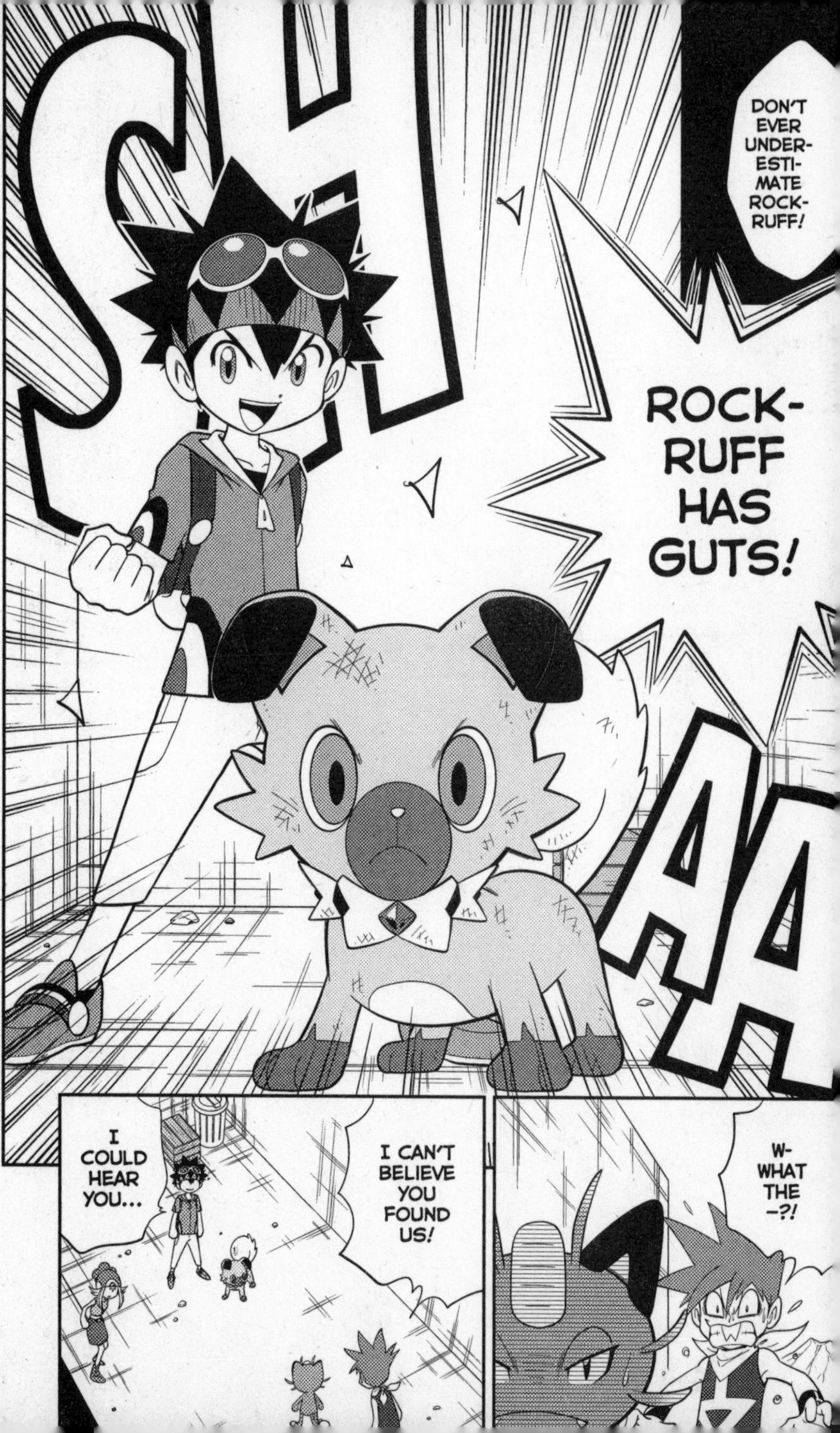
DON'T EVER UNDER-ESTI-MATE ROCK-RUFF!
ROCK-RUFF HAS GUTS!
W-WHAT THE-?!
I CAN'T BELIEVE YOU FOUND US!
I COULD HEAR YOU...

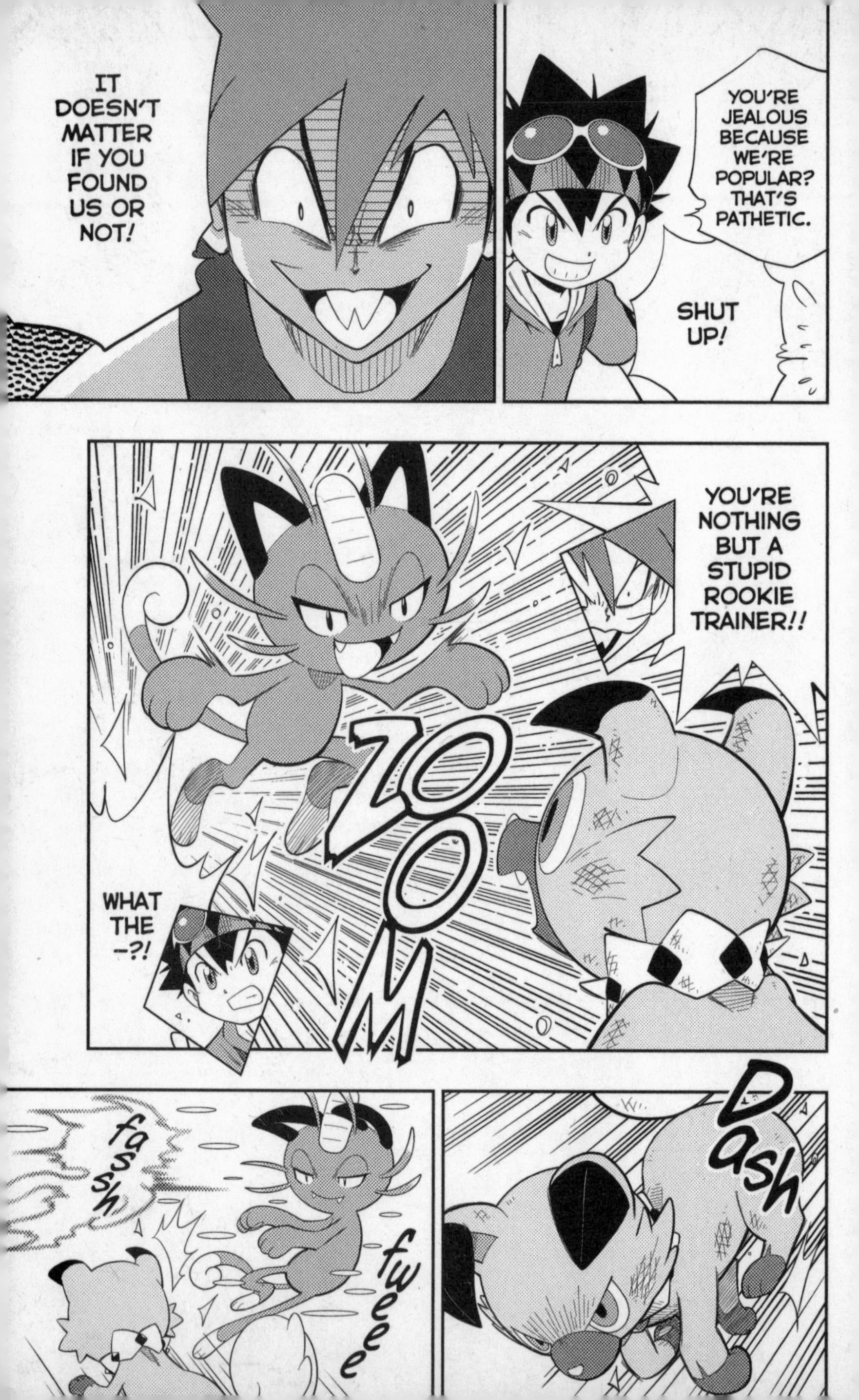
YOU'RE JEALOUS BECAUSE WE'RE POPULAR? THAT'S PATHETIC.
SHUT UP!
IT DOESN'T MATTER IF YOU FOUND US OR NOT!
YOU'RE NOTHING BUT A STUPID ROOKIE TRAINER!!
ZOOM
WHAT THE --?!
Dash
fash
fweeeee

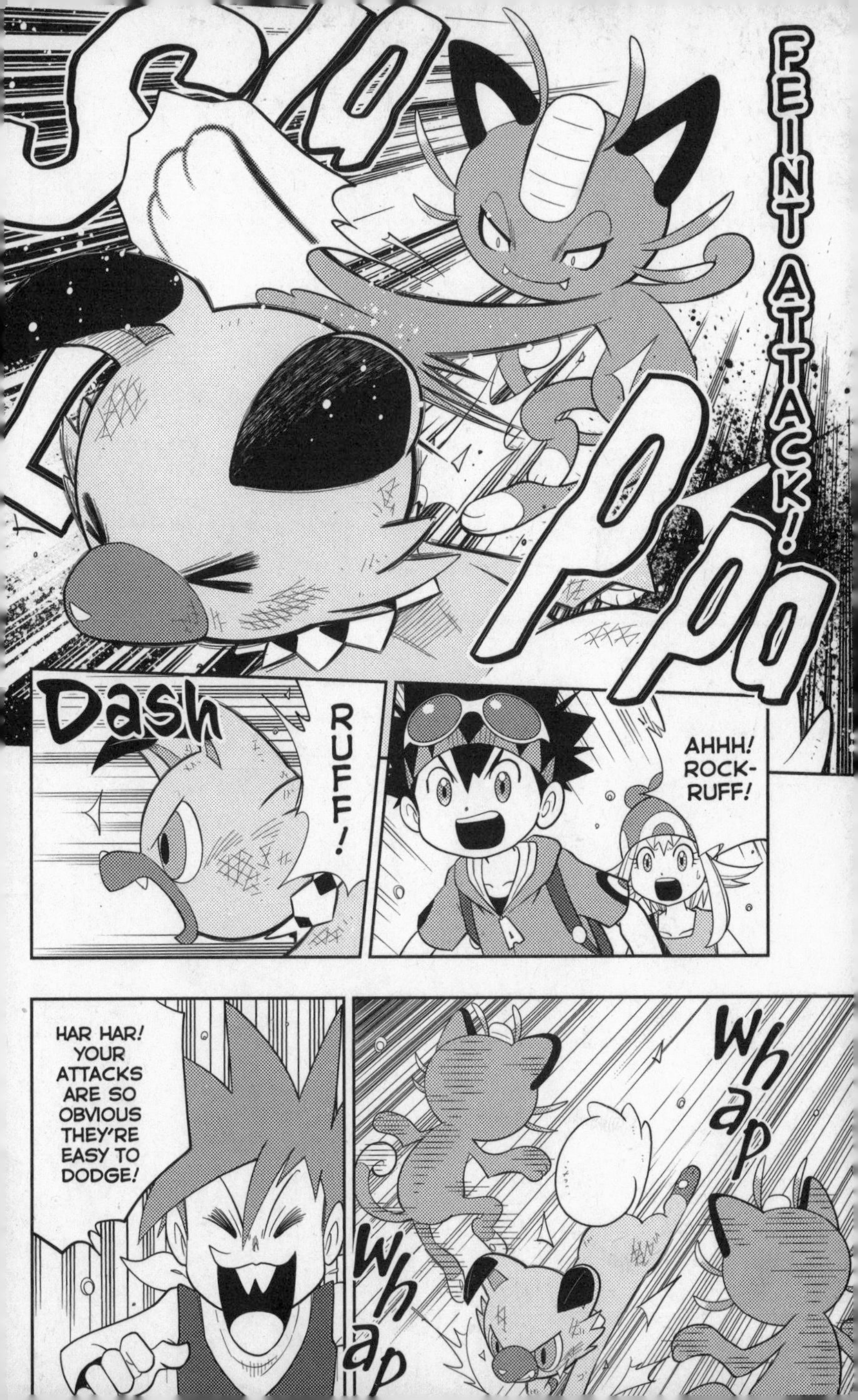
FEINT ATTACK!
AHHH! ROCK-RUFF!
RUFF!
Dash
Whap
Whap
HAR HAR! YOUR ATTACKS ARE SO OBVIOUS THEY'RE EASY TO DODGE!

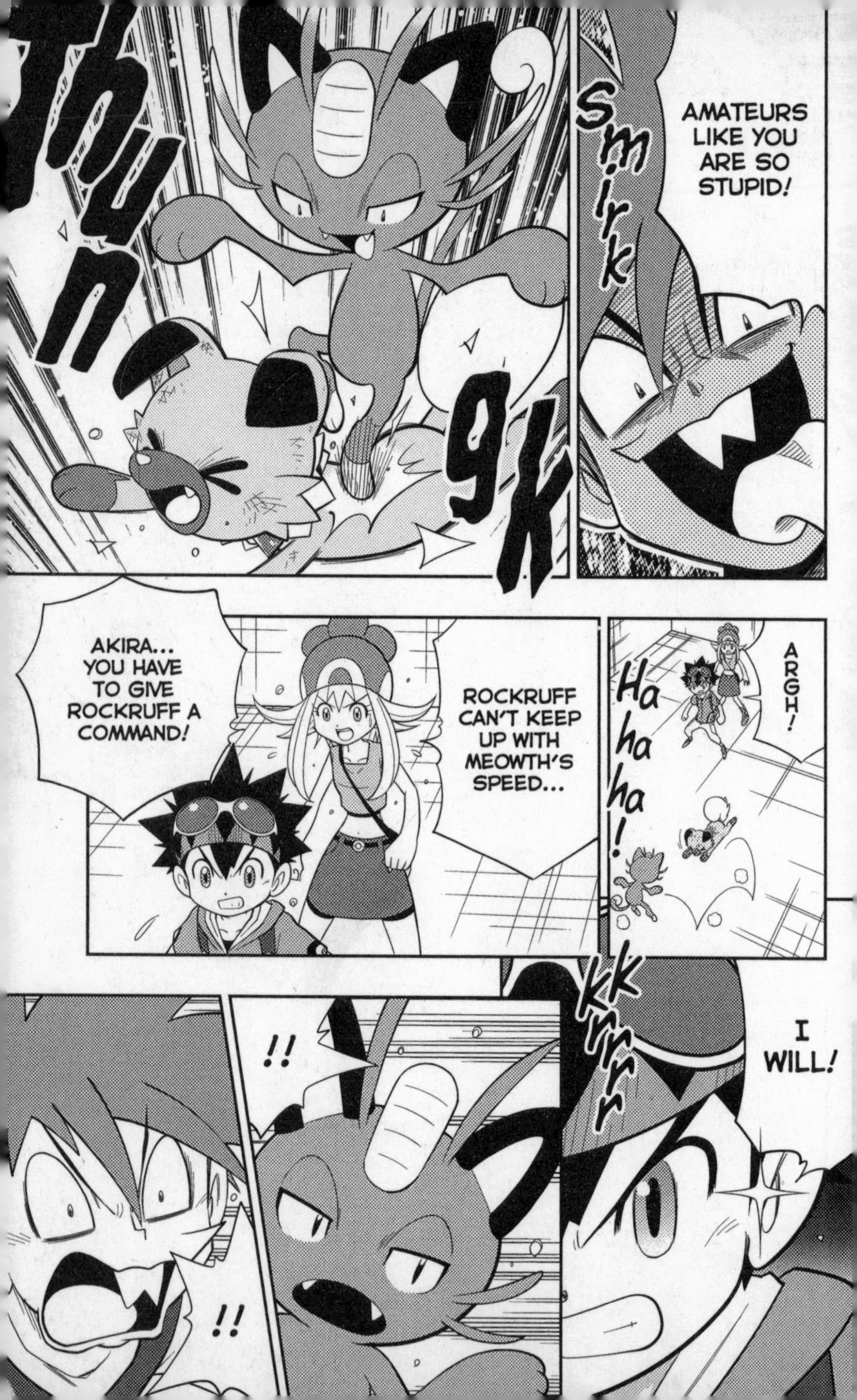
Smirk
AMATEURS LIKE YOU ARE SO STUPID!
Thoun
Gk
ARGH!
Hahaha!
ROCKRUFF CAN'T KEEP UP WITH MEOWTH'S SPEED...
AKIRA... YOU HAVE TO GIVE ROCKRUFF A COMMAND!
I WILL!
Kkrrrr
!!
!!

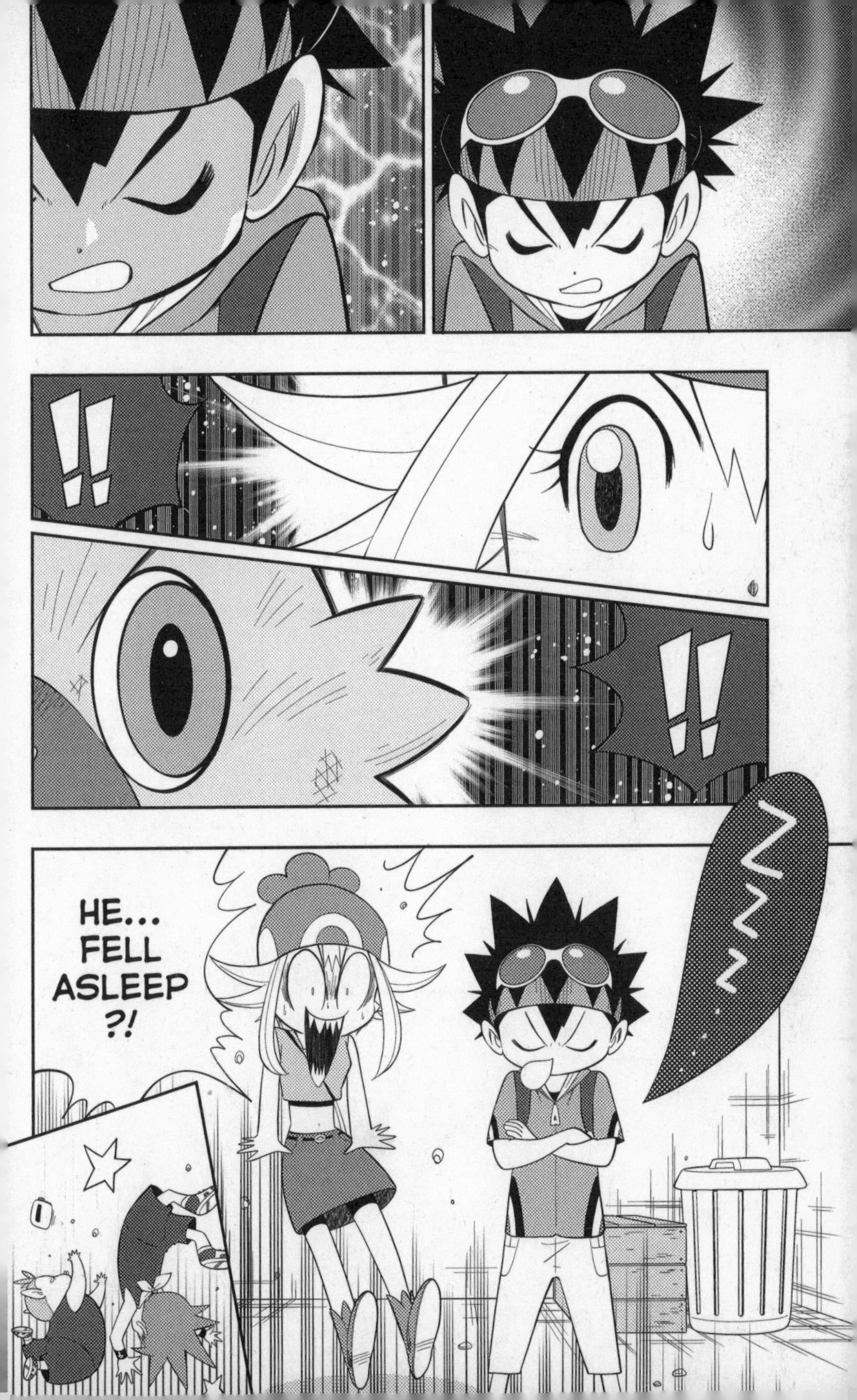
!!
!!
HE... FELL ASLEEP ?!
ZZZ

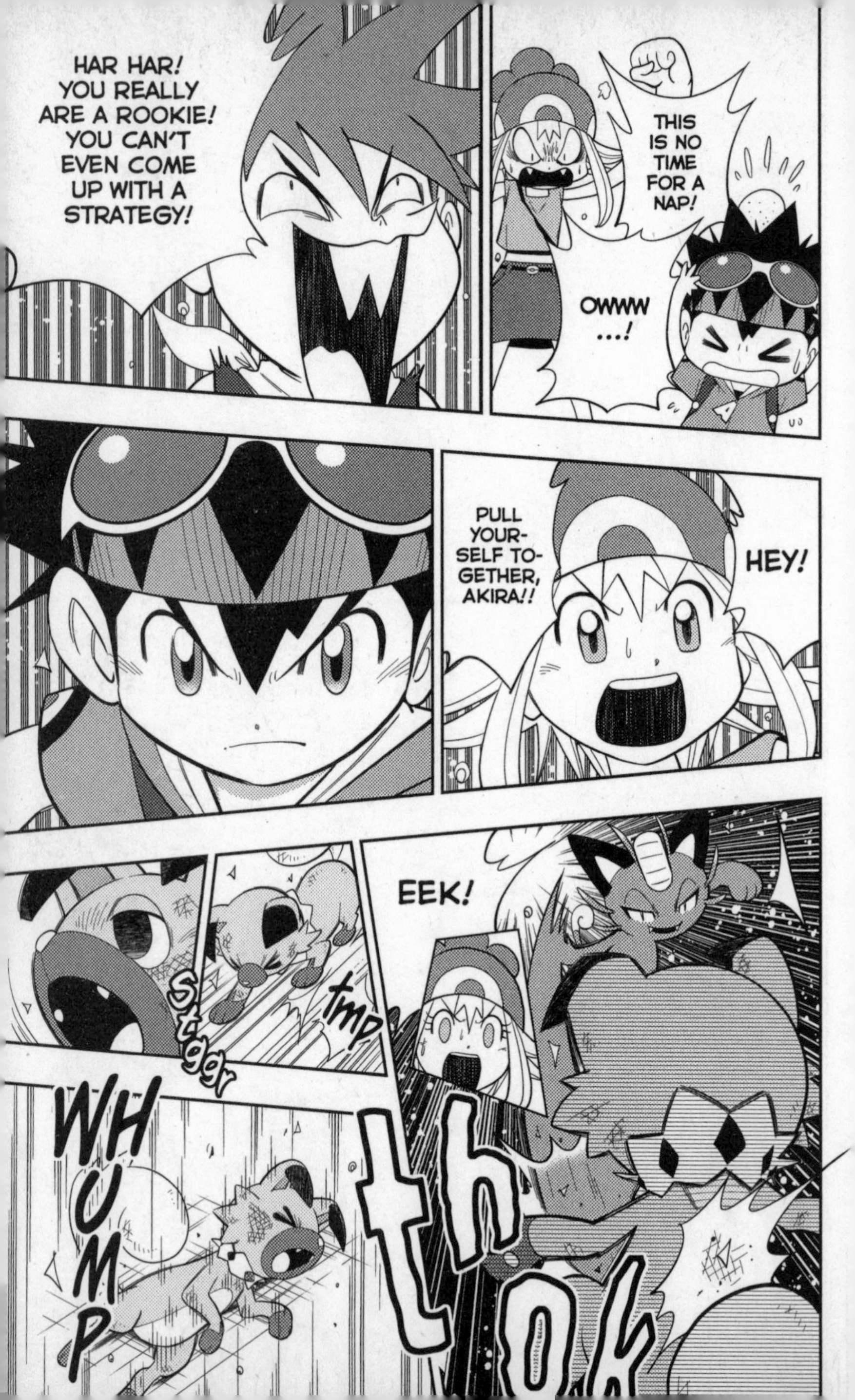
THIS IS NO TIME FOR A NAP!
OWWW ...!
HAR HAR! YOU REALLY ARE A ROOKIE! YOU CAN'T EVEN COME UP WITH A STRATEGY!
HEY!
PULL YOUR-SELF TO-GETHER, AKIRA!!
EEK!
thok
tmp
stggr
WHUMP

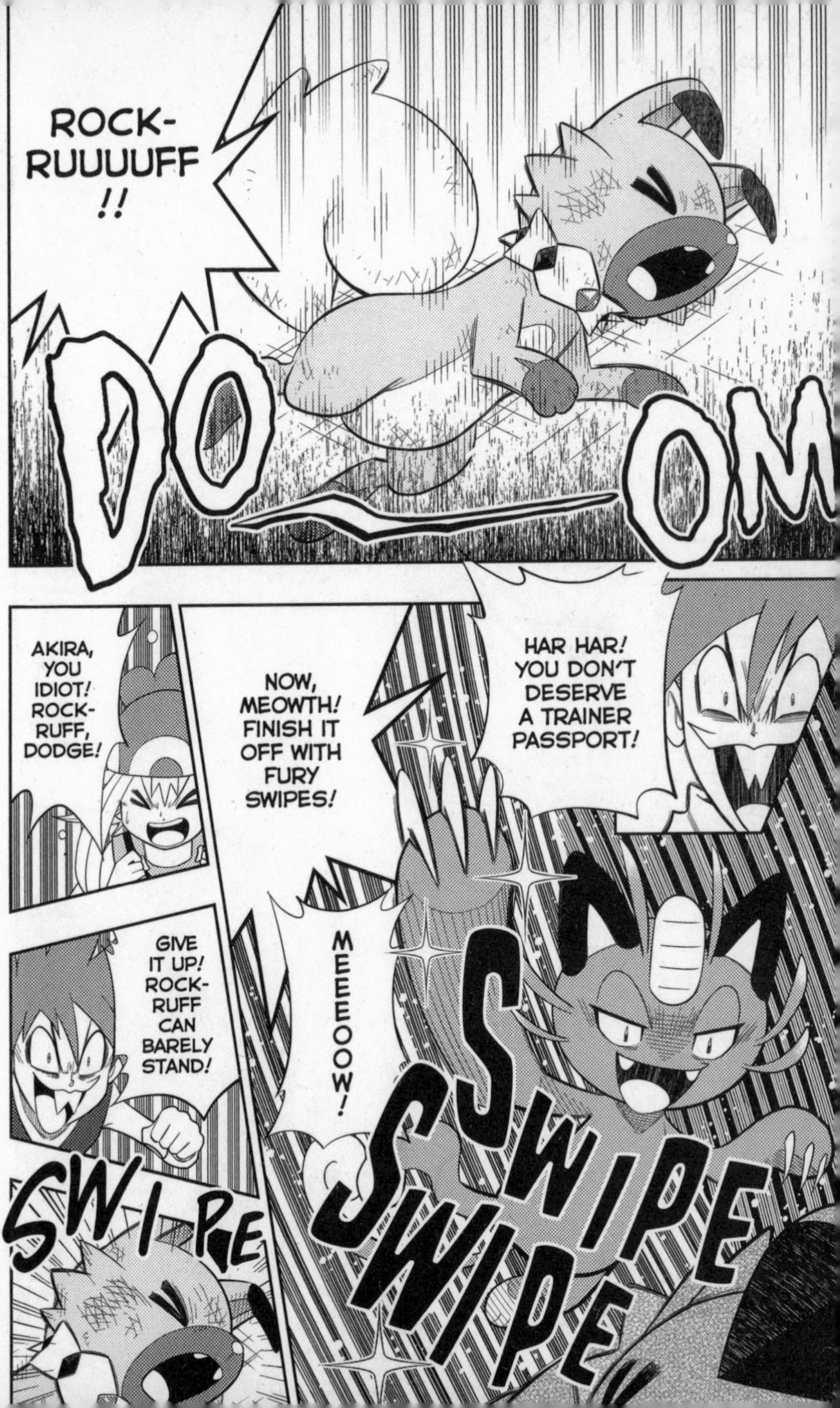

ROCK-RUUUUFF!!
DO
OM
HAR HAR! YOU DON'T DESERVE A TRAINER PASSPORT!
NOW, MEOWTH! FINISH IT OFF WITH FURY SWIPES!
AKIRA, YOU IDIOT! ROCK-RUFF, DODGE!
MEEEOOOW!
SWIPE
SWIPE
GIVE IT UP! ROCK-RUFF CAN BARELY STAND!
SWIPE

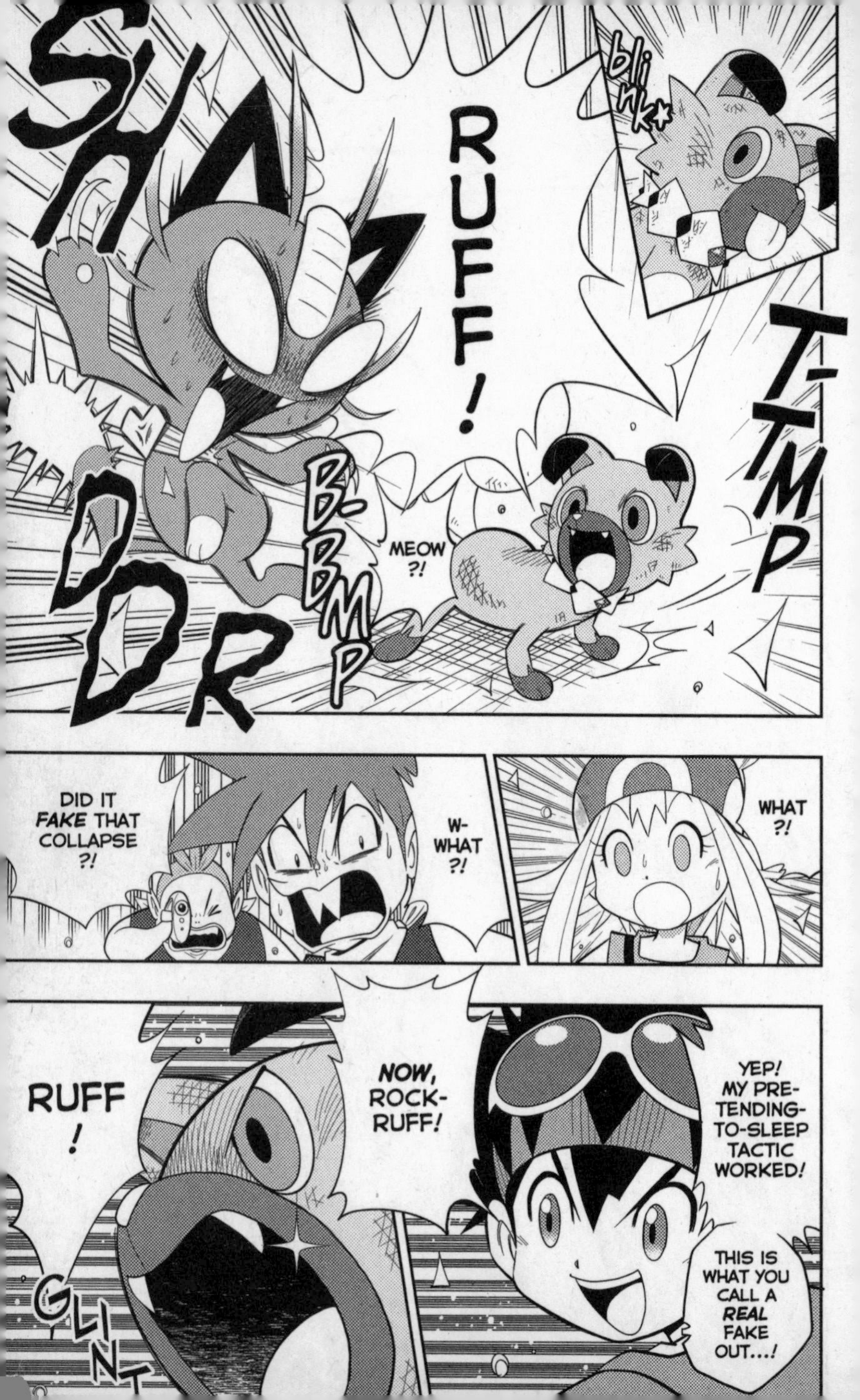
blink
RUFF!
T-TMP
SHADDR
B-BMP
MEOW?!
WHAT?!
W-WHAT?!
DID IT FAKE THAT COLLAPSE?!
YEP! MY PRE-TENDING-TO-SLEEP TACTIC WORKED!
THIS IS WHAT YOU CALL A REAL FAKE OUT...!
NOW, ROCK-RUFF!
RUFF!
GLINT

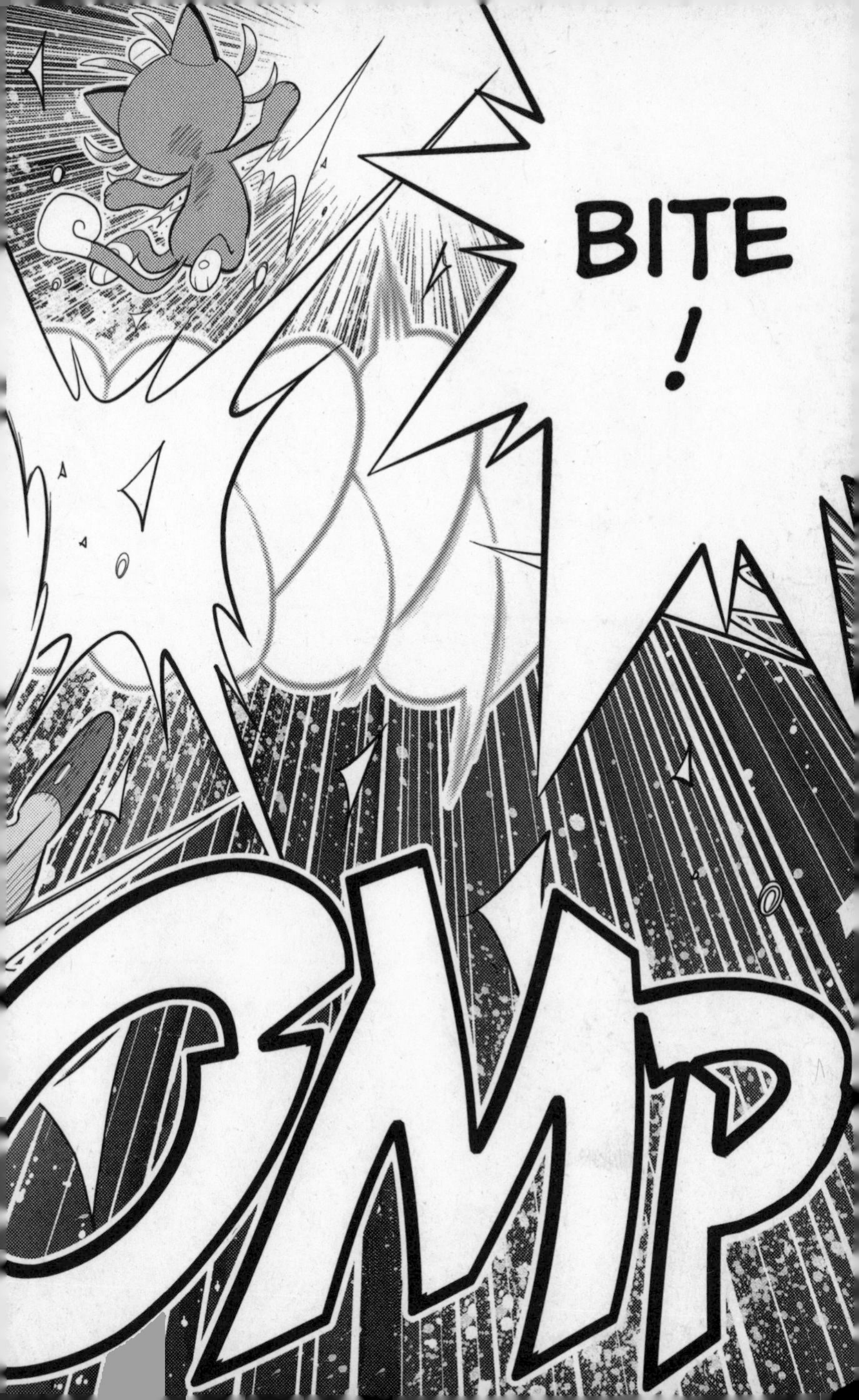
BITE!

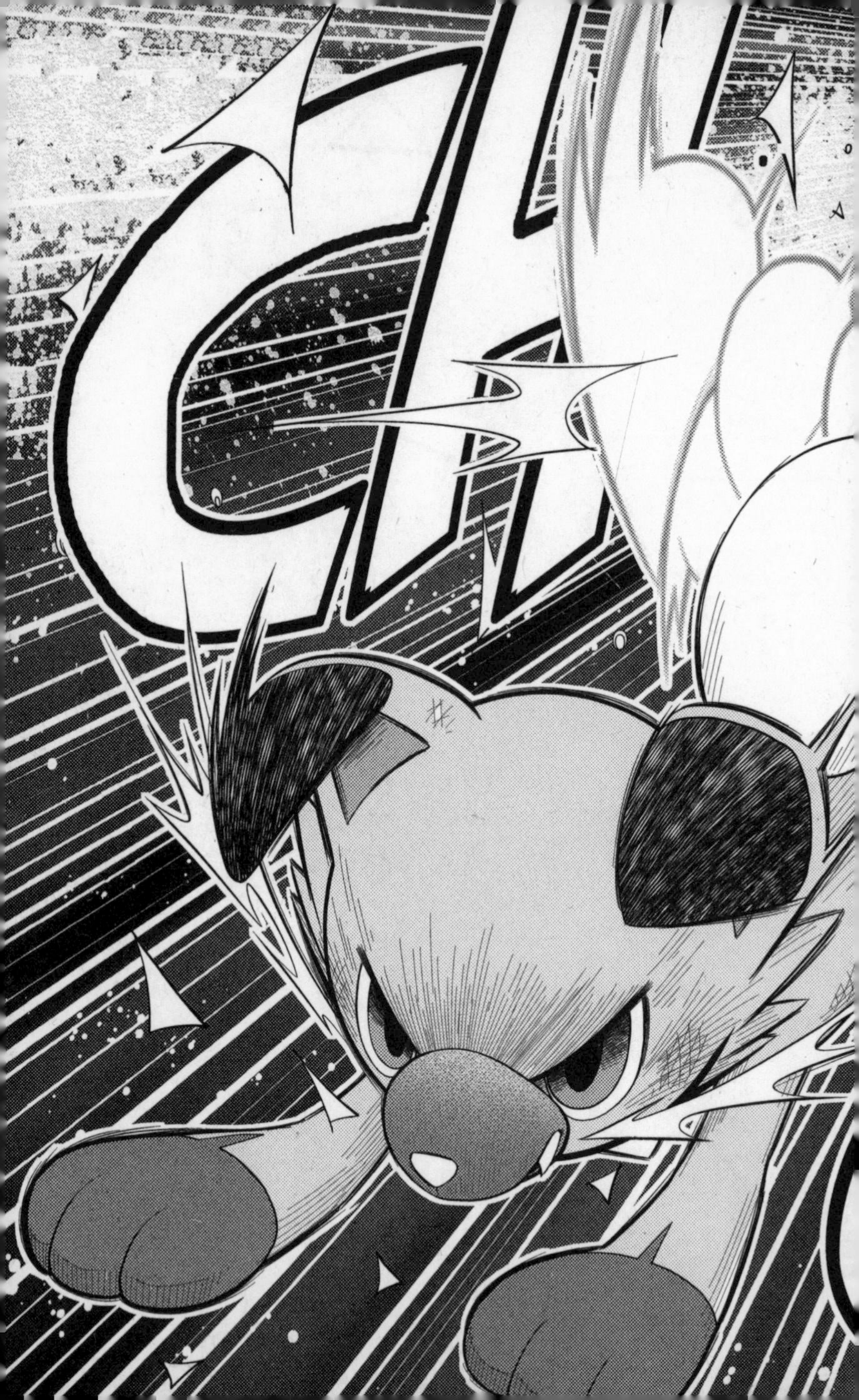

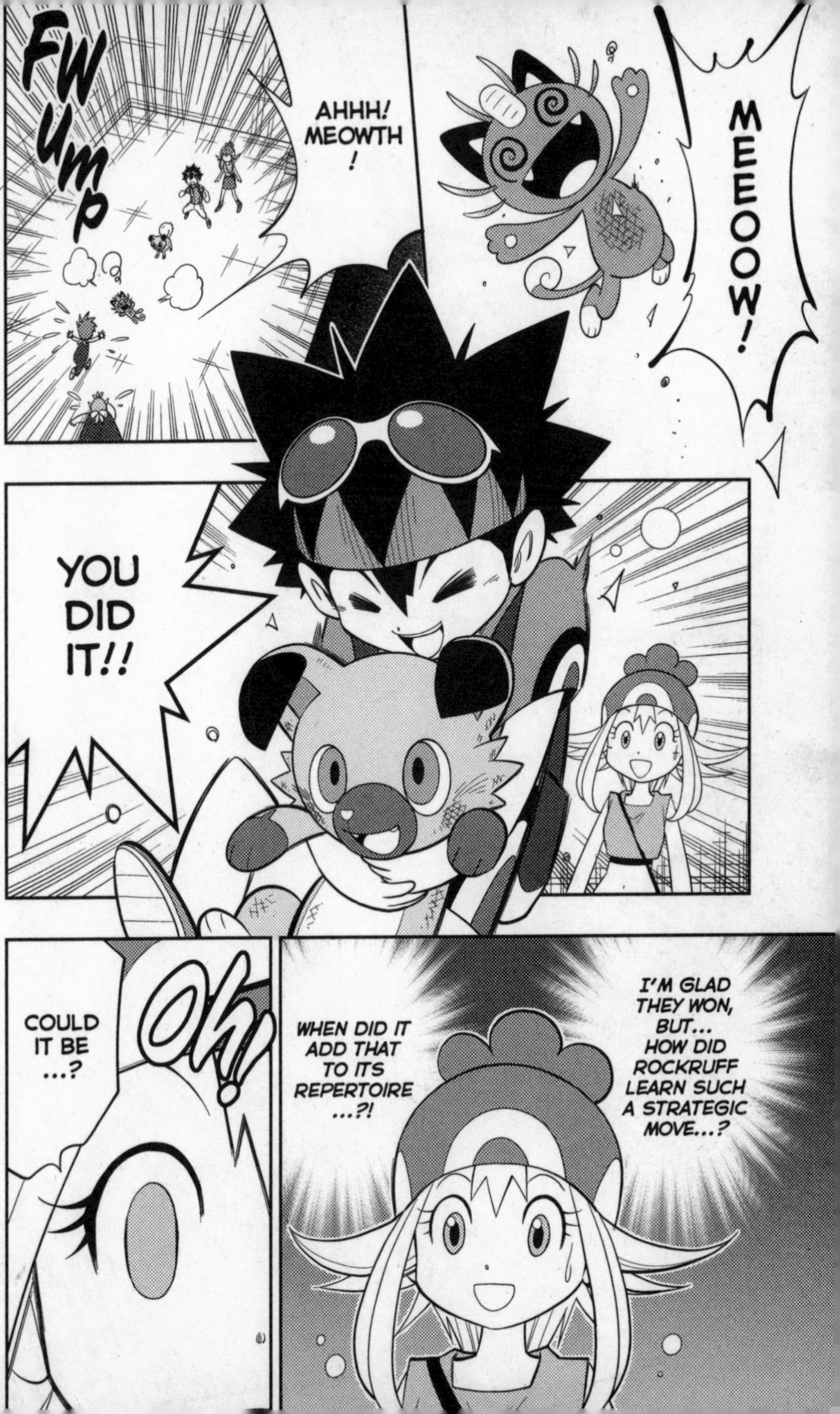
MEEOOOW!
AHHH! MEOWTH!
FWUMP
YOU DID IT!!
I'M GLAD THEY WON, BUT... HOW DID ROCKRUFF LEARN SUCH A STRATEGIC MOVE...?
WHEN DID IT ADD THAT TO ITS REPERTOIRE...?!
Oh!
COULD IT BE...?

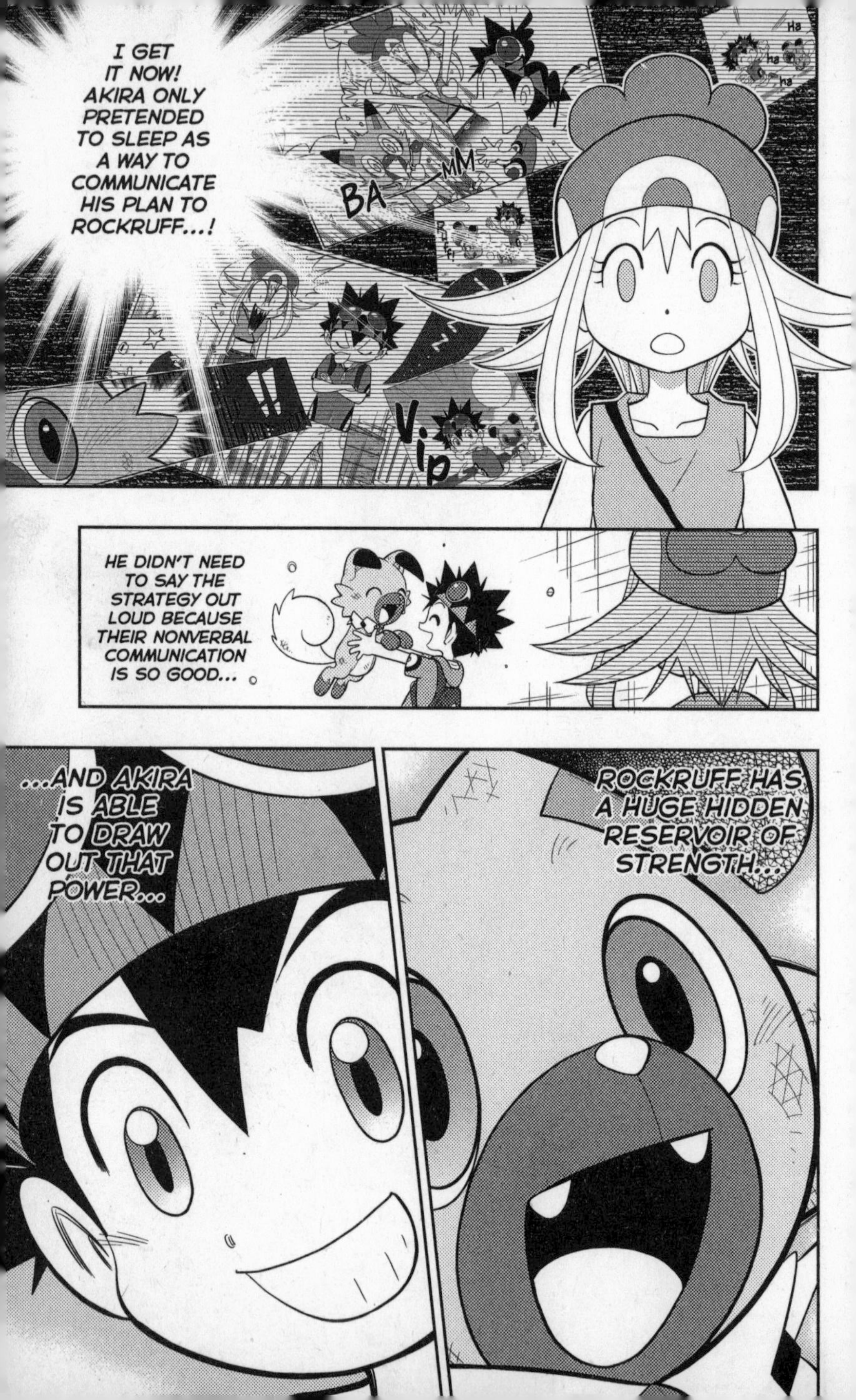
Ha
ha
ha
I GET IT NOW! AKIRA ONLY PRETENDED TO SLEEP AS A WAY TO COMMUNICATE HIS PLAN TO ROCKRUFF...!
BAMM
Vip
HE DIDN'T NEED TO SAY THE STRATEGY OUT LOUD BECAUSE THEIR NONVERBAL COMMUNICATION IS SO GOOD...
ROCKRUFF HAS A HUGE HIDDEN RESERVOIR OF STRENGTH...
...AND AKIRA IS ABLE TO DRAW OUT THAT POWER...

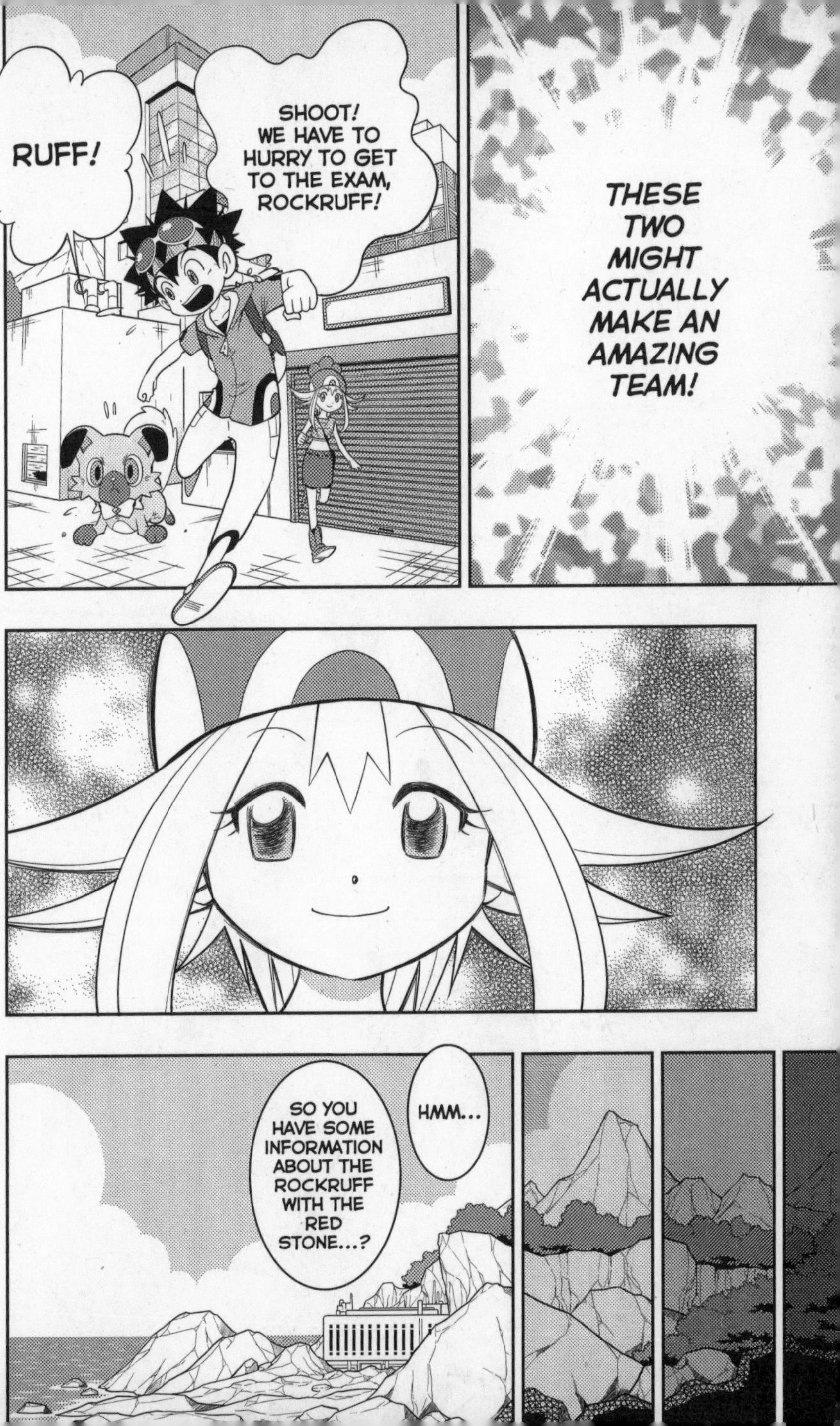
THESE TWO MIGHT ACTUALLY MAKE AN AMAZING TEAM!
SHOOT! WE HAVE TO HURRY TO GET TO THE EXAM, ROCKRUFF!
RUFF!
HMM...
SO YOU HAVE SOME INFORMATION ABOUT THE ROCKRUFF WITH THE RED STONE...?

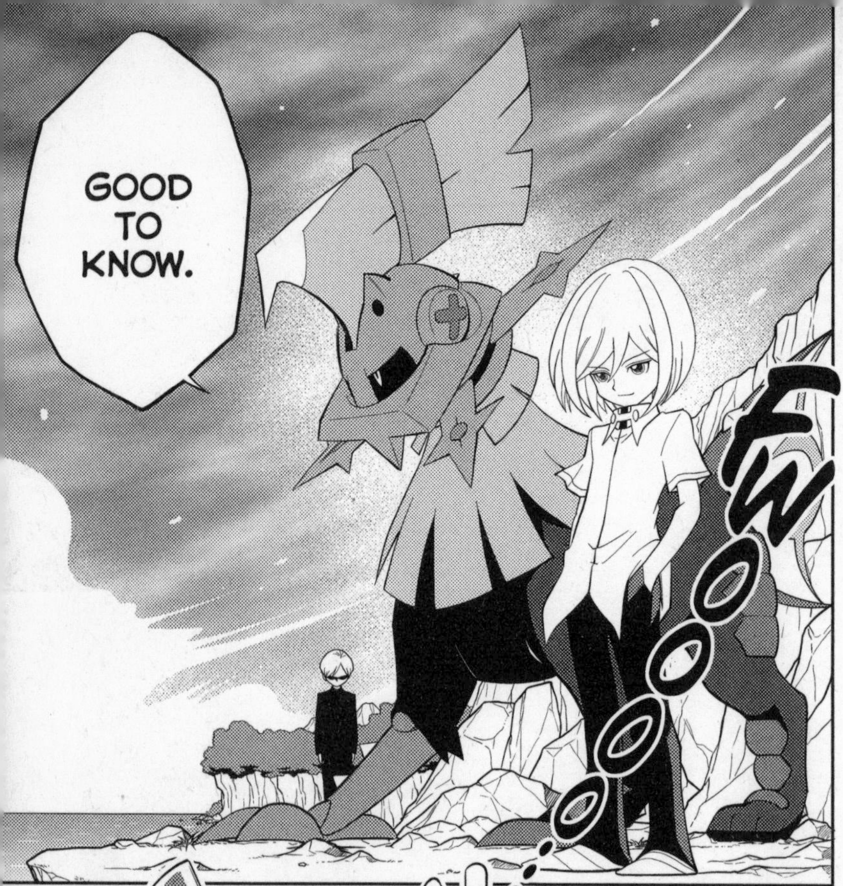
GOOD TO KNOW.
FWOOOOOO

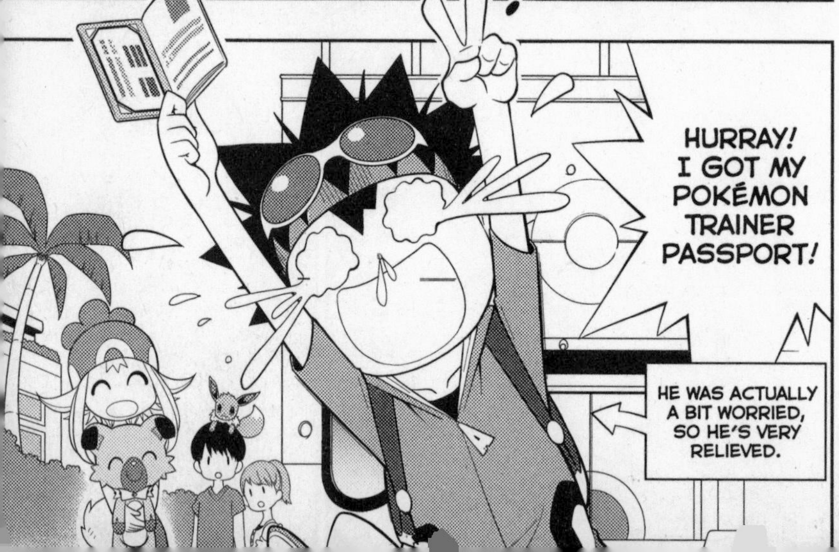
HURRAY! I GOT MY POKÉMON TRAINER PASSPORT!
HE WAS ACTUALLY A BIT WORRIED, SO HE'S VERY RELIEVED.

Event 3: Traveling Trainer Tokio

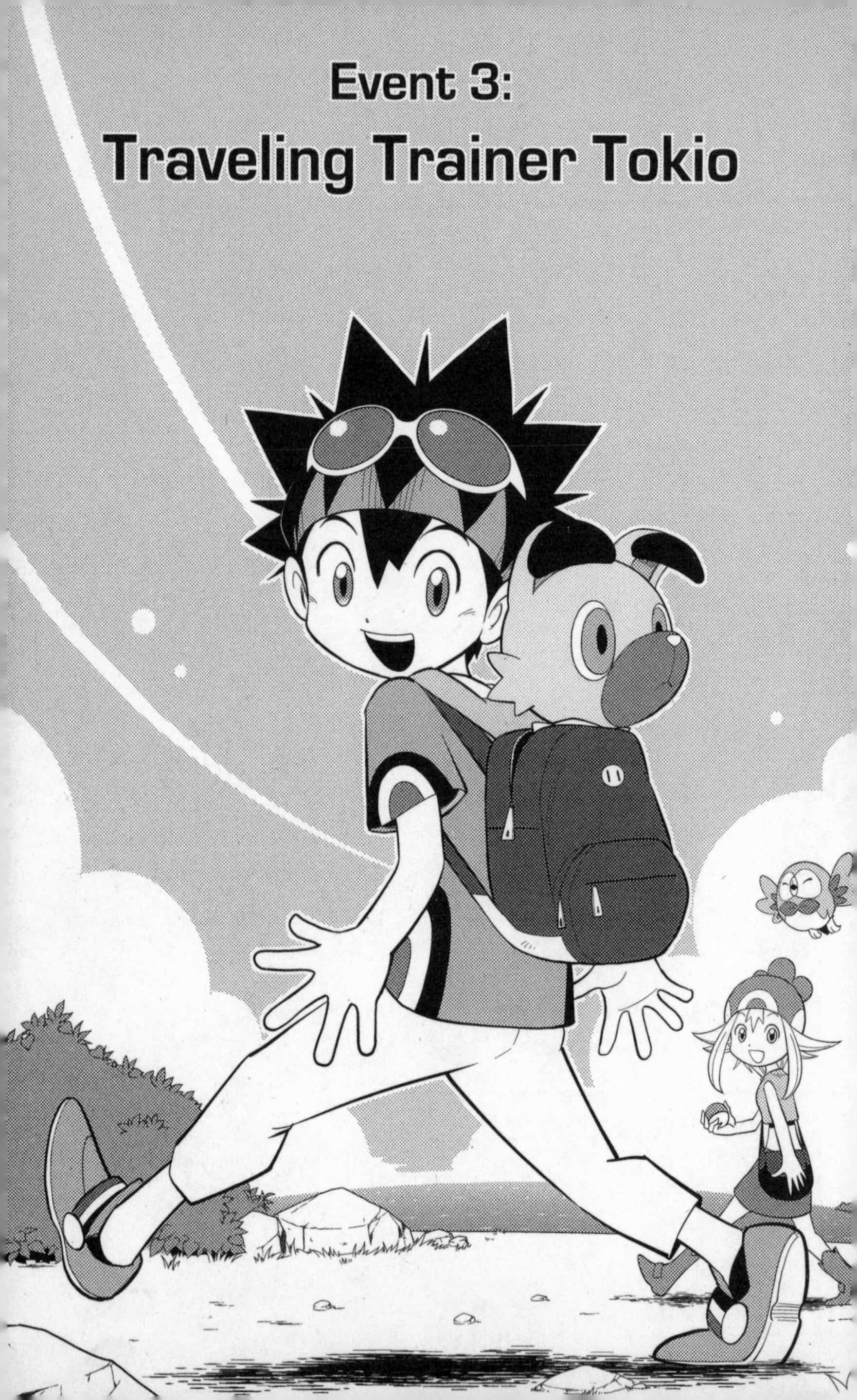

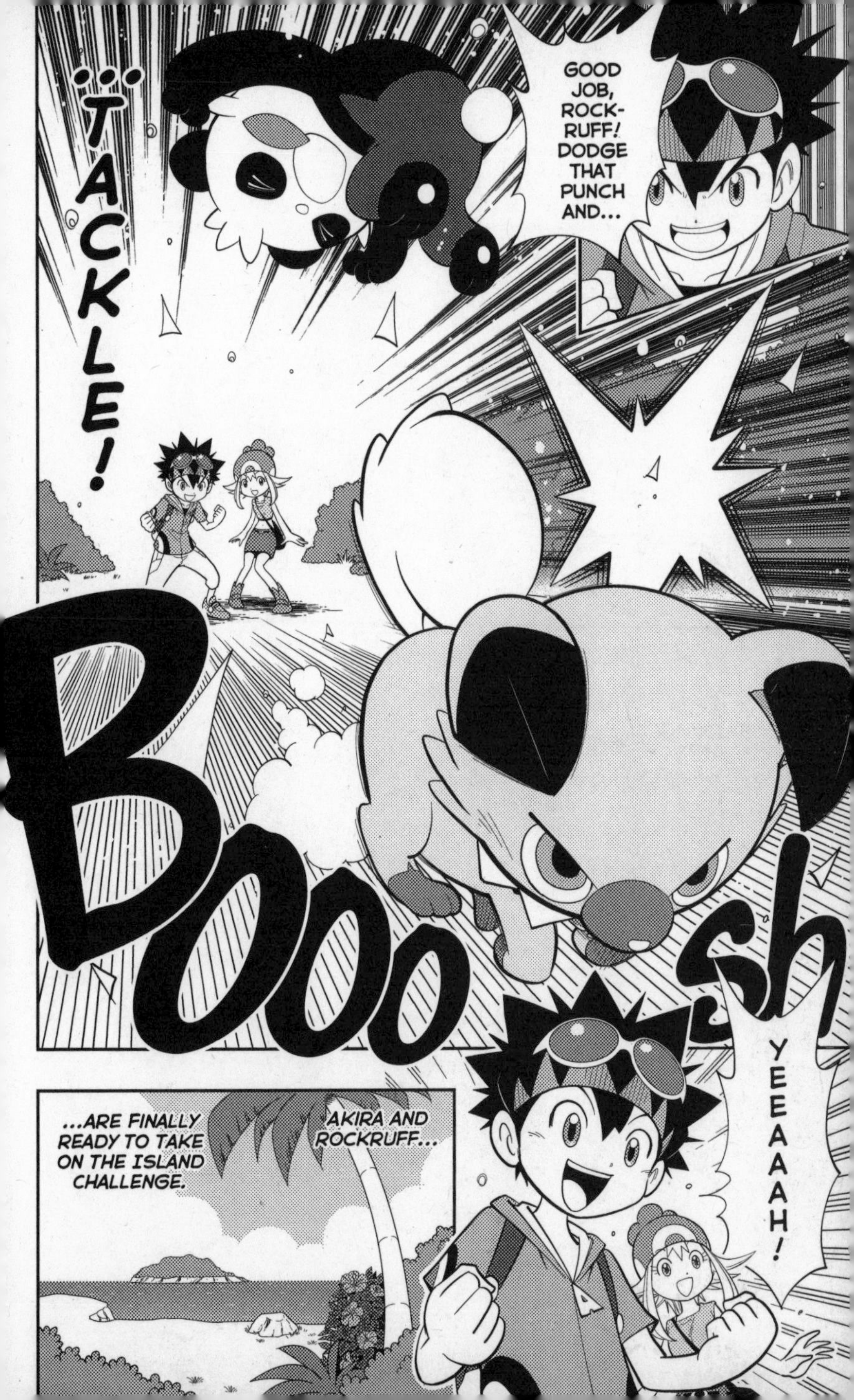
GOOD JOB, ROCK-RUFF! DODGE THAT PUNCH AND...
...TACKLE!
BOOOSH
YEEAAAAH!
AKIRA AND ROCKRUFF...
...ARE FINALLY READY TO TAKE ON THE ISLAND CHALLENGE.

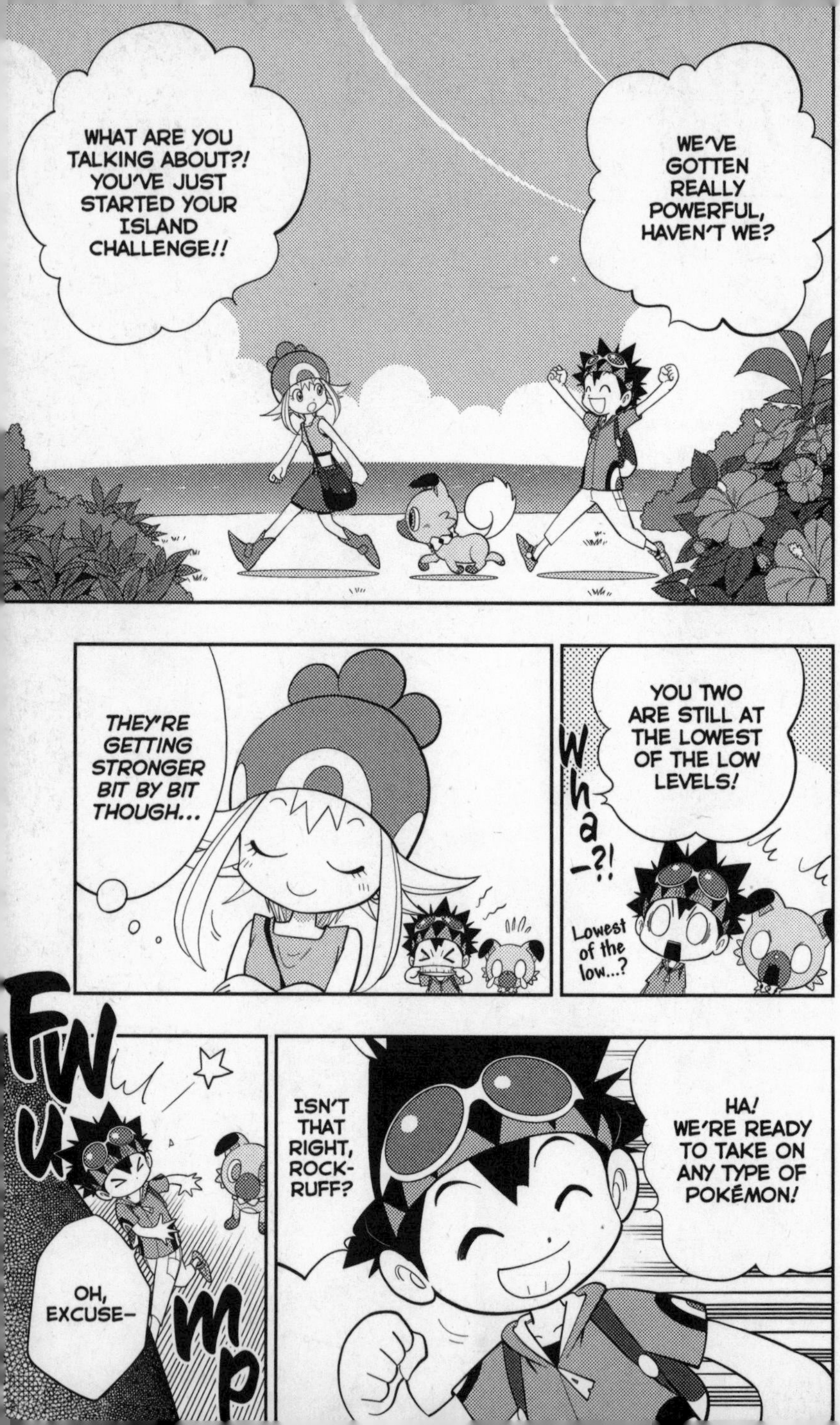
WE'VE GOTTEN REALLY POWERFUL, HAVEN'T WE?
WHAT ARE YOU TALKING ABOUT?! YOU'VE JUST STARTED YOUR ISLAND CHALLENGE!!
YOU TWO ARE STILL AT THE LOWEST OF THE LOW LEVELS!
Wha-?!
Lowest of the low...?
THEY'RE GETTING STRONGER BIT BY BIT THOUGH...
HA! WE'RE READY TO TAKE ON ANY TYPE OF POKÉMON!
ISN'T THAT RIGHT, ROCK-RUFF?
FWUMP
OH, EXCUSE-

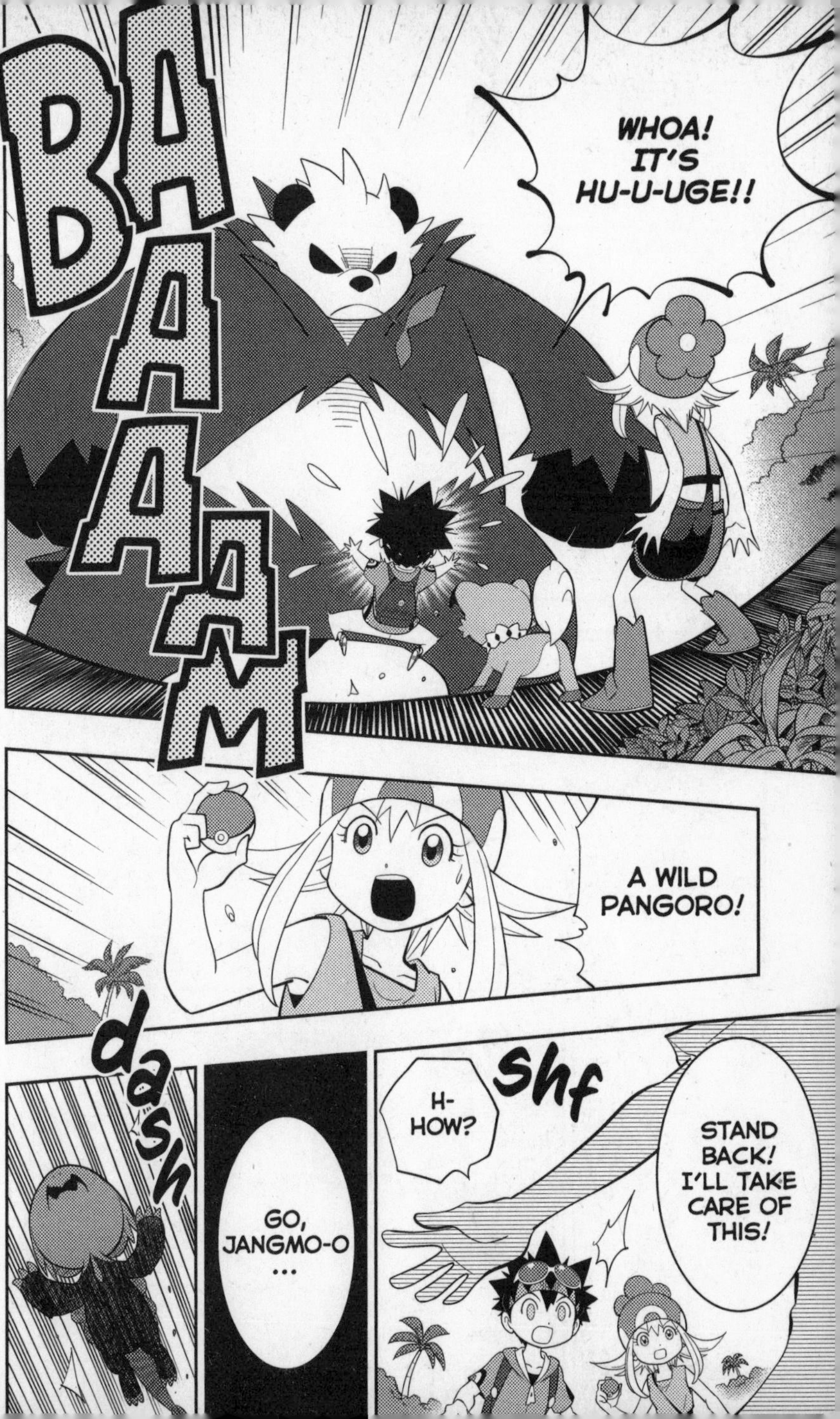
WHOA! IT'S HU-U-UGE!!
BAAAAAM
A WILD PANGORO!
STAND BACK! I'LL TAKE CARE OF THIS!
Shf
H- HOW?
GO, JANGMO-O ...
dash

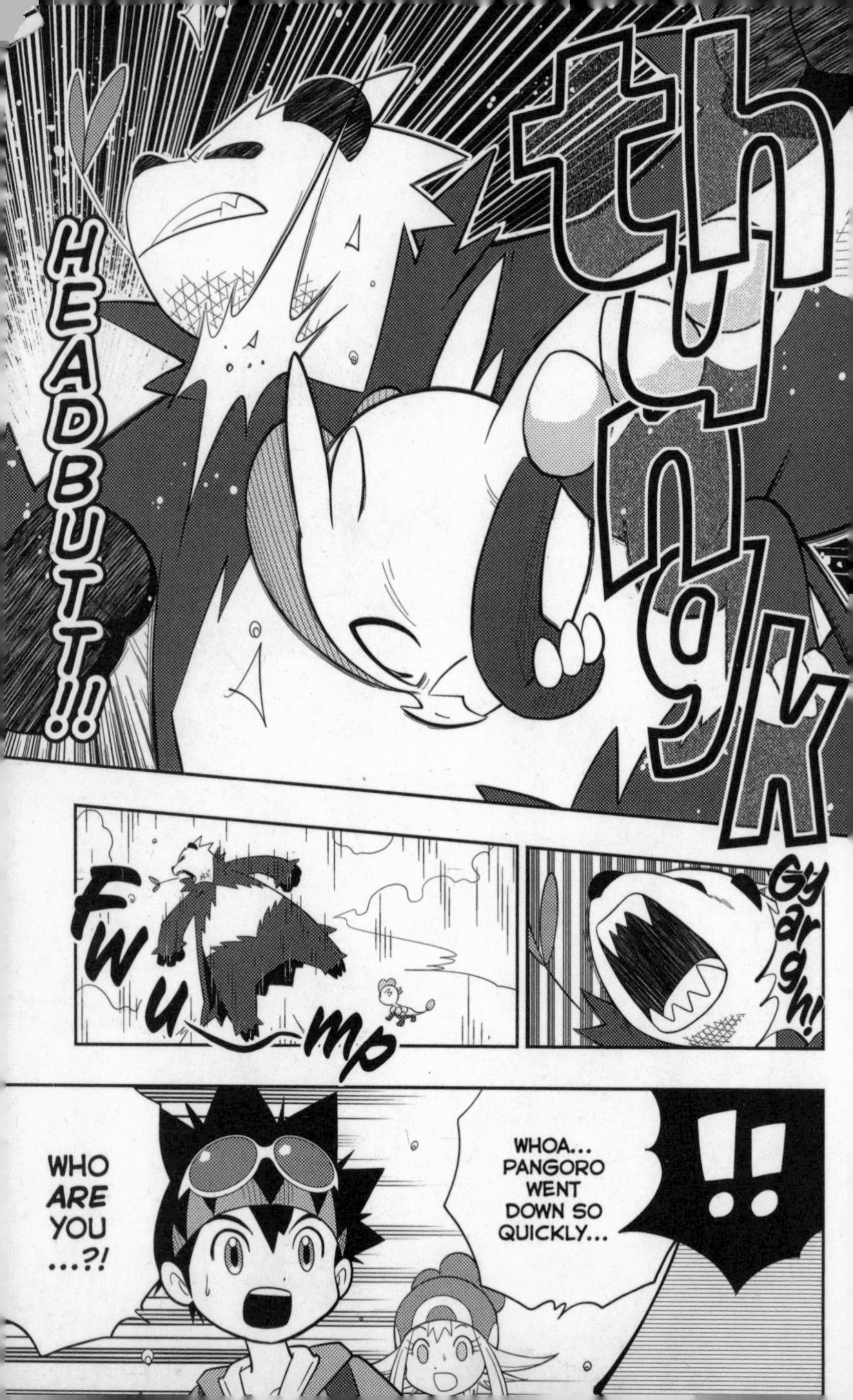
thungk
HEADBUTT!!
Gyargh!
Fwuuump
!!
WHOA... PANGORO WENT DOWN SO QUICKLY...
WHO ARE YOU ...?!

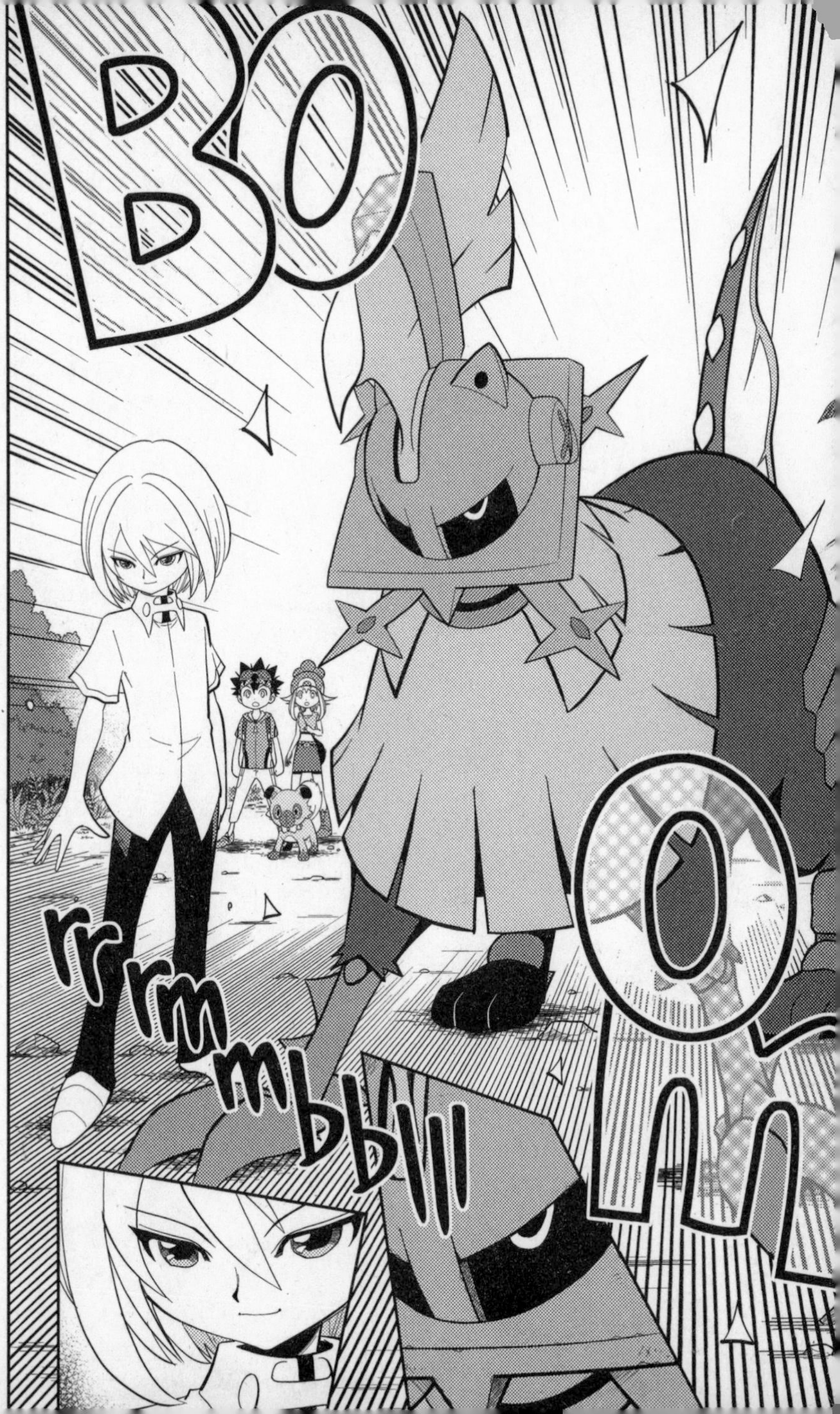
BOOM
rrrmmbbll

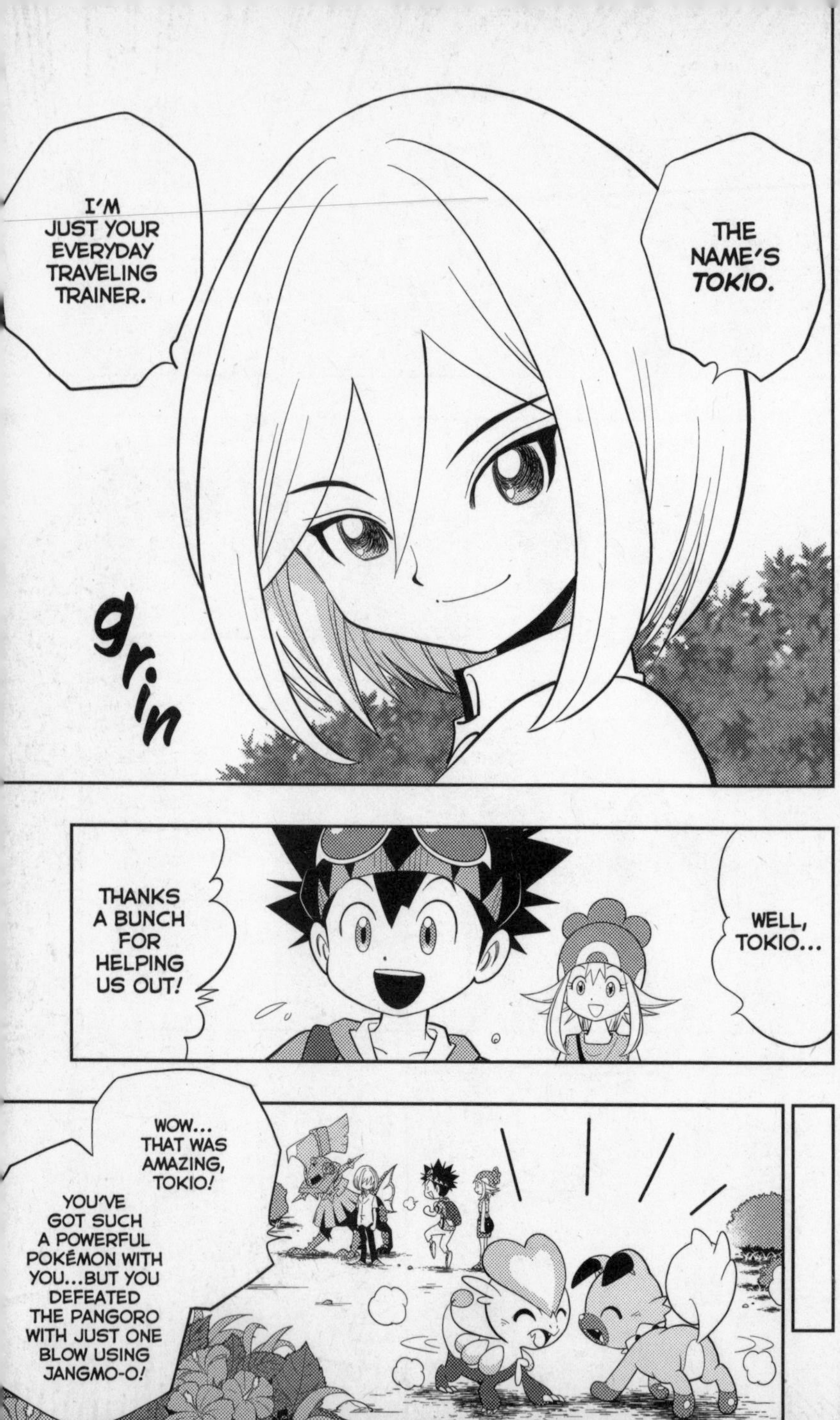
THE NAME'S *TOKIO*.
I'M JUST YOUR EVERYDAY TRAVELING TRAINER.
grin
WELL, TOKIO...
THANKS A BUNCH FOR HELPING US OUT!
WOW... THAT WAS AMAZING, TOKIO!
YOU'VE GOT SUCH A POWERFUL POKéMON WITH YOU...BUT YOU DEFEATED THE PANGORO WITH JUST ONE BLOW USING JANGMO-O!

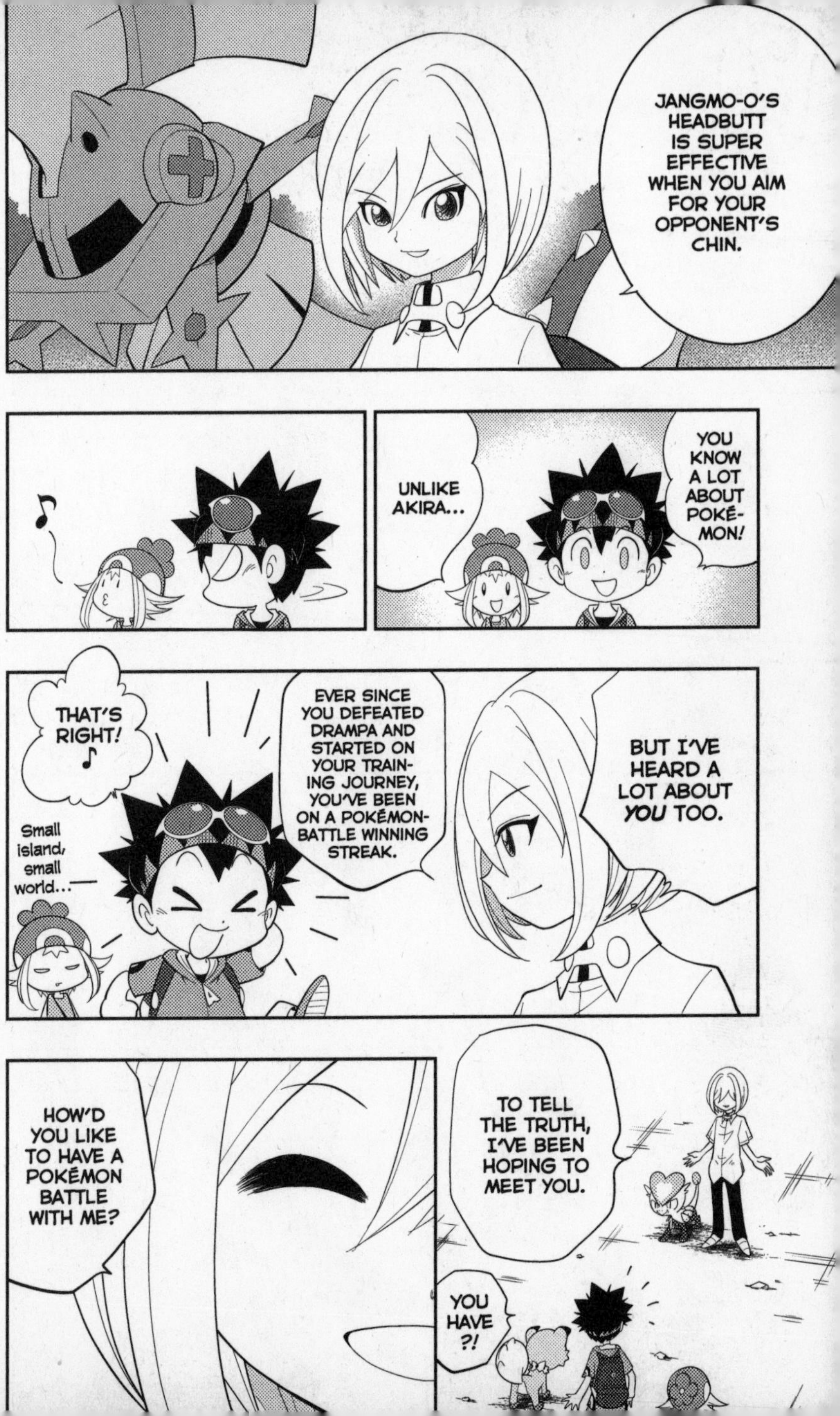
JANGMO-O'S HEADBUTT IS SUPER EFFECTIVE WHEN YOU AIM FOR YOUR OPPONENT'S CHIN.
YOU KNOW A LOT ABOUT POKÉMON!
UNLIKE AKIRA...
♪
BUT I'VE HEARD A LOT ABOUT *YOU* TOO.
EVER SINCE YOU DEFEATED DRAMPA AND STARTED ON YOUR TRAINING JOURNEY, YOU'VE BEEN ON A POKÉMON-BATTLE WINNING STREAK.
THAT'S RIGHT! ♪
Small island, small world...
TO TELL THE TRUTH, I'VE BEEN HOPING TO MEET YOU.
YOU HAVE?!
HOW'D YOU LIKE TO HAVE A POKÉMON BATTLE WITH ME?

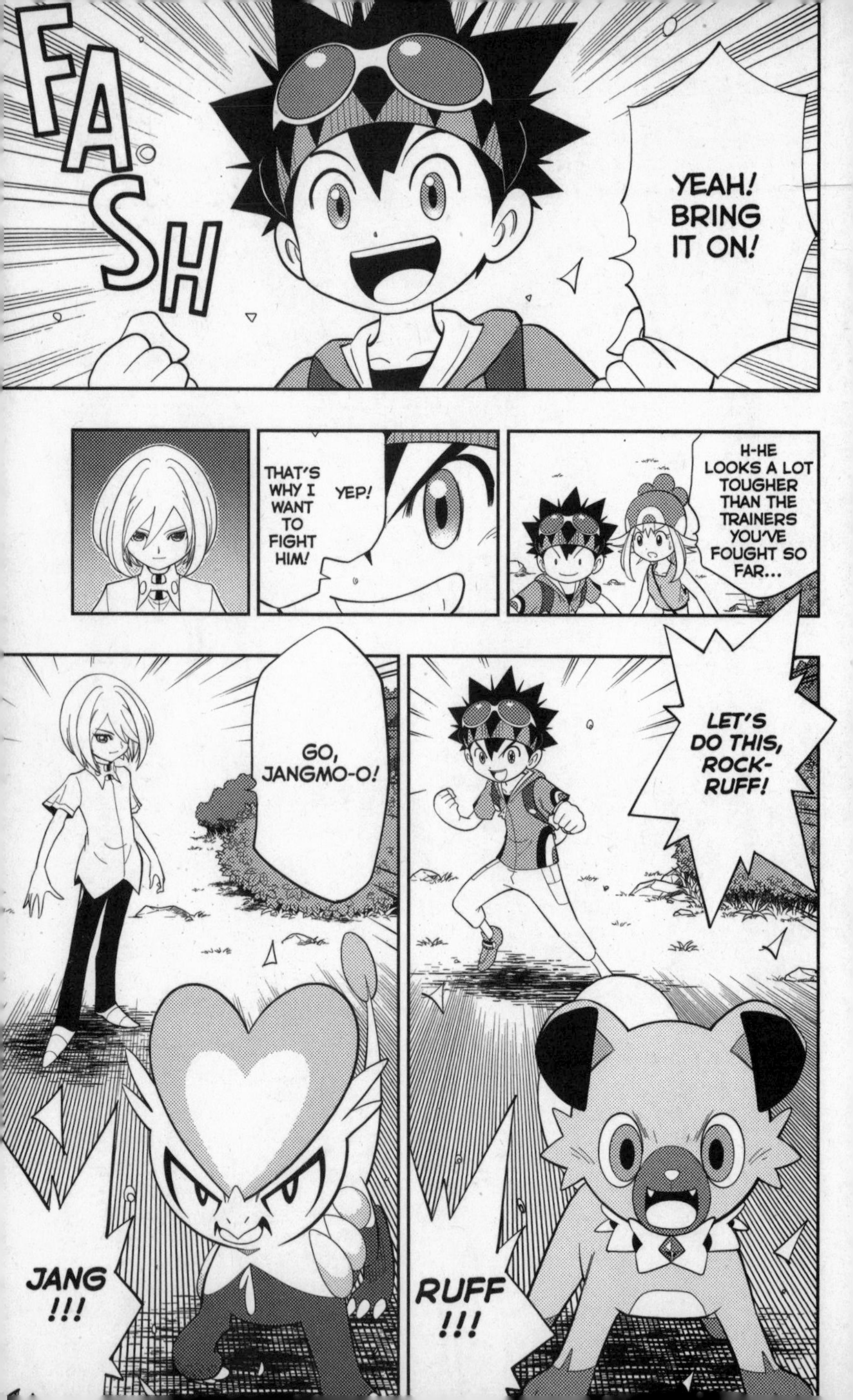
YEAH! BRING IT ON!
FASH
H-HE LOOKS A LOT TOUGHER THAN THE TRAINERS YOU'VE FOUGHT SO FAR...
YEP!
THAT'S WHY I WANT TO FIGHT HIM!
LET'S DO THIS, ROCK-RUFF!
RUFF !!!
GO, JANGMO-O!
JANG !!!

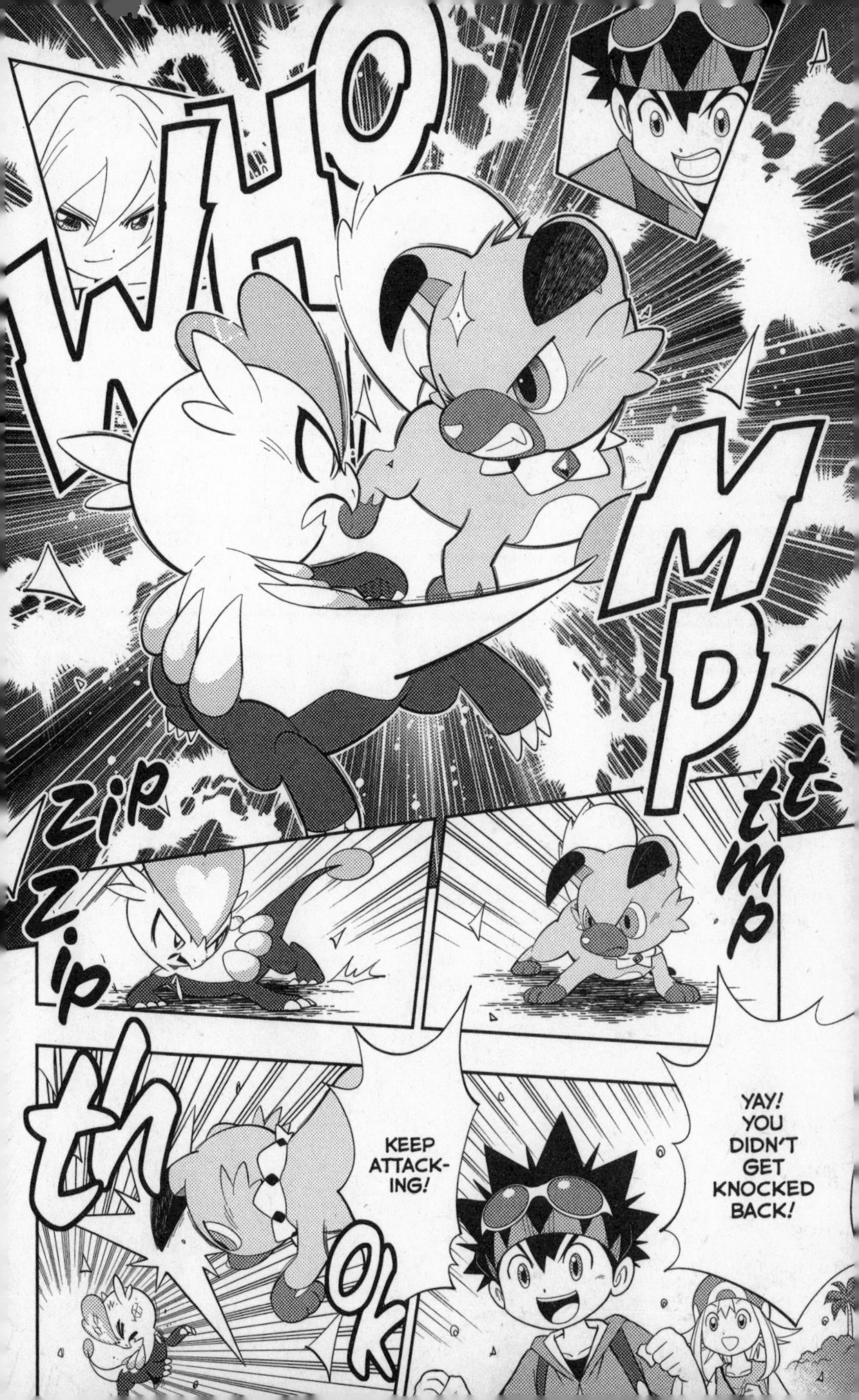
WHOMP
tt
tmp
Zip
Zip
YAY! YOU DIDN'T GET KNOCKED BACK!
KEEP ATTACK-ING!
thok

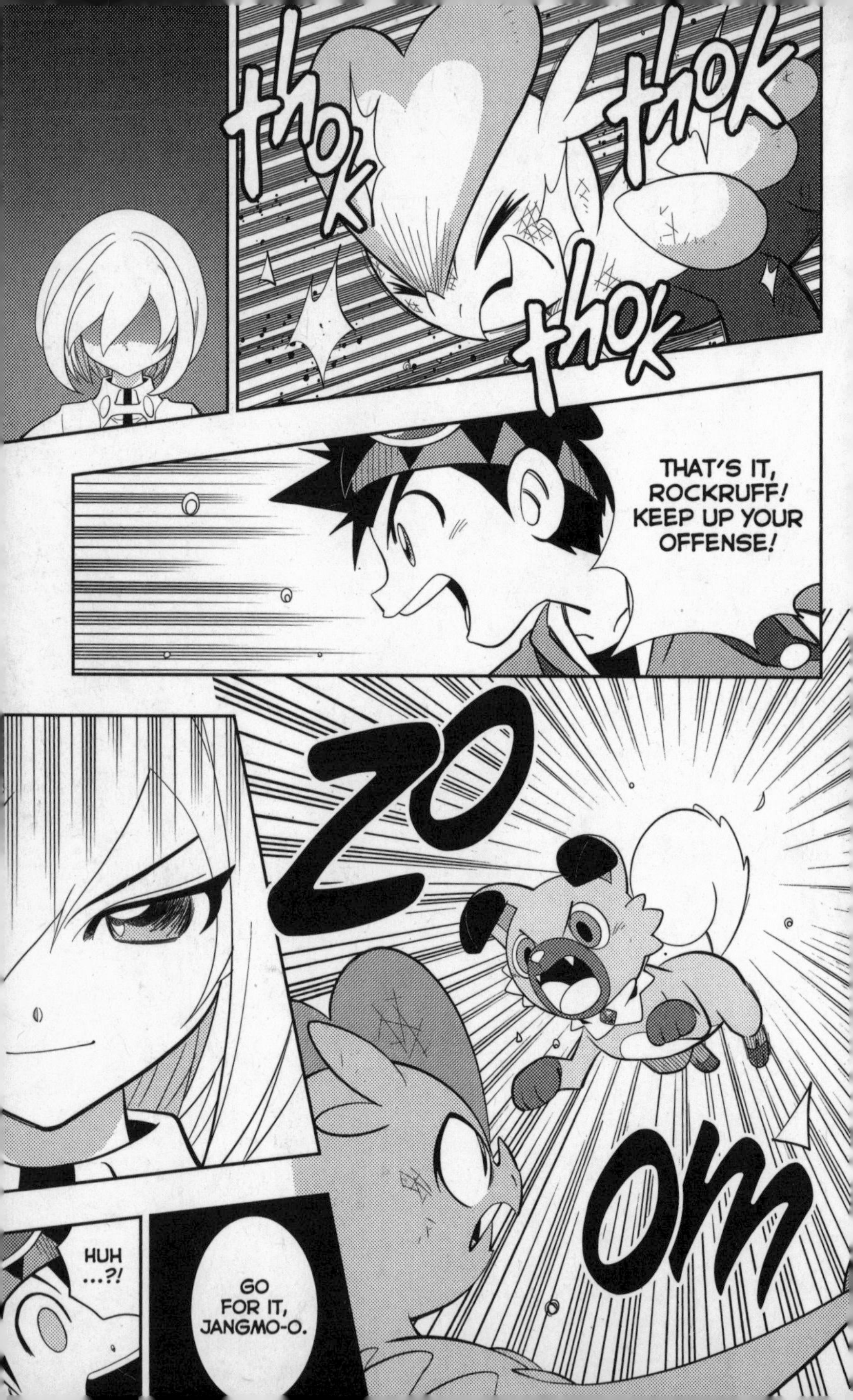
thok
thok
thok
THAT'S IT, ROCKRUFF! KEEP UP YOUR OFFENSE!
ZOOM
GO FOR IT, JANGMO-O.
HUH ...?!

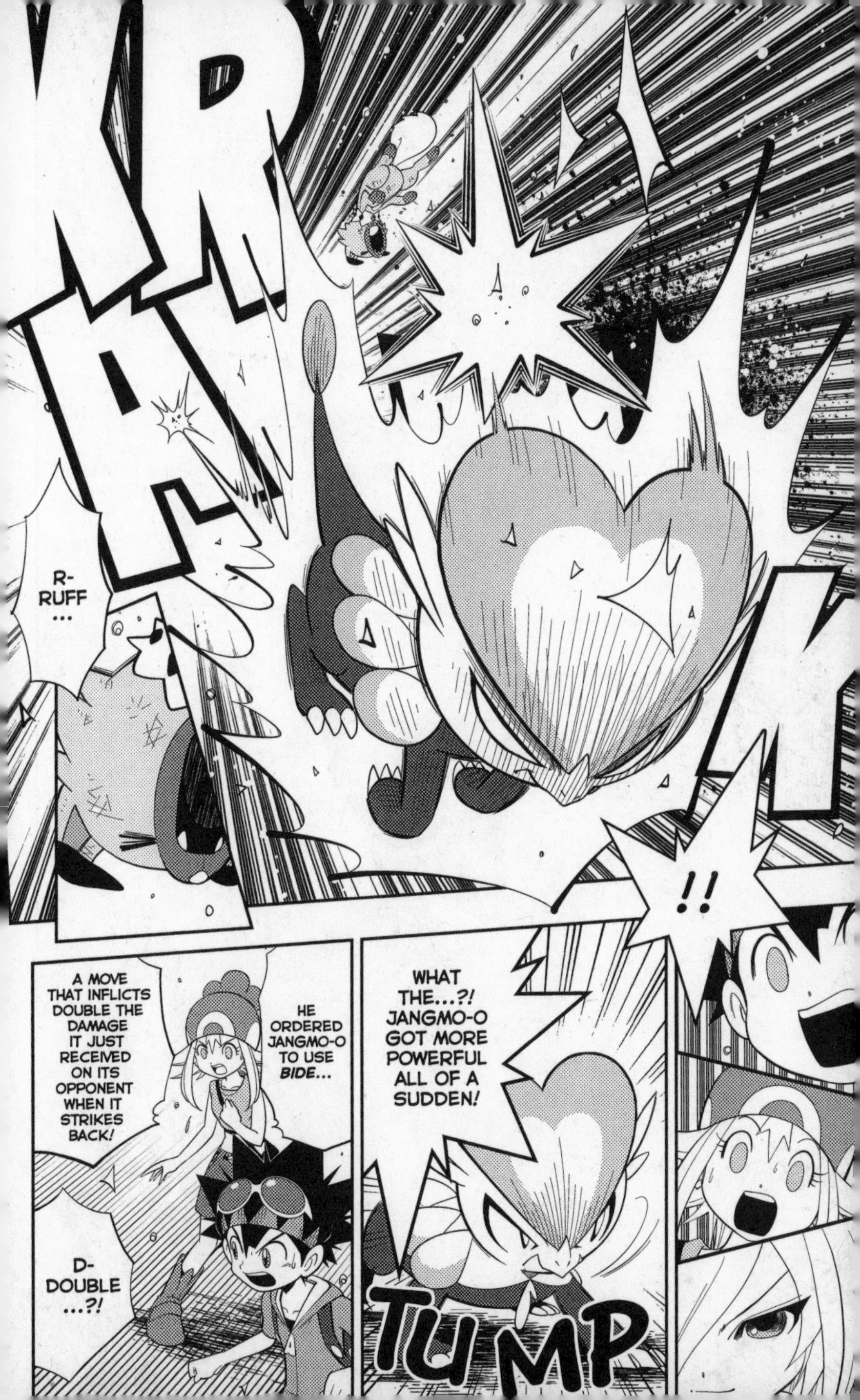
R-RUFF...
!!
WHAT THE...?! JANGMO-O GOT MORE POWERFUL ALL OF A SUDDEN!
TUMP
HE ORDERED JANGMO-O TO USE *BIDE*...
A MOVE THAT INFLICTS DOUBLE THE DAMAGE IT JUST RECEIVED ON ITS OPPONENT WHEN IT STRIKES BACK!
D-DOUBLE...?!

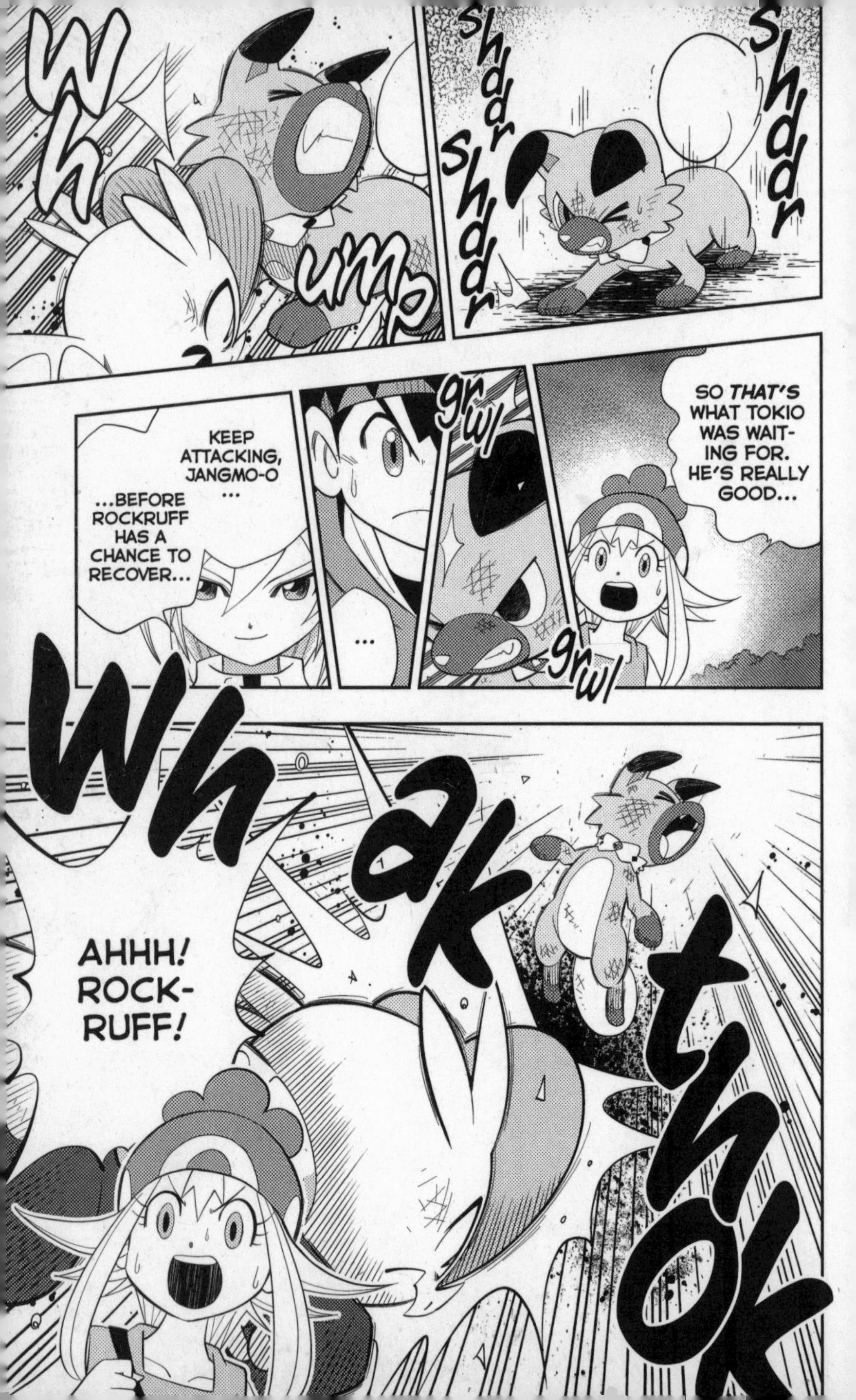
Shddr
Shddr
Shddr
Shddr
Whump
SO THAT'S WHAT TOKIO WAS WAIT-ING FOR. HE'S REALLY GOOD...
grwl
grwl
...
KEEP ATTACKING, JANGMO-O...
...BEFORE ROCKRUFF HAS A CHANCE TO RECOVER...
Whakthok
AHHH! ROCK-RUFF!

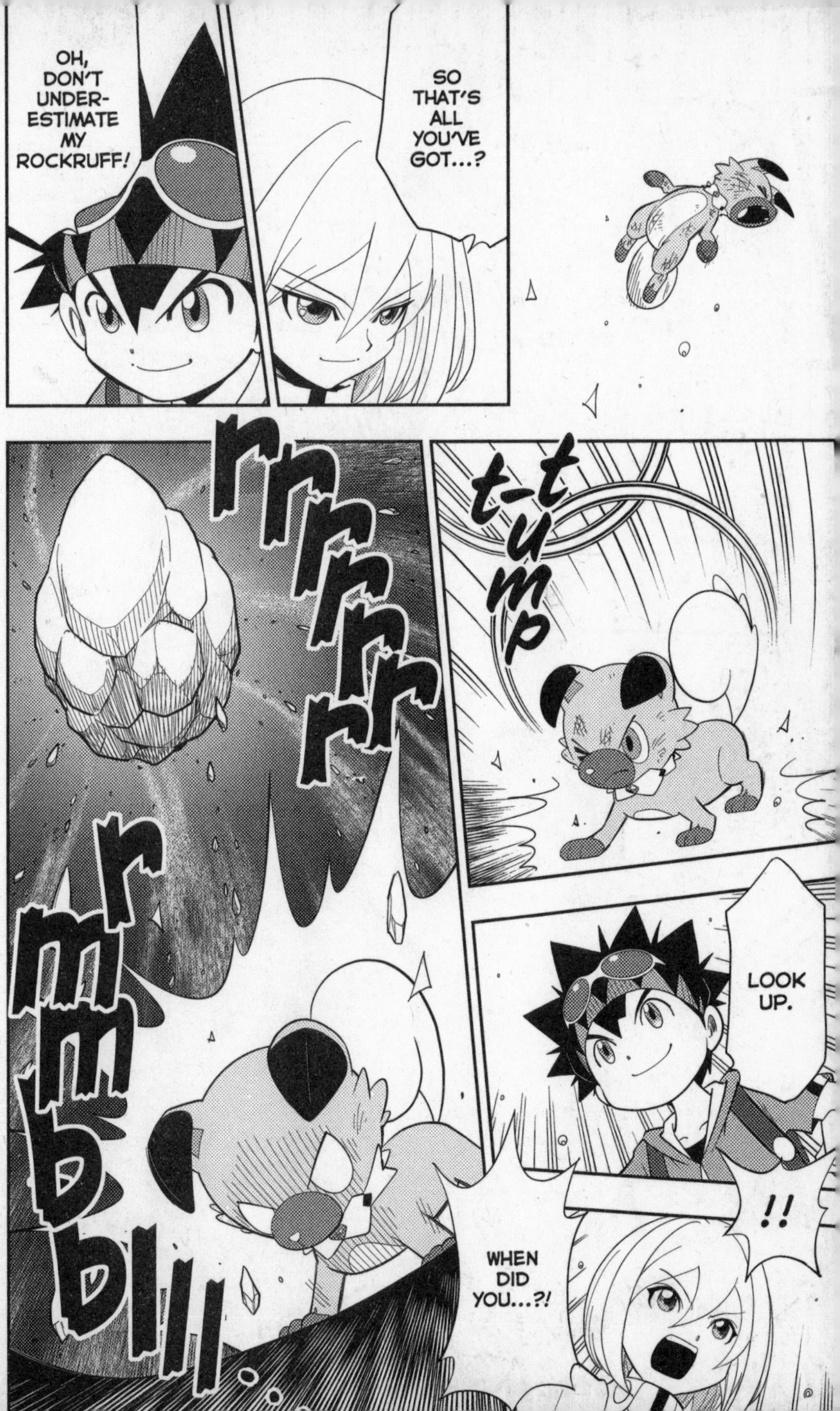
SO THAT'S ALL YOU'VE GOT...?
OH, DON'T UNDER-ESTIMATE MY ROCKRUFF!
t-tump
LOOK UP.
!!
WHEN DID YOU...?!
rrrrrrr
rmmbbll...

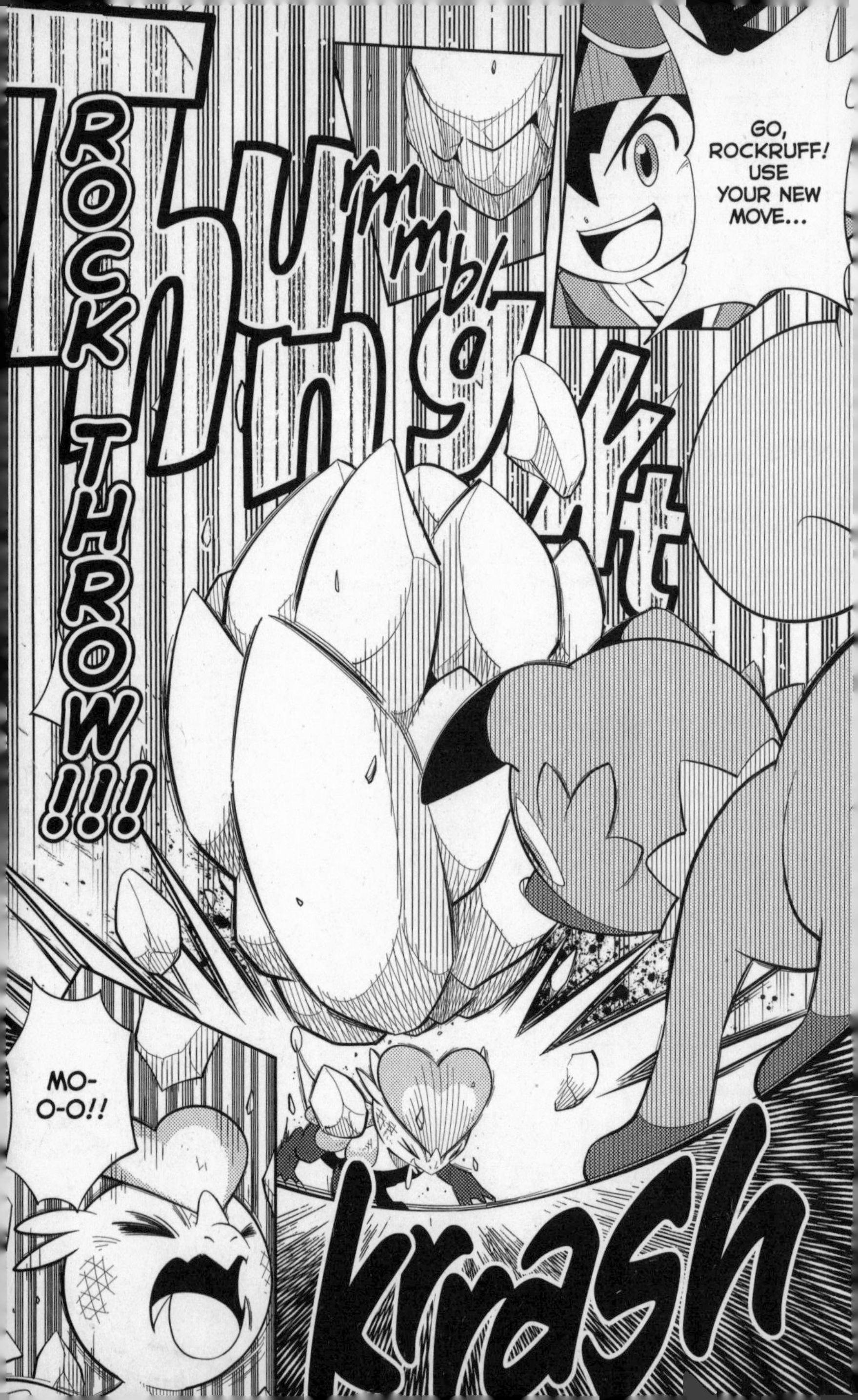
GO, ROCKRUFF! USE YOUR NEW MOVE...
ROCK THROW!!!
MO-O-O!!
krrash

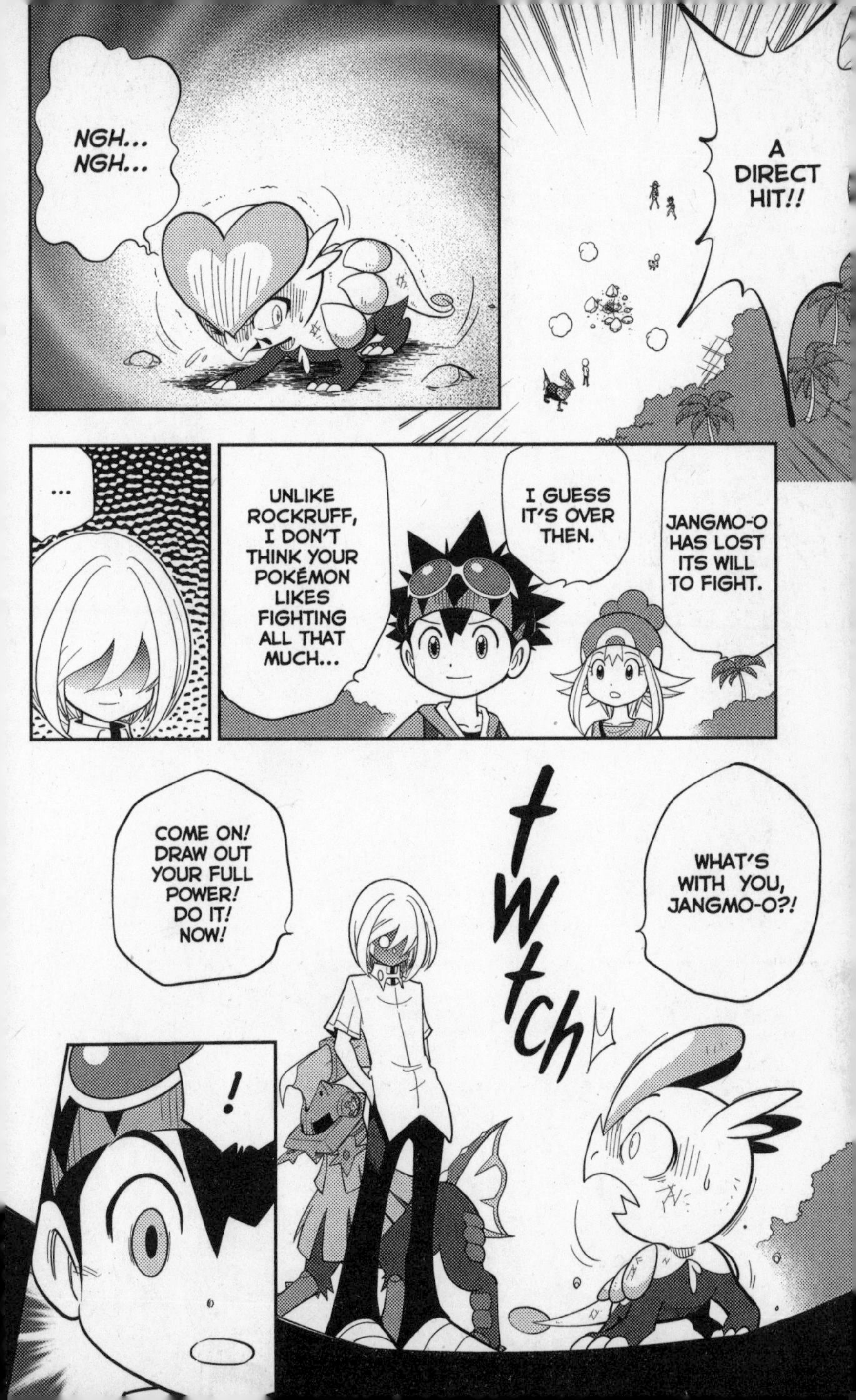
A DIRECT HIT!!
NGH... NGH...
JANGMO-O HAS LOST ITS WILL TO FIGHT.
I GUESS IT'S OVER THEN.
UNLIKE ROCKRUFF, I DON'T THINK YOUR POKÉMON LIKES FIGHTING ALL THAT MUCH...
...
WHAT'S WITH YOU, JANGMO-O?!
twitch
COME ON! DRAW OUT YOUR FULL POWER! DO IT! NOW!
!

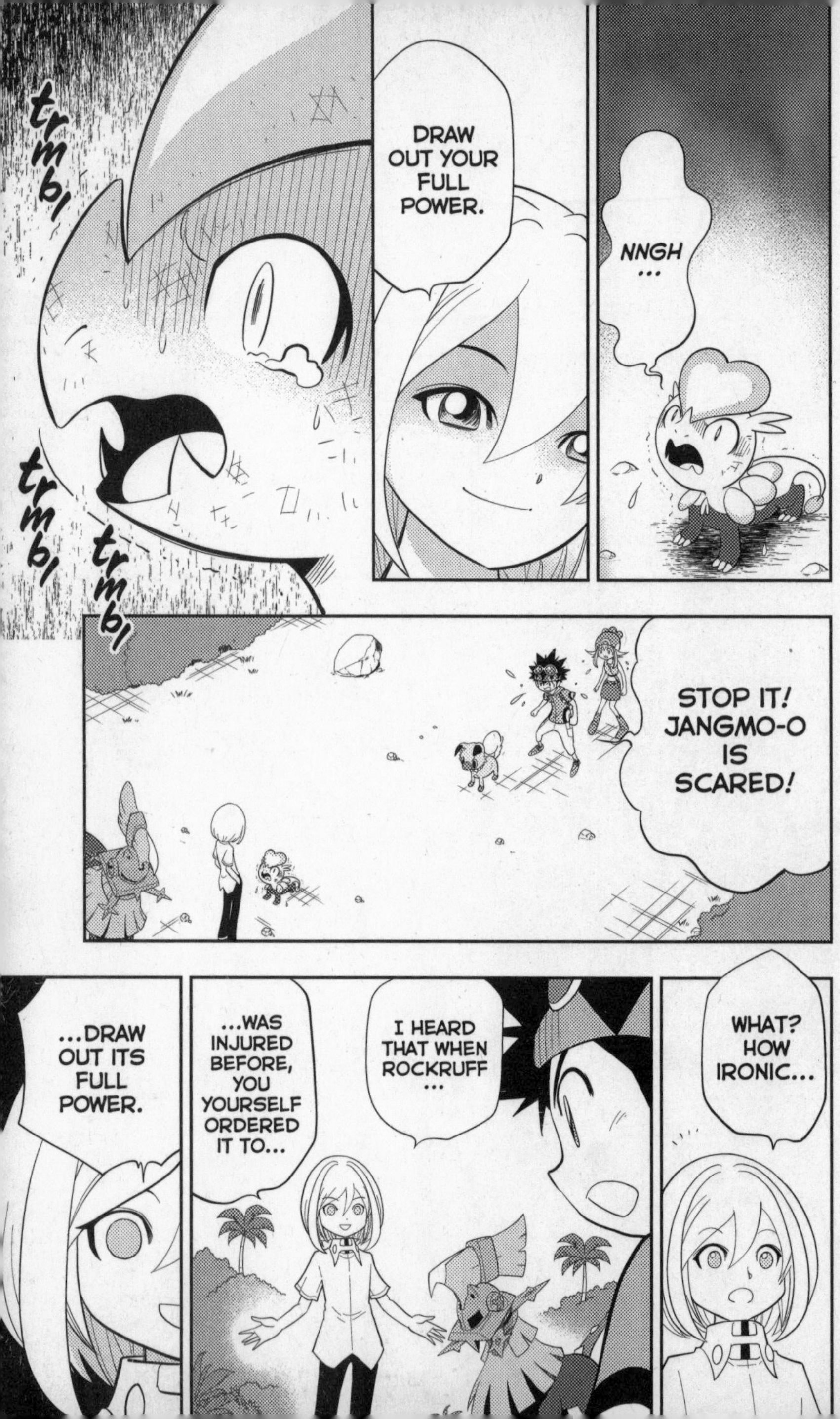
NNGH...
DRAW OUT YOUR FULL POWER.
trmbl
trmbl
trmbl
STOP IT! JANGMO-O IS SCARED!
WHAT? HOW IRONIC...
I HEARD THAT WHEN ROCKRUFF...
...WAS INJURED BEFORE, YOU YOURSELF ORDERED IT TO...
...DRAW OUT ITS FULL POWER.

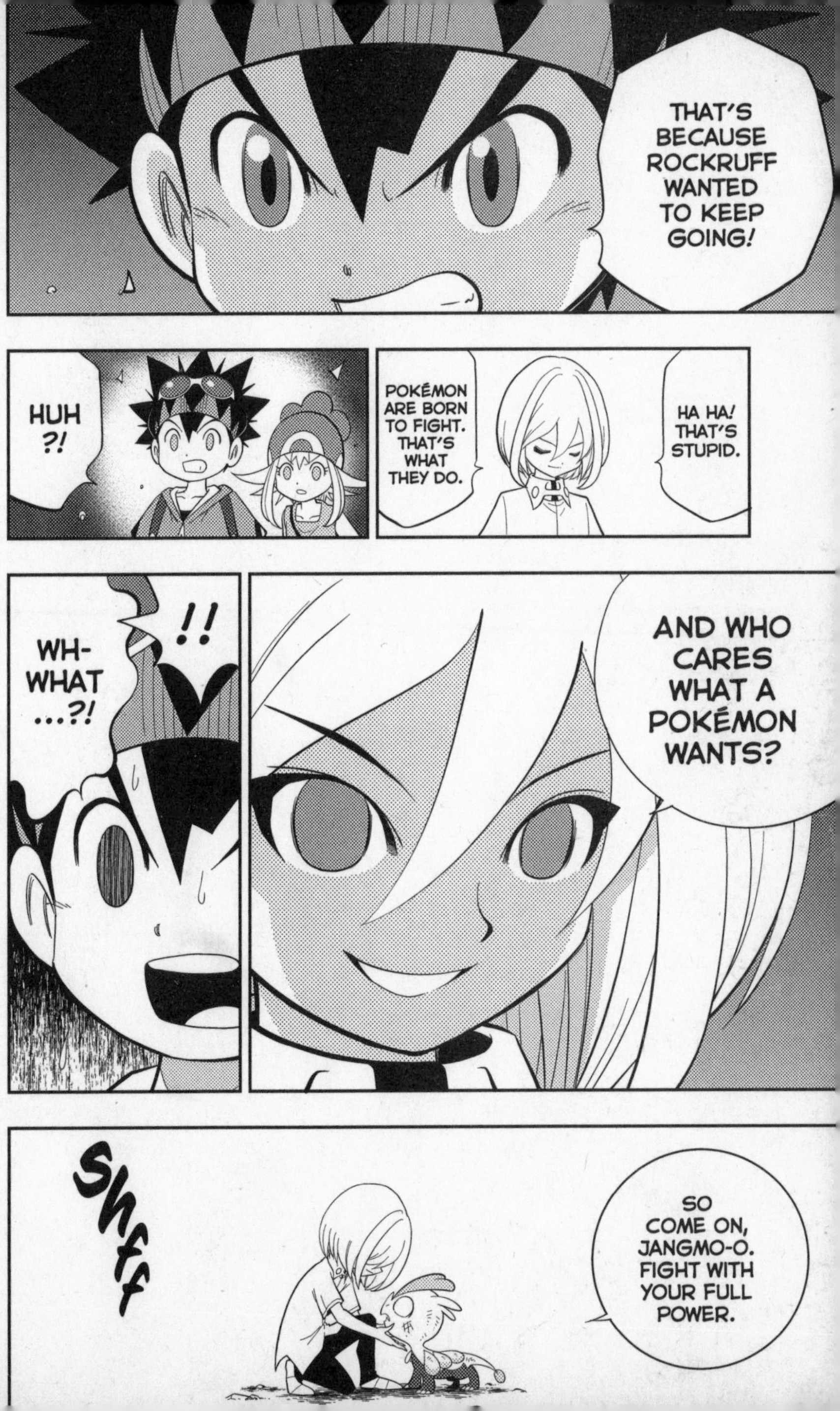
THAT'S BECAUSE ROCKRUFF WANTED TO KEEP GOING!
HA HA! THAT'S STUPID.
POKÉMON ARE BORN TO FIGHT. THAT'S WHAT THEY DO.
HUH ?!
AND WHO CARES WHAT A POKÉMON WANTS?
!!
WH-WHAT ...?!
SO COME ON, JANGMO-O. FIGHT WITH YOUR FULL POWER.
SNFF

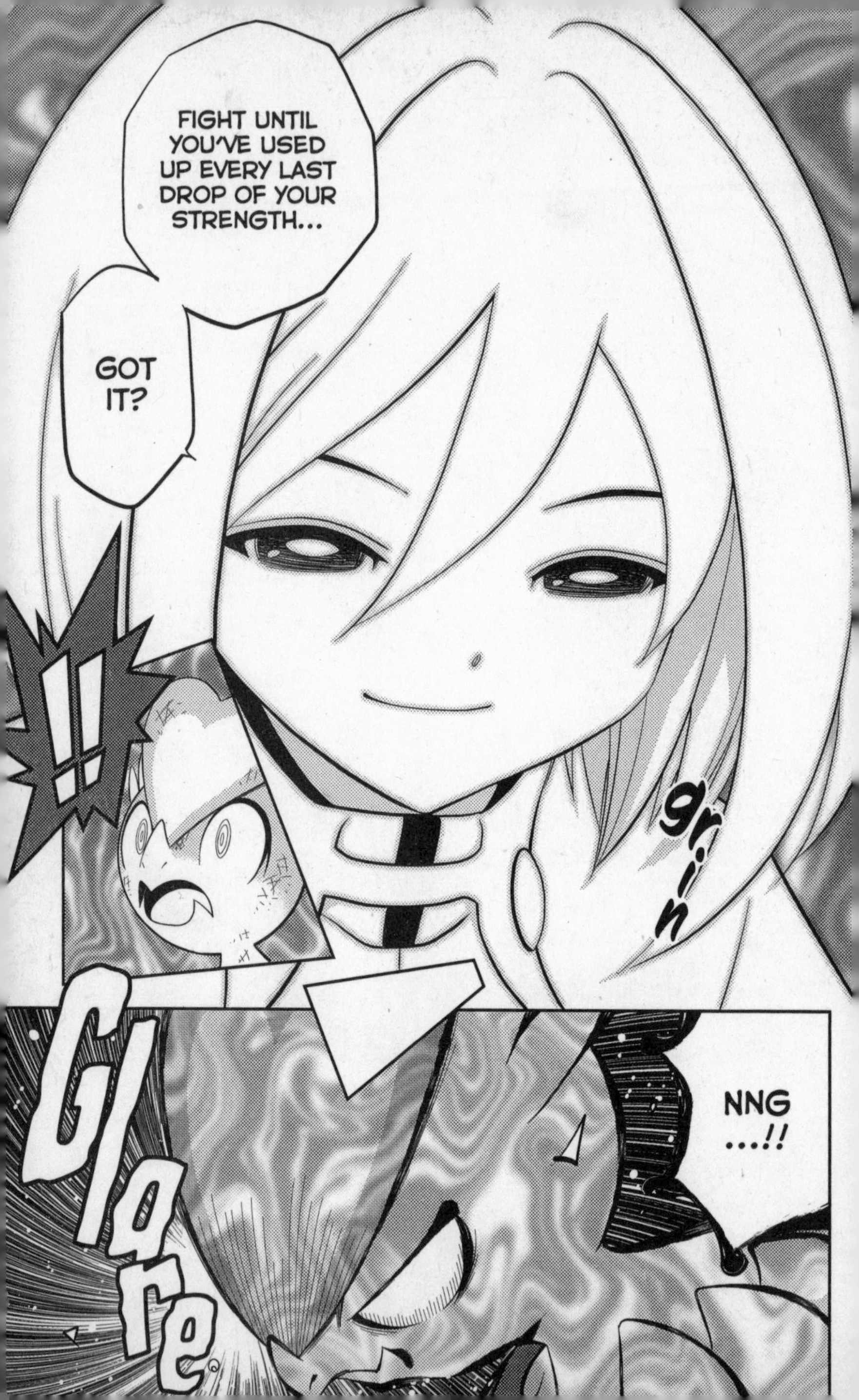
FIGHT UNTIL YOU'VE USED UP EVERY LAST DROP OF YOUR STRENGTH...
GOT IT?
grin
!!
NNG ...!!
Glare

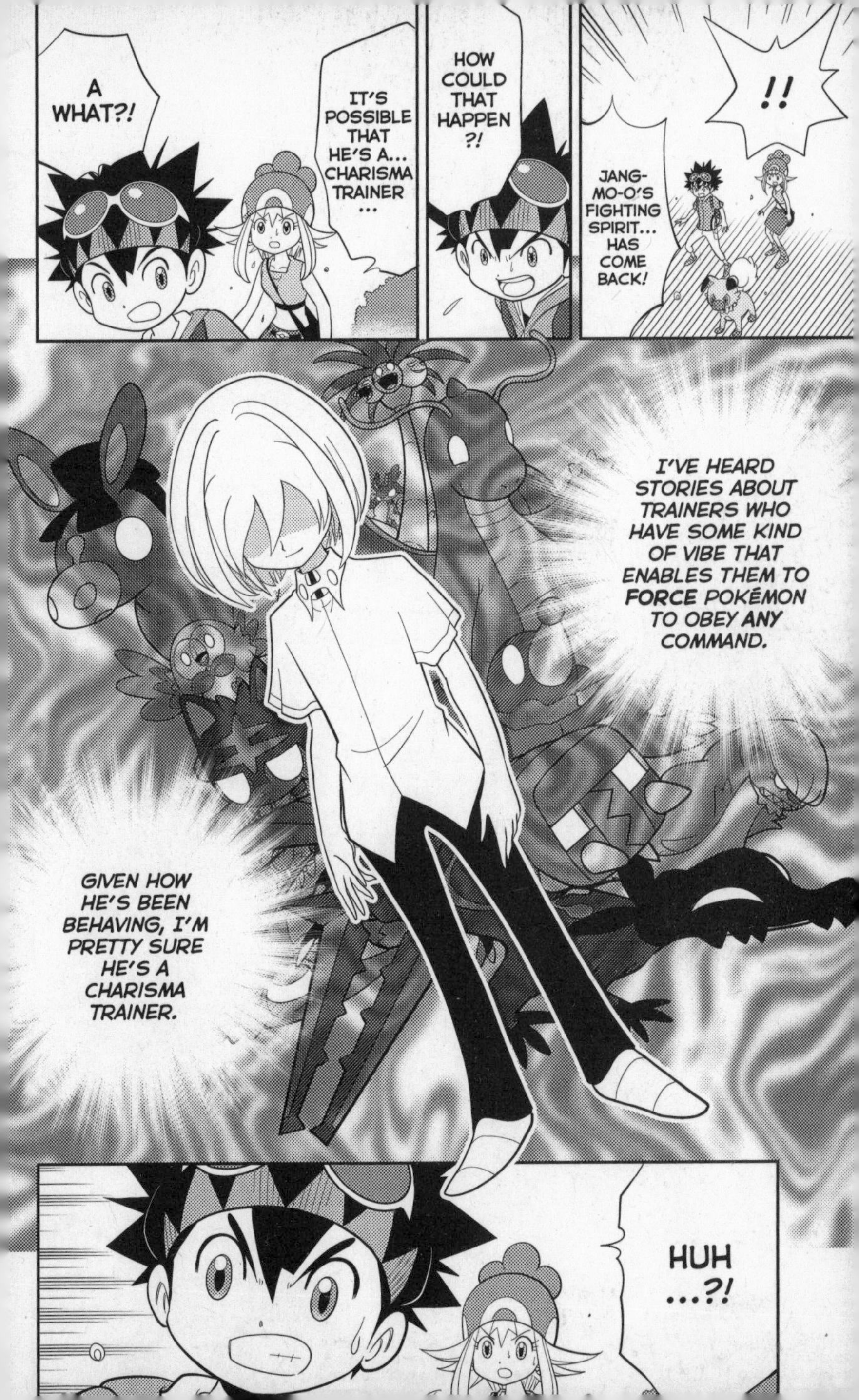
!!
JANG-MO-O'S FIGHTING SPIRIT... HAS COME BACK!
HOW COULD THAT HAPPEN ?!
IT'S POSSIBLE THAT HE'S A... CHARISMA TRAINER ...
A WHAT?!
I'VE HEARD STORIES ABOUT TRAINERS WHO HAVE SOME KIND OF VIBE THAT ENABLES THEM TO FORCE POKÉMON TO OBEY ANY COMMAND.
GIVEN HOW HE'S BEEN BEHAVING, I'M PRETTY SURE HE'S A CHARISMA TRAINER.
HUH ...?!

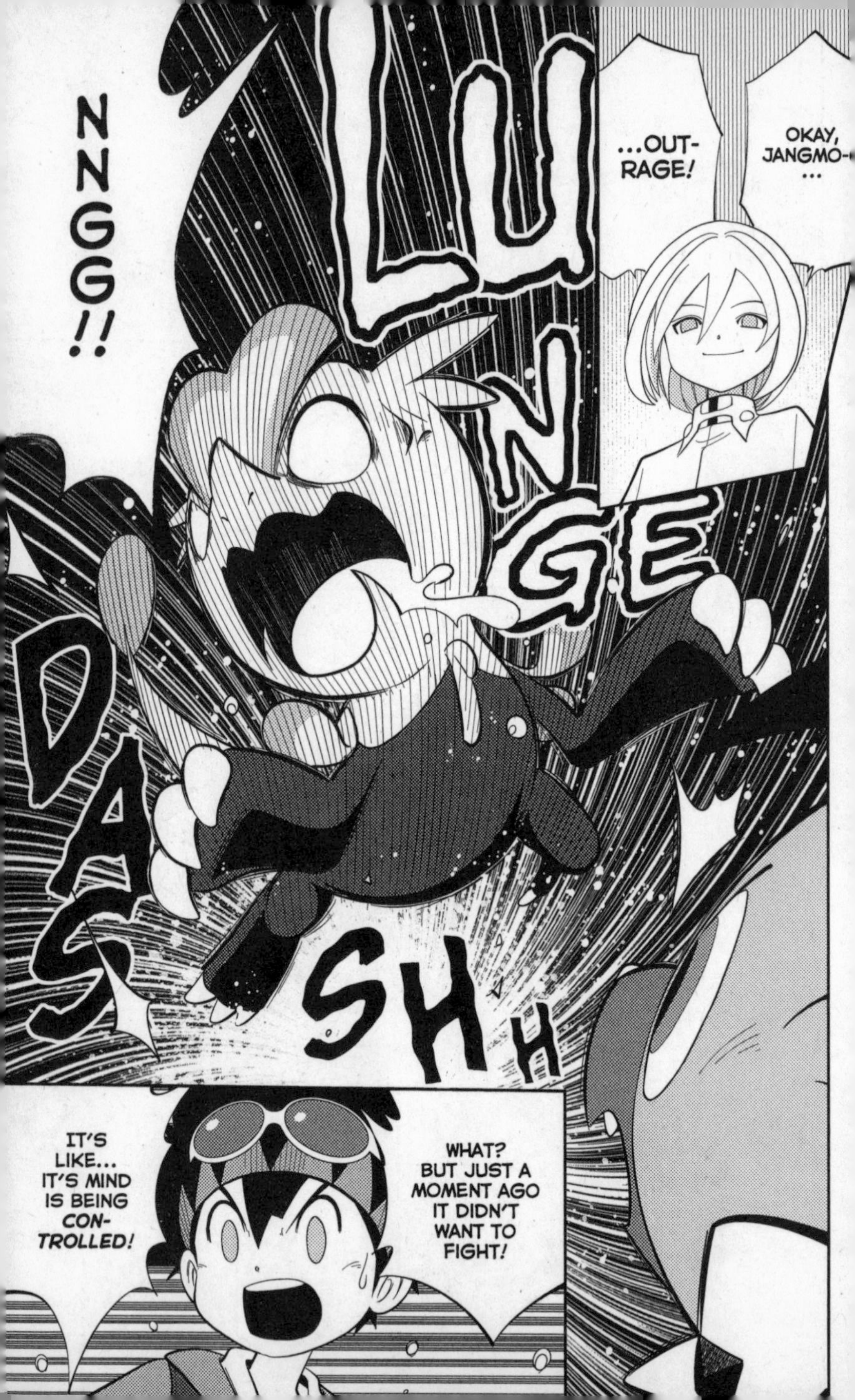
OKAY, JANGMO-...
...OUT-RAGE!
LUNGE
NNGG!!
DASHH
WHAT? BUT JUST A MOMENT AGO IT DIDN'T WANT TO FIGHT!
IT'S LIKE... IT'S MIND IS BEING CON-TROLLED!

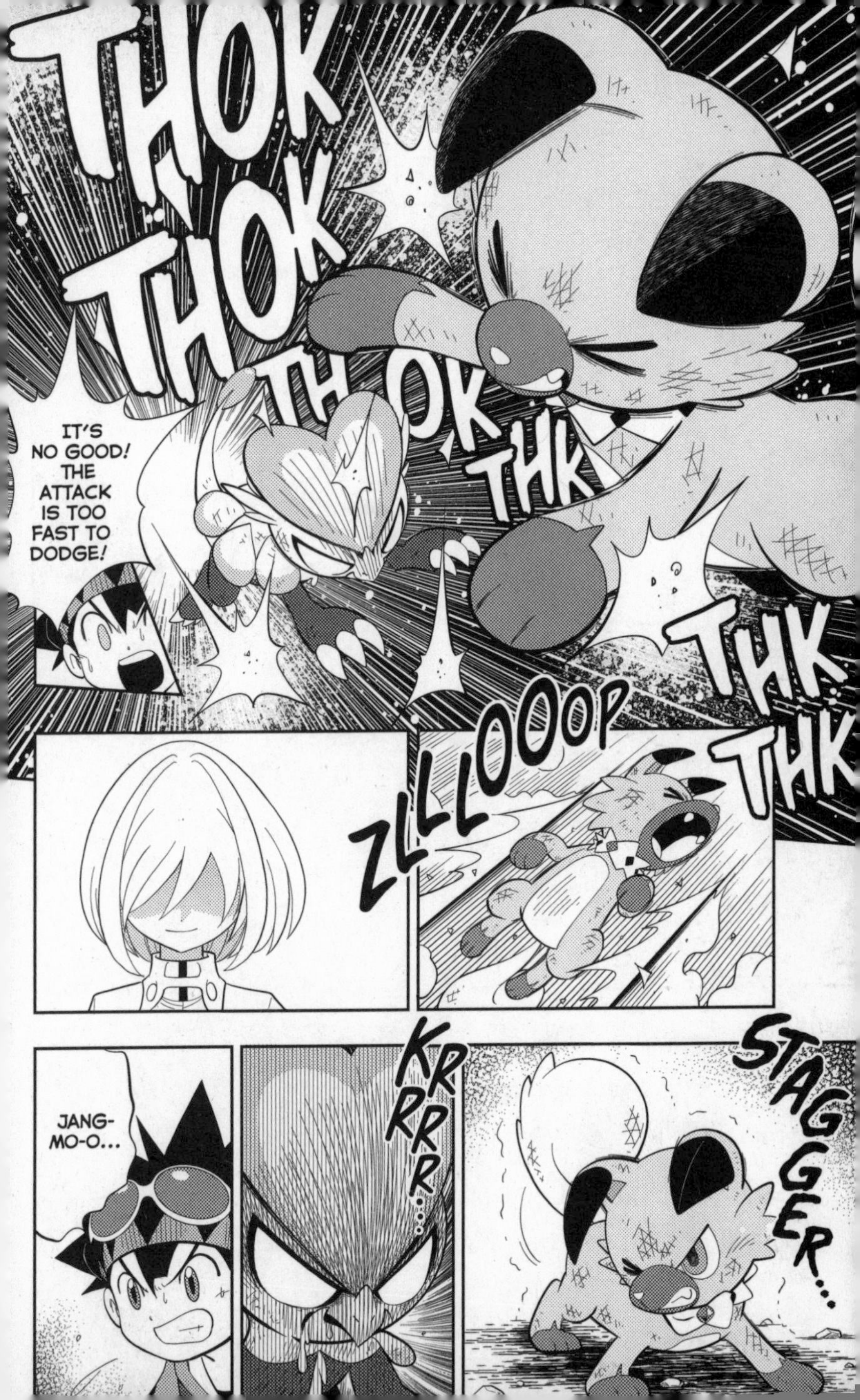
THOK
THOK
TH OK
THK
IT'S NO GOOD! THE ATTACK IS TOO FAST TO DODGE!
THK
THK
ZLLLOOOP
STAGGER...
KRRRR...
JANG-MO-O...

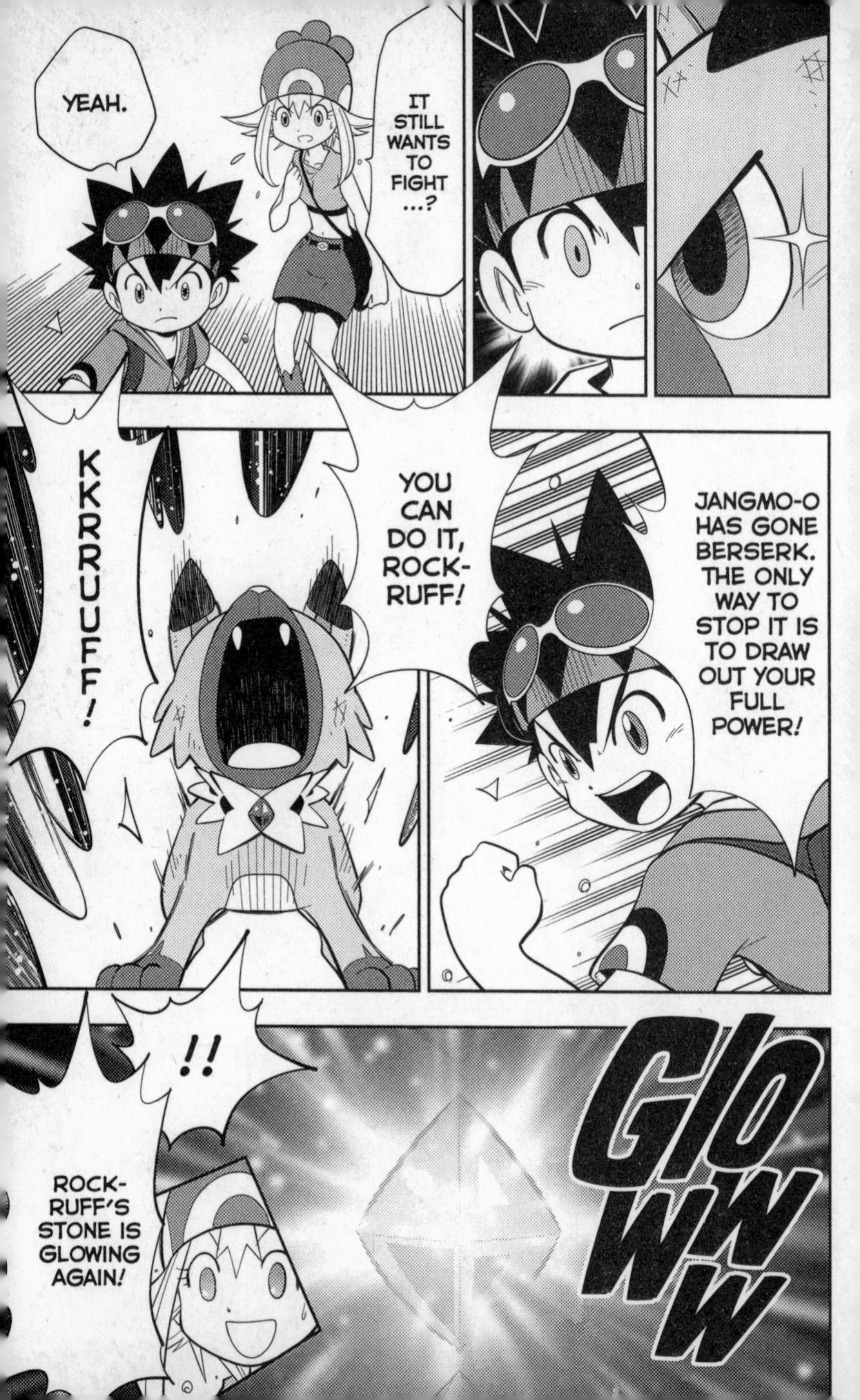

IT STILL WANTS TO FIGHT...?
YEAH.
JANGMO-O HAS GONE BERSERK. THE ONLY WAY TO STOP IT IS TO DRAW OUT YOUR FULL POWER!
YOU CAN DO IT, ROCK-RUFF!
KKRRUUFF!
GLOWWW
!!
ROCK-RUFF'S STONE IS GLOWING AGAIN!

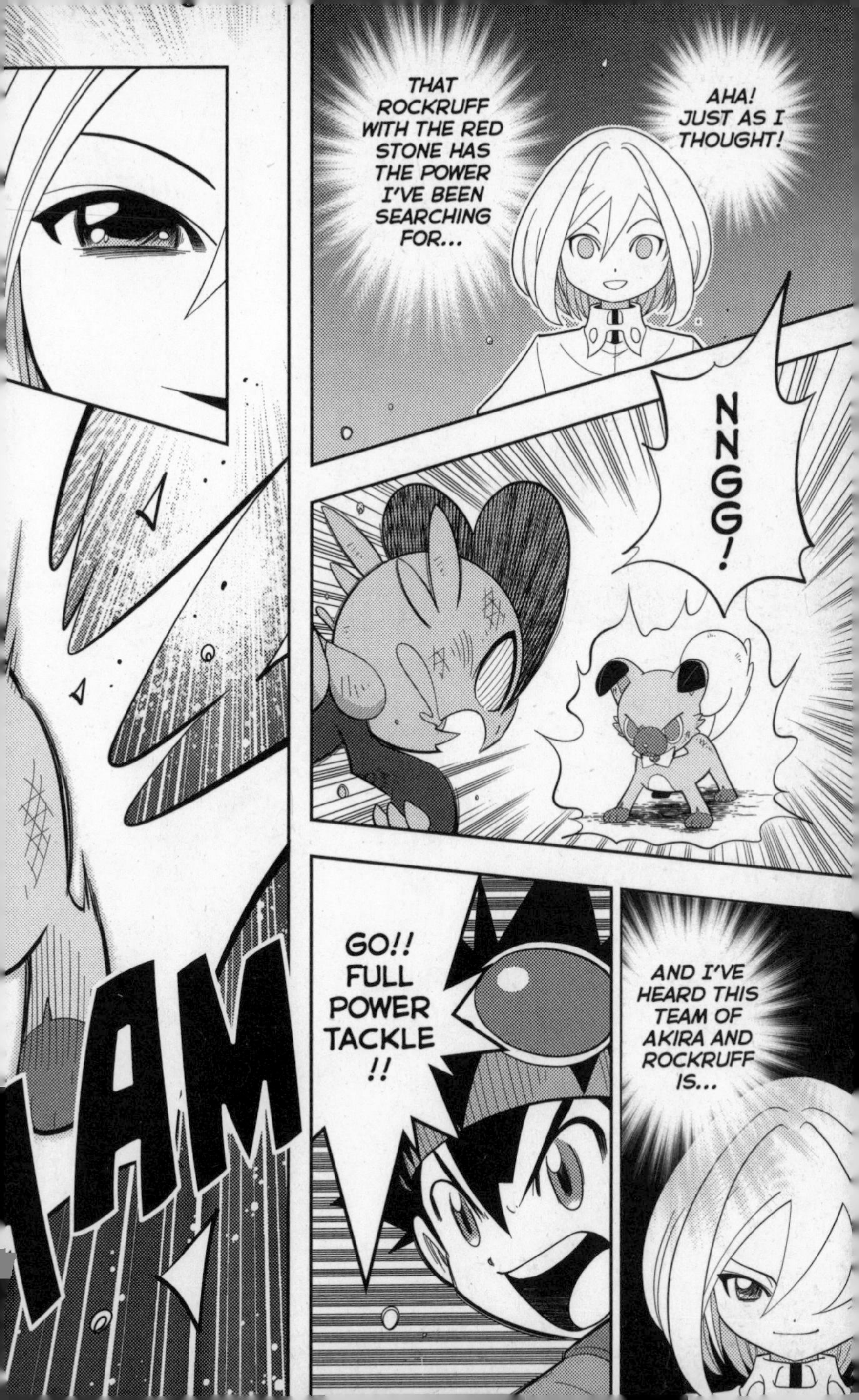
AHA! JUST AS I THOUGHT!
THAT ROCKRUFF WITH THE RED STONE HAS THE POWER I'VE BEEN SEARCHING FOR...
NNGG!
AND I'VE HEARD THIS TEAM OF AKIRA AND ROCKRUFF IS...
GO!! FULL POWER TACKLE!!
AM

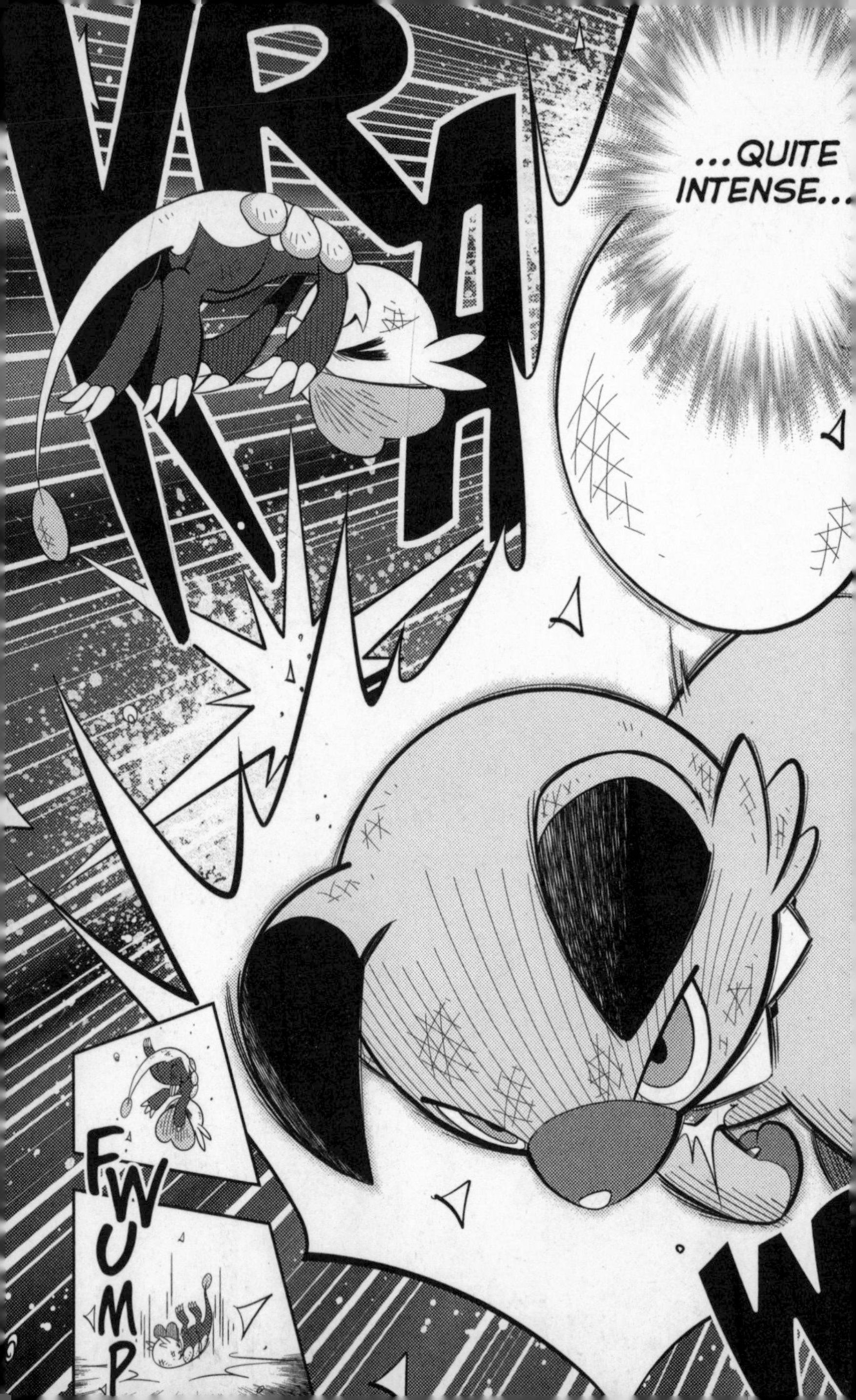
...QUITE INTENSE...
FWUMP

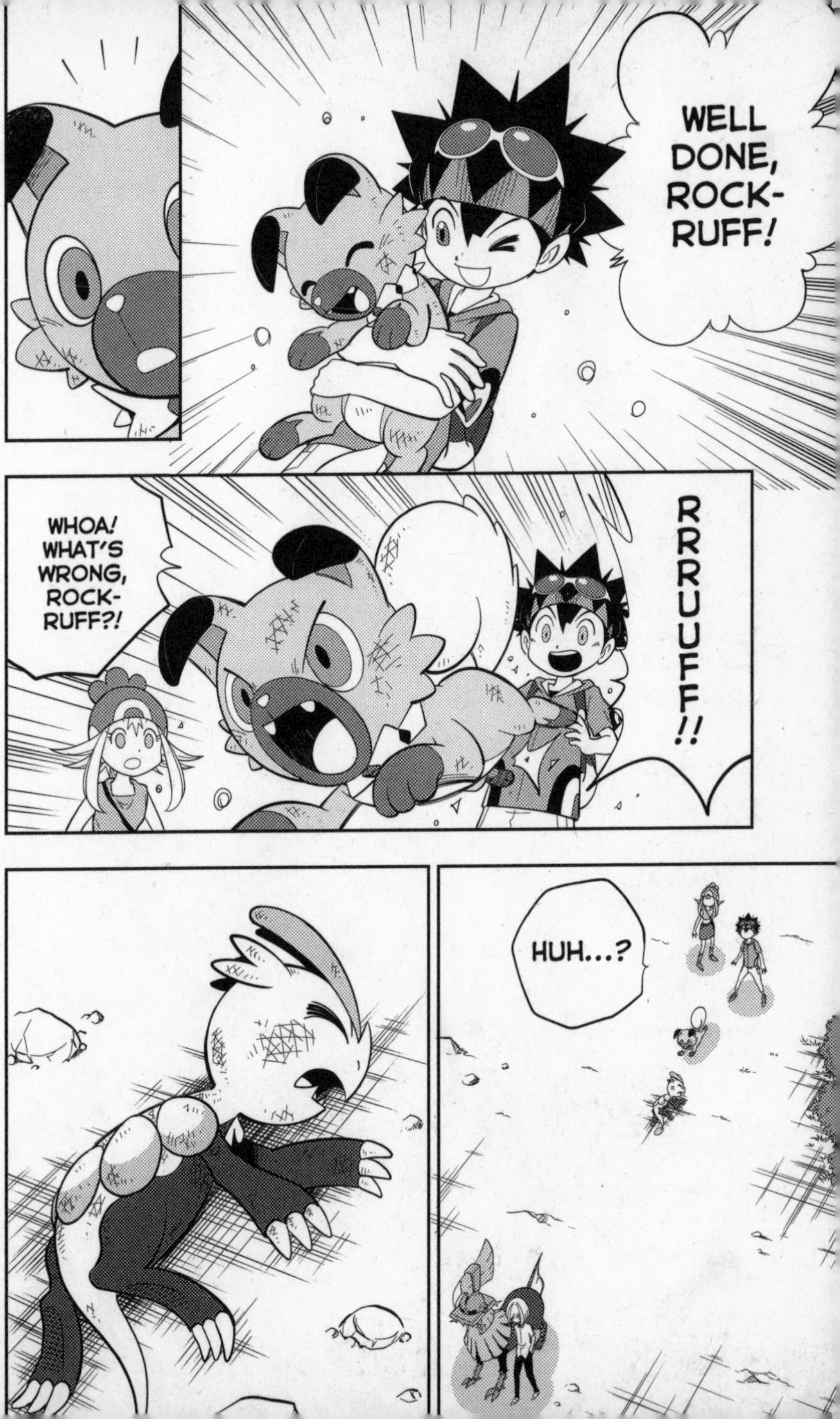
WELL DONE, ROCK-RUFF!
RRRUUFF!!
WHOA! WHAT'S WRONG, ROCK-RUFF?!
HUH...?

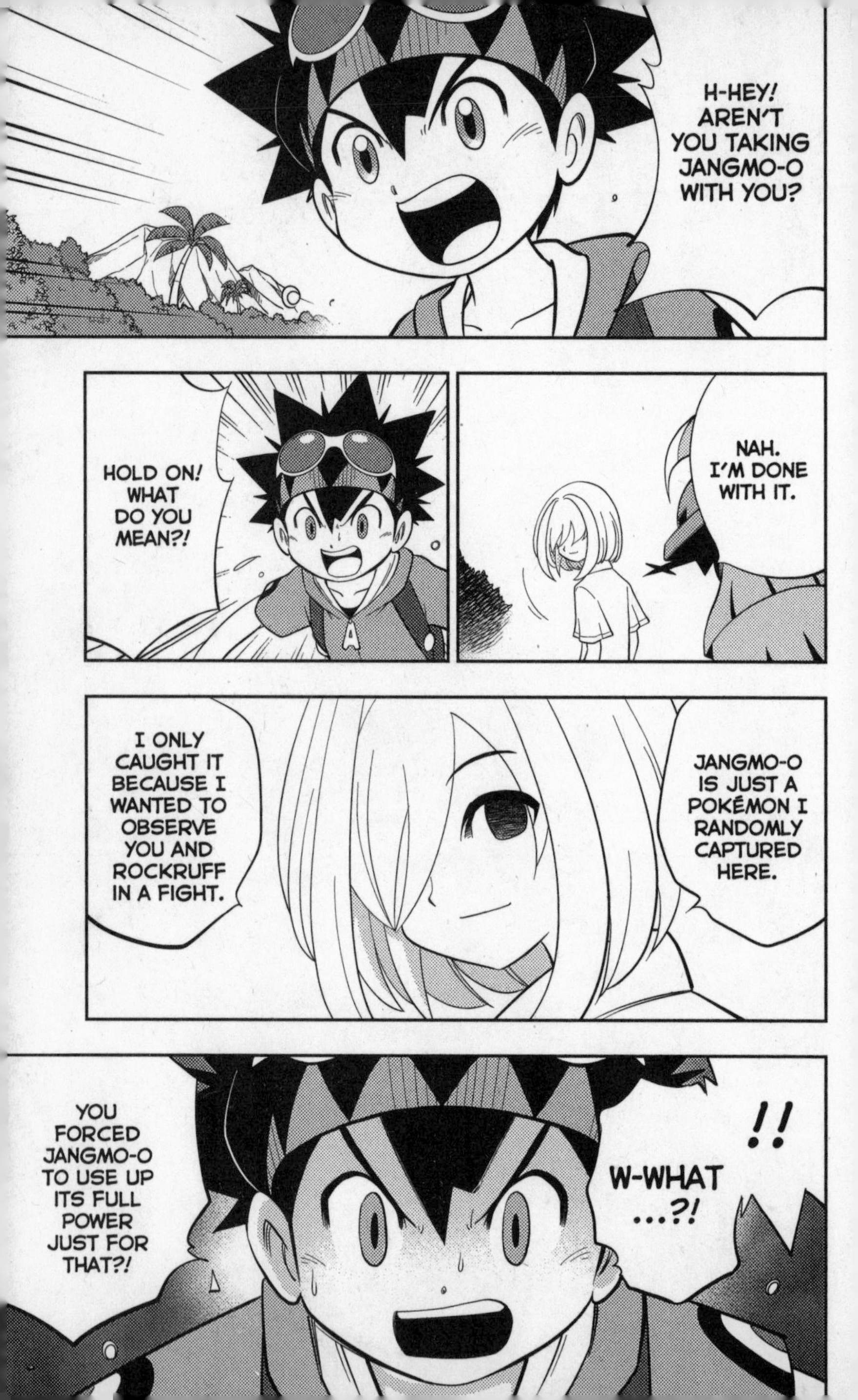
H-HEY! AREN'T YOU TAKING JANGMO-O WITH YOU?
NAH. I'M DONE WITH IT.
HOLD ON! WHAT DO YOU MEAN?!
JANGMO-O IS JUST A POKÉMON I RANDOMLY CAPTURED HERE.
I ONLY CAUGHT IT BECAUSE I WANTED TO OBSERVE YOU AND ROCKRUFF IN A FIGHT.
!!
W-WHAT ...?!
YOU FORCED JANGMO-O TO USE UP ITS FULL POWER JUST FOR THAT?!

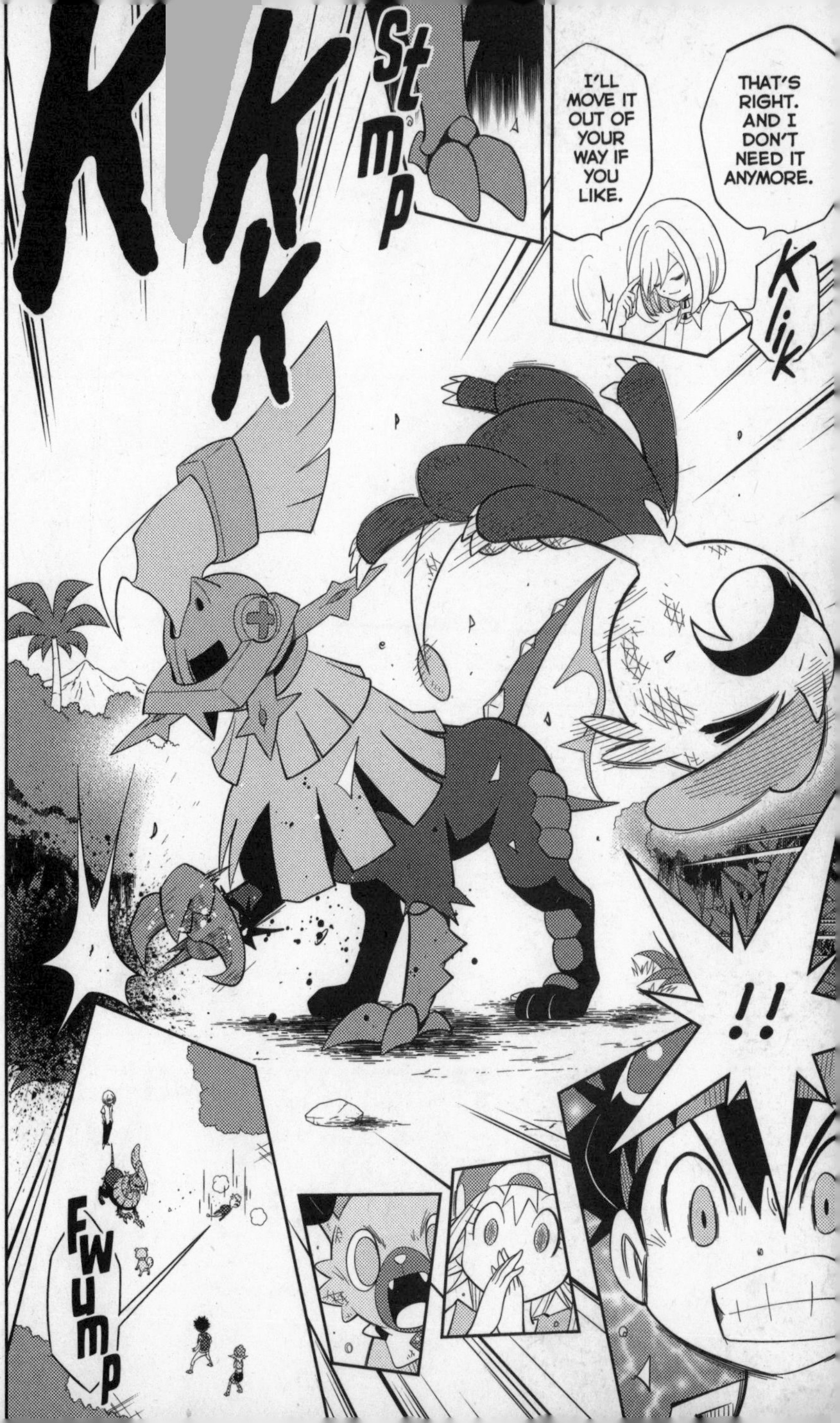

THAT'S RIGHT. AND I DON'T NEED IT ANYMORE.
I'LL MOVE IT OUT OF YOUR WAY IF YOU LIKE.
Klik
Stmp
KKKK
!!
Fwump

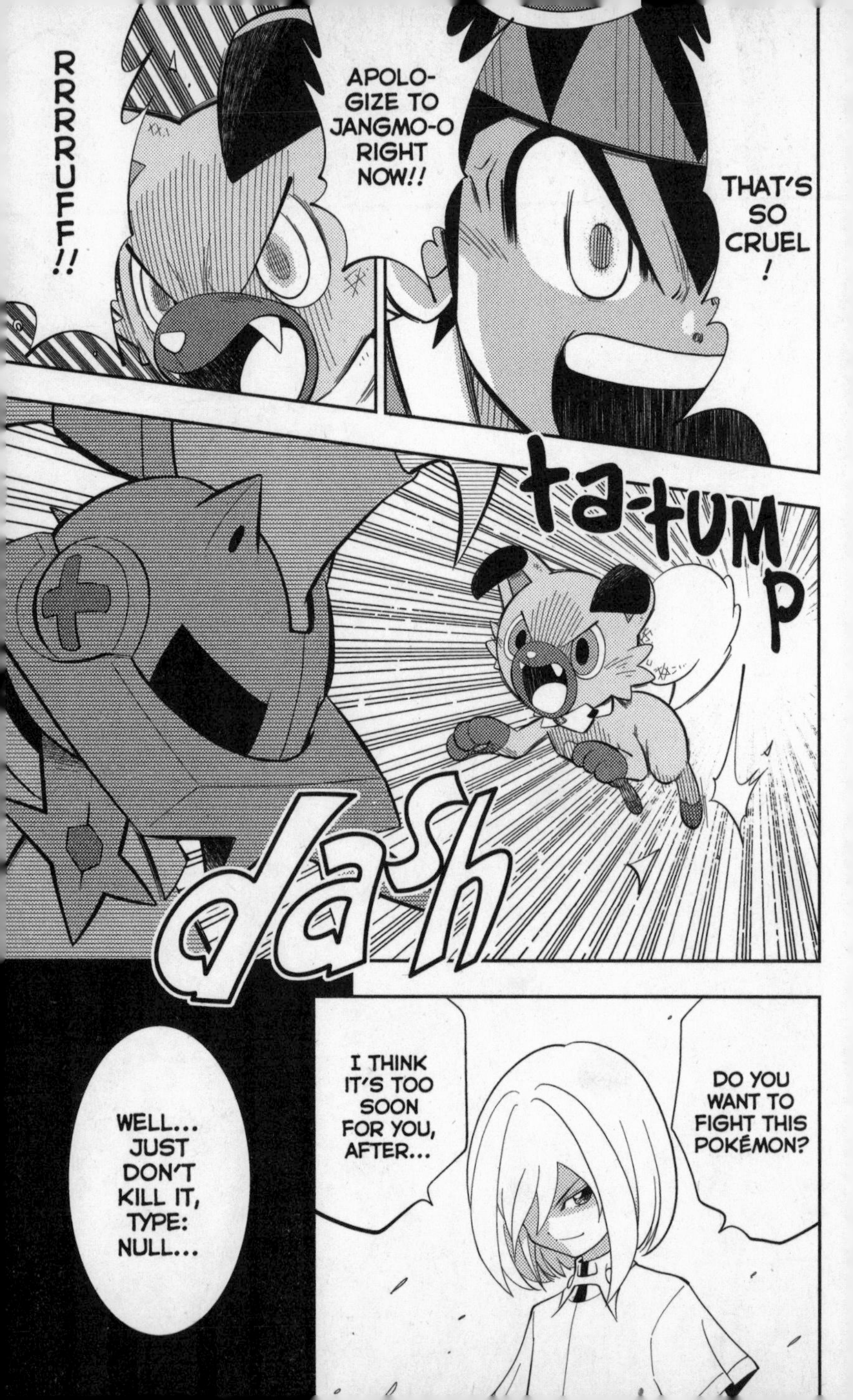
THAT'S SO CRUEL!
APOLOGIZE TO JANGMO-O RIGHT NOW!!
RRRRUFF!!
ta-tump
dash
DO YOU WANT TO FIGHT THIS POKÉMON?
I THINK IT'S TOO SOON FOR YOU, AFTER...
WELL... JUST DON'T KILL IT, TYPE: NULL...

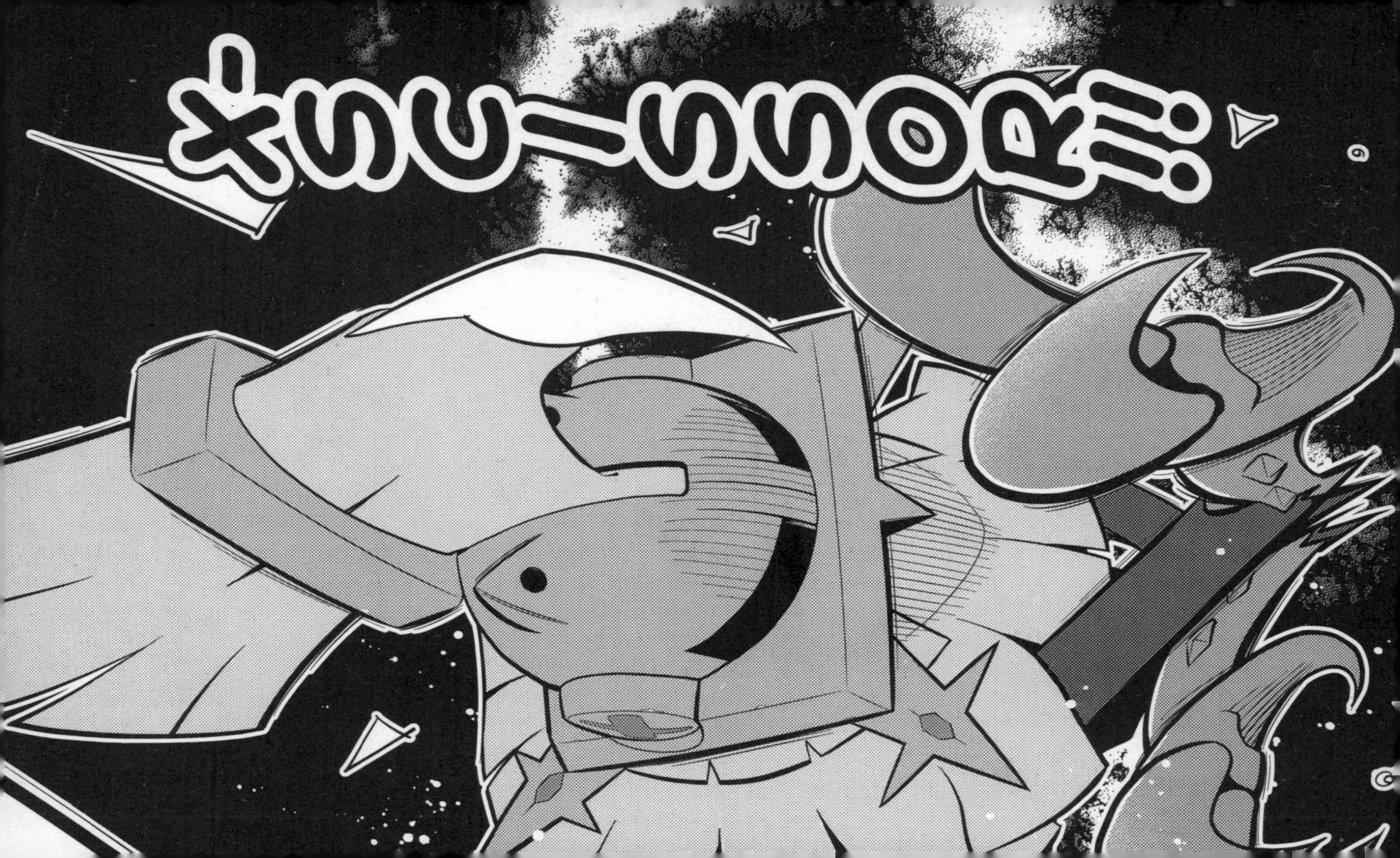
X-SCISSOR!!

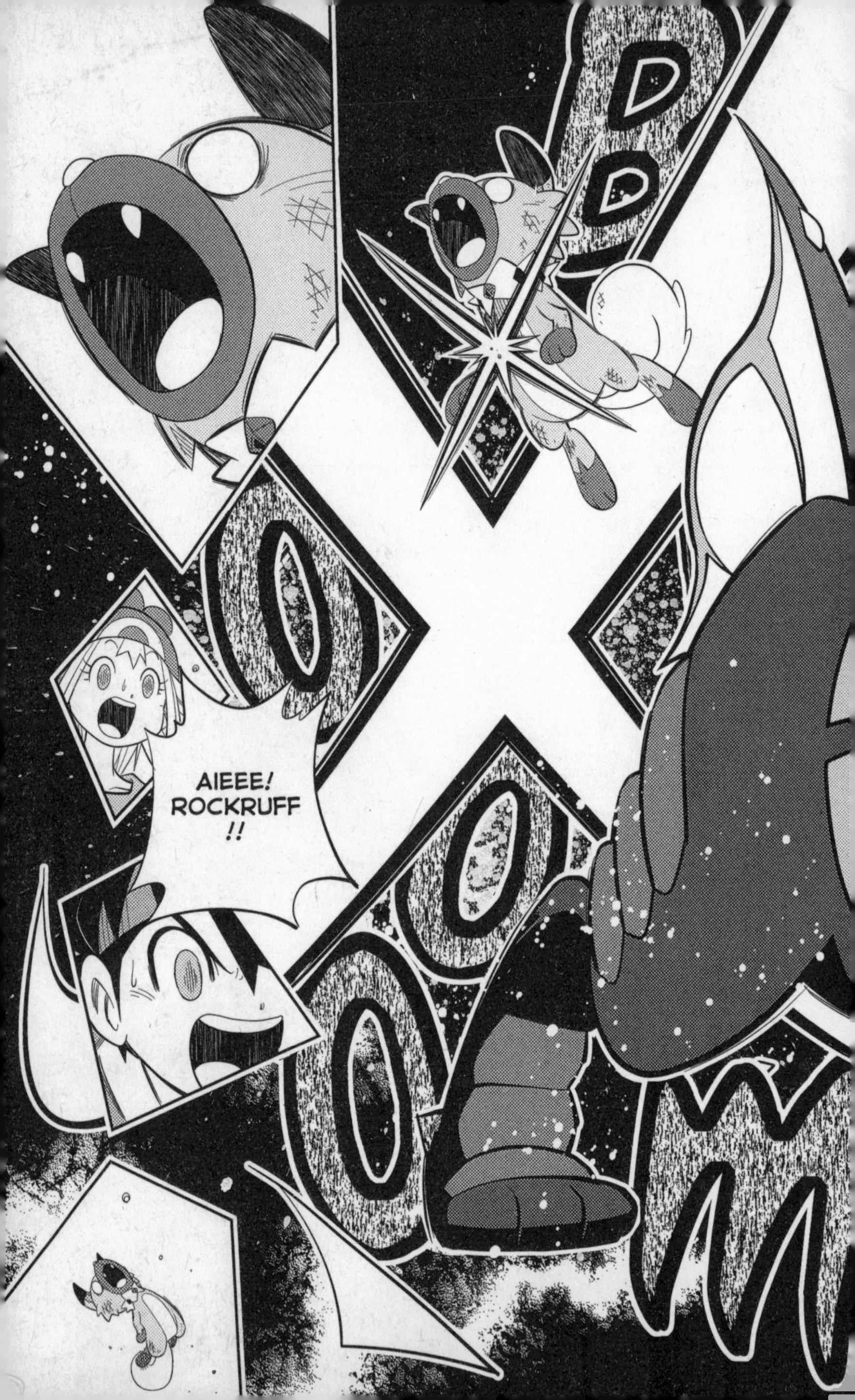
AIEEE! ROCKRUFF !!

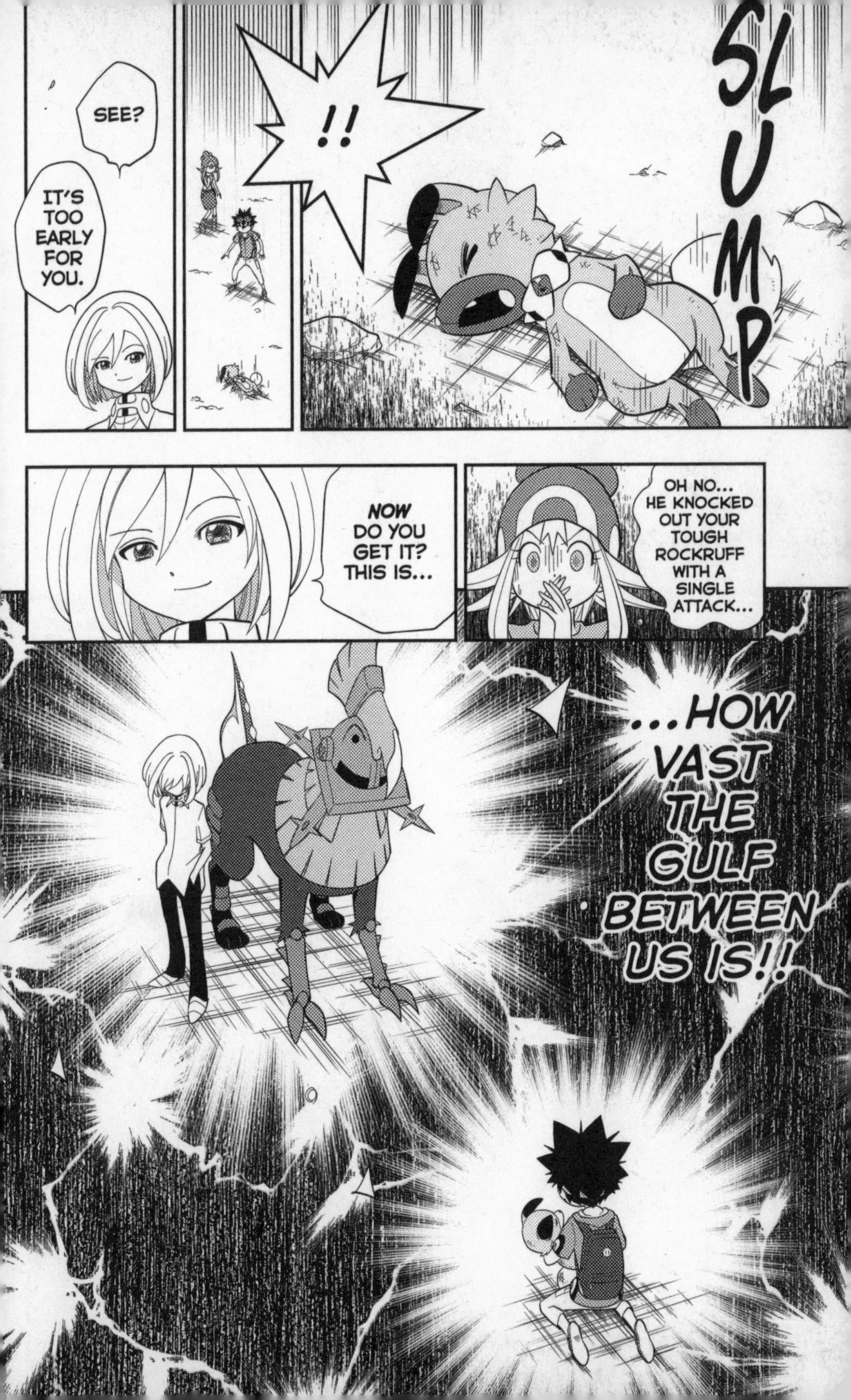
SLUMP
!!
SEE?
IT'S TOO EARLY FOR YOU.
OH NO... HE KNOCKED OUT YOUR TOUGH ROCKRUFF WITH A SINGLE ATTACK...
NOW DO YOU GET IT? THIS IS...
...HOW VAST THE GULF BETWEEN US IS!!

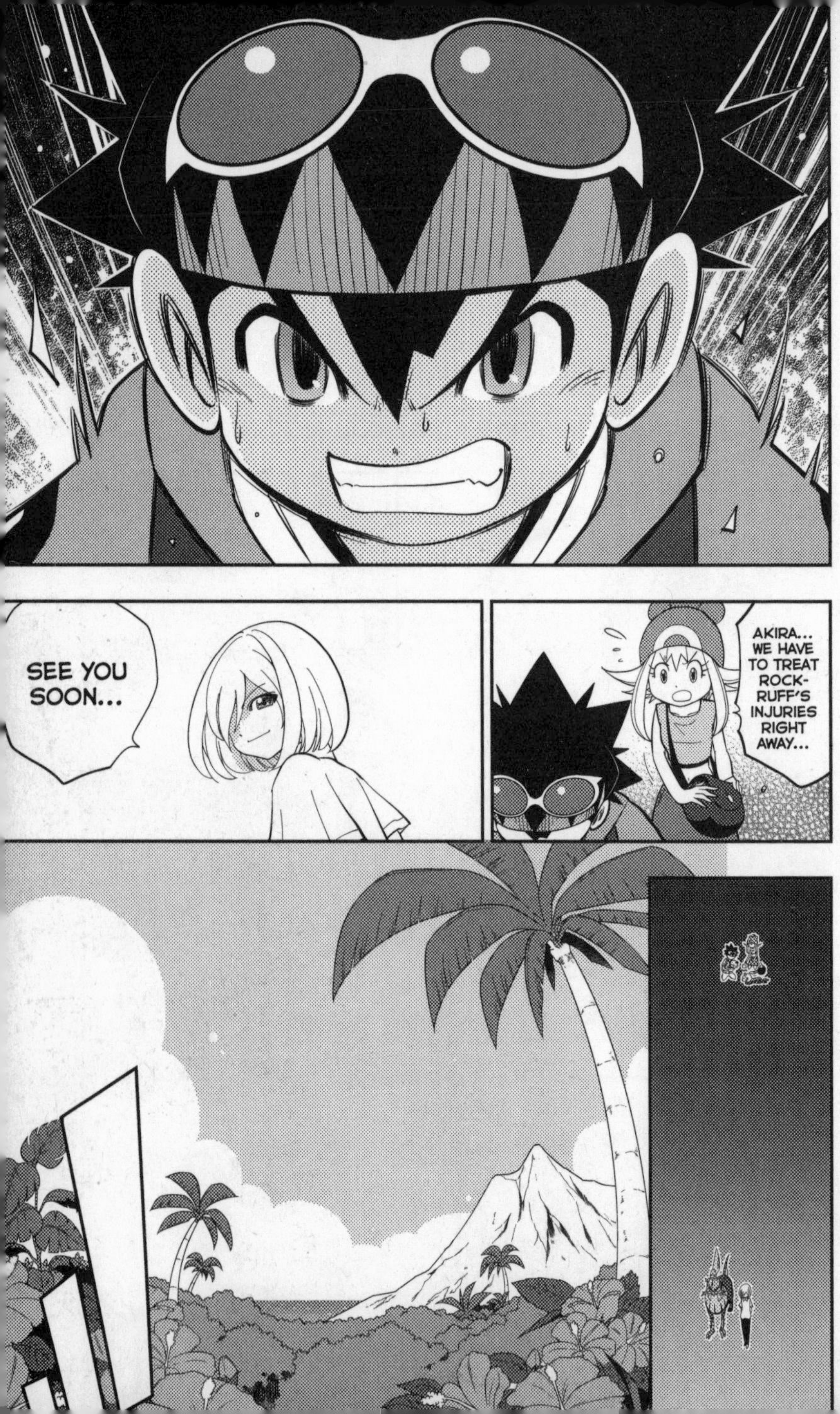
AKIRA... WE HAVE TO TREAT ROCK-RUFF'S INJURIES RIGHT AWAY...
SEE YOU SOON...

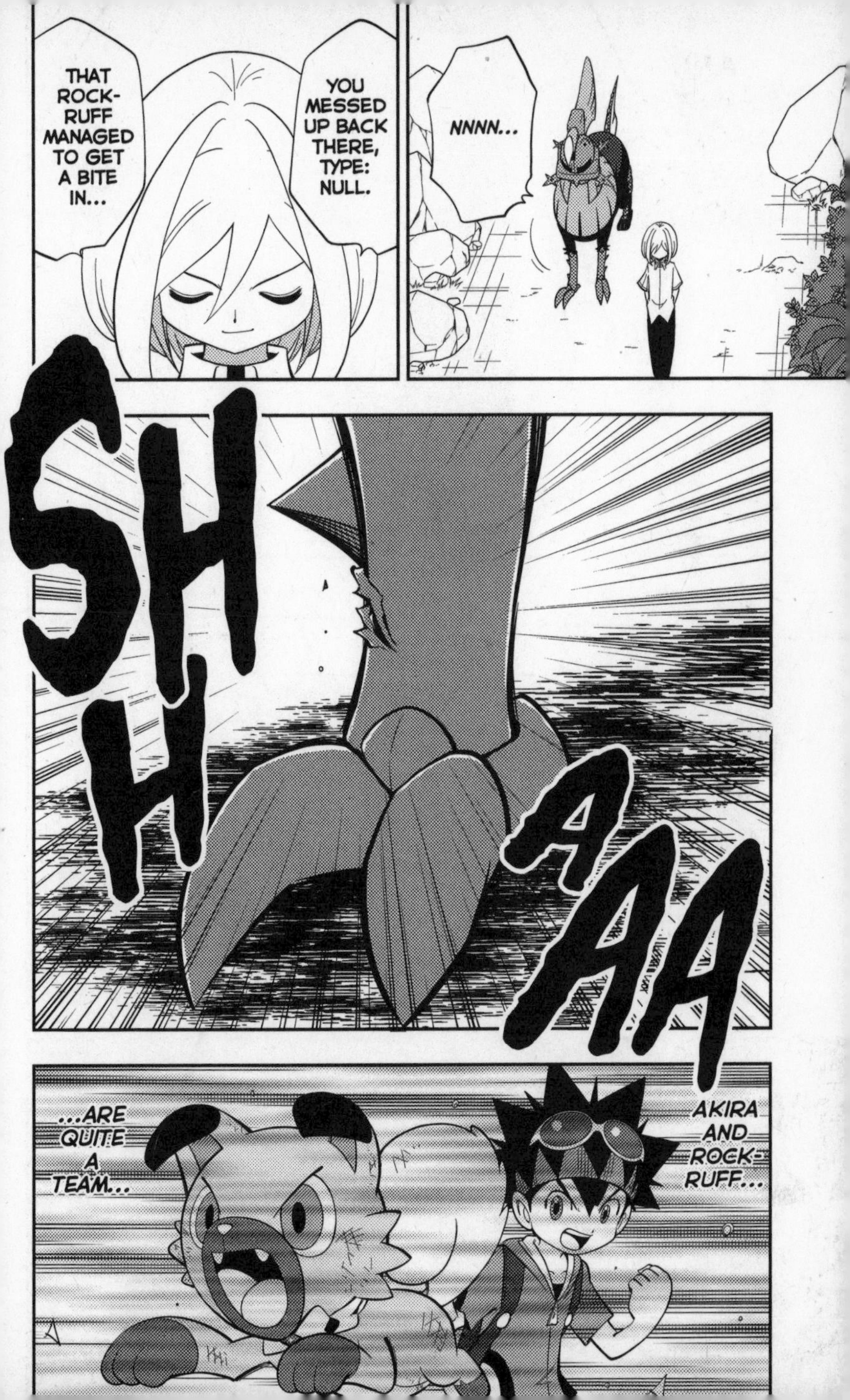
NNNN...
YOU MESSED UP BACK THERE, TYPE: NULL.
THAT ROCKRUFF MANAGED TO GET A BITE IN...
SHHAAA
AKIRA AND ROCKRUFF...
...ARE QUITE A TEAM...

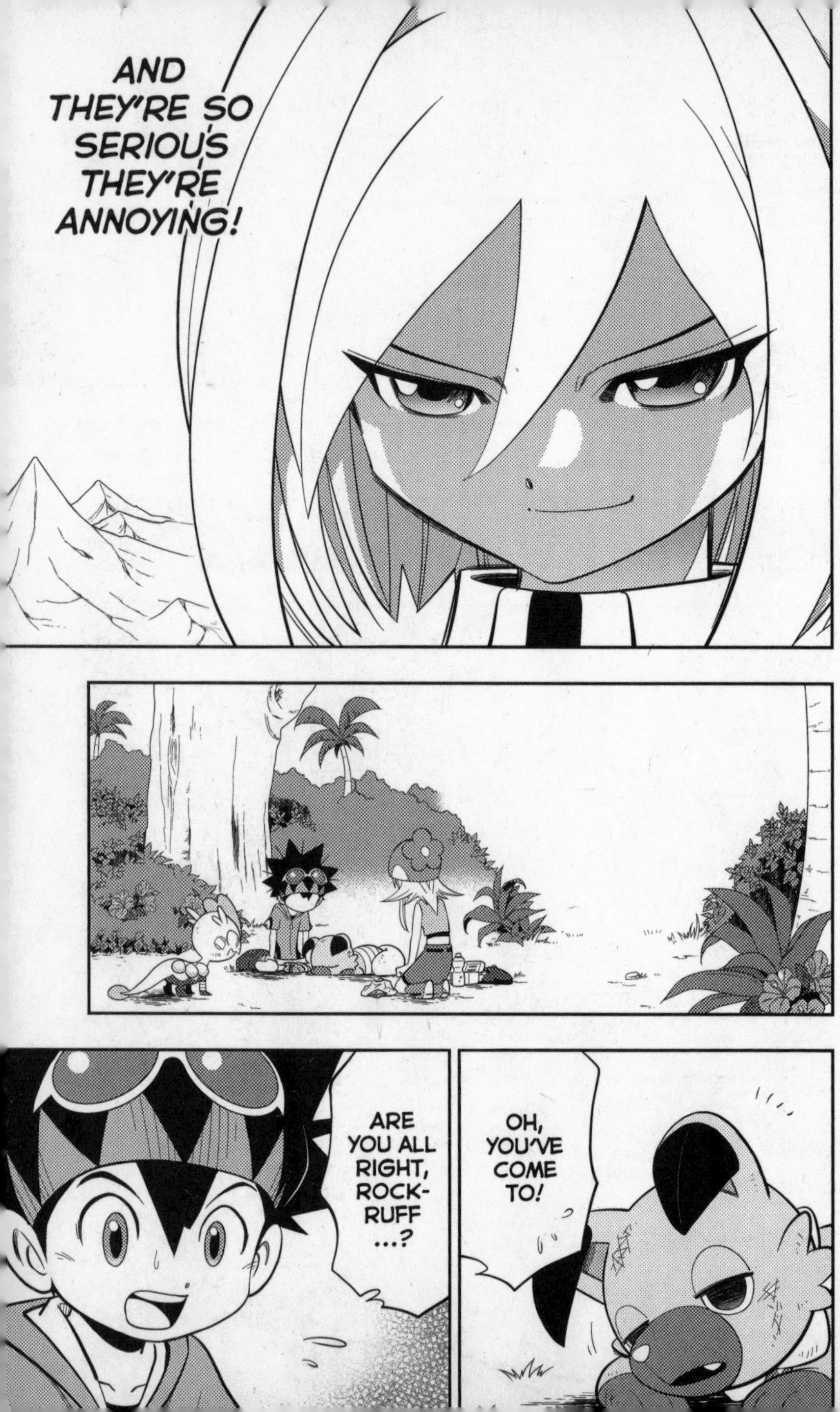
AND THEY'RE SO SERIOUS THEY'RE ANNOYING!
OH, YOU'VE COME TO!
ARE YOU ALL RIGHT, ROCK-RUFF ...?

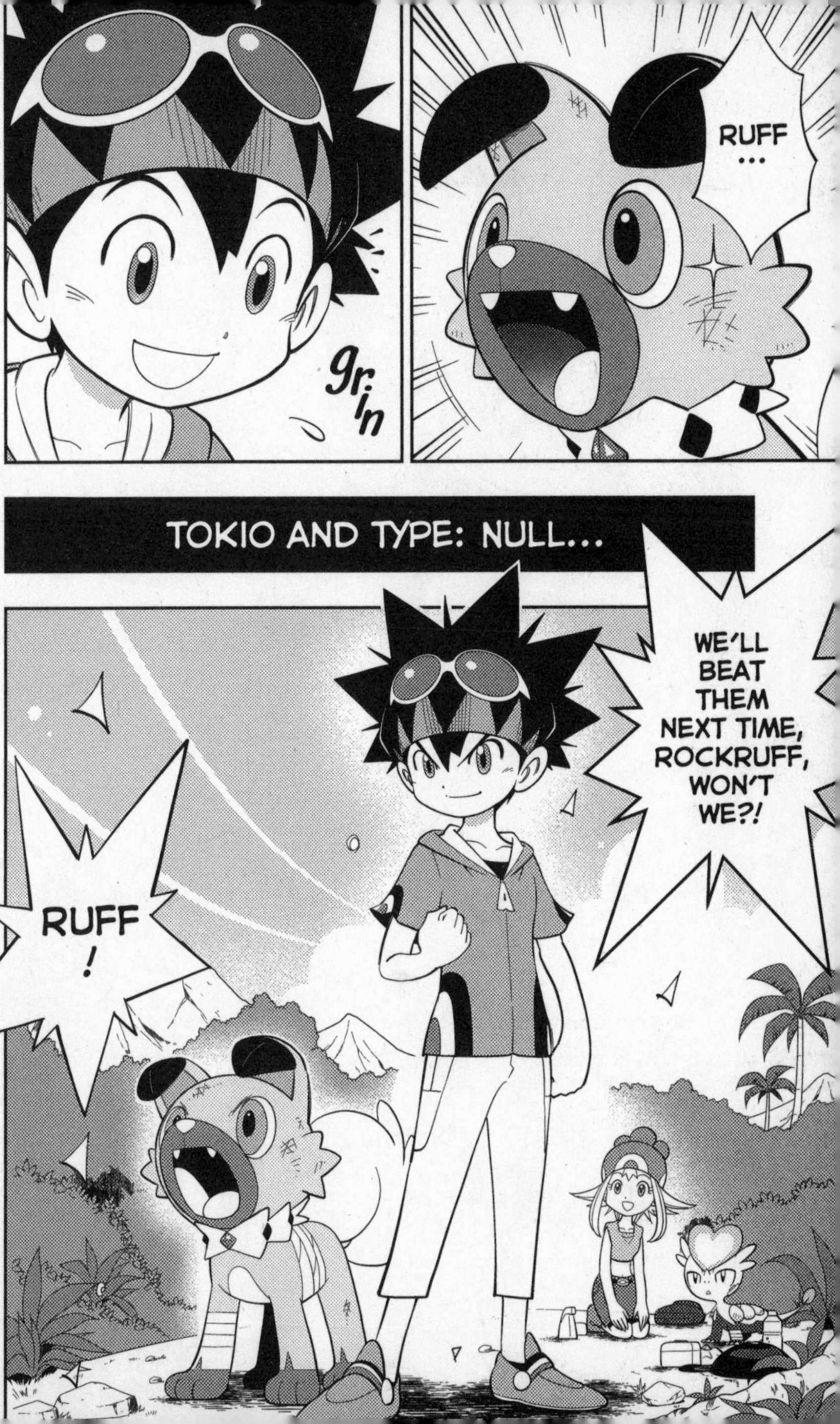
RUFF ...
grin
TOKIO AND TYPE: NULL...
WE'LL BEAT THEM NEXT TIME, ROCKRUFF, WON'T WE?!
RUFF !

Event 4: Mastering the Z-Move!

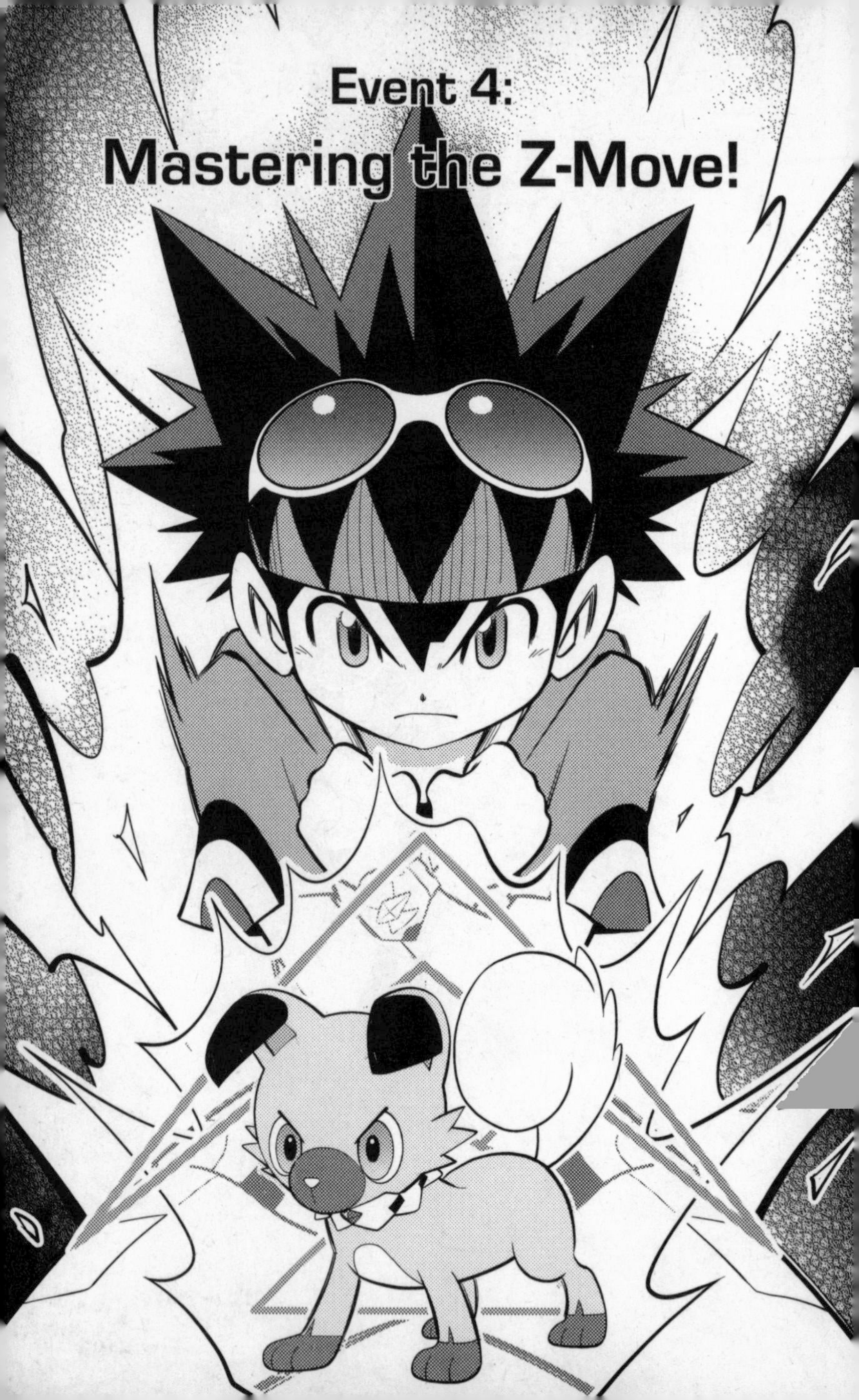

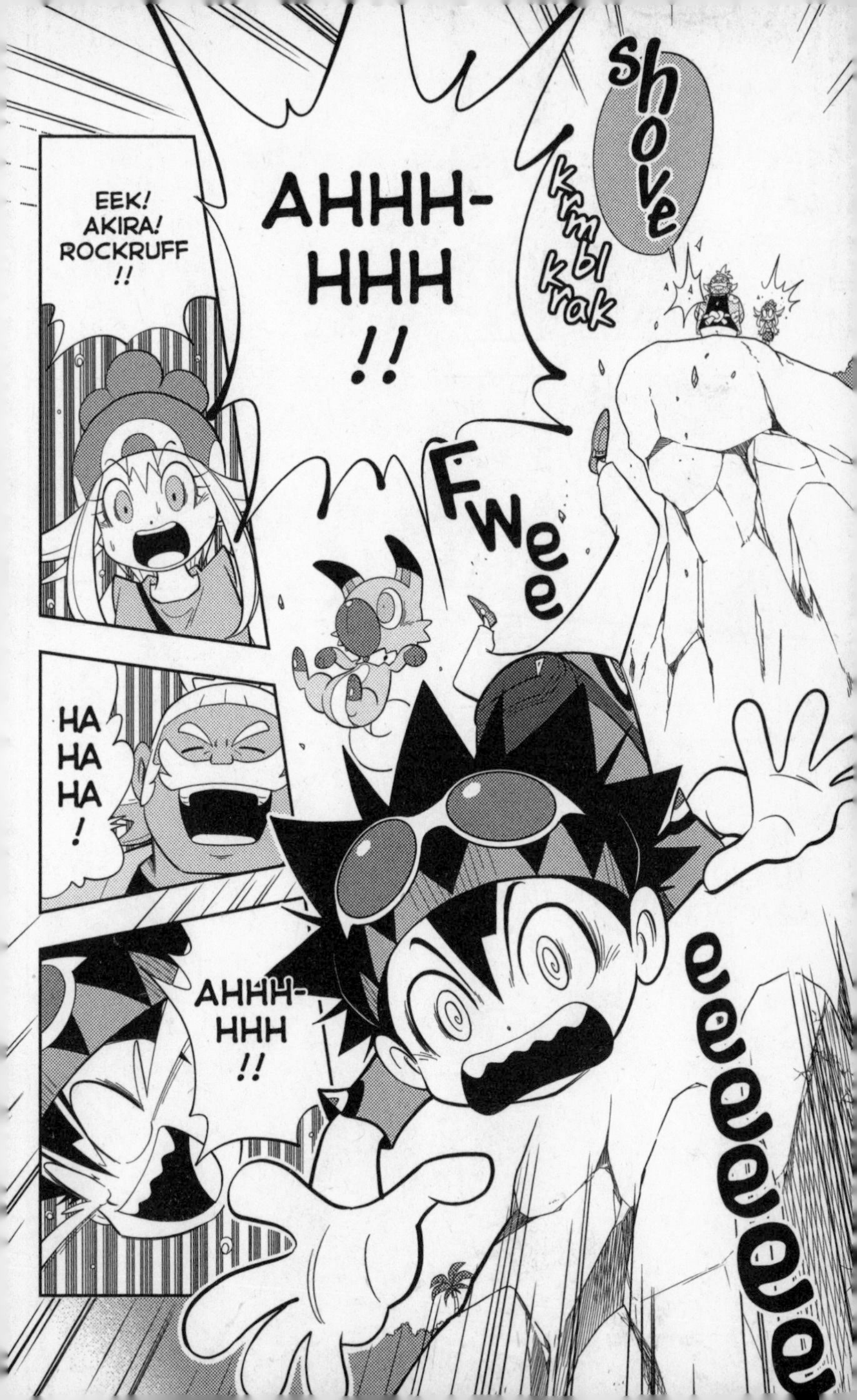
shove
krmbl krak
AHHH-HHH!!
Fwee
eeeeeeeee
EEK! AKIRA! ROCKRUFF!!
HA HA HA!
AHHH-HHH!!

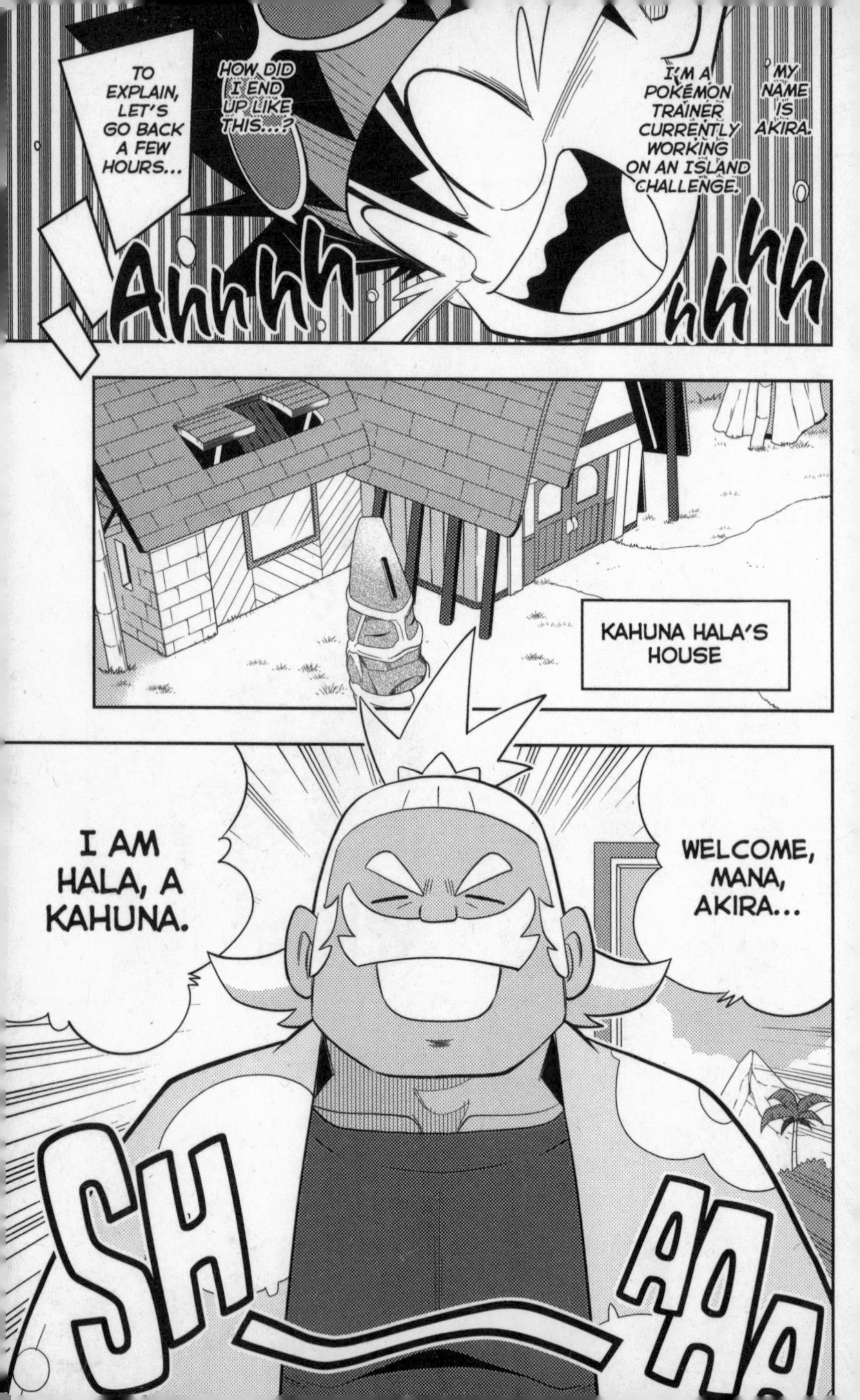
MY NAME IS AKIRA.
I'M A POKÉMON TRAINER CURRENTLY WORKING ON AN ISLAND CHALLENGE.
HOW DID I END UP LIKE THIS...?
TO EXPLAIN, LET'S GO BACK A FEW HOURS...
!Ahhhh hhhh
KAHUNA HALA'S HOUSE
WELCOME, MANA, AKIRA...
I AM HALA, A KAHUNA.
SH—AAA

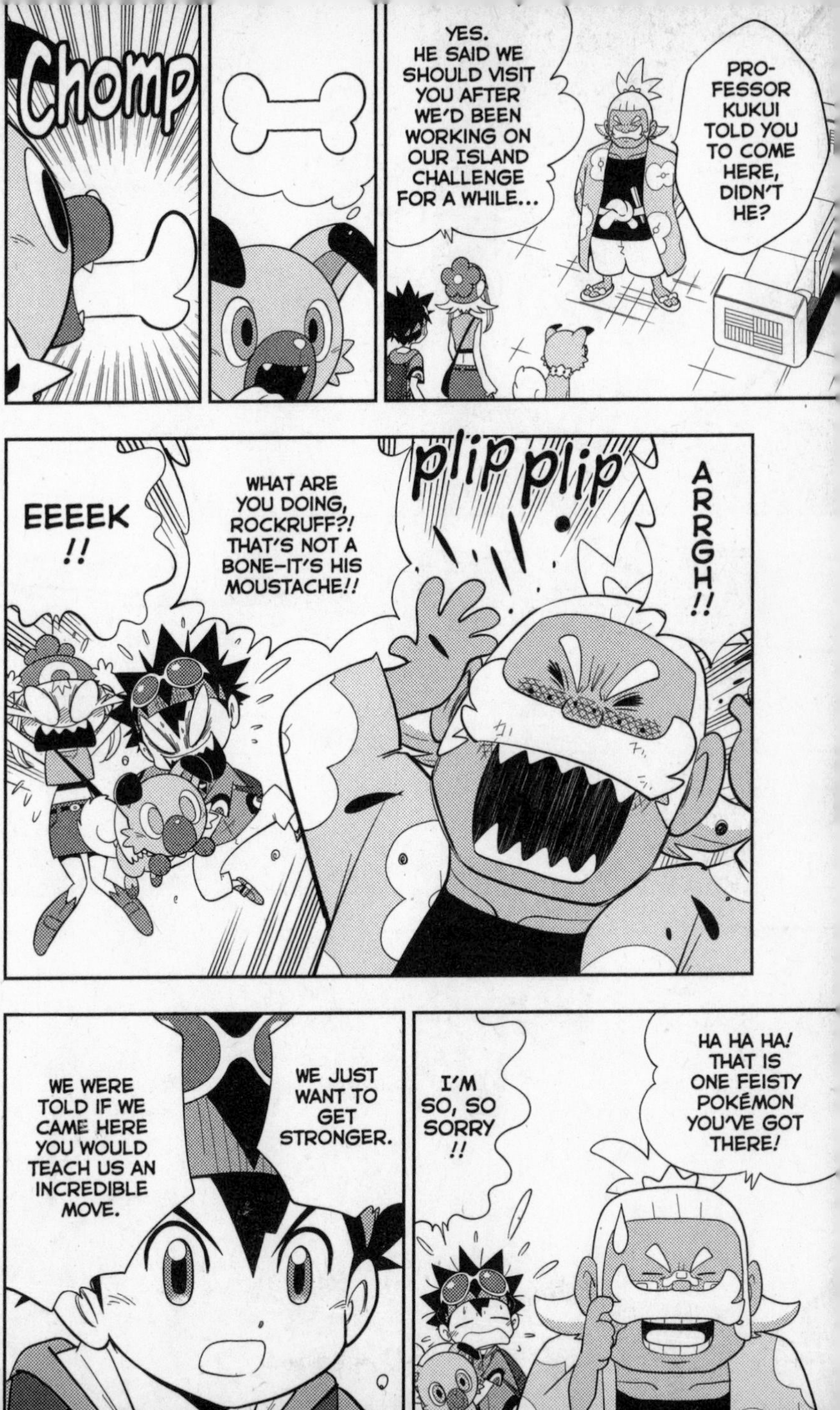
PROFESSOR KUKUI TOLD YOU TO COME HERE, DIDN'T HE?
YES. HE SAID WE SHOULD VISIT YOU AFTER WE'D BEEN WORKING ON OUR ISLAND CHALLENGE FOR A WHILE...
Chomp
ARRGH!!
plip plip
WHAT ARE YOU DOING, ROCKRUFF?! THAT'S NOT A BONE—IT'S HIS MOUSTACHE!!
EEEEK!!
HA HA HA! THAT IS ONE FEISTY POKÉMON YOU'VE GOT THERE!
I'M SO, SO SORRY!!
WE JUST WANT TO GET STRONGER.
WE WERE TOLD IF WE CAME HERE YOU WOULD TEACH US AN INCREDIBLE MOVE.

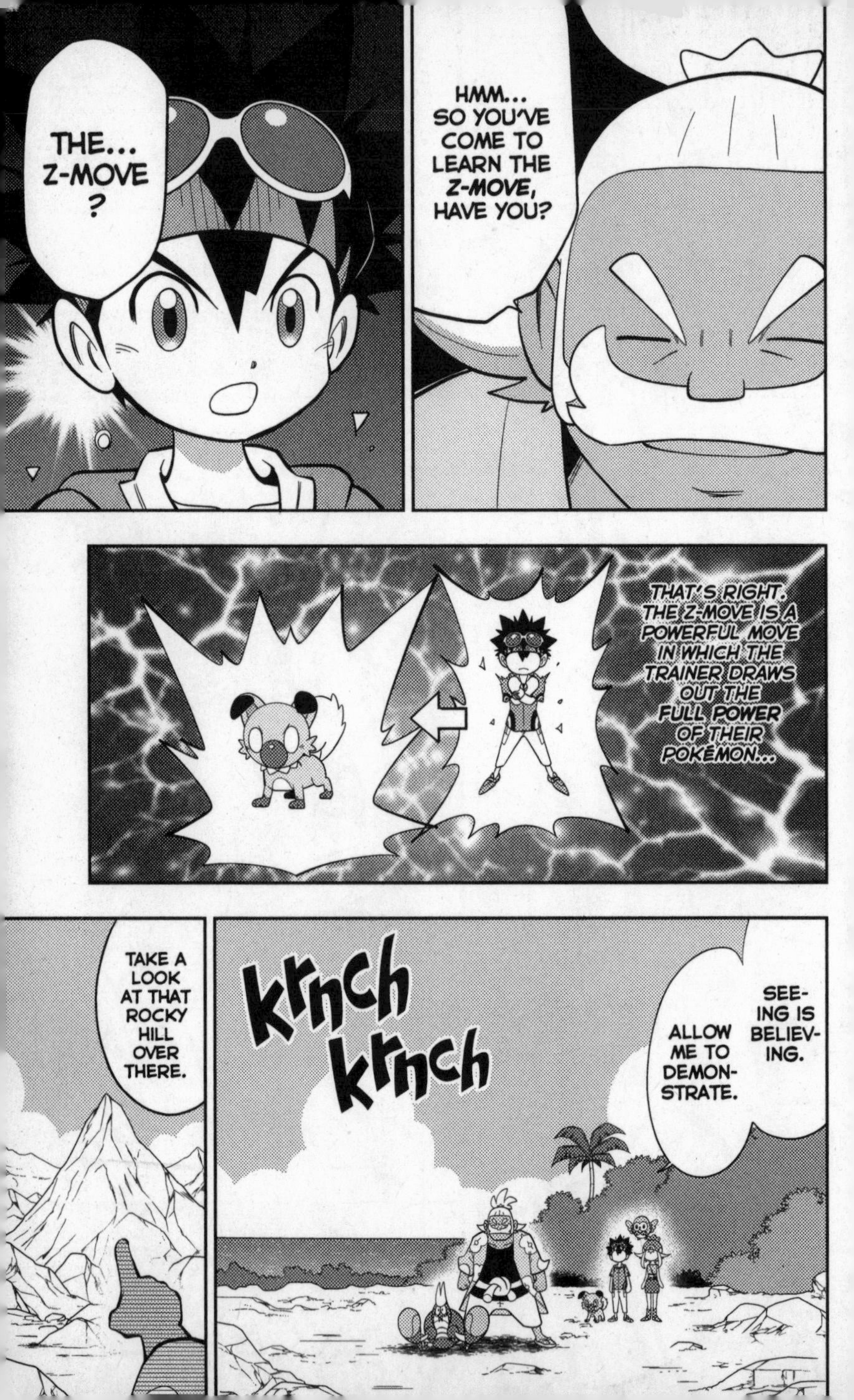
HMM... SO YOU'VE COME TO LEARN THE *Z-MOVE*, HAVE YOU?
THE... Z-MOVE?
THAT'S RIGHT. THE Z-MOVE IS A POWERFUL MOVE IN WHICH THE TRAINER DRAWS OUT THE FULL POWER OF THEIR POKÉMON...
SEE-ING IS BELIEV-ING.
ALLOW ME TO DEMON-STRATE.
krnch krnch
TAKE A LOOK AT THAT ROCKY HILL OVER THERE.

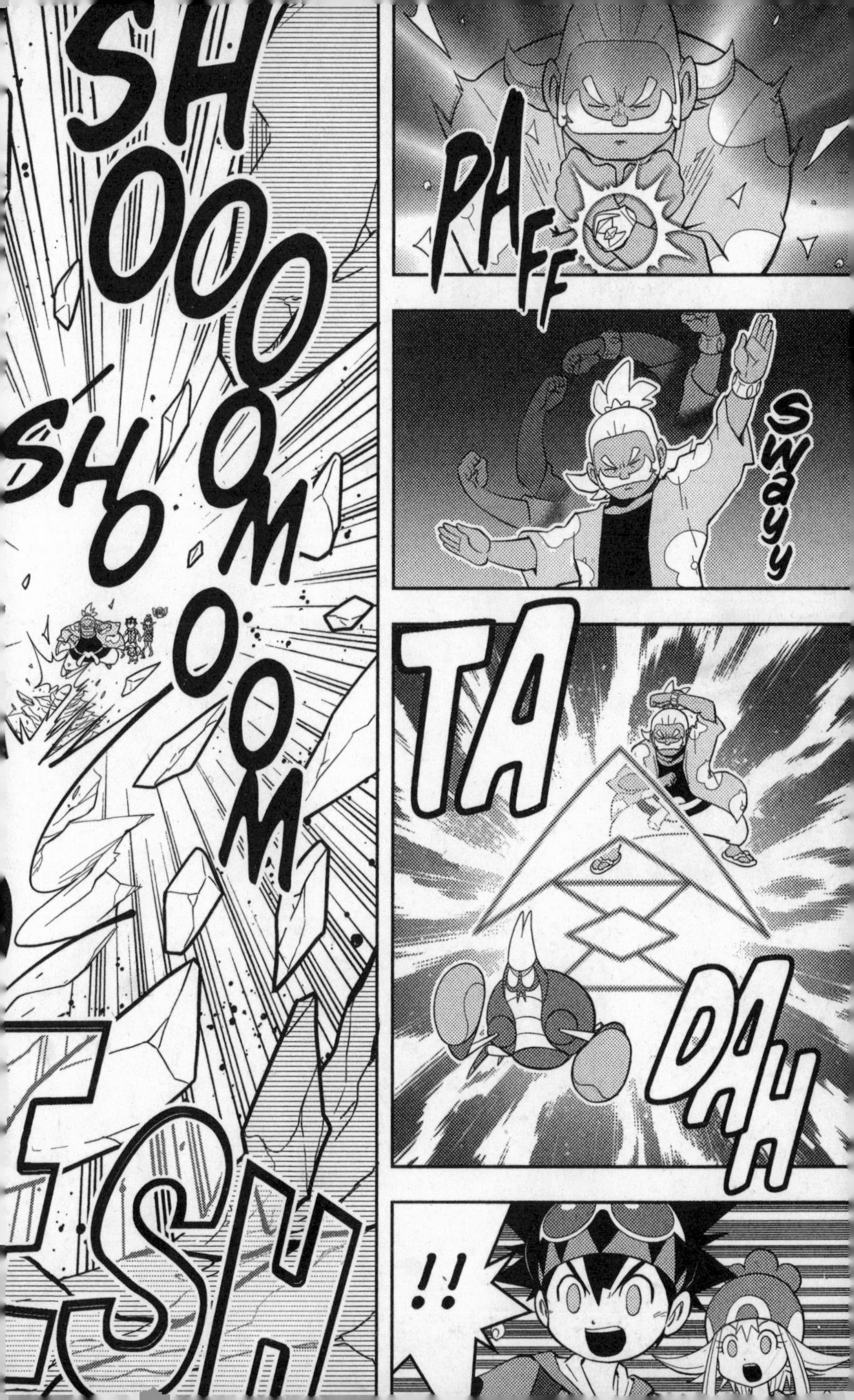
PAFF
SWAYY
TA DAH
!!
SHOOOOOOM
SHOOOM
SH

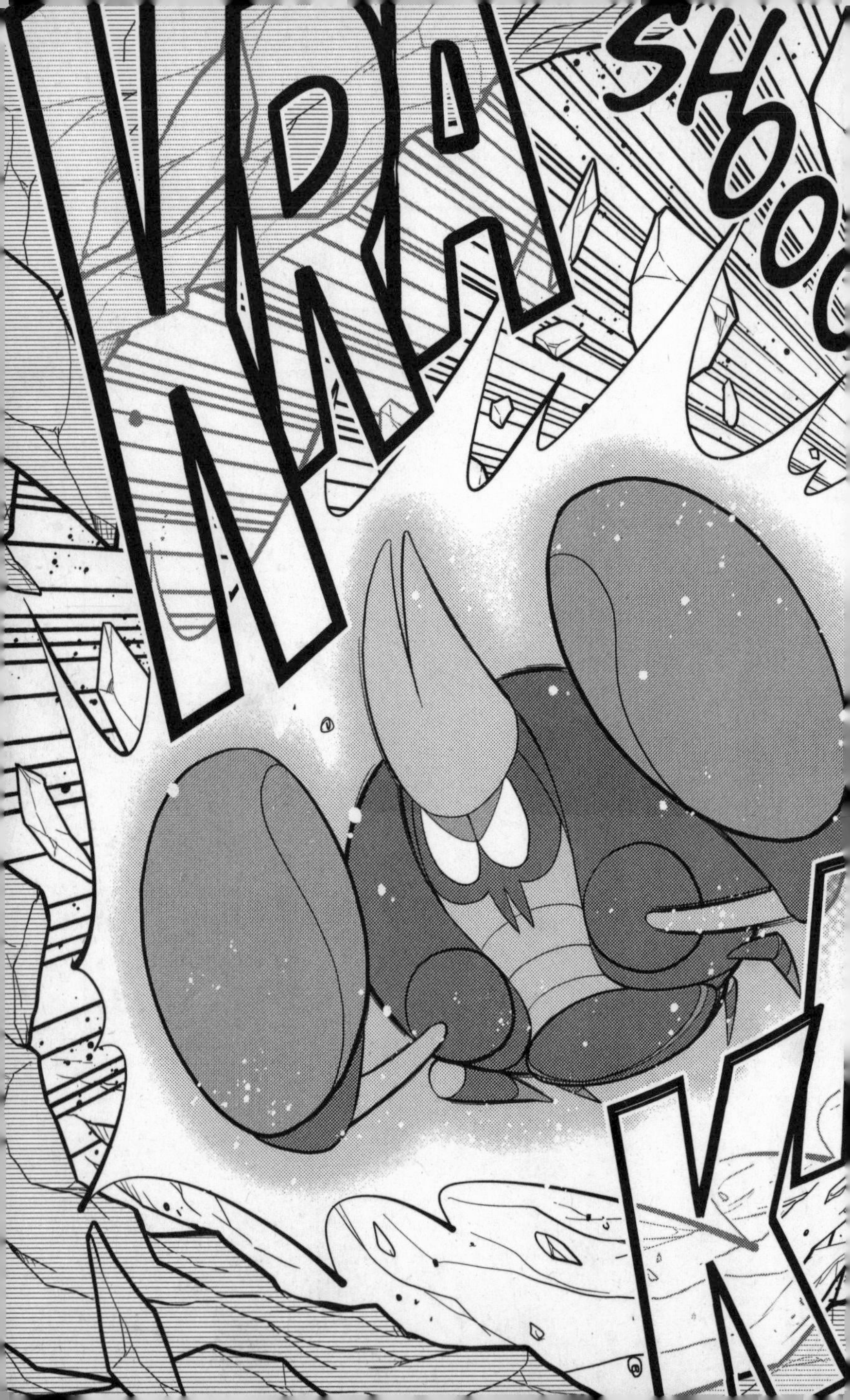
SHOO

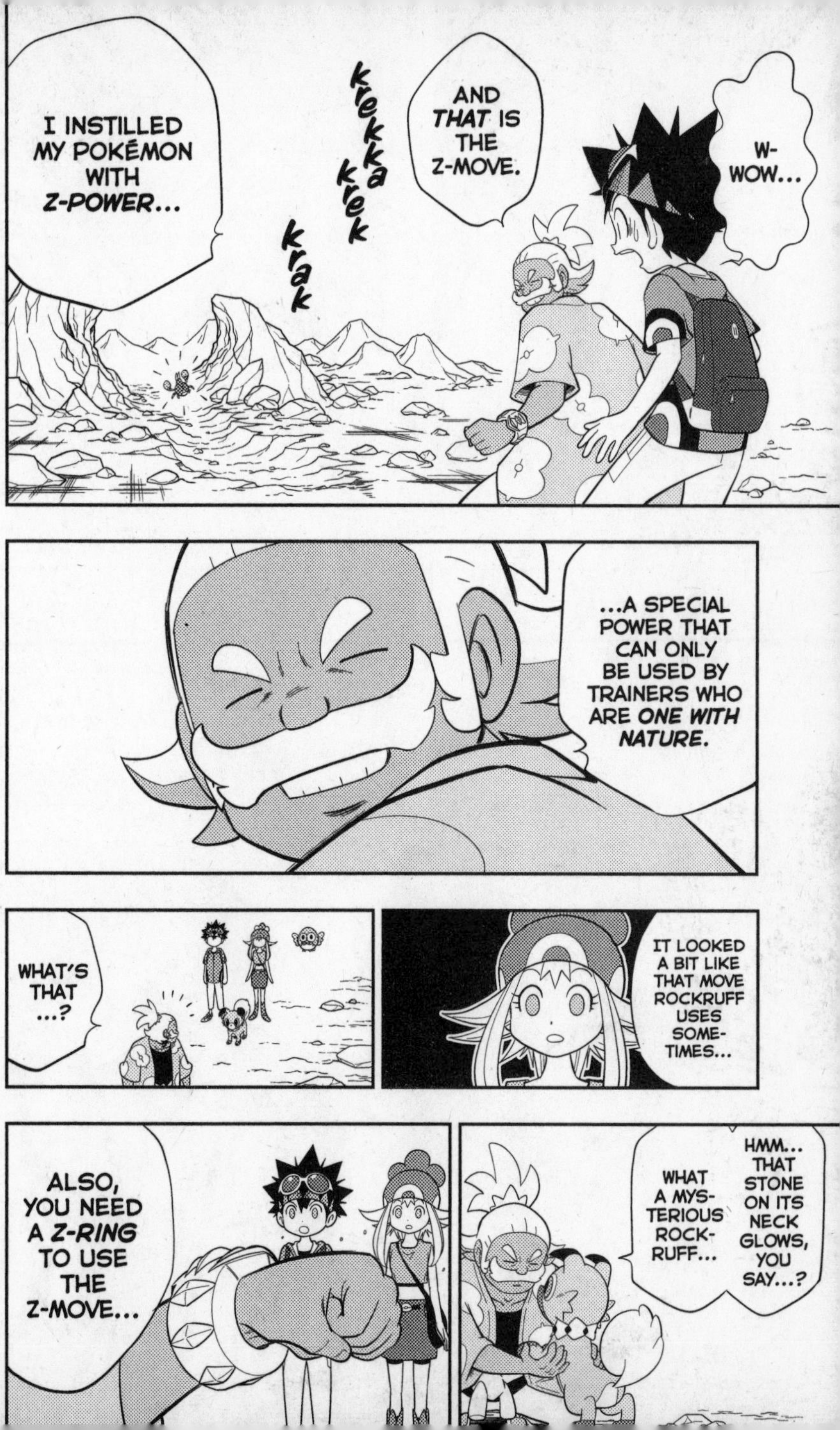
W-WOW...
AND THAT IS THE Z-MOVE.
krekka krek krak
I INSTILLED MY POKÉMON WITH Z-POWER...
...A SPECIAL POWER THAT CAN ONLY BE USED BY TRAINERS WHO ARE ONE WITH NATURE.
IT LOOKED A BIT LIKE THAT MOVE ROCKRUFF USES SOME-TIMES...
WHAT'S THAT ...?
HMM... THAT STONE ON ITS NECK GLOWS, YOU SAY...?
WHAT A MYS-TERIOUS ROCK-RUFF...
ALSO, YOU NEED A Z-RING TO USE THE Z-MOVE...

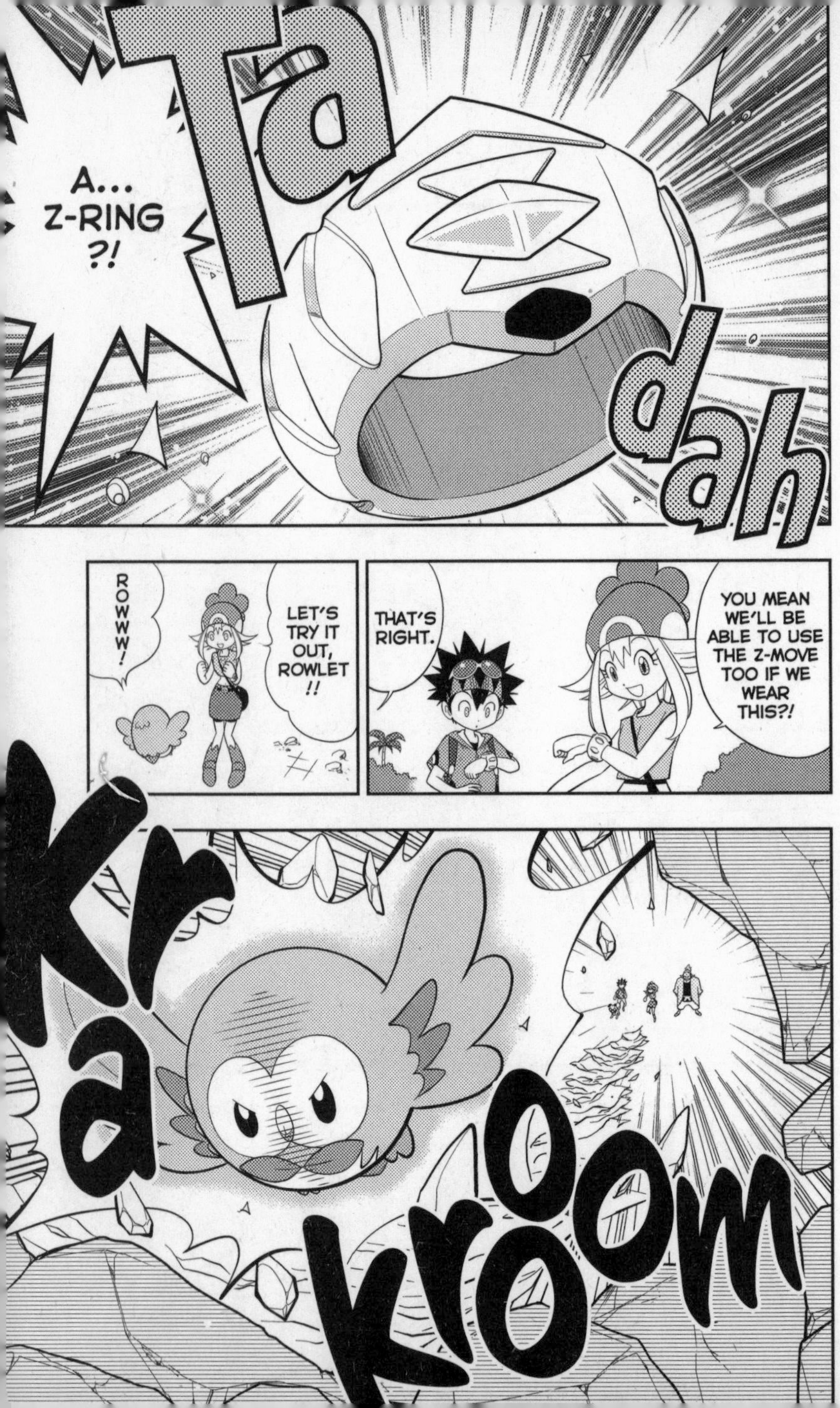
Ta
dah
A... Z-RING ?!
YOU MEAN WE'LL BE ABLE TO USE THE Z-MOVE TOO IF WE WEAR THIS?!
THAT'S RIGHT.
LET'S TRY IT OUT, ROWLET!!
ROWWW!
Ka
kroom

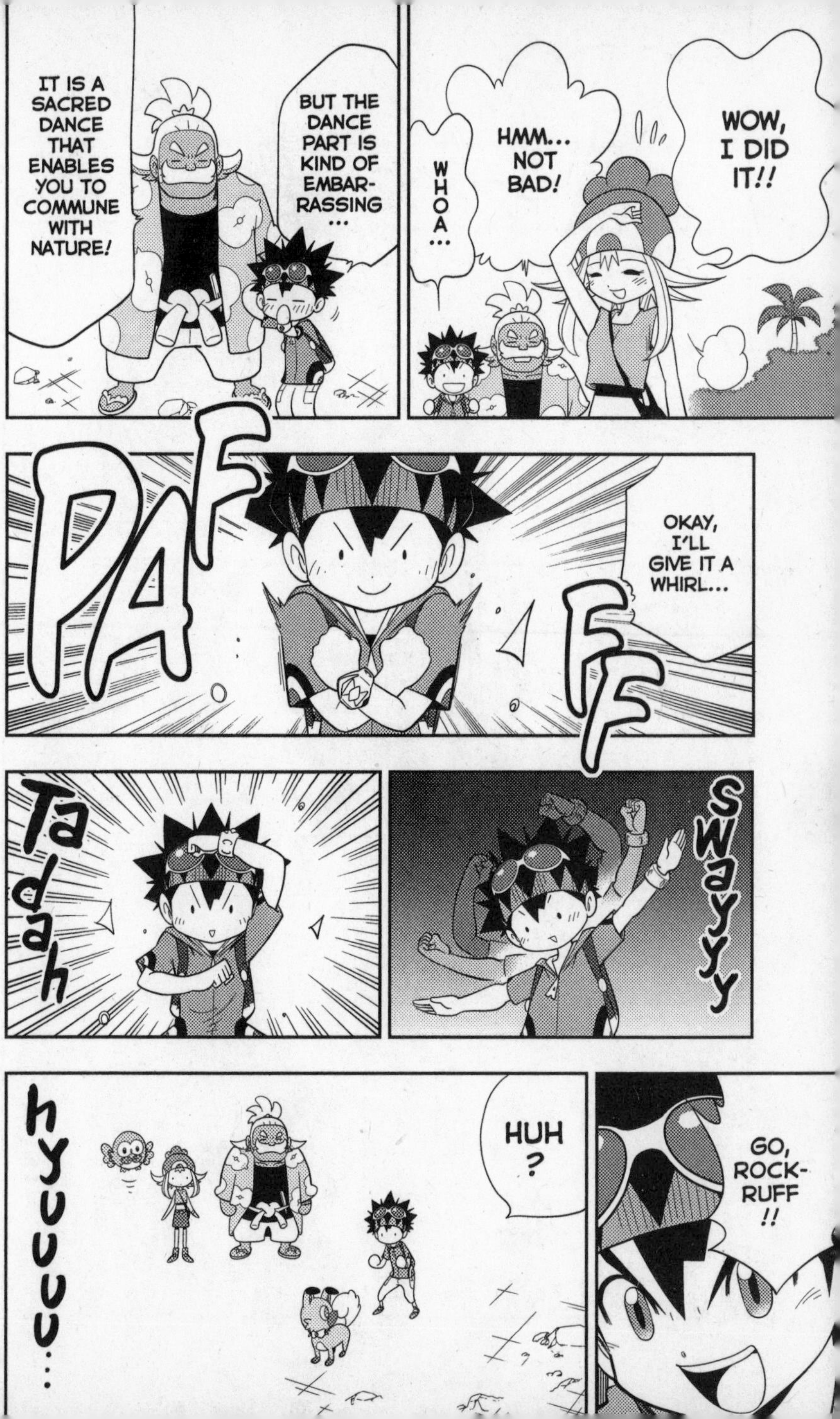
WOW, I DID IT!!
HMM... NOT BAD!
WHOA...
BUT THE DANCE PART IS KIND OF EMBARRASSING...
IT IS A SACRED DANCE THAT ENABLES YOU TO COMMUNE WITH NATURE!
OKAY, I'LL GIVE IT A WHIRL...
PAFF
SWAYYY
Ta dah
GO, ROCKRUFF!!
HUH?
hyuuuuu...

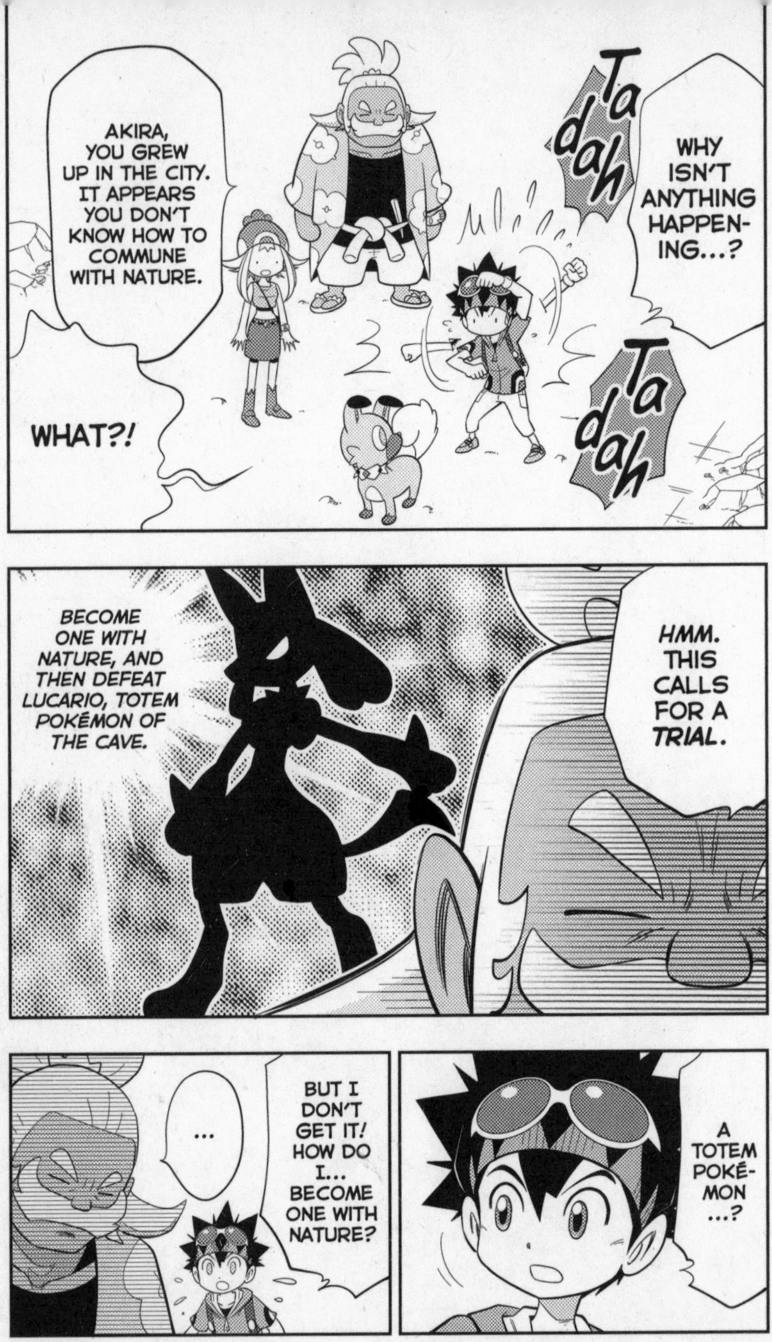
Ta dah
WHY ISN'T ANYTHING HAPPEN-ING...?
Ta dah
AKIRA, YOU GREW UP IN THE CITY. IT APPEARS YOU DON'T KNOW HOW TO COMMUNE WITH NATURE.
WHAT?!
HMM. THIS CALLS FOR A *TRIAL*.
BECOME ONE WITH NATURE, AND THEN DEFEAT LUCARIO, TOTEM POKÉMON OF THE CAVE.
A TOTEM POKÉ-MON ...?
BUT I DON'T GET IT! HOW DO I... BECOME ONE WITH NATURE?
...

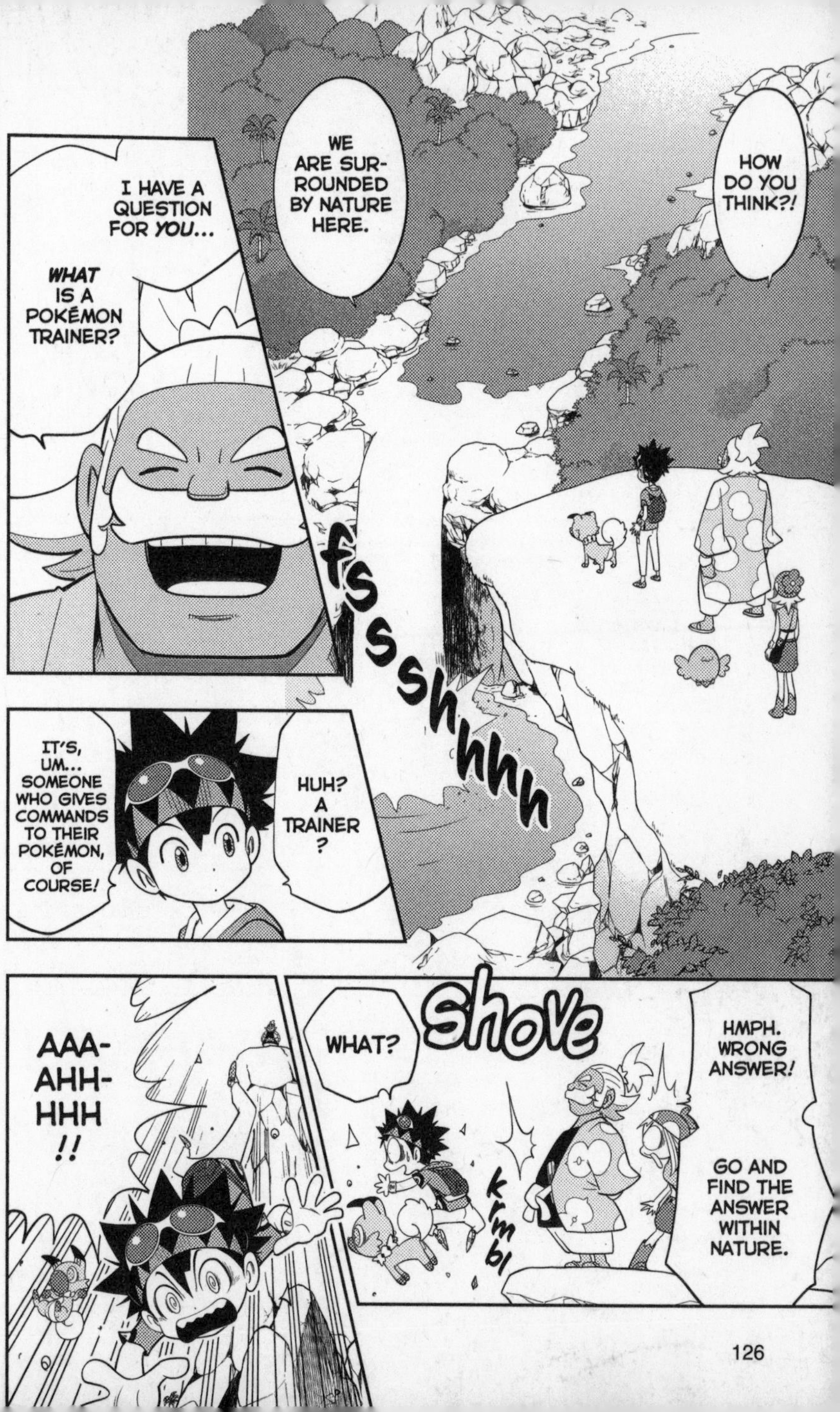
HOW DO YOU THINK?!
WE ARE SURROUNDED BY NATURE HERE.
fsssshhhhh
I HAVE A QUESTION FOR *YOU*...
WHAT IS A POKÉMON TRAINER?
HUH? A TRAINER?
IT'S, UM... SOMEONE WHO GIVES COMMANDS TO THEIR POKÉMON, OF COURSE!
HMPH. WRONG ANSWER!
GO AND FIND THE ANSWER WITHIN NATURE.
shove
WHAT?
krmbl
AAA-AHH-HHH!!

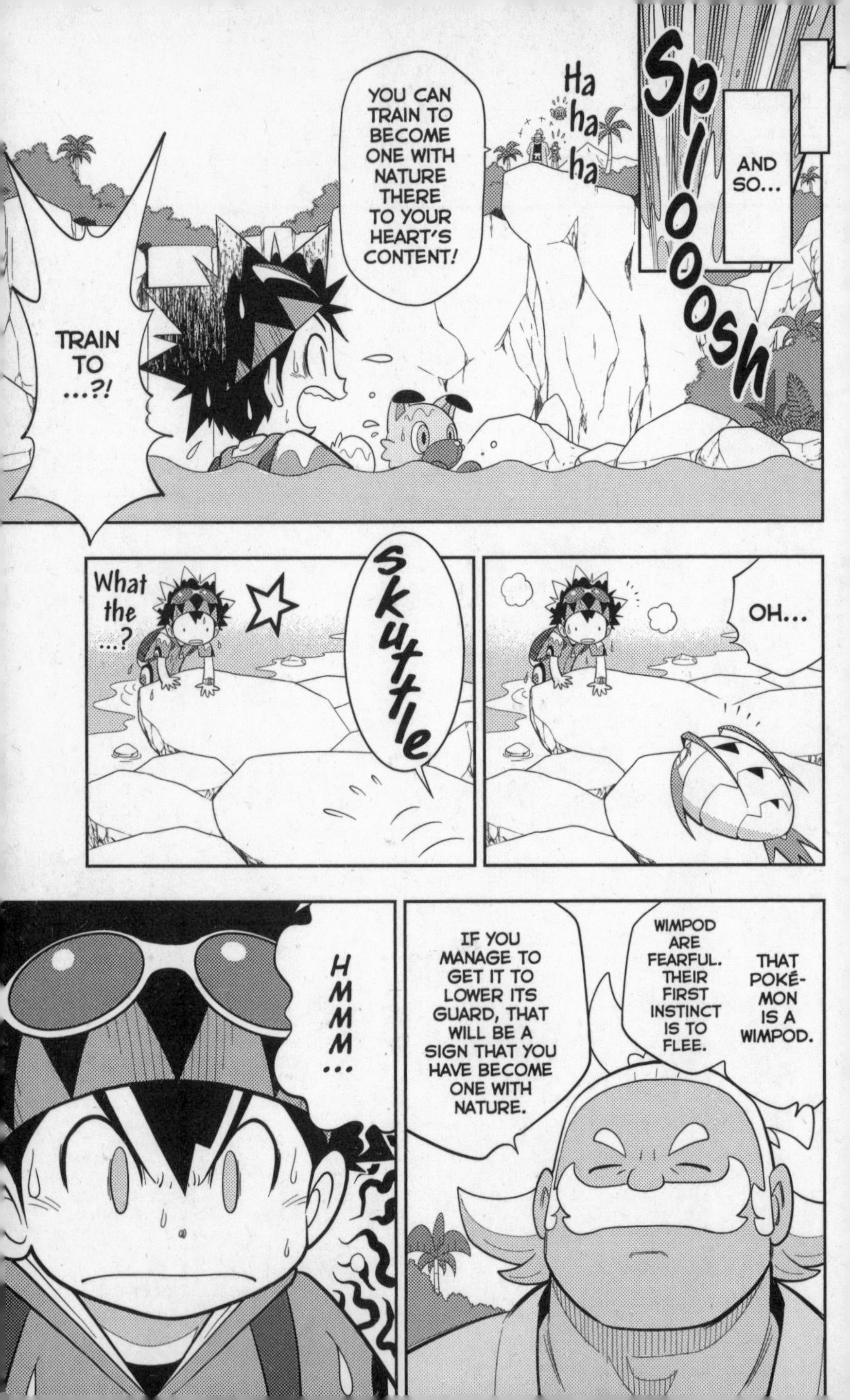
AND SO...
Splooooosh
Ha ha ha
YOU CAN TRAIN TO BECOME ONE WITH NATURE THERE TO YOUR HEART'S CONTENT!
TRAIN TO ...?!
OH...
Skuttle
What the ...?
THAT POKÉ-MON IS A WIMPOD.
WIMPOD ARE FEARFUL. THEIR FIRST INSTINCT IS TO FLEE.
IF YOU MANAGE TO GET IT TO LOWER ITS GUARD, THAT WILL BE A SIGN THAT YOU HAVE BECOME ONE WITH NATURE.
HMMM...

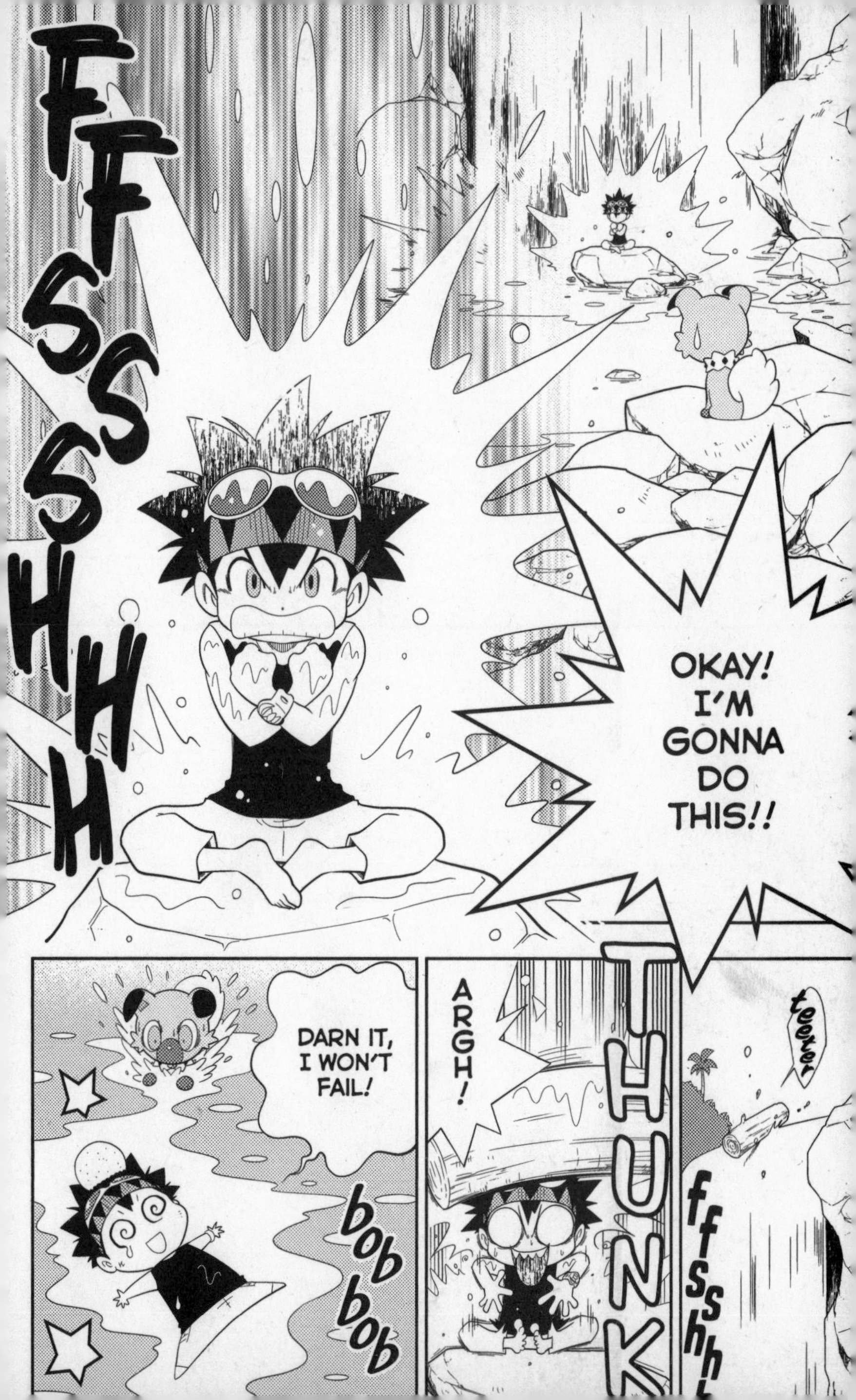
FFSSSHHH
OKAY! I'M GONNA DO THIS!!
teeter
THUNK
ARGH!
ffsshh
DARN IT, I WON'T FAIL!
bob bob

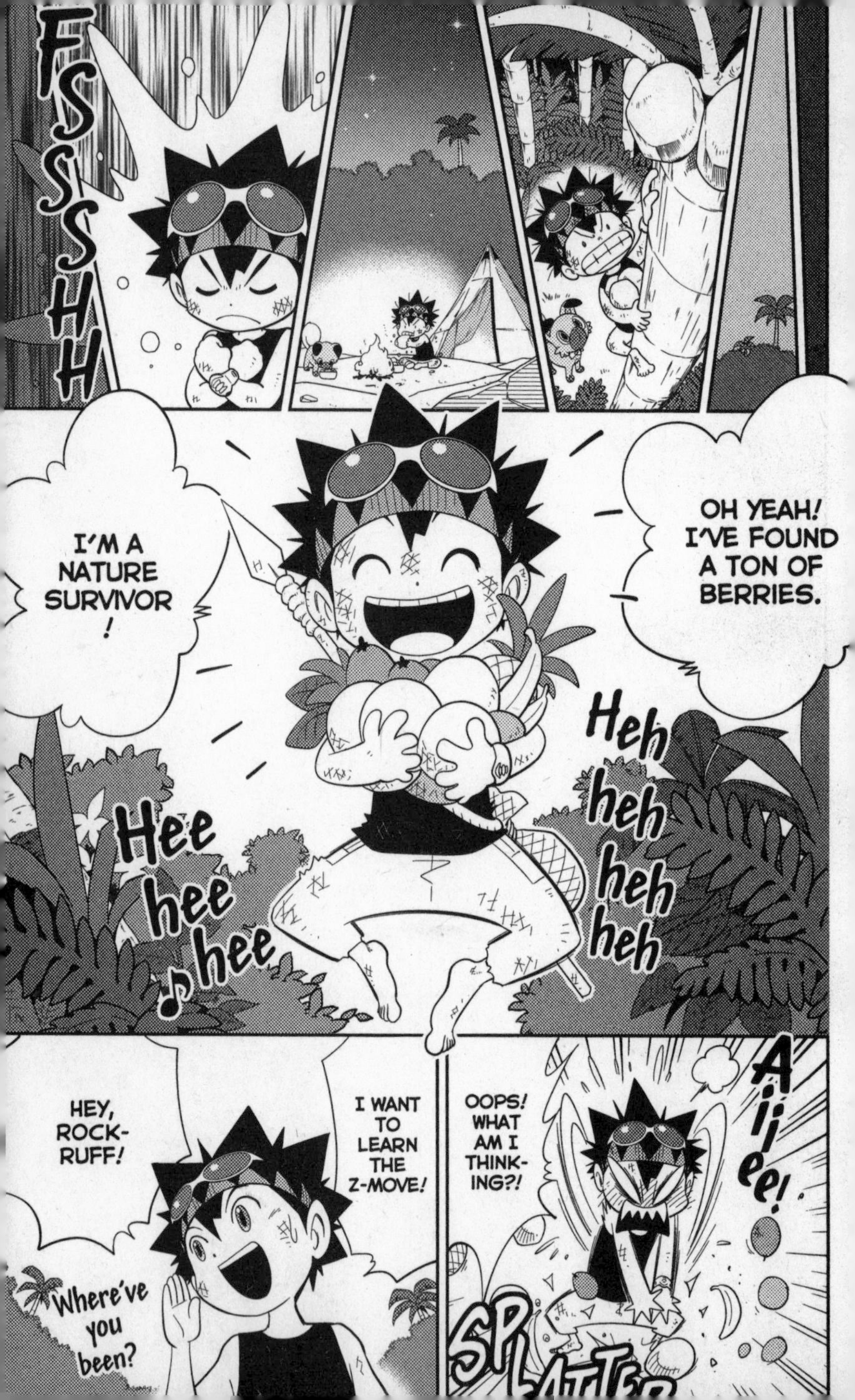
FSSSHH
OH YEAH! I'VE FOUND A TON OF BERRIES.
I'M A NATURE SURVIVOR!
Heh heh heh heh
Hee hee hee
Aiiee!
OOPS! WHAT AM I THINKING?!
SP
I WANT TO LEARN THE Z-MOVE!
HEY, ROCK-RUFF!
Where've you been?

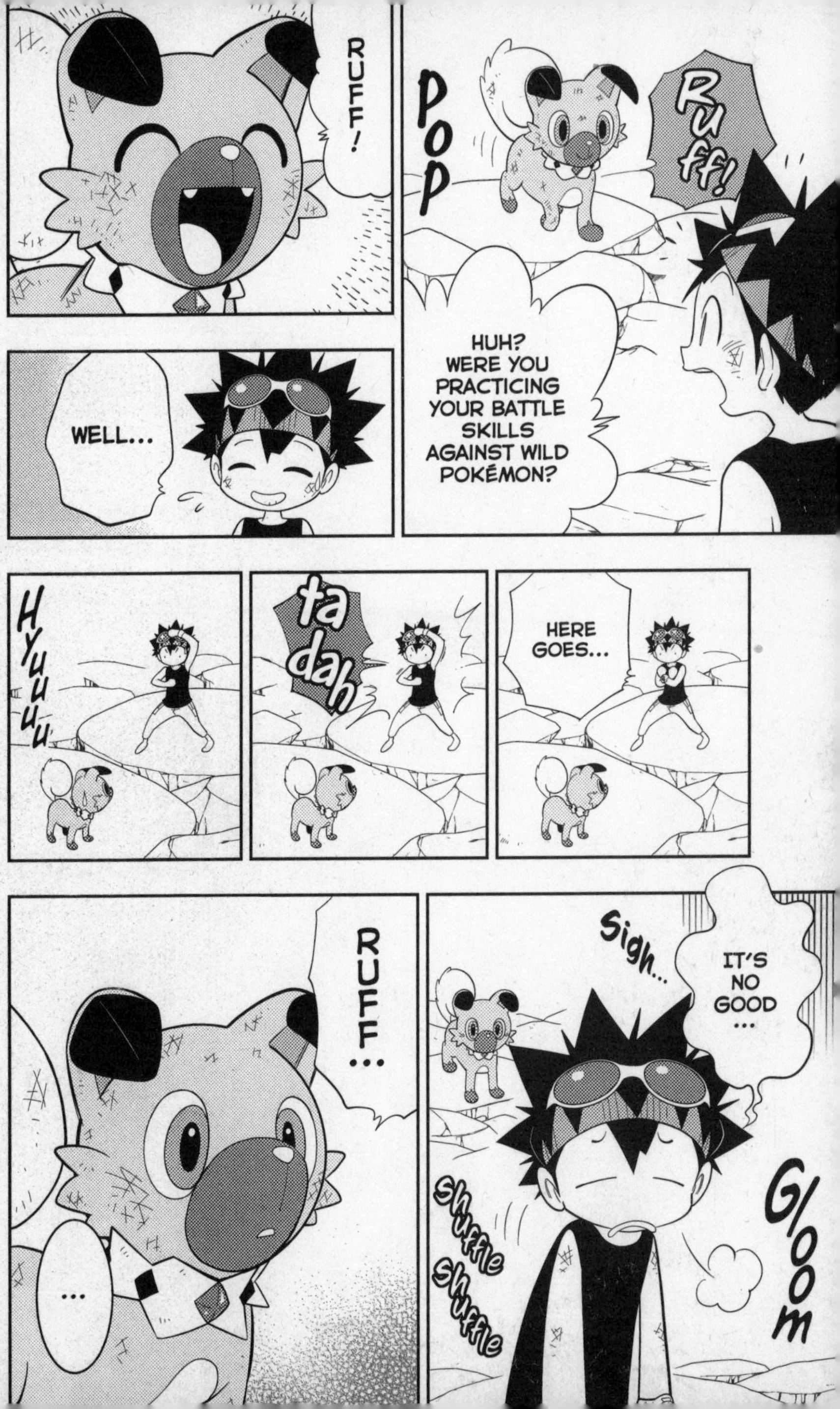
Pop
Ruff!
HUH? WERE YOU PRACTICING YOUR BATTLE SKILLS AGAINST WILD POKÉMON?
RUFF!
WELL...
HERE GOES...
ta dah
Hyuuuuu
Sigh...
IT'S NO GOOD ...
Gloom
shuffle shuffle
RUFF...
...

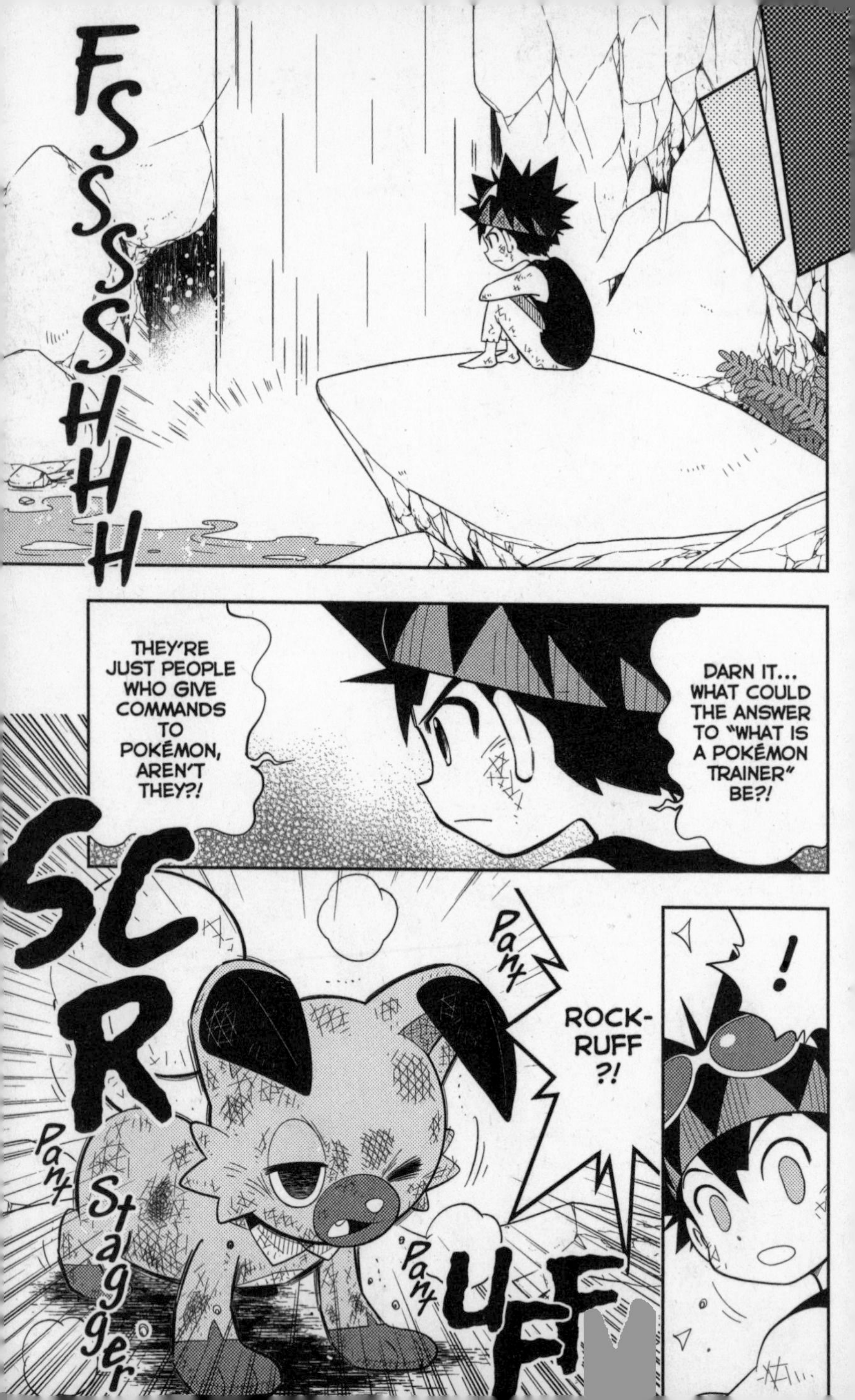
FSSSSHHHH
DARN IT... WHAT COULD THE ANSWER TO "WHAT IS A POKÉMON TRAINER" BE?!
THEY'RE JUST PEOPLE WHO GIVE COMMANDS TO POKÉMON, AREN'T THEY?!
SCRUFF
!
ROCK-RUFF?!
Pant
Pant
Stagger
Pant

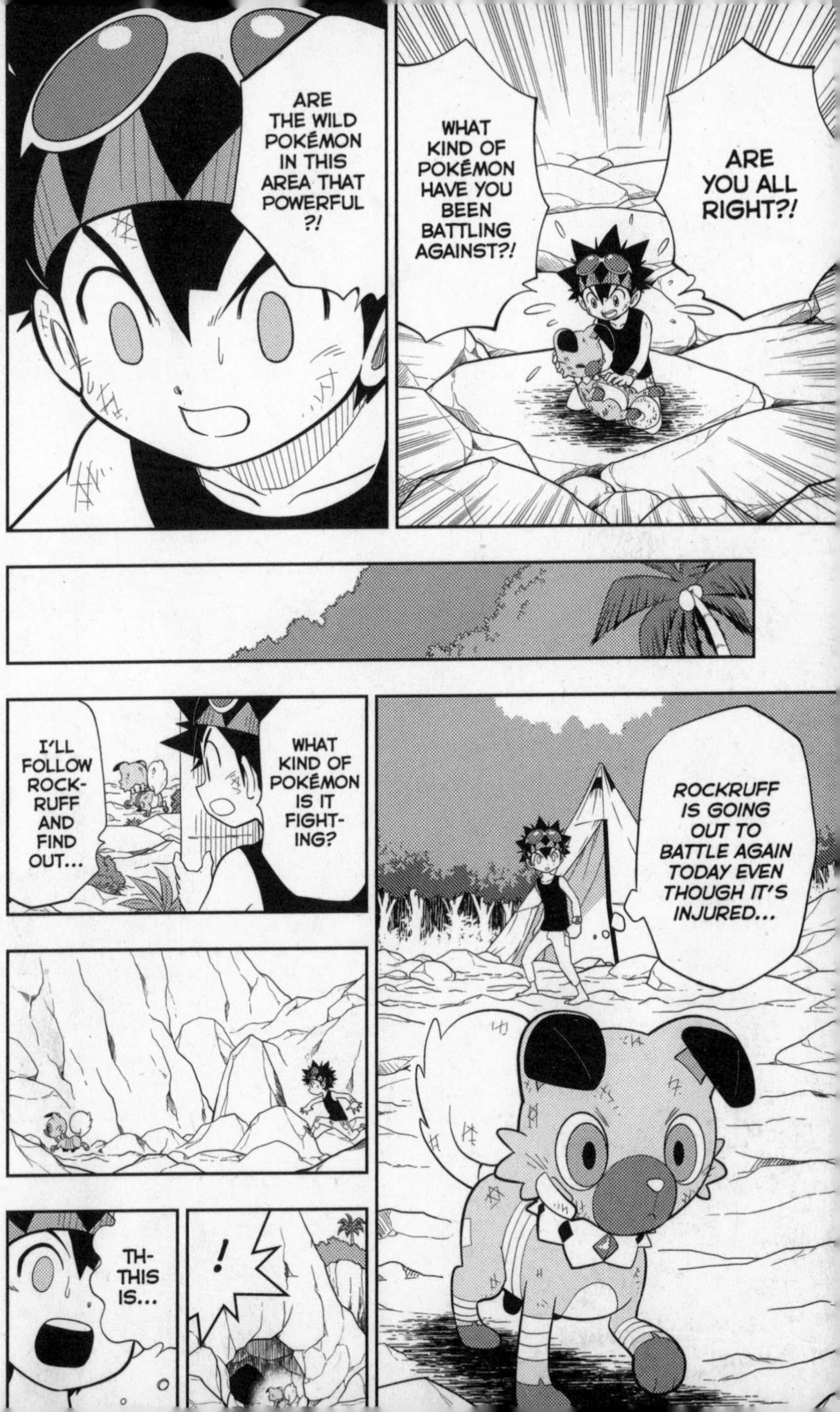
ARE YOU ALL RIGHT?!
WHAT KIND OF POKÉMON HAVE YOU BEEN BATTLING AGAINST?!
ARE THE WILD POKÉMON IN THIS AREA THAT POWERFUL?!
ROCKRUFF IS GOING OUT TO BATTLE AGAIN TODAY EVEN THOUGH IT'S INJURED...
WHAT KIND OF POKÉMON IS IT FIGHTING?
I'LL FOLLOW ROCKRUFF AND FIND OUT...
!
TH-THIS IS...

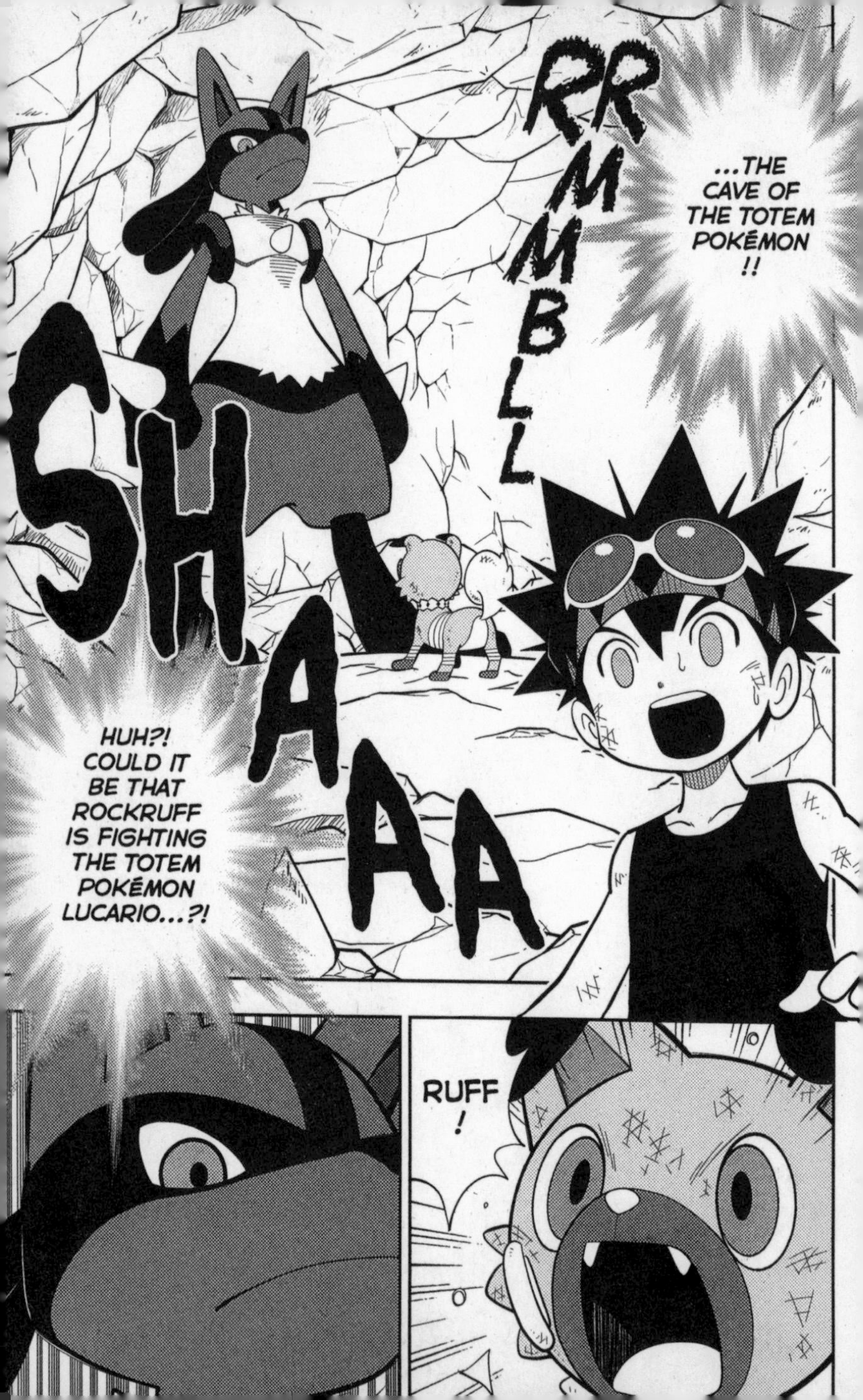
...THE CAVE OF THE TOTEM POKÉMON !!
RRMMBLL
SHAAAA
HUH?! COULD IT BE THAT ROCKRUFF IS FIGHTING THE TOTEM POKÉMON LUCARIO...?!
RUFF !

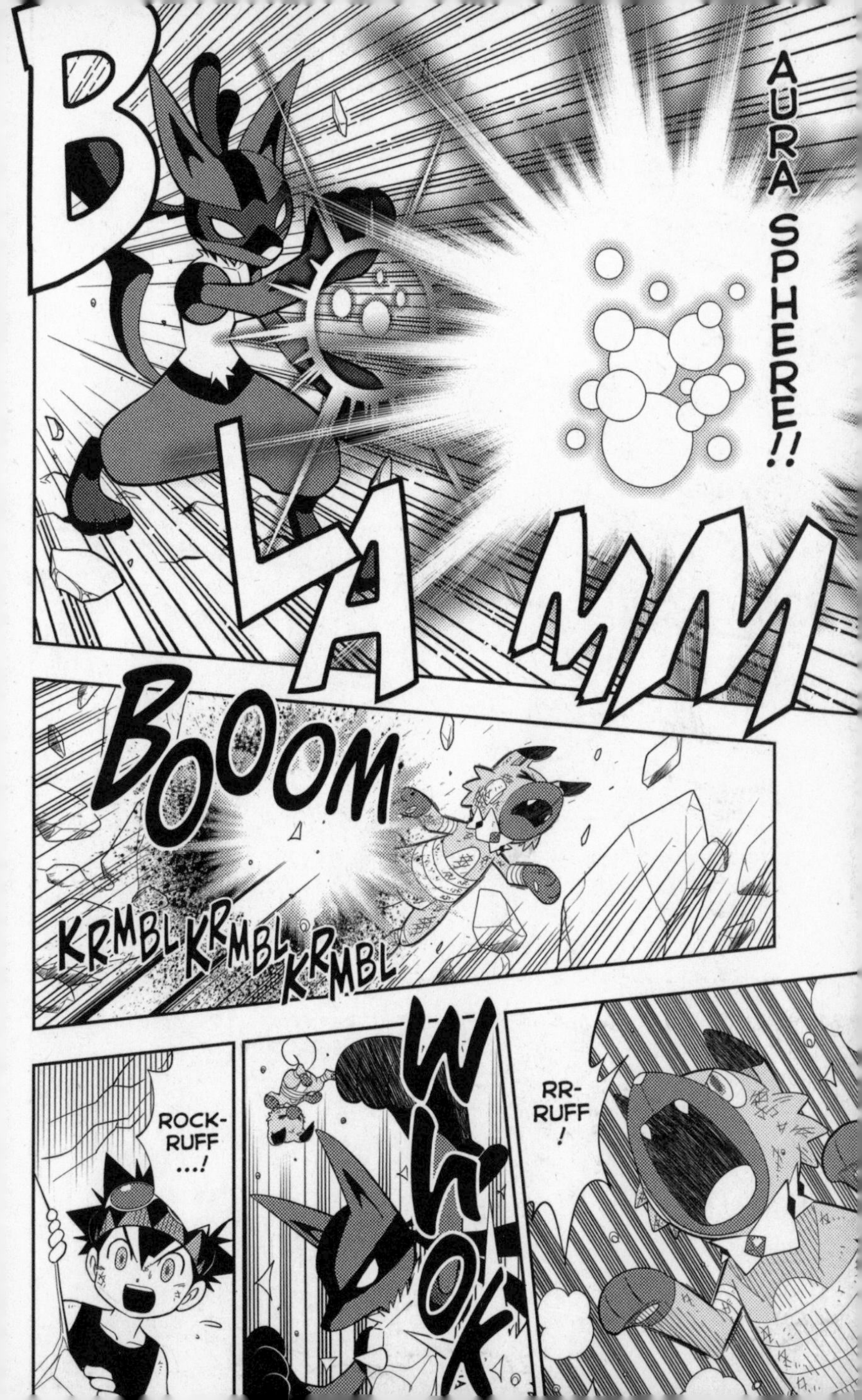
AURA SPHERE!!
BLAMM
BOOOM
KRMBL KRMBL KRMBL
RR-RUFF!
WHOK
ROCK-RUFF...!

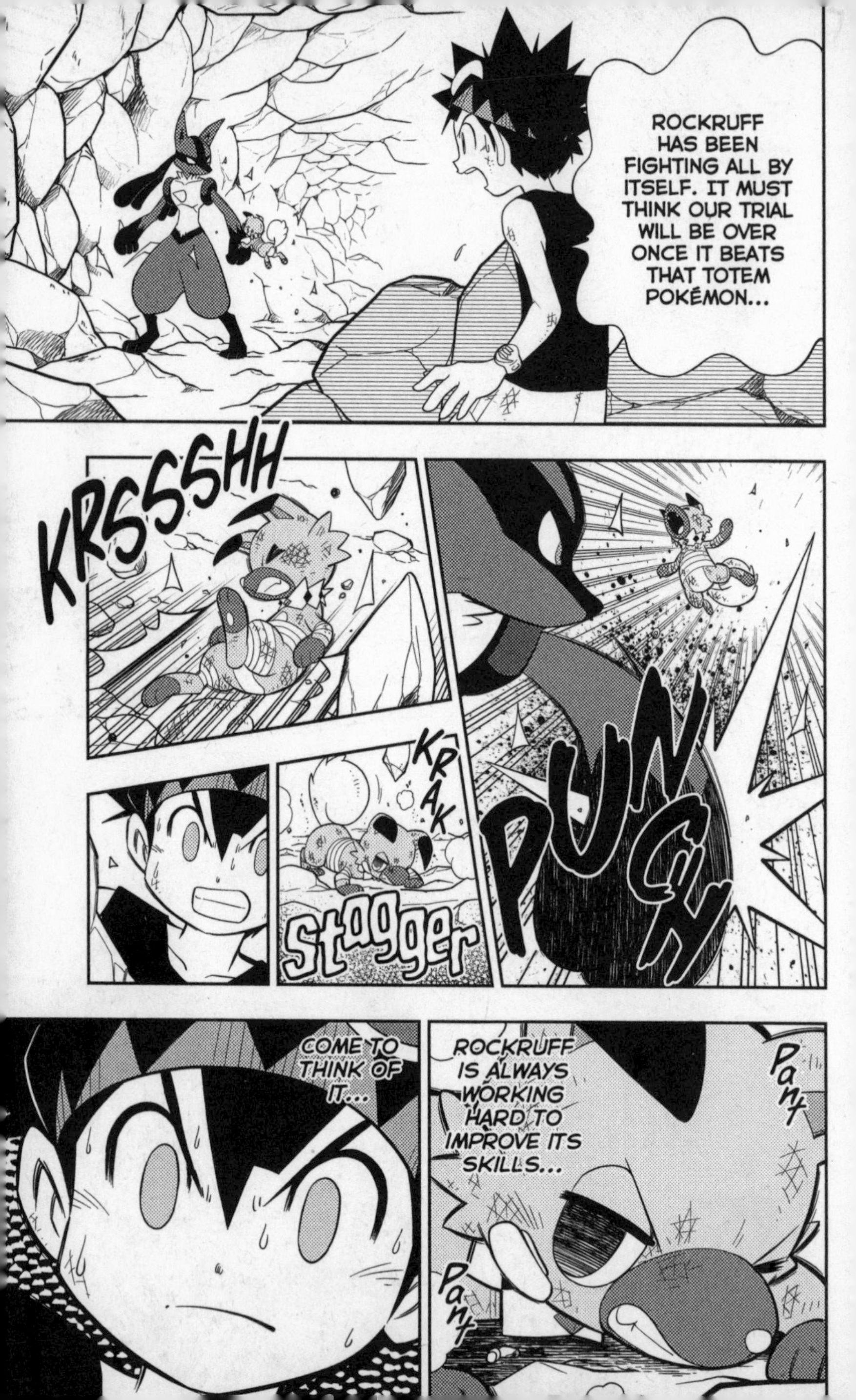
ROCKRUFF HAS BEEN FIGHTING ALL BY ITSELF. IT MUST THINK OUR TRIAL WILL BE OVER ONCE IT BEATS THAT TOTEM POKÉMON...
PUNCH
KRSSSHH
KRAK
stagger
Pant
ROCKRUFF IS ALWAYS WORKING HARD TO IMPROVE ITS SKILLS...
Pant
COME TO THINK OF IT...

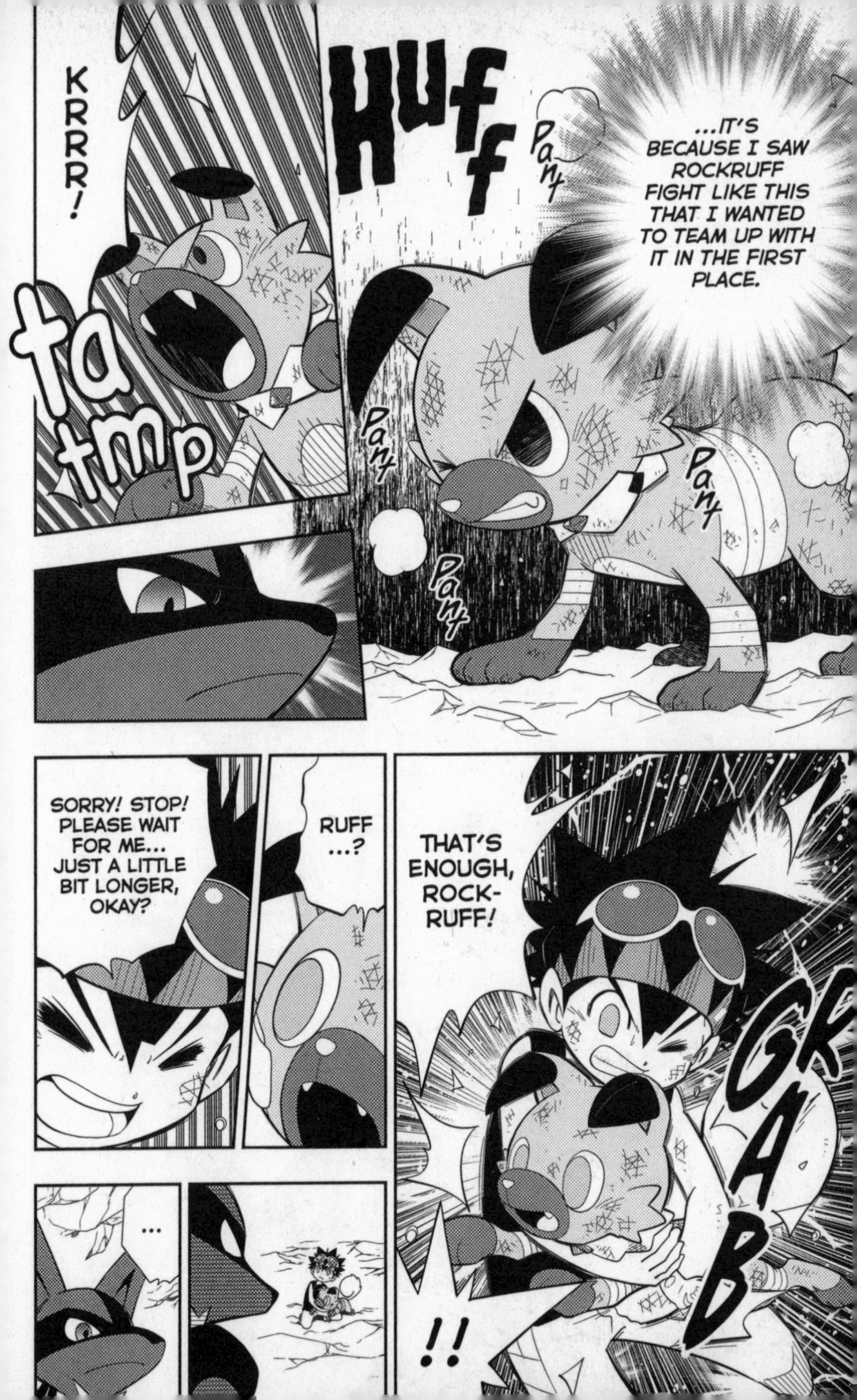
HUFF
Pant
...IT'S BECAUSE I SAW ROCKRUFF FIGHT LIKE THIS THAT I WANTED TO TEAM UP WITH IT IN THE FIRST PLACE.
Pant
Pant
Pant
KRRR!
ta
tmp
THAT'S ENOUGH, ROCK-RUFF!
GRAB
!!
RUFF ...?
SORRY! STOP! PLEASE WAIT FOR ME... JUST A LITTLE BIT LONGER, OKAY?
...

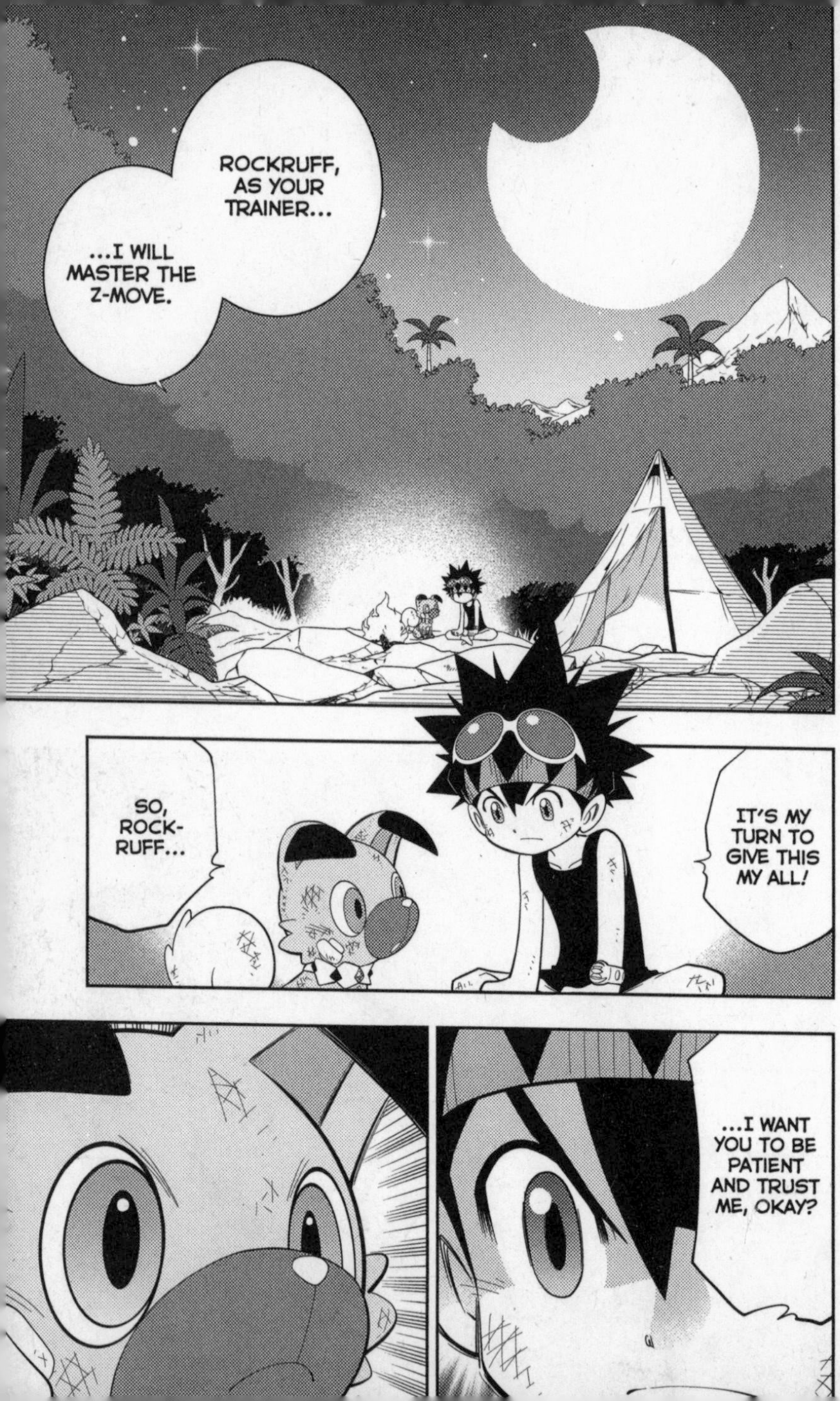
ROCKRUFF, AS YOUR TRAINER...
...I WILL MASTER THE Z-MOVE.
IT'S MY TURN TO GIVE THIS MY ALL!
SO, ROCK-RUFF...
...I WANT YOU TO BE PATIENT AND TRUST ME, OKAY?

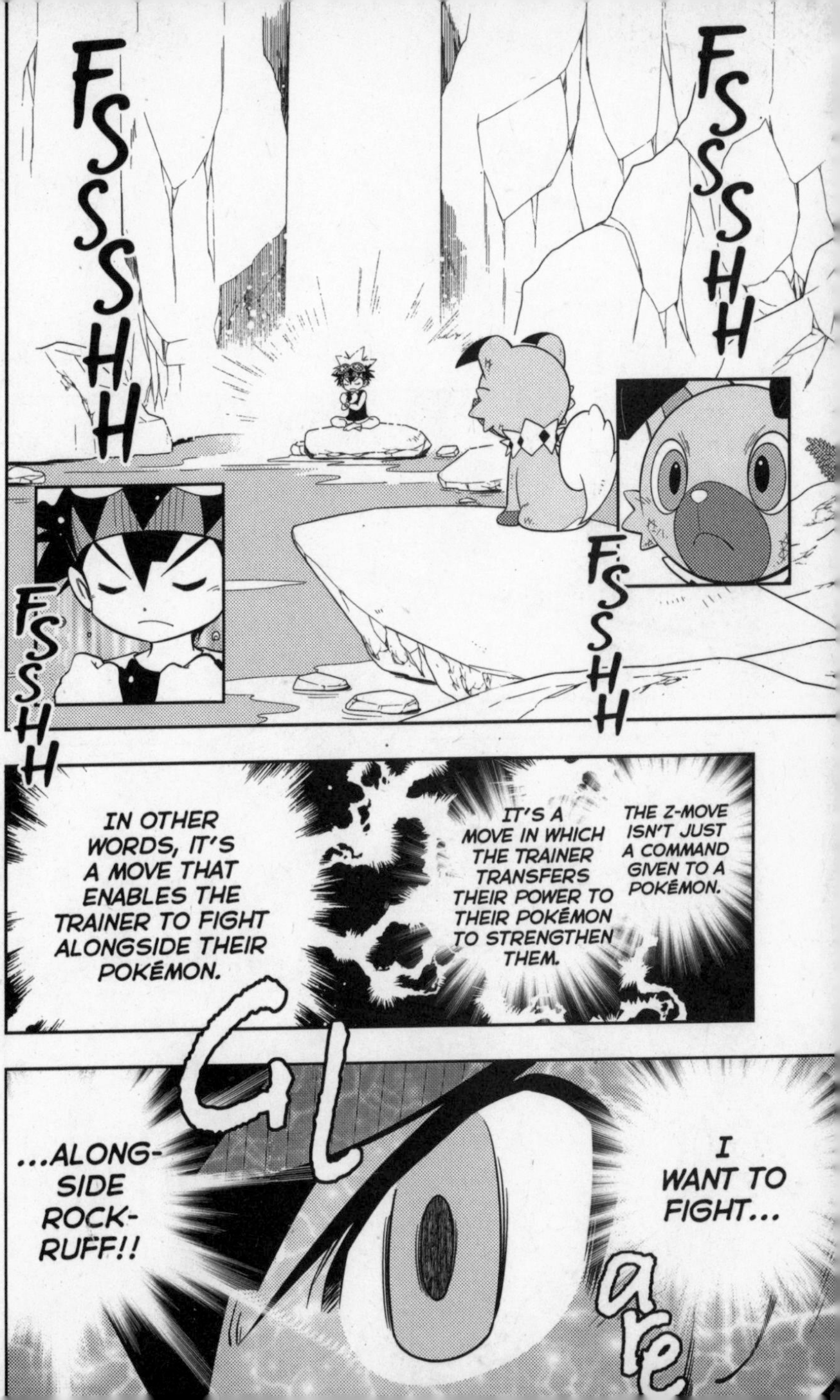
FSSSHH
FSSSHH
FSSHH
FSSHH
THE Z-MOVE ISN'T JUST A COMMAND GIVEN TO A POKéMON.
IT'S A MOVE IN WHICH THE TRAINER TRANSFERS THEIR POWER TO THEIR POKéMON TO STRENGTHEN THEM.
IN OTHER WORDS, IT'S A MOVE THAT ENABLES THE TRAINER TO FIGHT ALONGSIDE THEIR POKéMON.
I WANT TO FIGHT...
...ALONG-SIDE ROCK-RUFF!!
GLARE

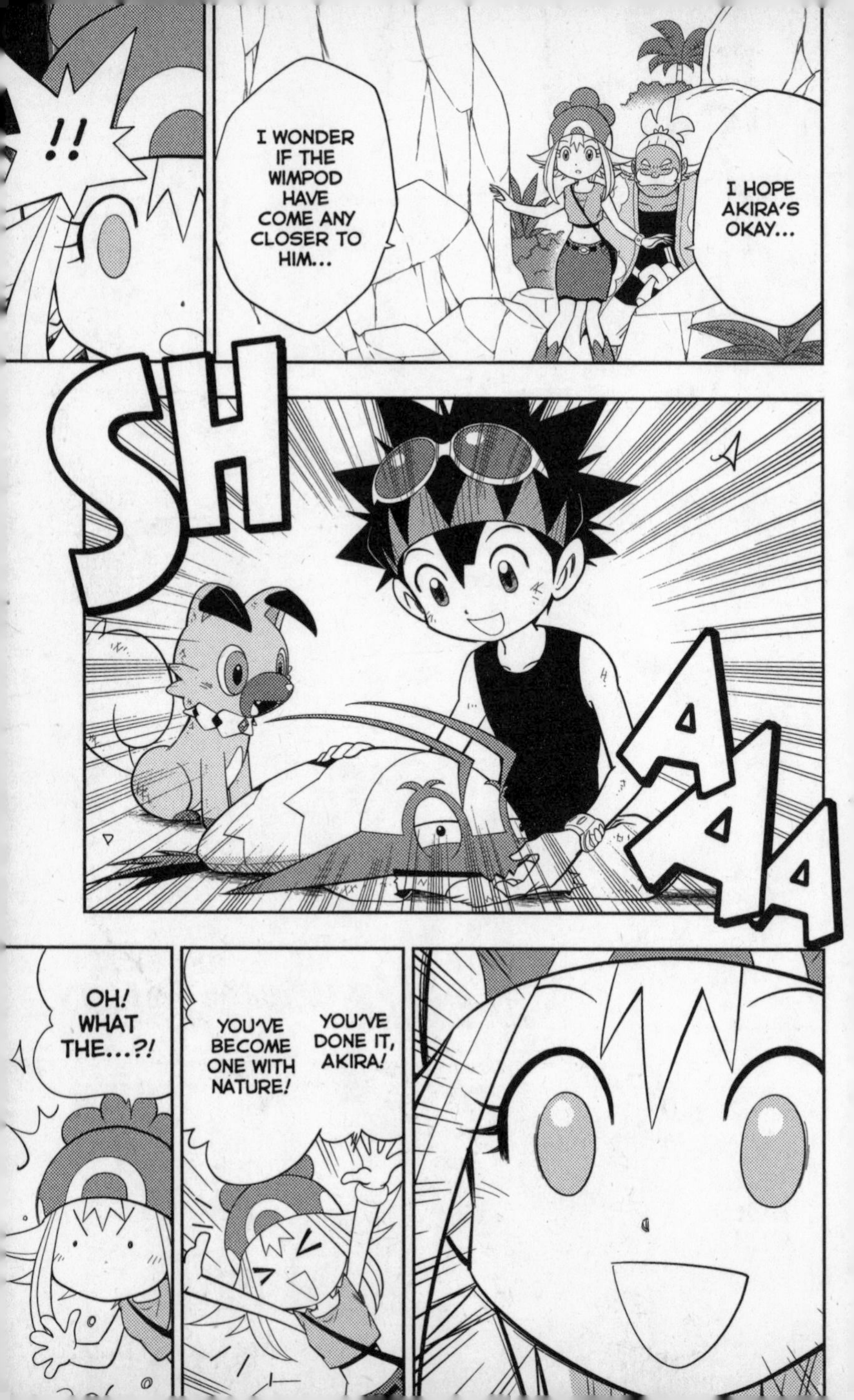
I HOPE AKIRA'S OKAY...
I WONDER IF THE WIMPOD HAVE COME ANY CLOSER TO HIM...
!!
SHAAA
YOU'VE DONE IT, AKIRA!
YOU'VE BECOME ONE WITH NATURE!
OH! WHAT THE...?!

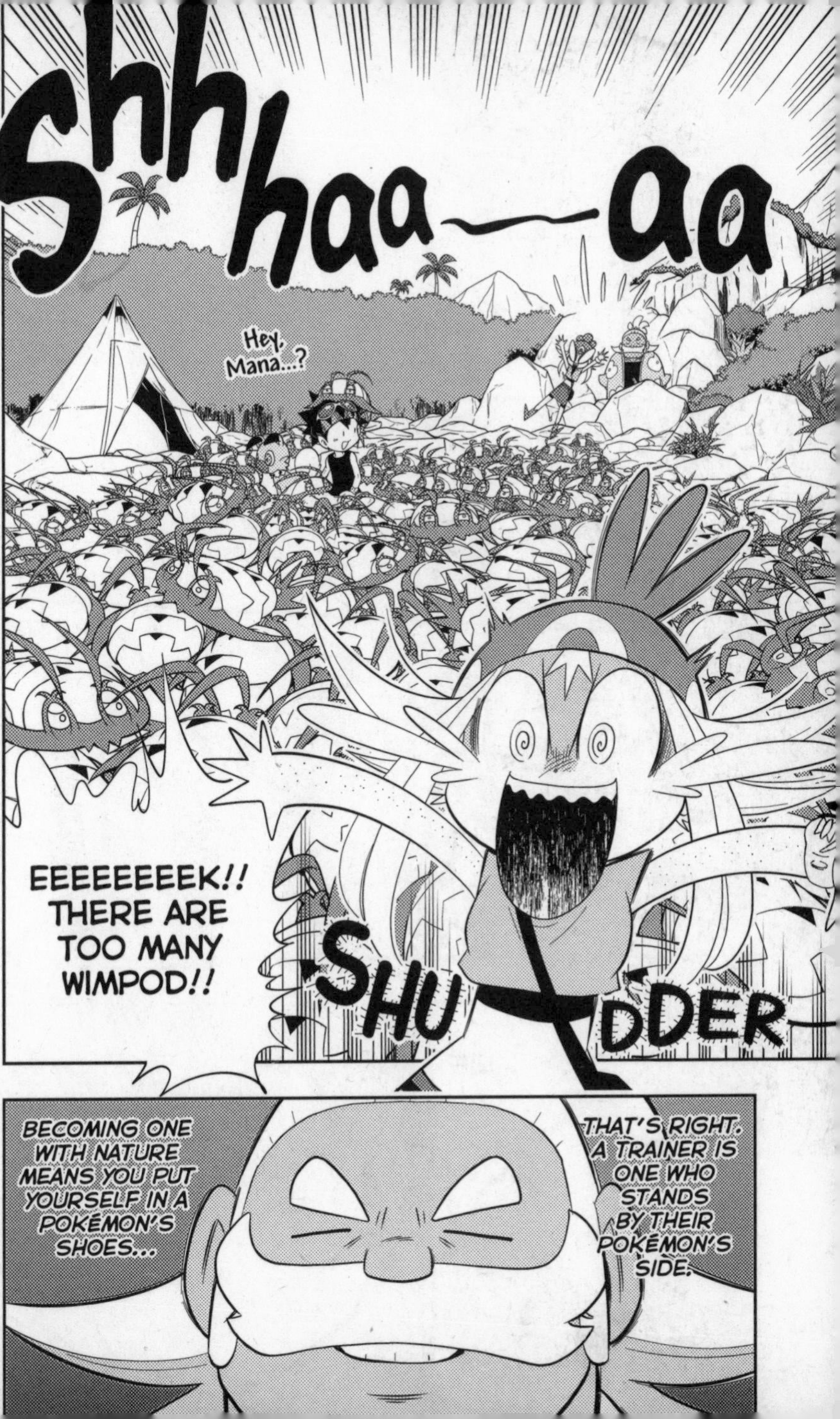
Shhhaa—aa
Hey, Mana...?
EEEEEEEEK!! THERE ARE TOO MANY WIMPOD!!
SHUDDER
THAT'S RIGHT. A TRAINER IS ONE WHO STANDS BY THEIR POKÉMON'S SIDE.
BECOMING ONE WITH NATURE MEANS YOU PUT YOURSELF IN A POKÉMON'S SHOES...

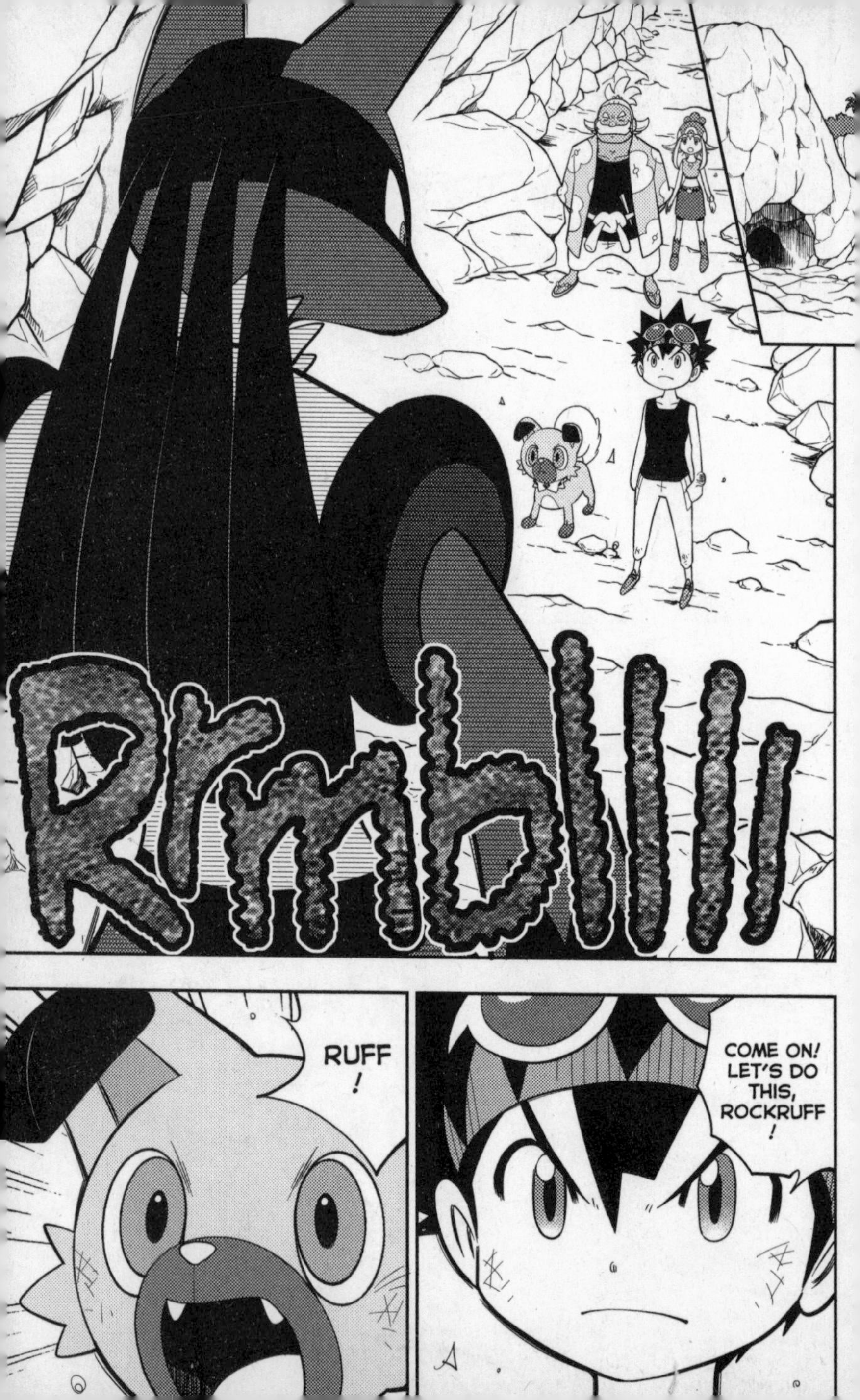
Rrmbllll
COME ON! LET'S DO THIS, ROCKRUFF!
RUFF!

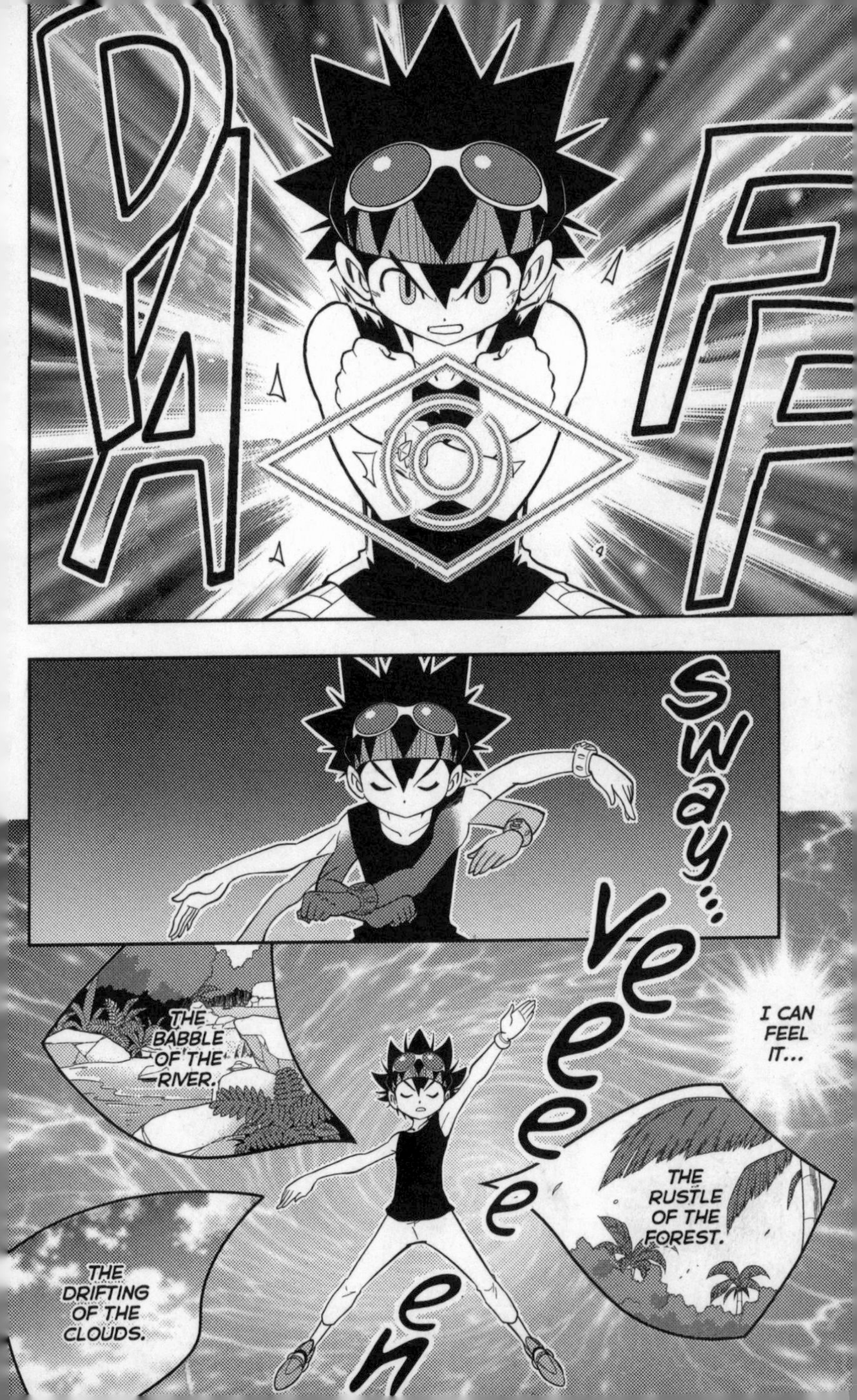
PAFF
sway...
I CAN FEEL IT...
Veeeeeen
THE RUSTLE OF THE FOREST.
THE BABBLE OF THE RIVER.
THE DRIFTING OF THE CLOUDS.

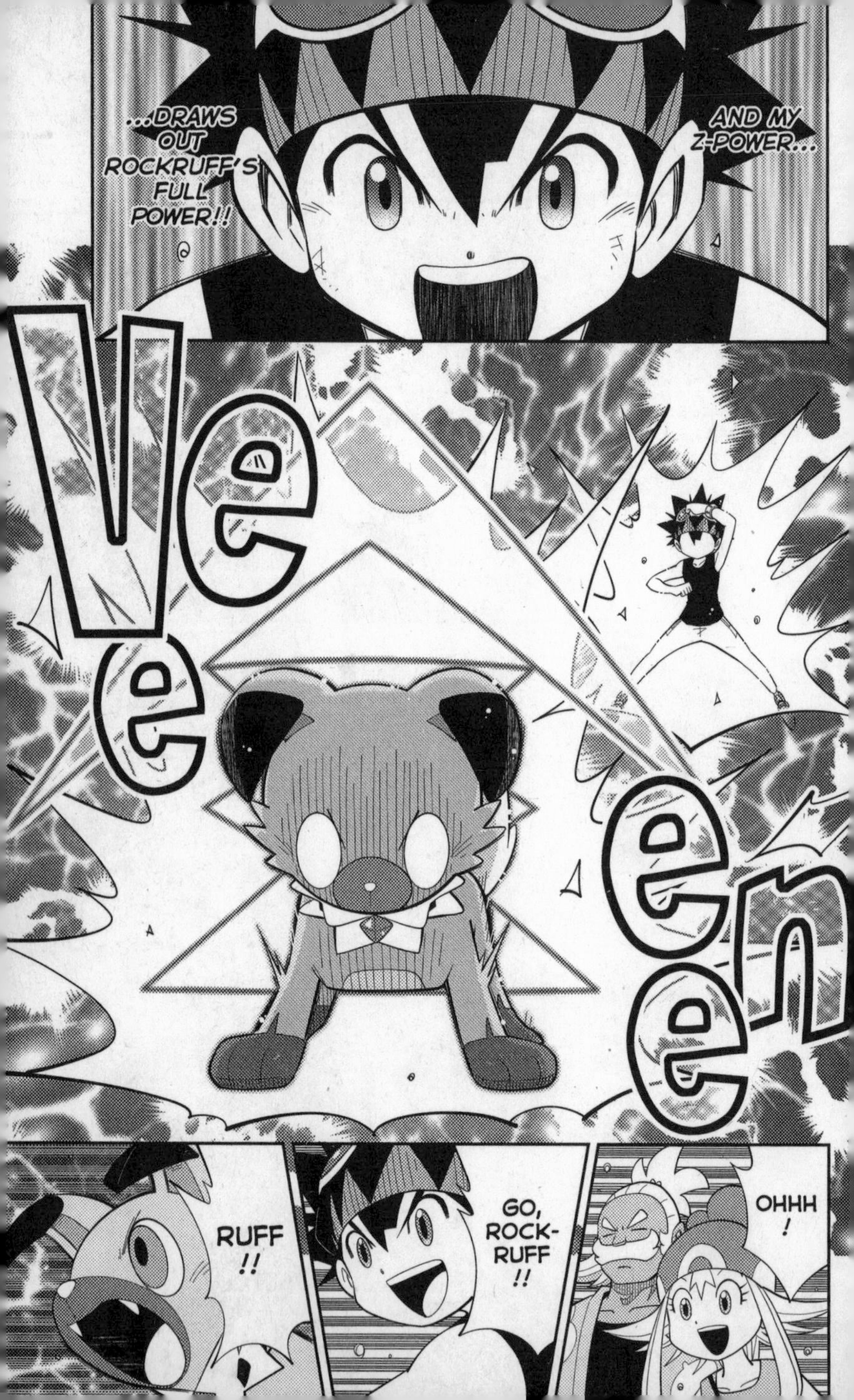
AND MY Z-POWER...
...DRAWS OUT ROCKRUFF'S FULL POWER!!
Veeeen
OHHH!
GO, ROCK-RUFF!!
RUFF!!

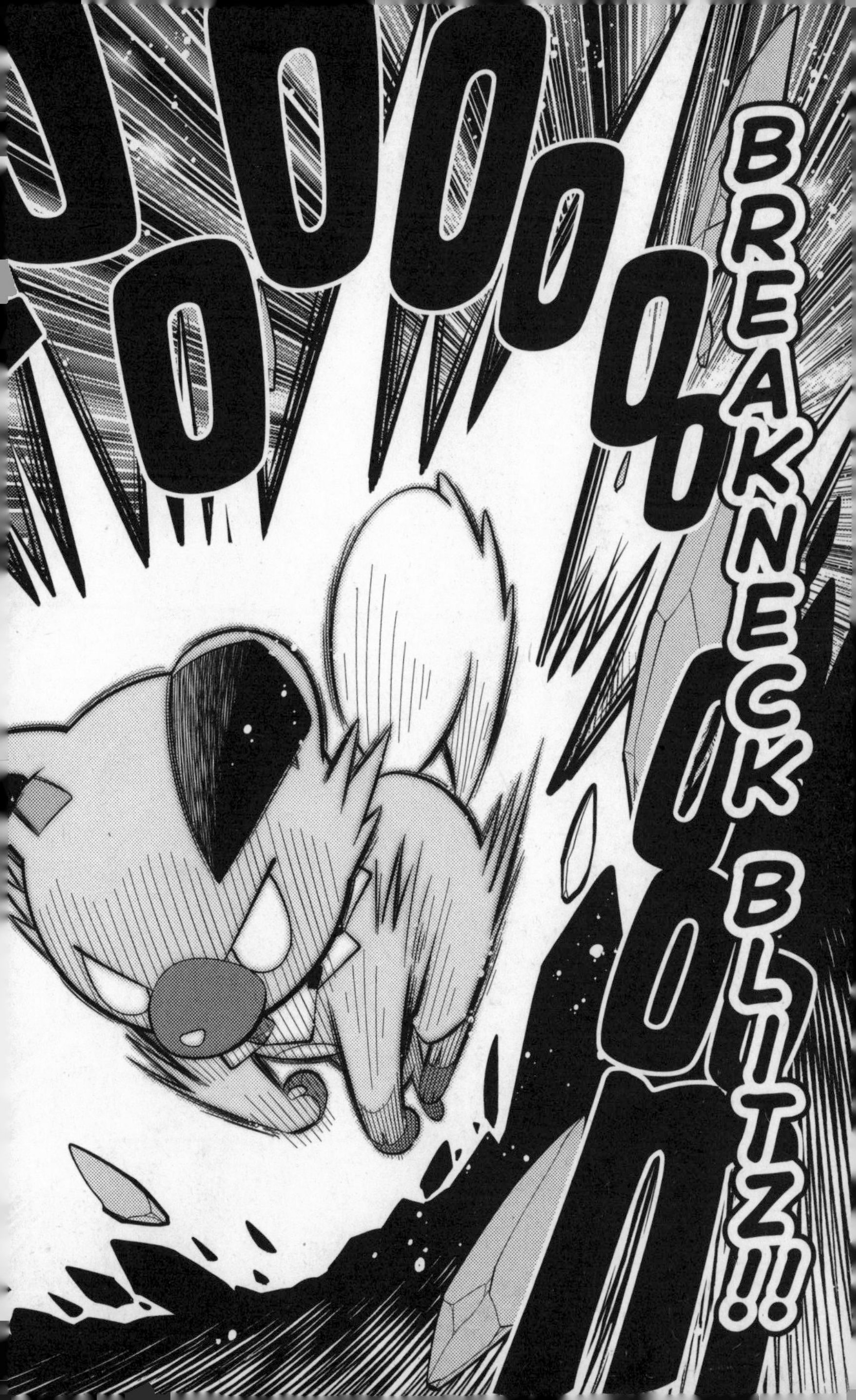
BREAKNECK BLITZ!!

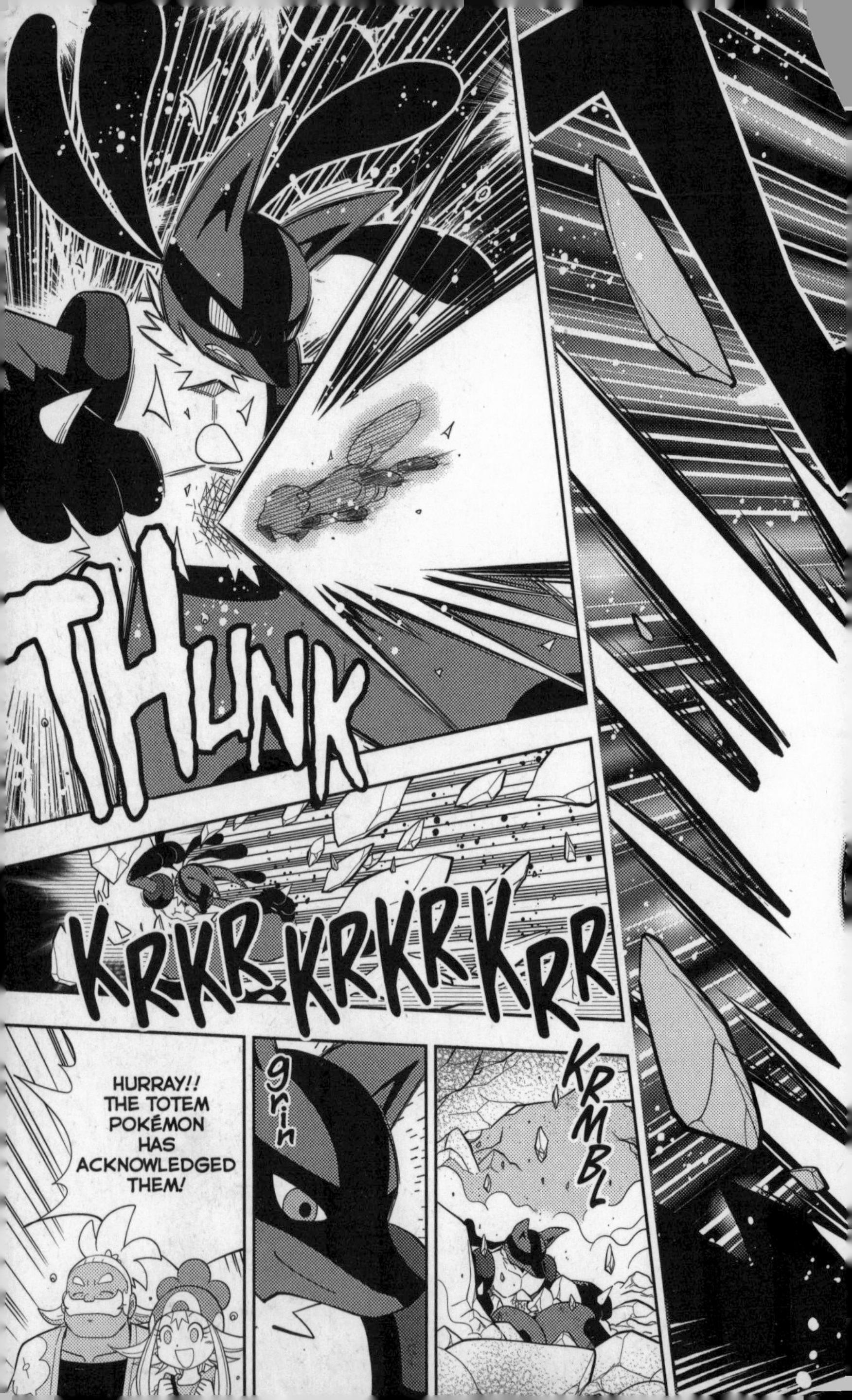
THUNK
KRKR KRKR KRR
KRMBL
grin
HURRAY!! THE TOTEM POKÉMON HAS ACKNOWLEDGED THEM!

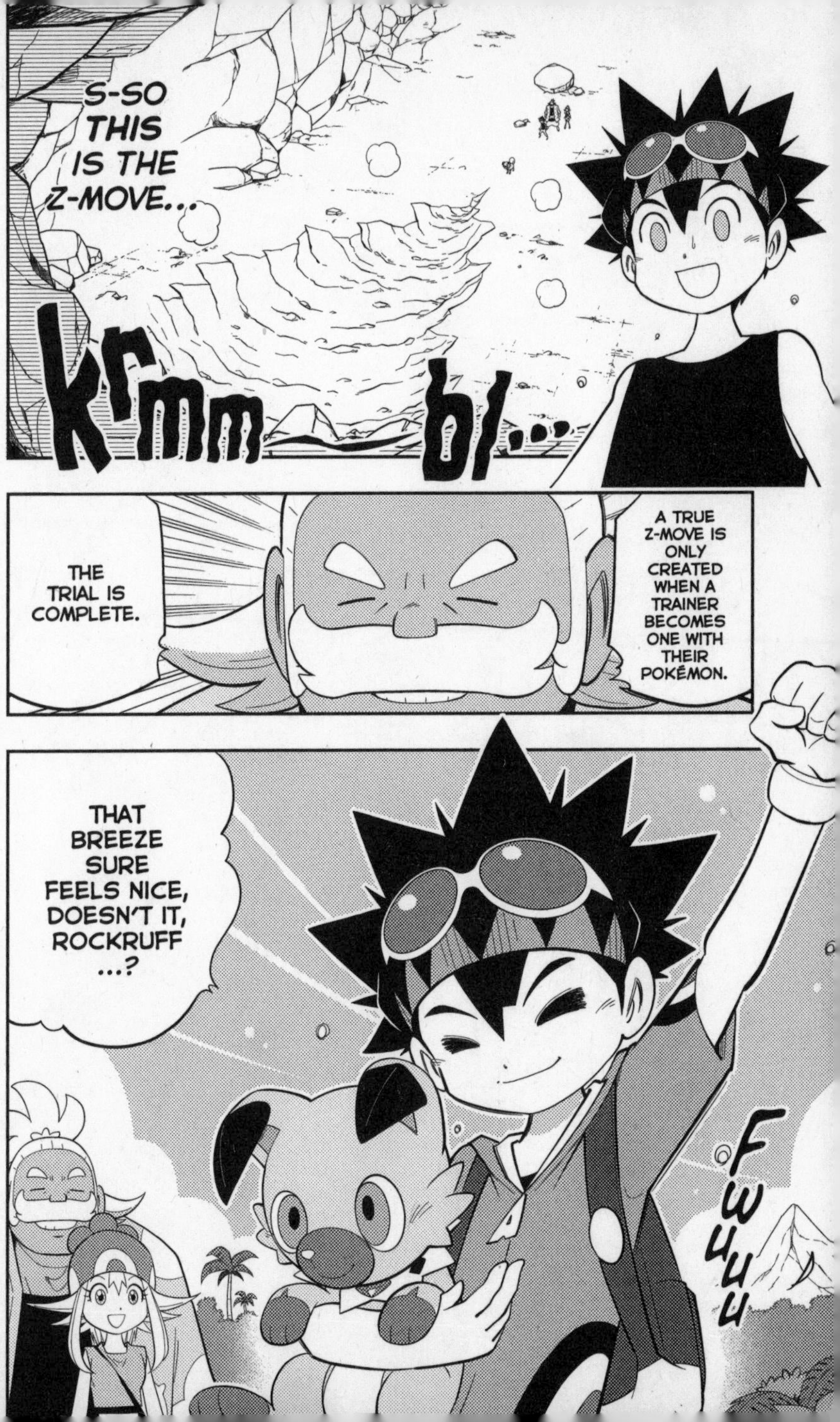
S-SO THIS IS THE Z-MOVE...
krmm bl...
A TRUE Z-MOVE IS ONLY CREATED WHEN A TRAINER BECOMES ONE WITH THEIR POKÉMON.
THE TRIAL IS COMPLETE.
THAT BREEZE SURE FEELS NICE, DOESN'T IT, ROCKRUFF ...?
Fwuuu

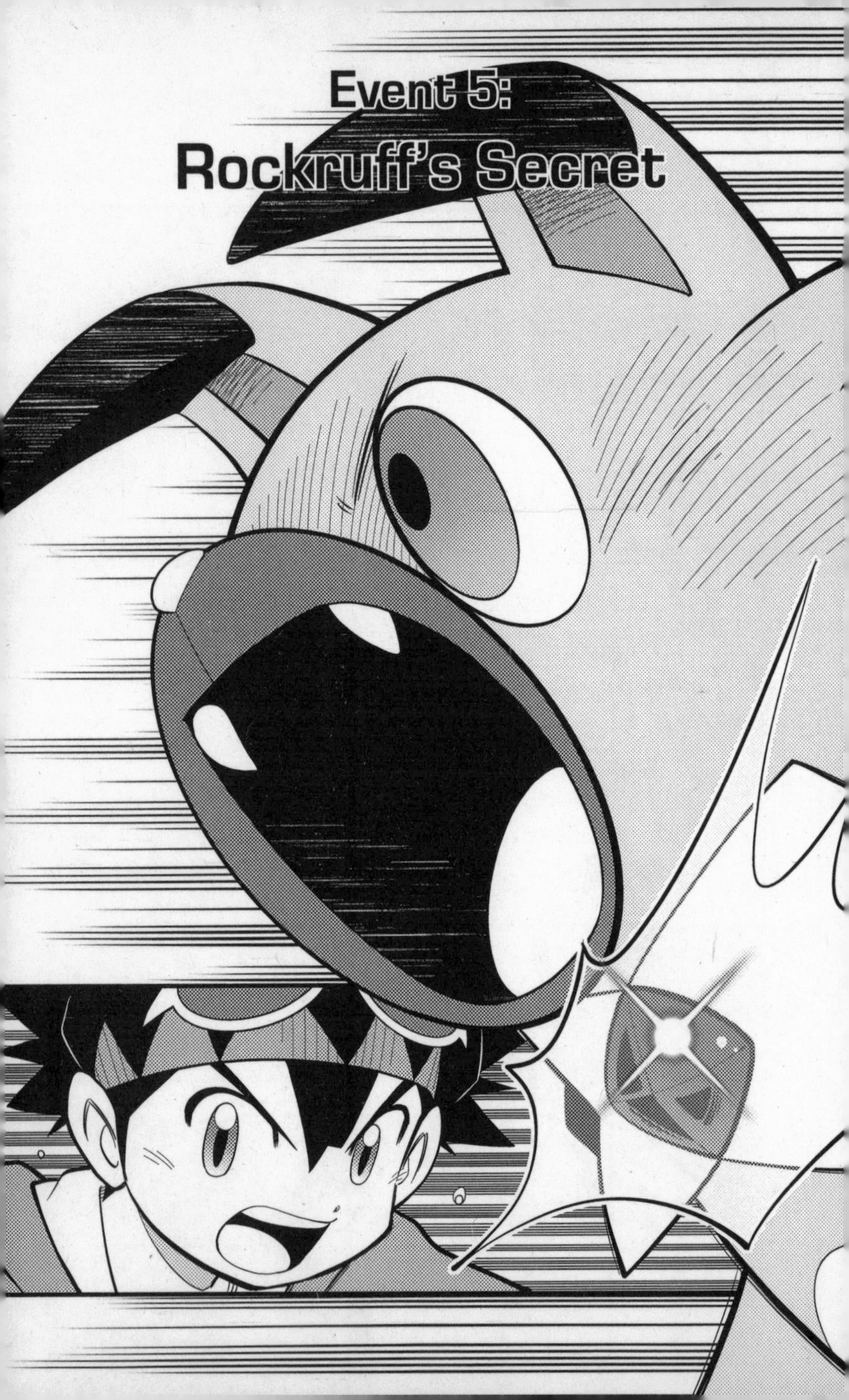
Event 5:
Rockruff's Secret

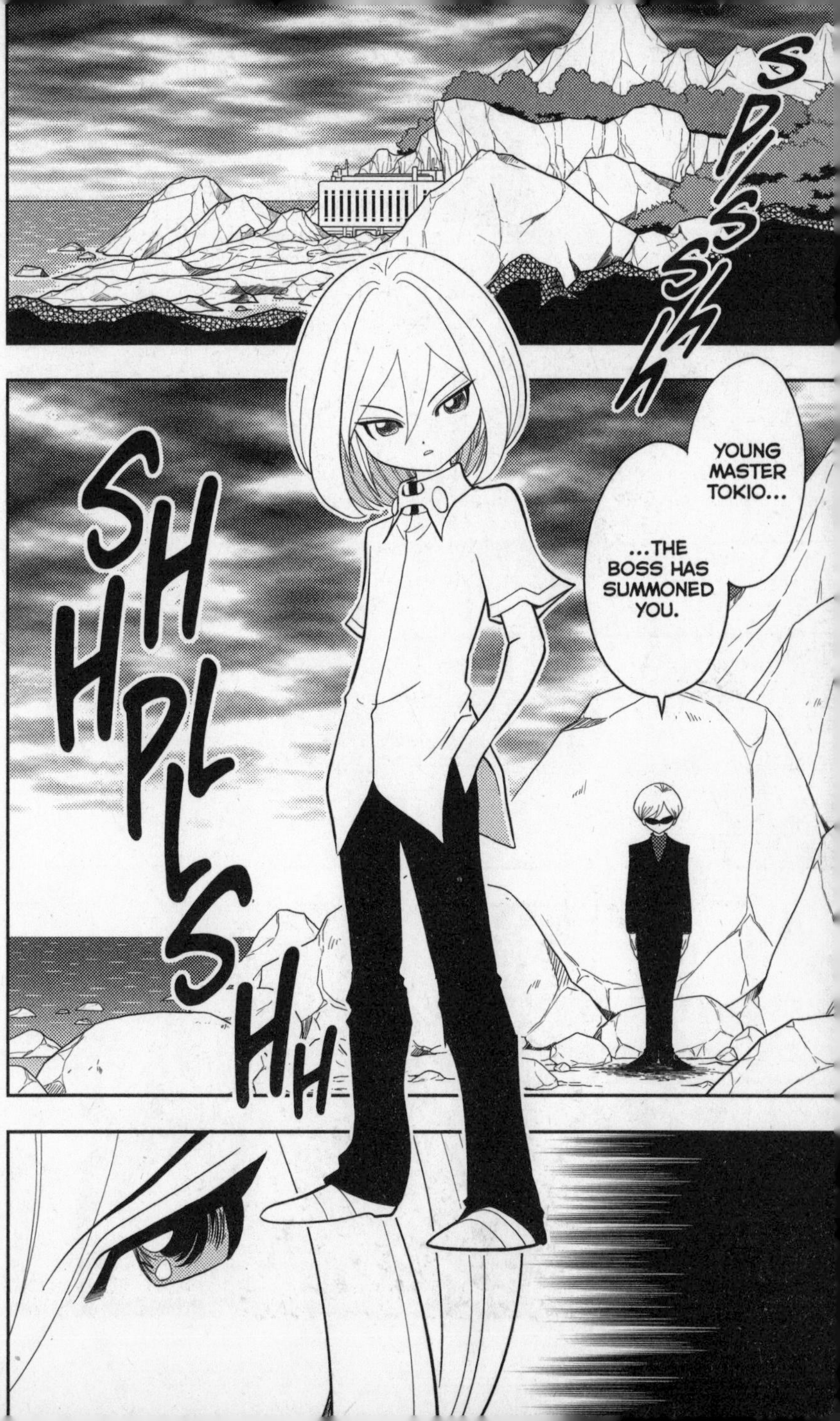
SPLISSHH
YOUNG MASTER TOKIO...
...THE BOSS HAS SUMMONED YOU.
SHHPLLSHH

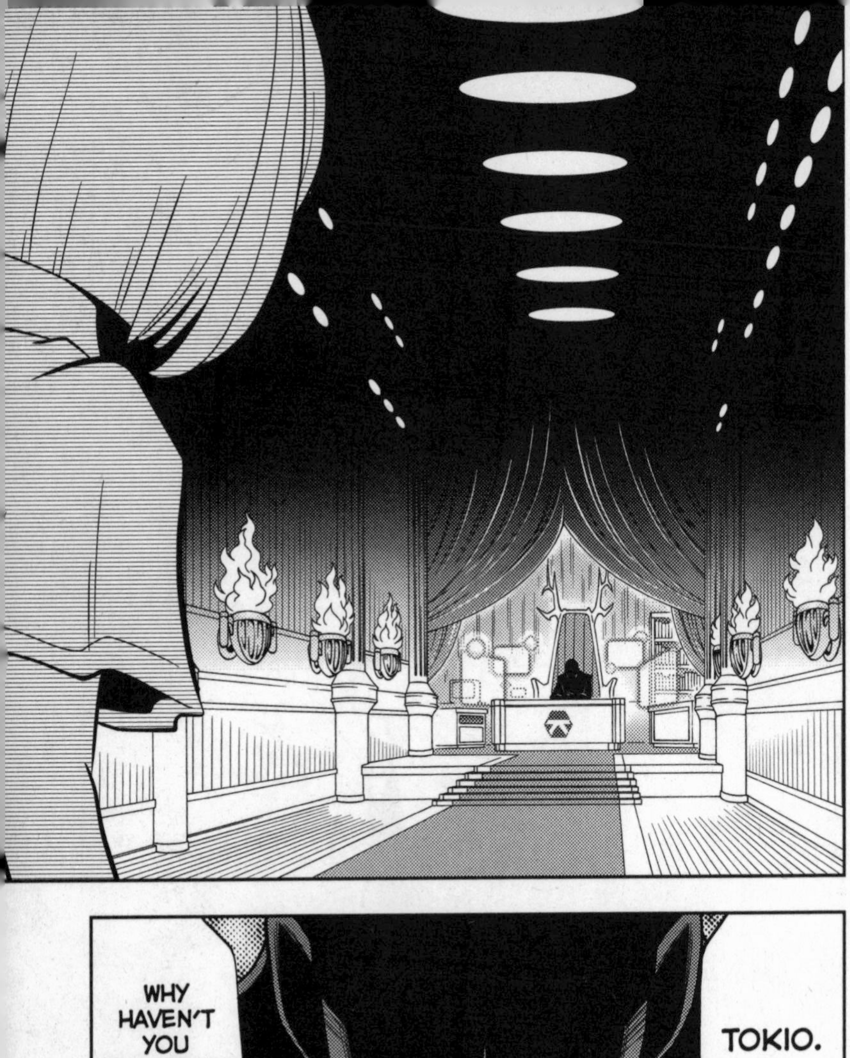

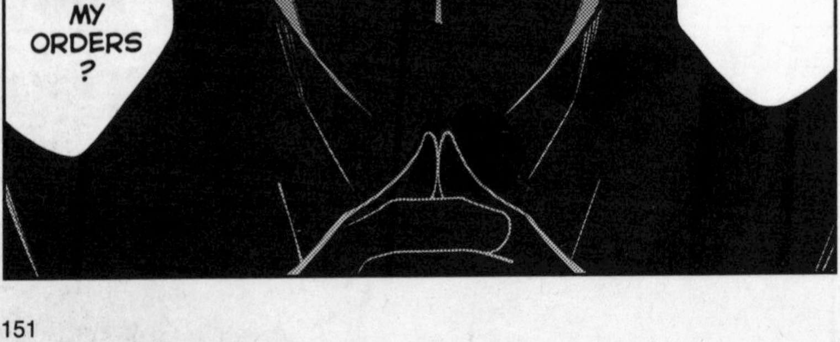
TOKIO.
WHY HAVEN'T YOU FOLLOWED MY ORDERS?

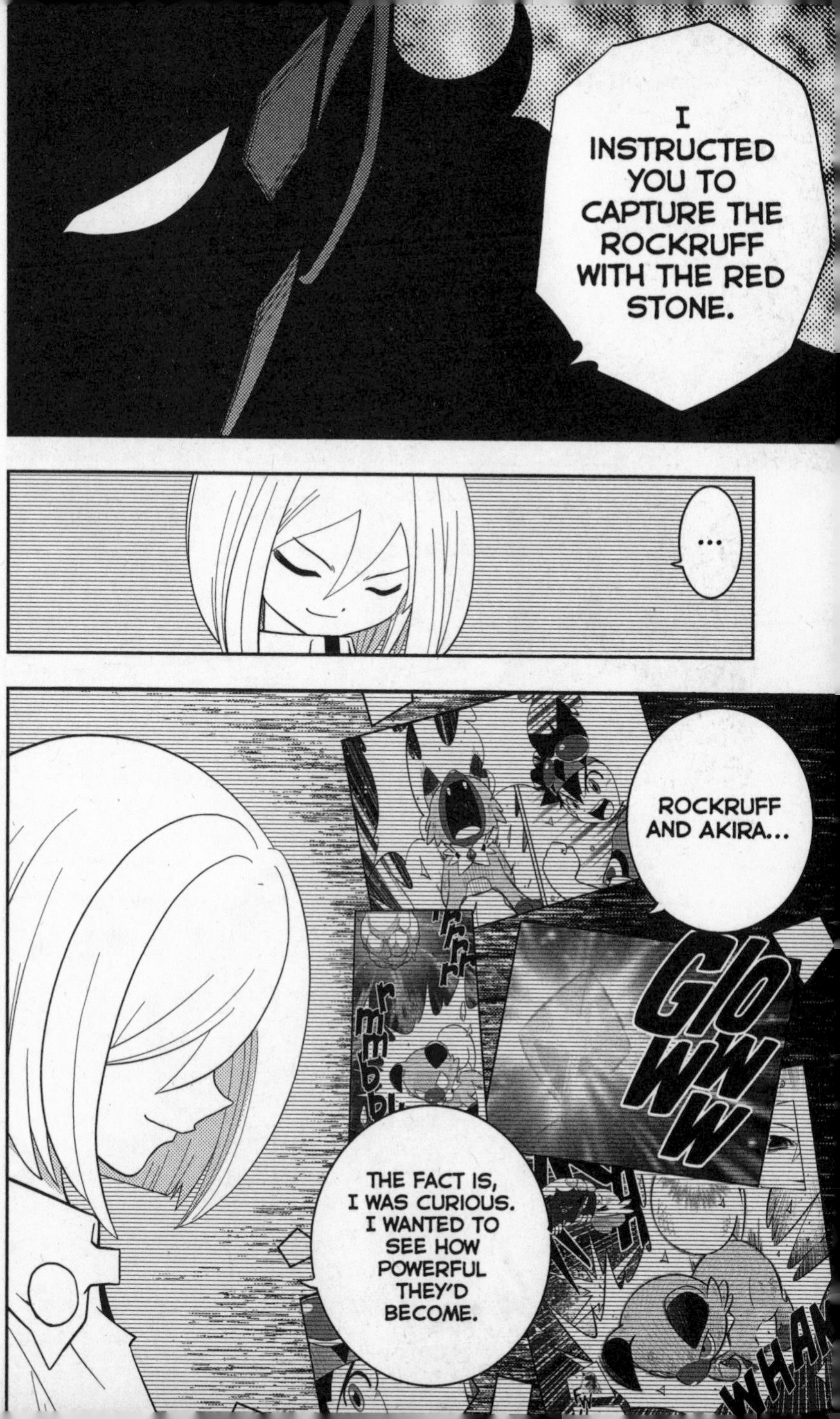
I INSTRUCTED YOU TO CAPTURE THE ROCKRUFF WITH THE RED STONE.
...
ROCKRUFF AND AKIRA...
GLOWWW
THE FACT IS, I WAS CURIOUS. I WANTED TO SEE HOW POWERFUL THEY'D BECOME.

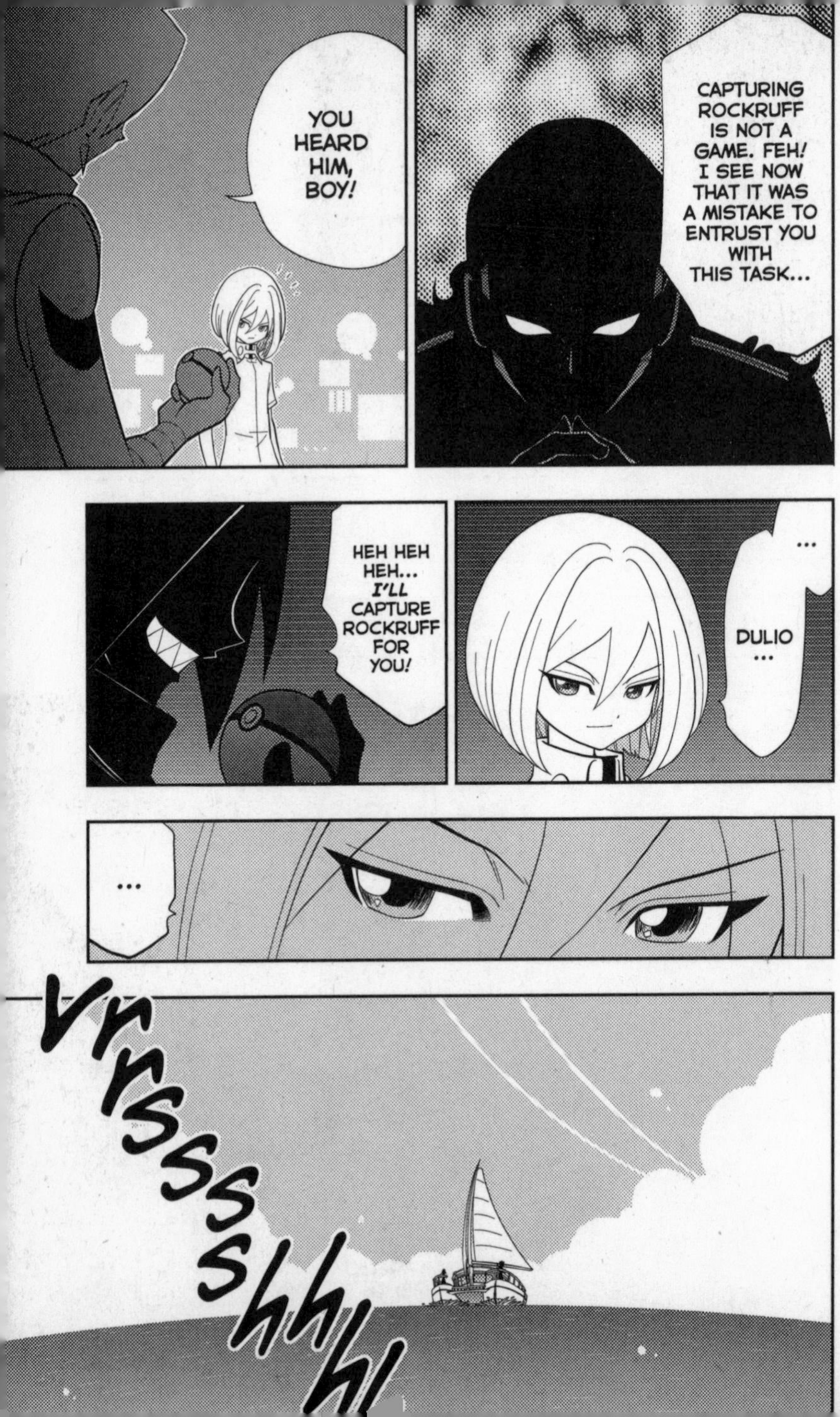
CAPTURING ROCKRUFF IS NOT A GAME. FEH! I SEE NOW THAT IT WAS A MISTAKE TO ENTRUST YOU WITH THIS TASK...
YOU HEARD HIM, BOY!
...
DULIO...
HEH HEH HEH... *I'LL* CAPTURE ROCKRUFF FOR YOU!
...
vrsssshhh!

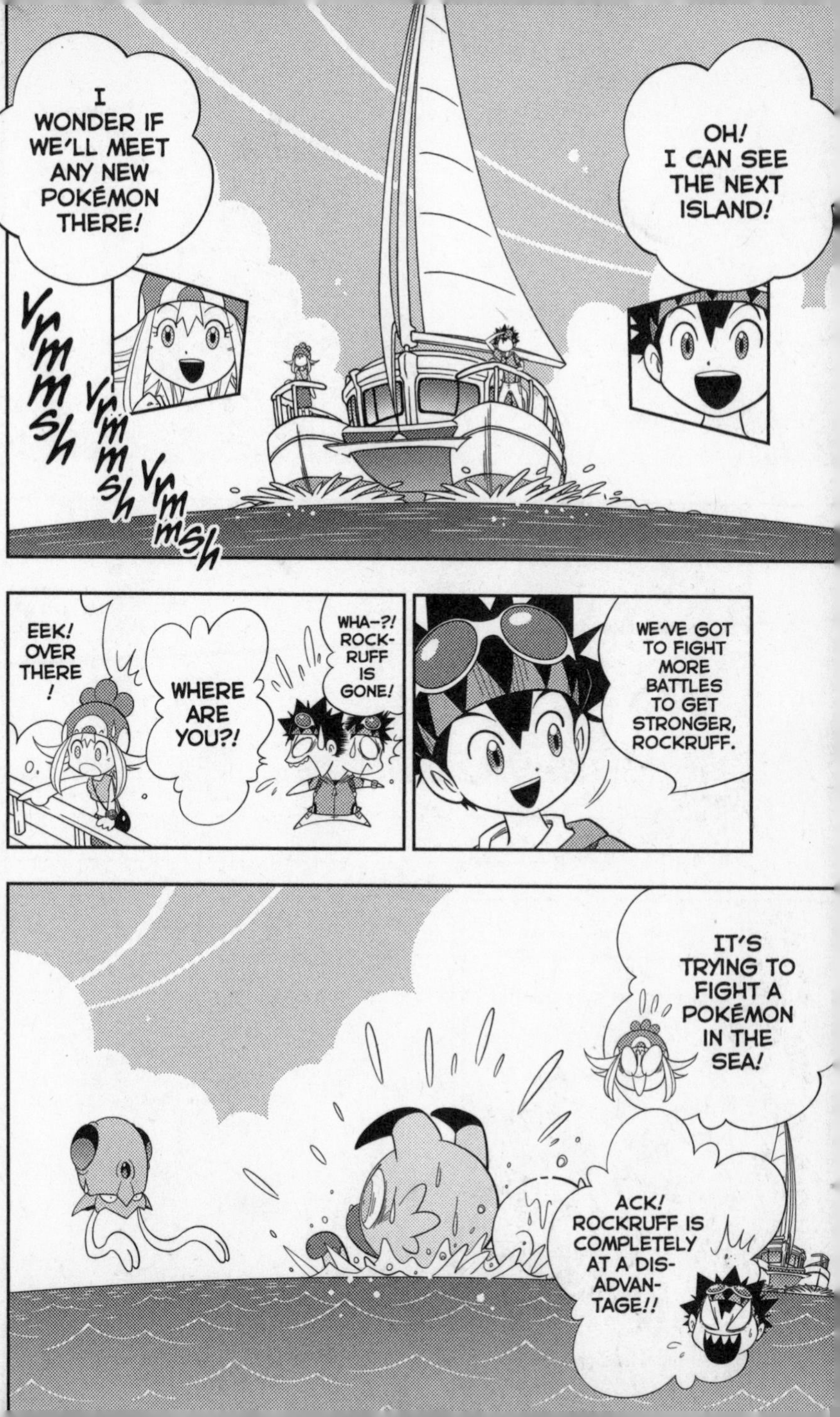
OH! I CAN SEE THE NEXT ISLAND!
I WONDER IF WE'LL MEET ANY NEW POKÉMON THERE!
Vrmmsh Vrmmsh Vrmmsh
WE'VE GOT TO FIGHT MORE BATTLES TO GET STRONGER, ROCKRUFF.
WHA-?! ROCK-RUFF IS GONE!
WHERE ARE YOU?!
EEK! OVER THERE!
IT'S TRYING TO FIGHT A POKÉMON IN THE SEA!
ACK! ROCKRUFF IS COMPLETELY AT A DIS-ADVAN-TAGE!!

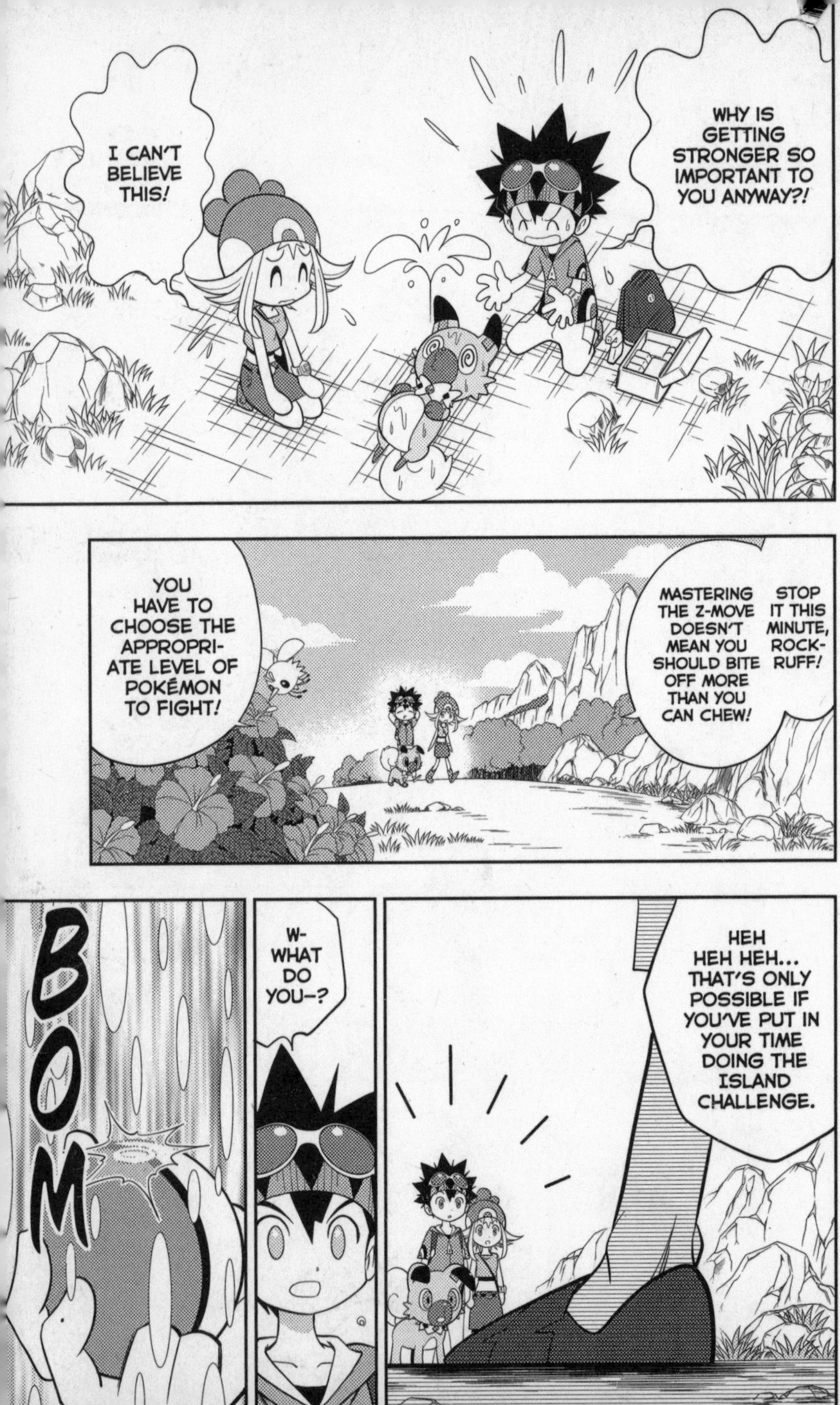
WHY IS GETTING STRONGER SO IMPORTANT TO YOU ANYWAY?!
I CAN'T BELIEVE THIS!
STOP IT THIS MINUTE, ROCKRUFF!
MASTERING THE Z-MOVE DOESN'T MEAN YOU SHOULD BITE OFF MORE THAN YOU CAN CHEW!
YOU HAVE TO CHOOSE THE APPROPRIATE LEVEL OF POKÉMON TO FIGHT!
HEH HEH HEH... THAT'S ONLY POSSIBLE IF YOU'VE PUT IN YOUR TIME DOING THE ISLAND CHALLENGE.
W-WHAT DO YOU-?
BOOM

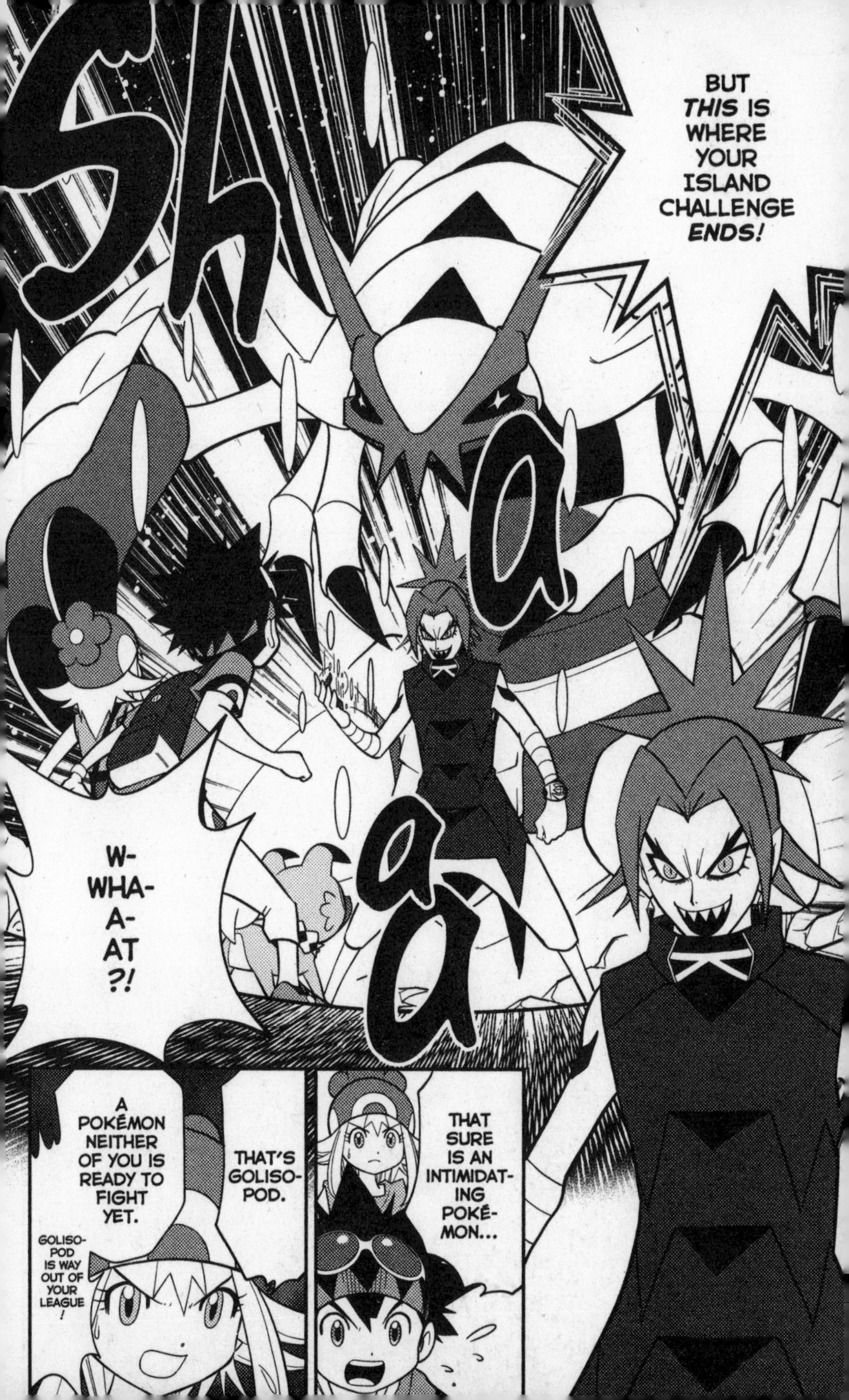
BUT THIS IS WHERE YOUR ISLAND CHALLENGE ENDS!
Shaaa
W-WHA-A-AT?!
THAT SURE IS AN INTIMIDAT-ING POKÉ-MON...
THAT'S GOLISO-POD.
A POKÉMON NEITHER OF YOU IS READY TO FIGHT YET.
GOLISO-POD IS WAY OUT OF YOUR LEAGUE!

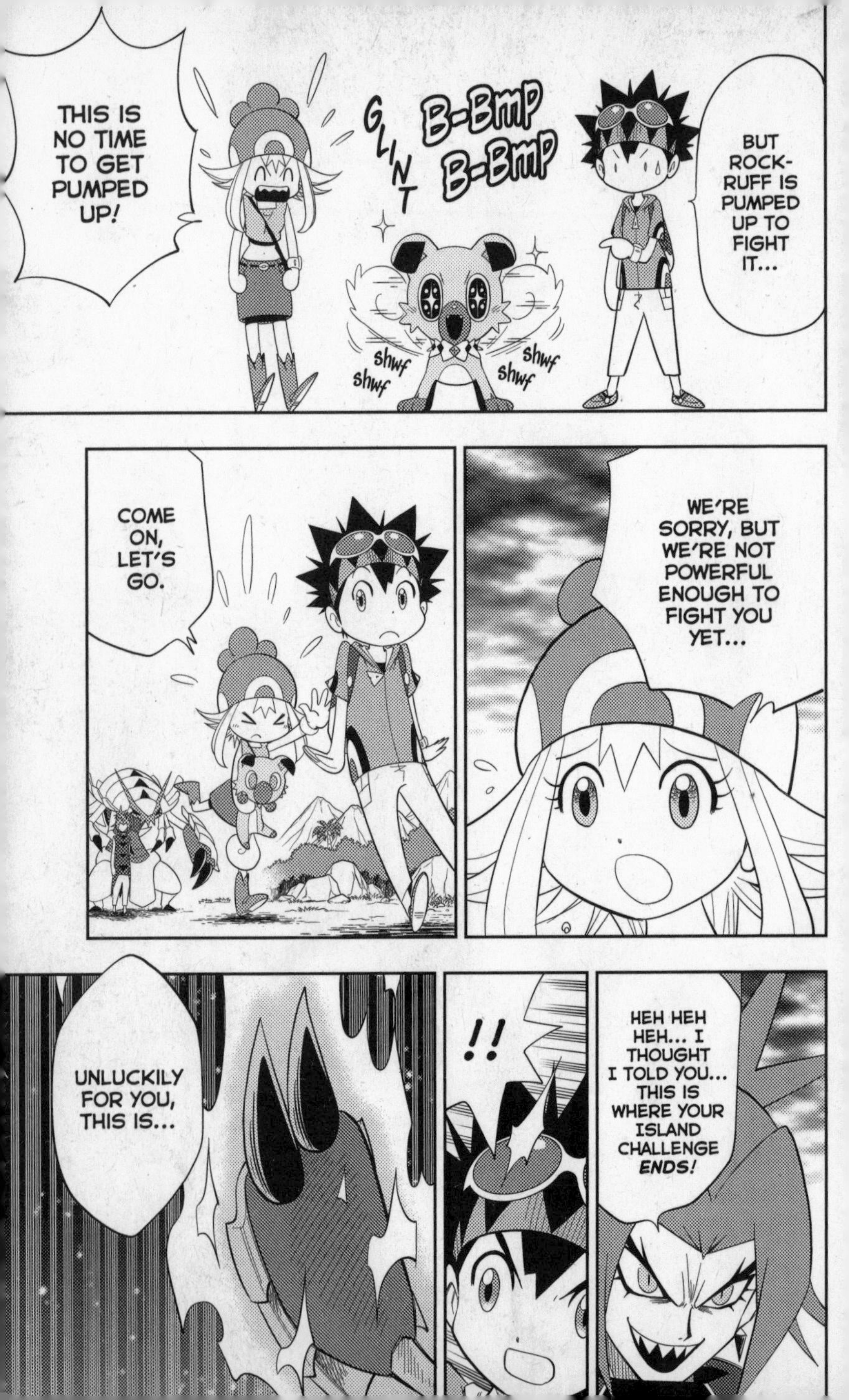
BUT ROCK-RUFF IS PUMPED UP TO FIGHT IT...
B-Bmp B-Bmp
GLINT
shwf shwf
shwf shwf
THIS IS NO TIME TO GET PUMPED UP!
WE'RE SORRY, BUT WE'RE NOT POWERFUL ENOUGH TO FIGHT YOU YET...
COME ON, LET'S GO.
HEH HEH HEH... I THOUGHT I TOLD YOU... THIS IS WHERE YOUR ISLAND CHALLENGE *ENDS!*
!!
UNLUCKILY FOR YOU, THIS IS...

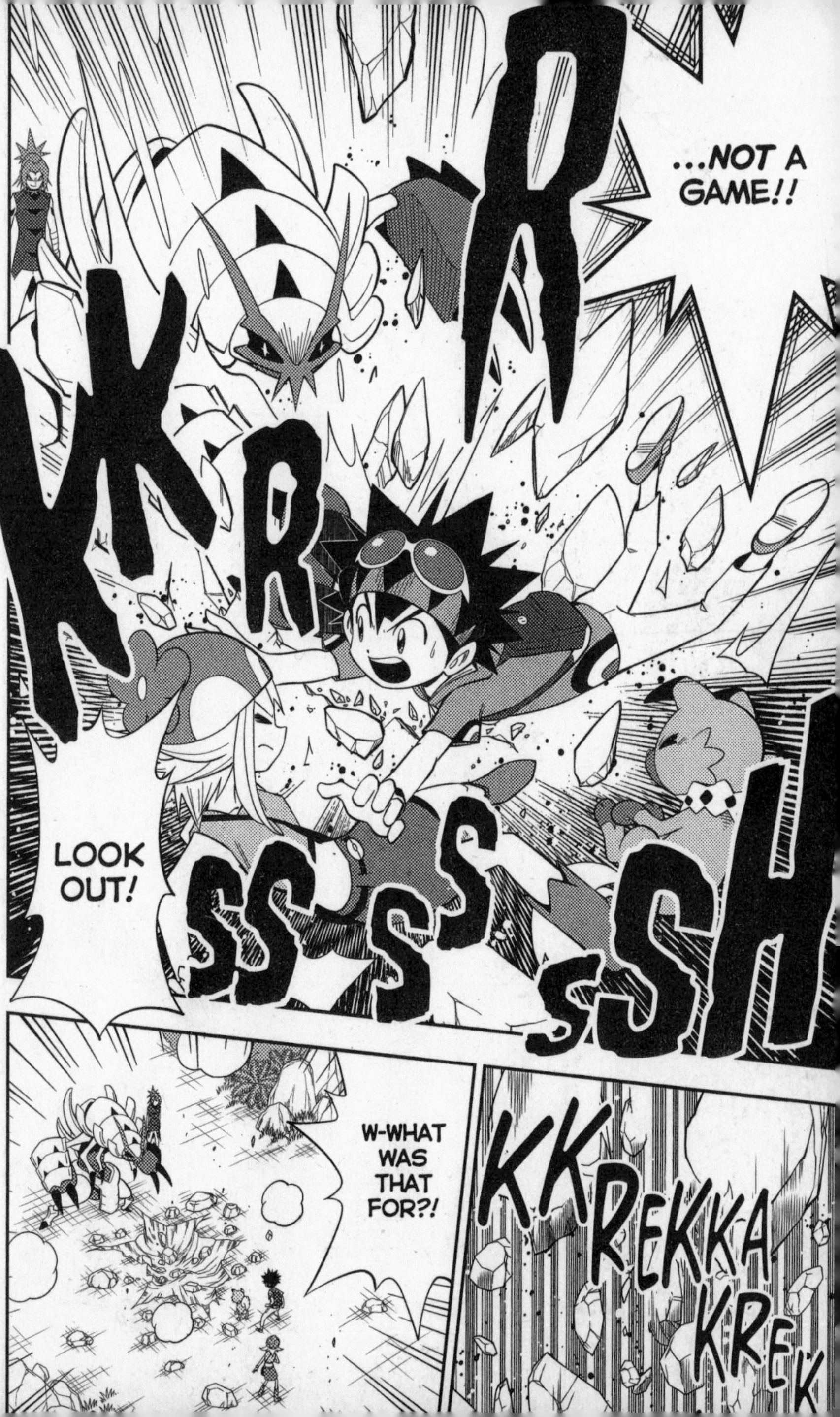
...NOT A GAME!!
LOOK OUT!
KKREKKA KREK
W-WHAT WAS THAT FOR?!

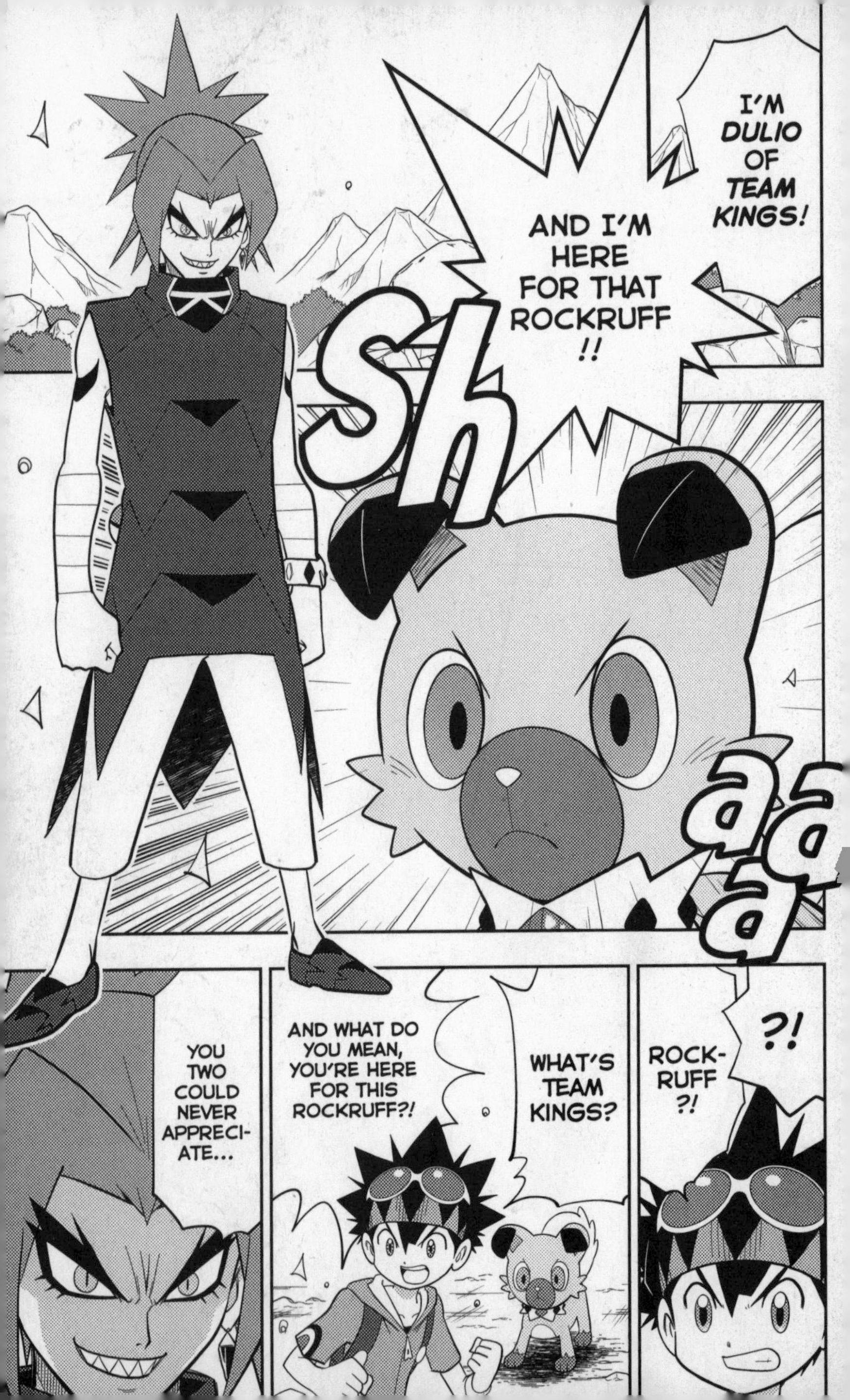
I'M DULIO OF TEAM KINGS!
AND I'M HERE FOR THAT ROCKRUFF!!
Shaaaa
?!
ROCK-RUFF?!
WHAT'S TEAM KINGS?
AND WHAT DO YOU MEAN, YOU'RE HERE FOR THIS ROCKRUFF?!
YOU TWO COULD NEVER APPRECI-ATE...

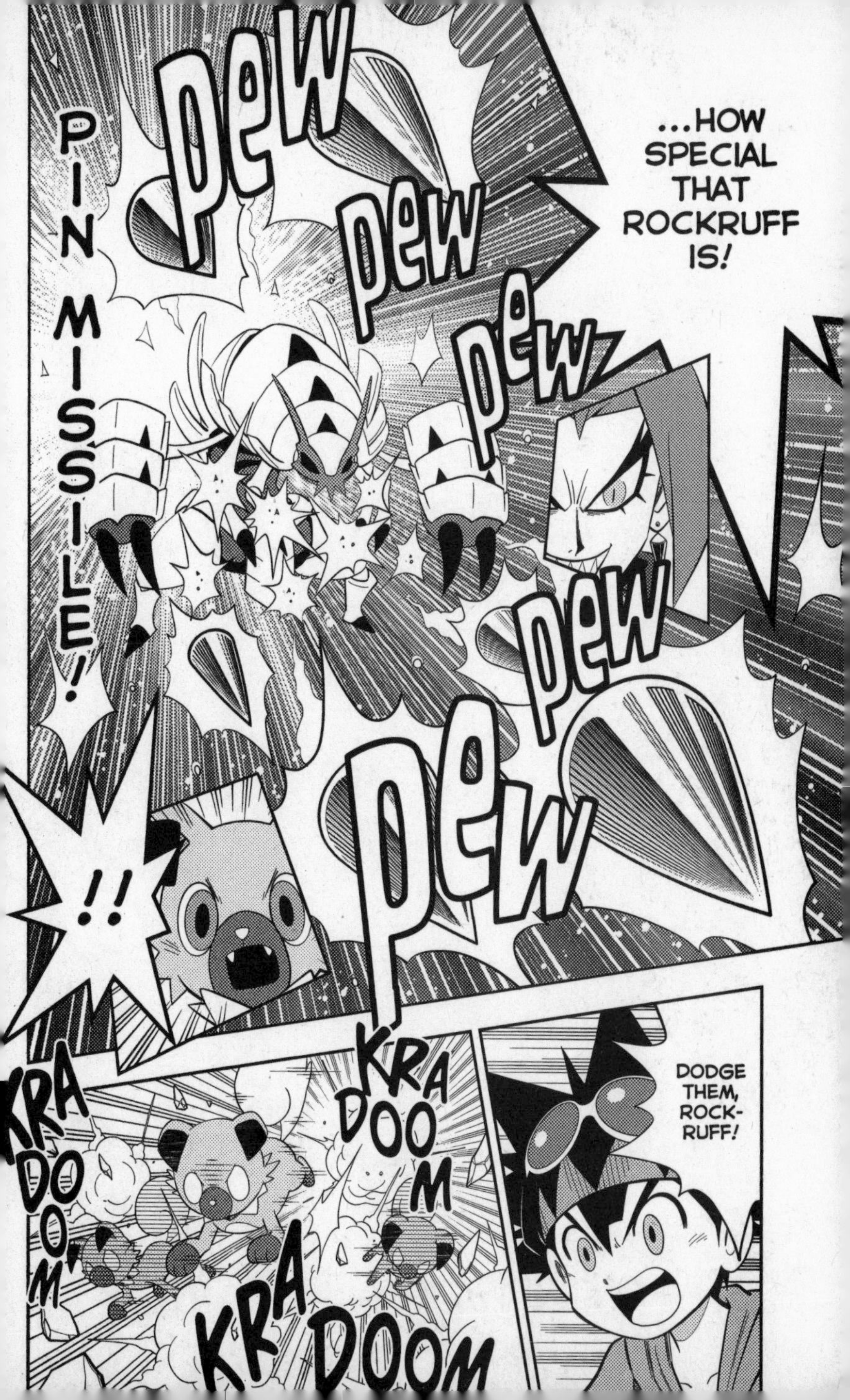
...HOW SPECIAL THAT ROCKRUFF IS!
PIN MISSILE!
PEW PEW PEW PEW PEW
!!
DODGE THEM, ROCK-RUFF!
KRA DOOM
KRA DOOM
KRA DOOM

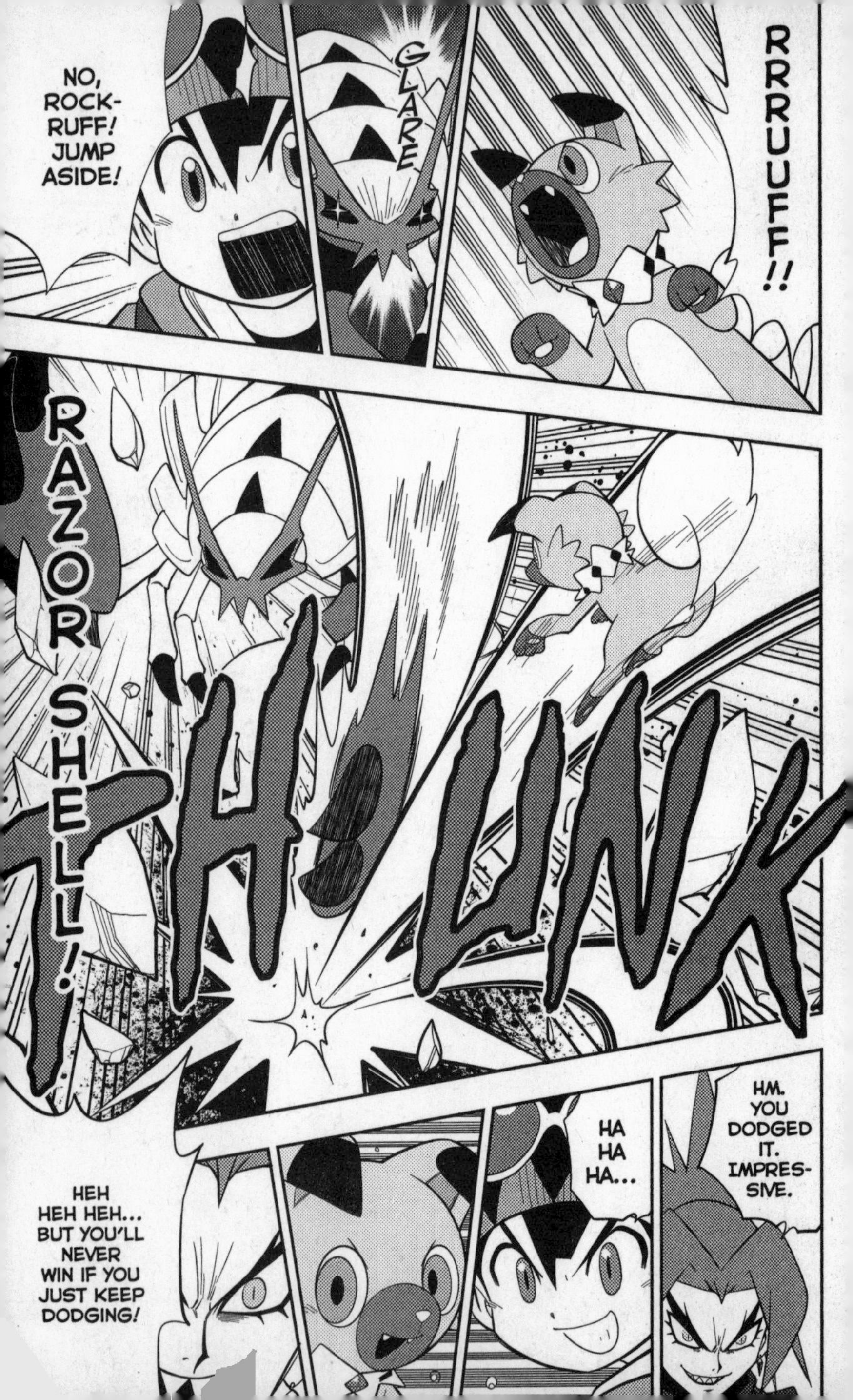
RRRUUFF!!
GLARE
NO, ROCK-RUFF! JUMP ASIDE!
RAZOR SHELL!
THUNK
HM. YOU DODGED IT. IMPRES-SIVE.
HA HA HA...
HEH HEH HEH... BUT YOU'LL NEVER WIN IF YOU JUST KEEP DODGING!

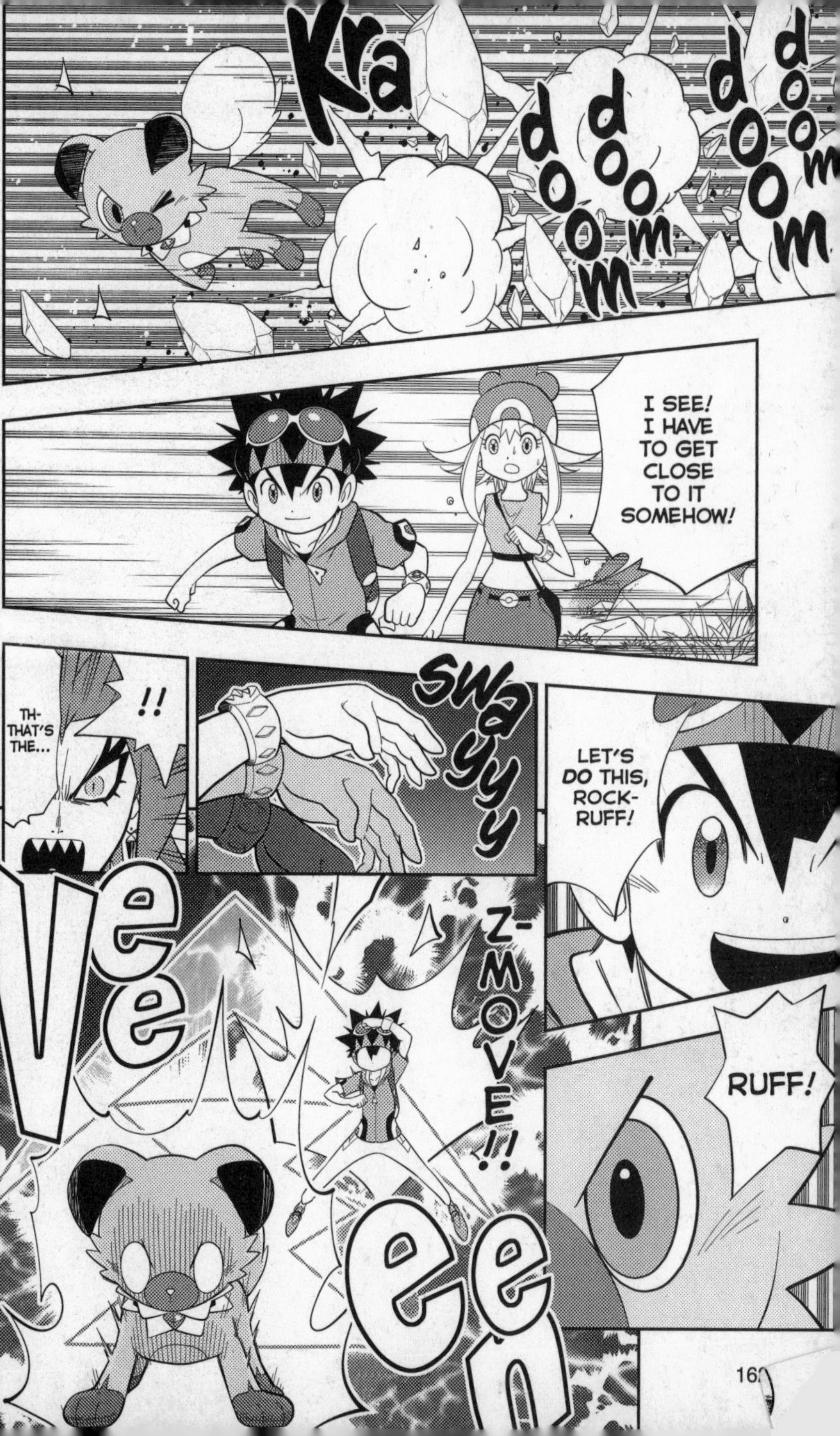
Kra
doom doom doom doom
I SEE! I HAVE TO GET CLOSE TO IT SOMEHOW!
LET'S DO THIS, ROCK-RUFF!
SWAYYY
!!
TH-THAT'S THE...
RUFF!
Z-MOVE!!!
Veeen

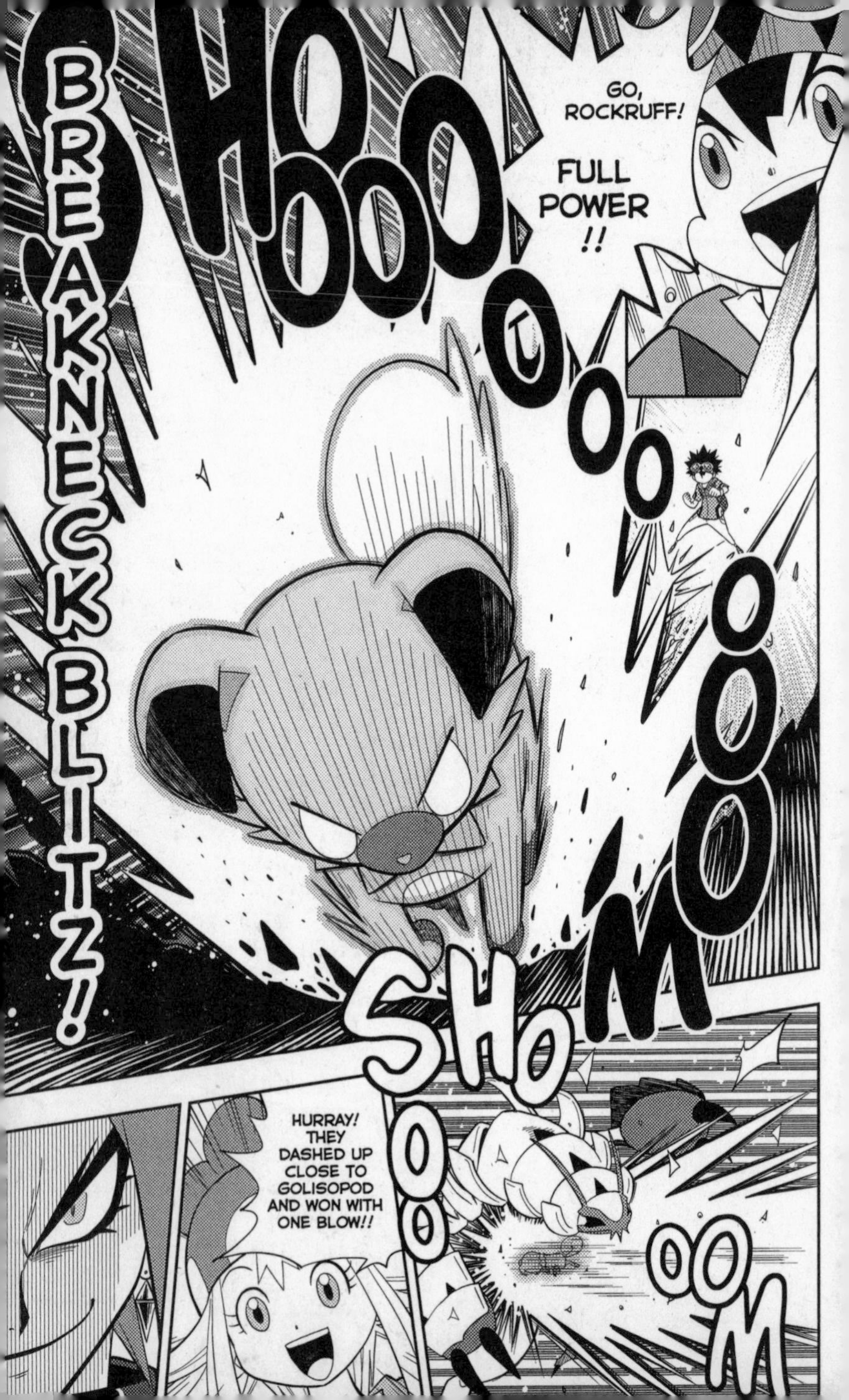
GO, ROCKRUFF!
FULL POWER!!
HOOOOOOOOOOOM
BREAKNECK BLITZ!
SHOOOOOM
HURRAY! THEY DASHED UP CLOSE TO GOLISOPOD AND WON WITH ONE BLOW!!
OOOM

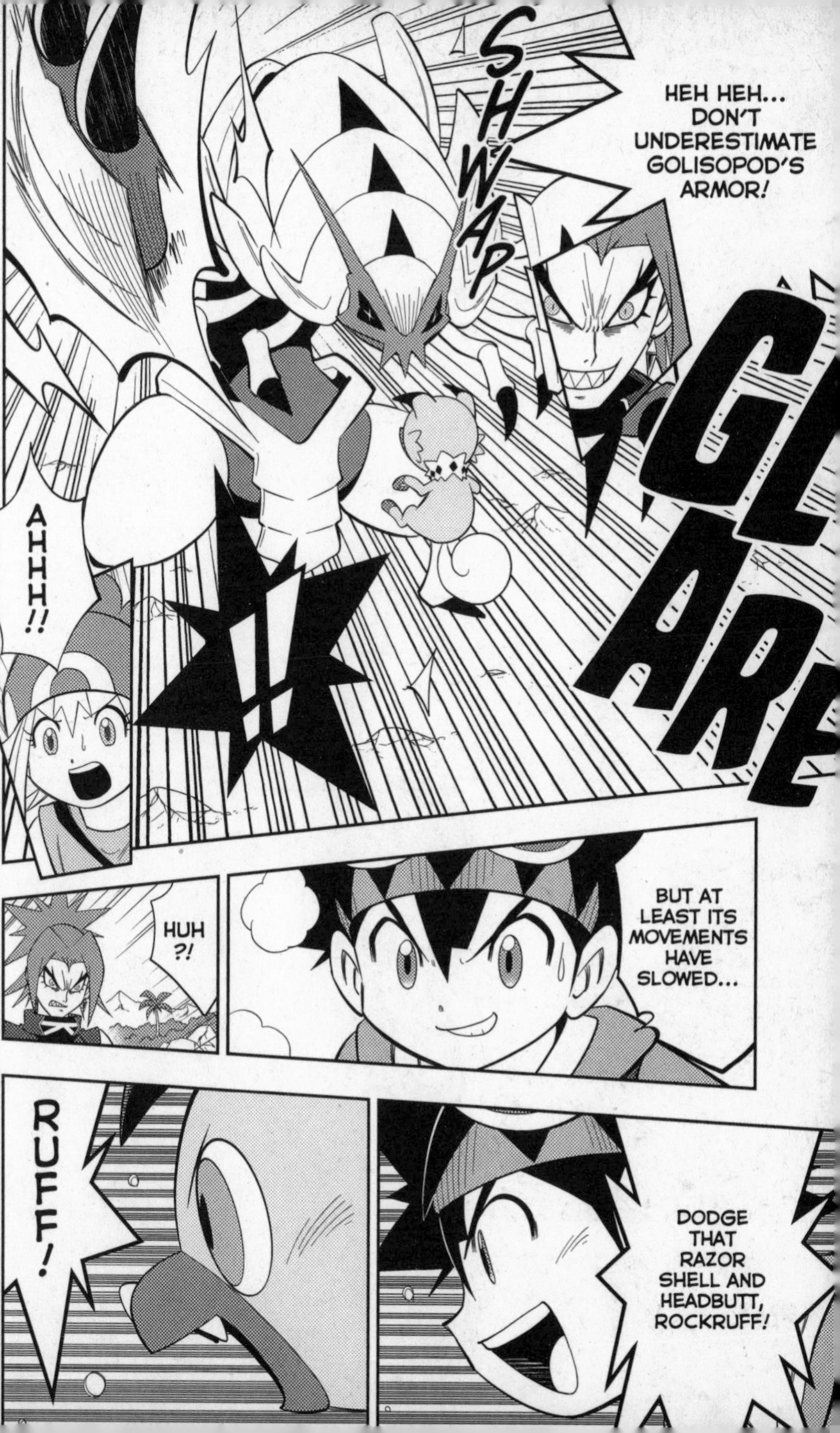
HEH HEH... DON'T UNDERESTIMATE GOLISOPOD'S ARMOR!
SHWAP
AHHH!!
!!
BUT AT LEAST ITS MOVEMENTS HAVE SLOWED...
HUH?!
DODGE THAT RAZOR SHELL AND HEADBUTT, ROCKRUFF!
RUFF!

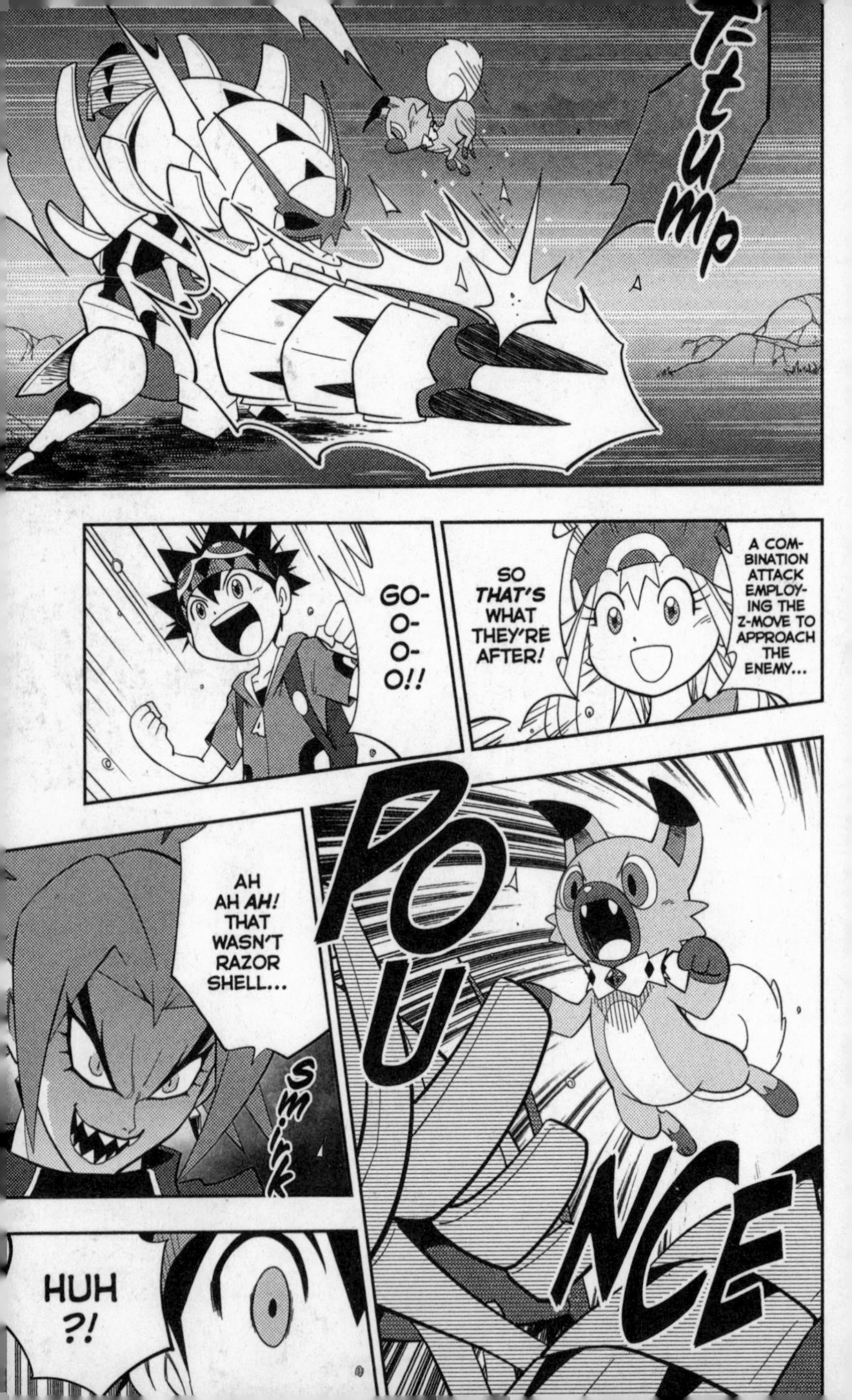
fttump
A COMBINATION ATTACK EMPLOYING THE Z-MOVE TO APPROACH THE ENEMY...
SO *THAT'S* WHAT THEY'RE AFTER!
GO-O-O-O!!
POUNCE
AH AH *AH*! THAT WASN'T RAZOR SHELL...
smirk
HUH ?!

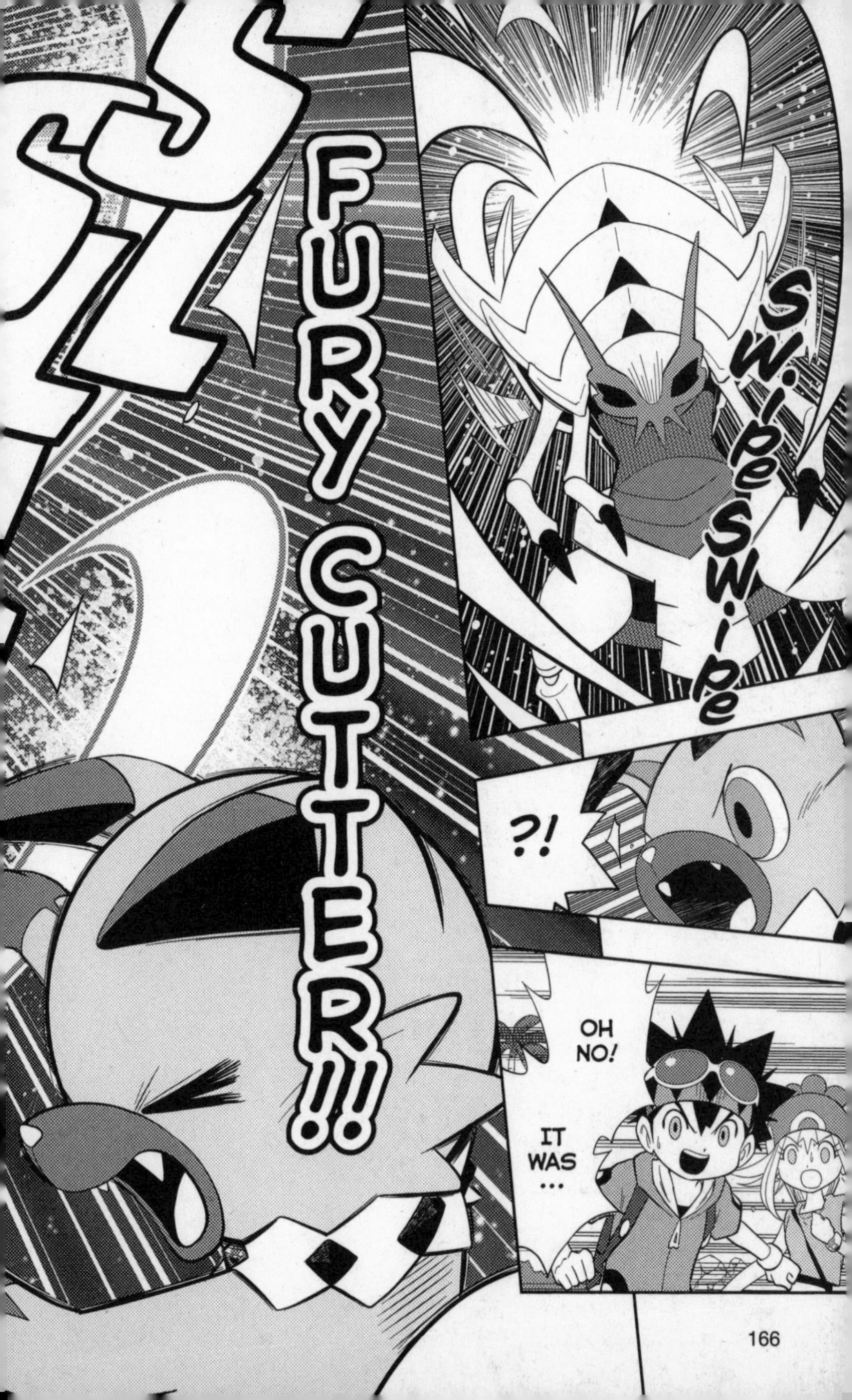
SWIPE SWIPE
?!
OH NO!
IT WAS...
FURY CUTTER!!

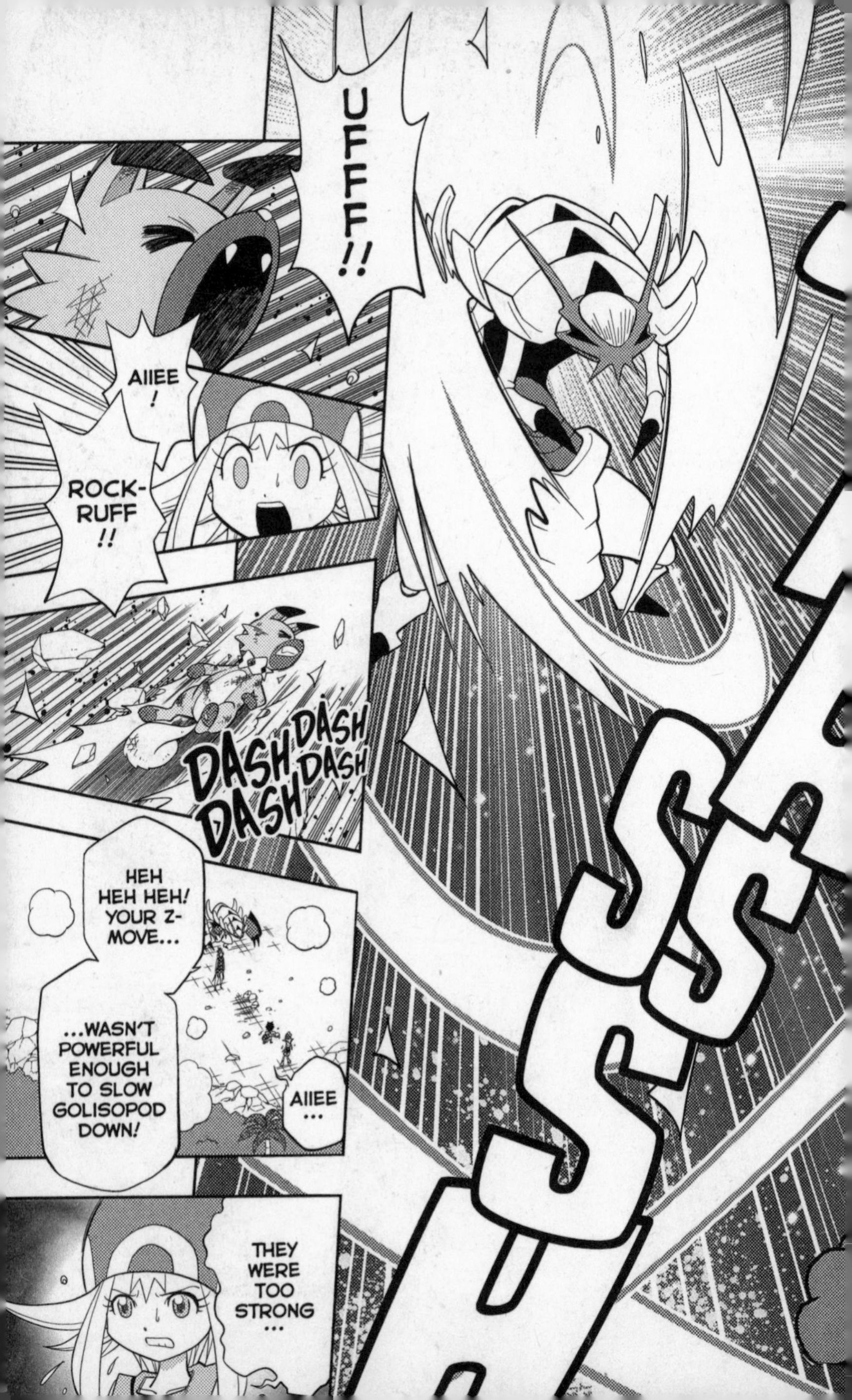
UFFF!!
AIIEE!
ROCK-RUFF!!
DASH DASH DASH DASH
HEH HEH HEH! YOUR Z-MOVE...
...WASN'T POWERFUL ENOUGH TO SLOW GOLISOPOD DOWN!
AIIEE...
THEY WERE TOO STRONG...

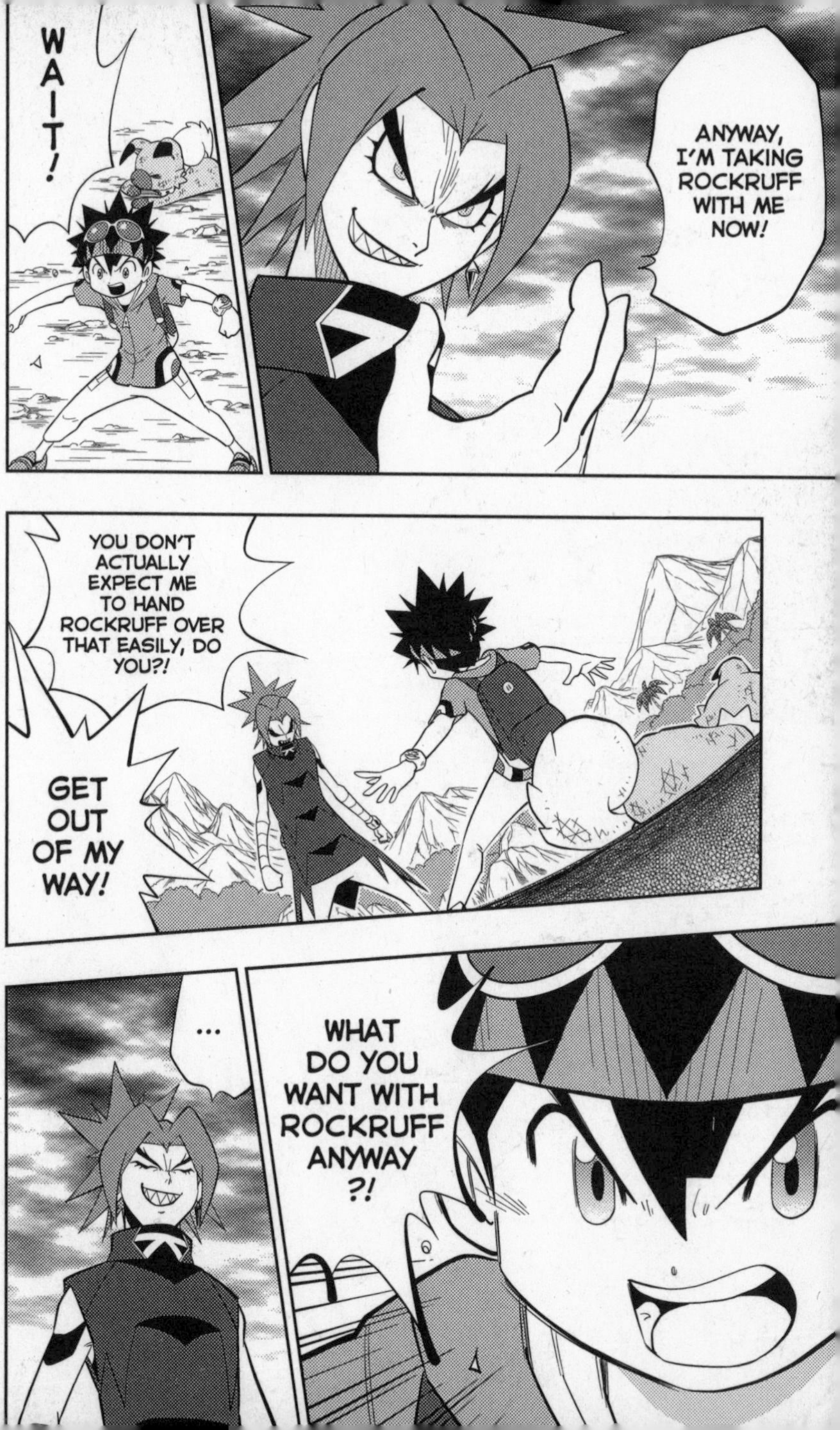
ANYWAY, I'M TAKING ROCKRUFF WITH ME NOW!
WAIT!
YOU DON'T ACTUALLY EXPECT ME TO HAND ROCKRUFF OVER THAT EASILY, DO YOU?!
GET OUT OF MY WAY!
WHAT DO YOU WANT WITH ROCKRUFF ANYWAY ?!
...

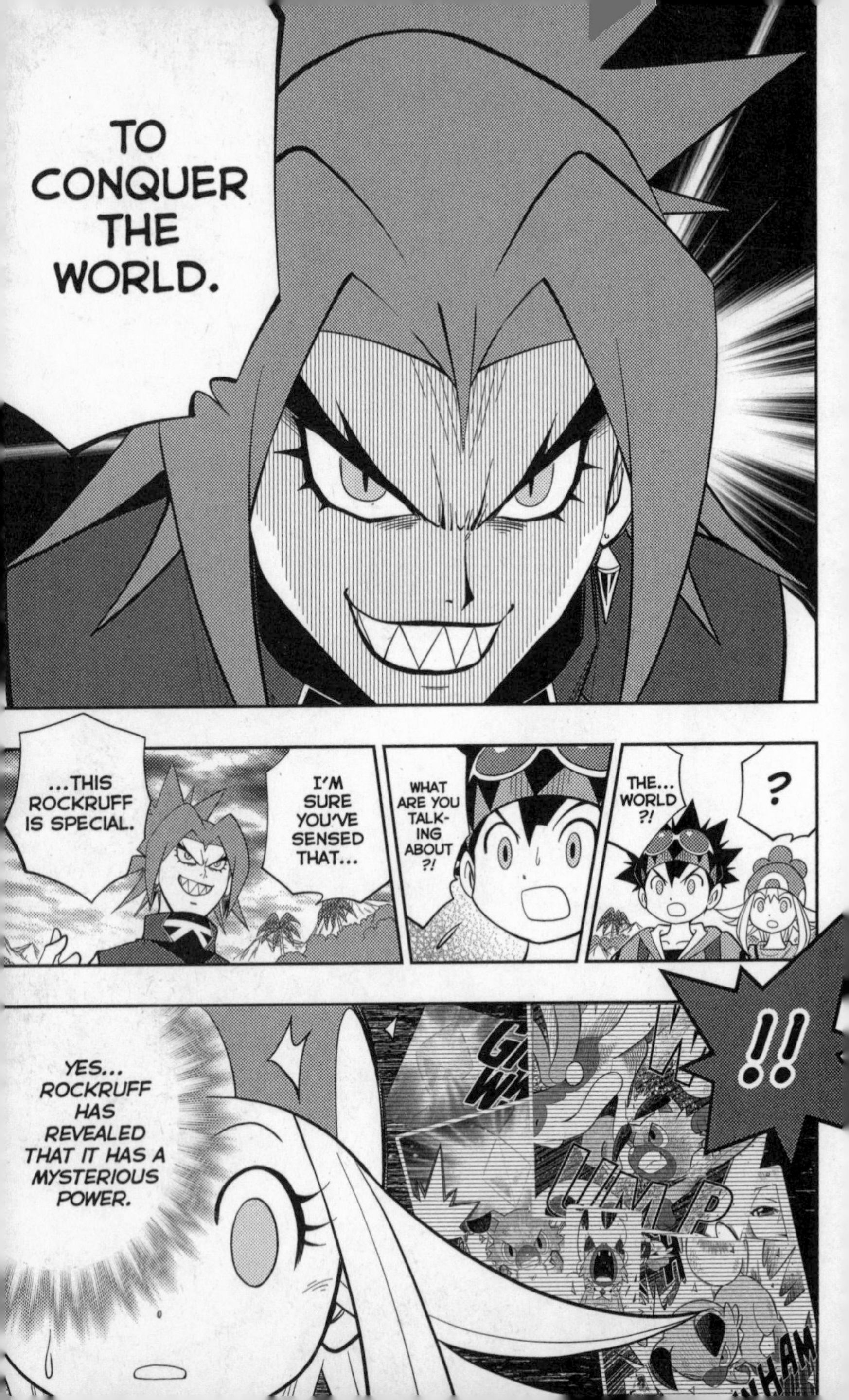
TO CONQUER THE WORLD.
?
THE... WORLD ?!
WHAT ARE YOU TALK-ING ABOUT ?!
I'M SURE YOU'VE SENSED THAT...
...THIS ROCKRUFF IS SPECIAL.
!!
YES... ROCKRUFF HAS REVEALED THAT IT HAS A MYSTERIOUS POWER.

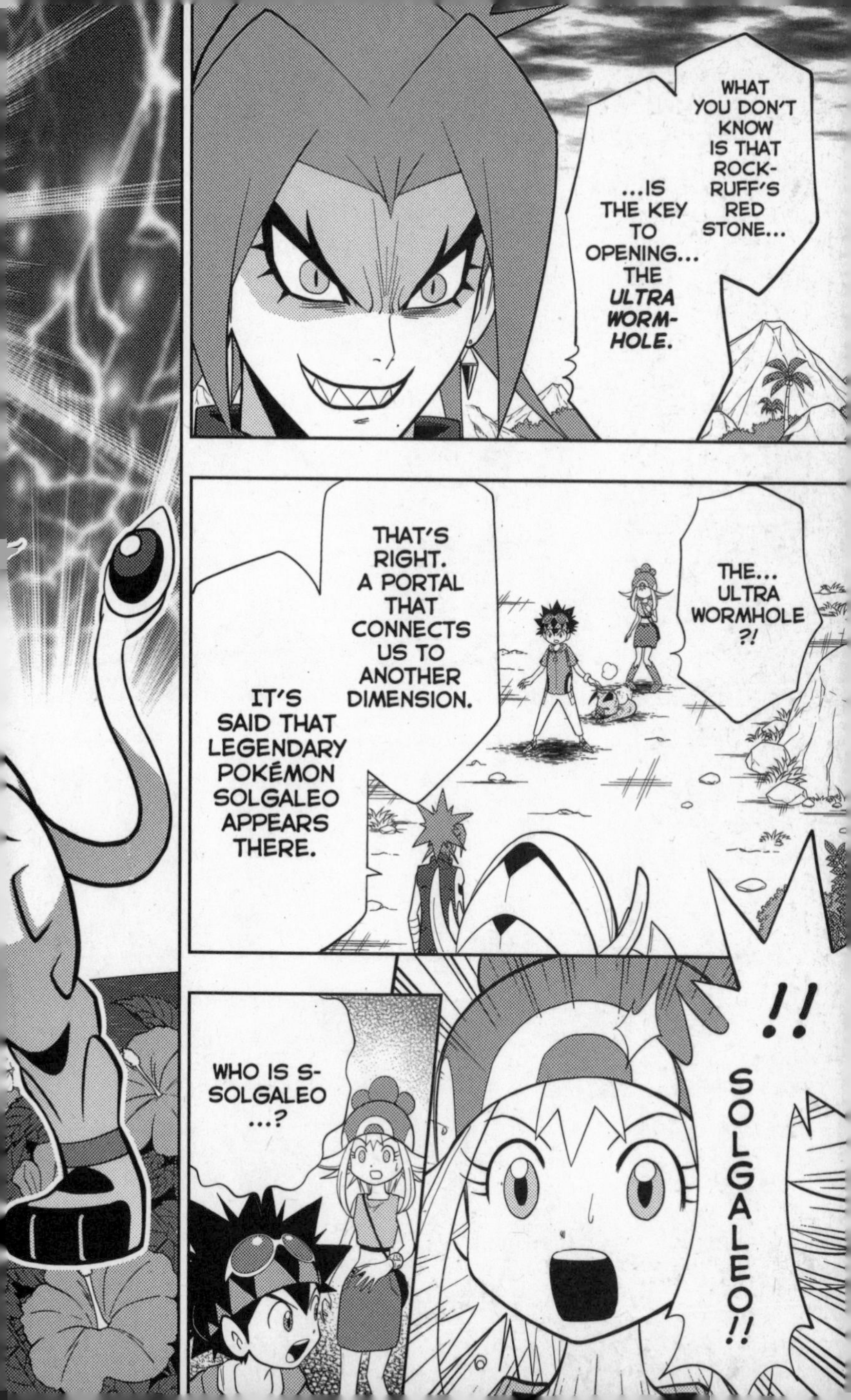
WHAT YOU DON'T KNOW IS THAT ROCK-RUFF'S RED STONE...
...IS THE KEY TO OPENING... THE *ULTRA WORM-HOLE.*
THE... ULTRA WORMHOLE ?!
THAT'S RIGHT. A PORTAL THAT CONNECTS US TO ANOTHER DIMENSION.
IT'S SAID THAT LEGENDARY POKÉMON SOLGALEO APPEARS THERE.
!!
SOLGALEO!!
WHO IS S-SOLGALEO ...?

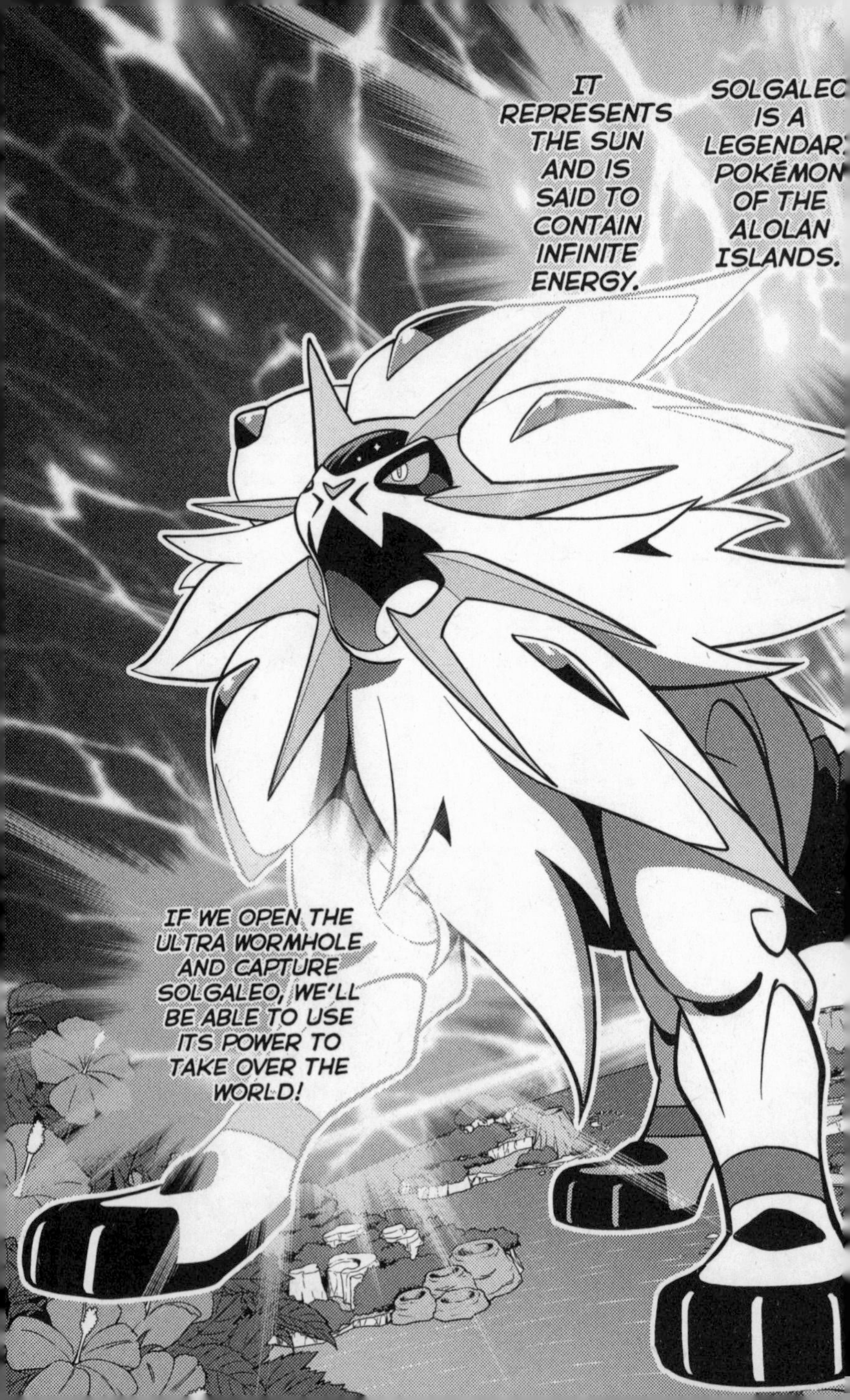
SOLGALEO IS A LEGENDARY POKÉMON OF THE ALOLAN ISLANDS.
IT REPRESENTS THE SUN AND IS SAID TO CONTAIN INFINITE ENERGY.
IF WE OPEN THE ULTRA WORMHOLE AND CAPTURE SOLGALEO, WE'LL BE ABLE TO USE ITS POWER TO TAKE OVER THE WORLD!

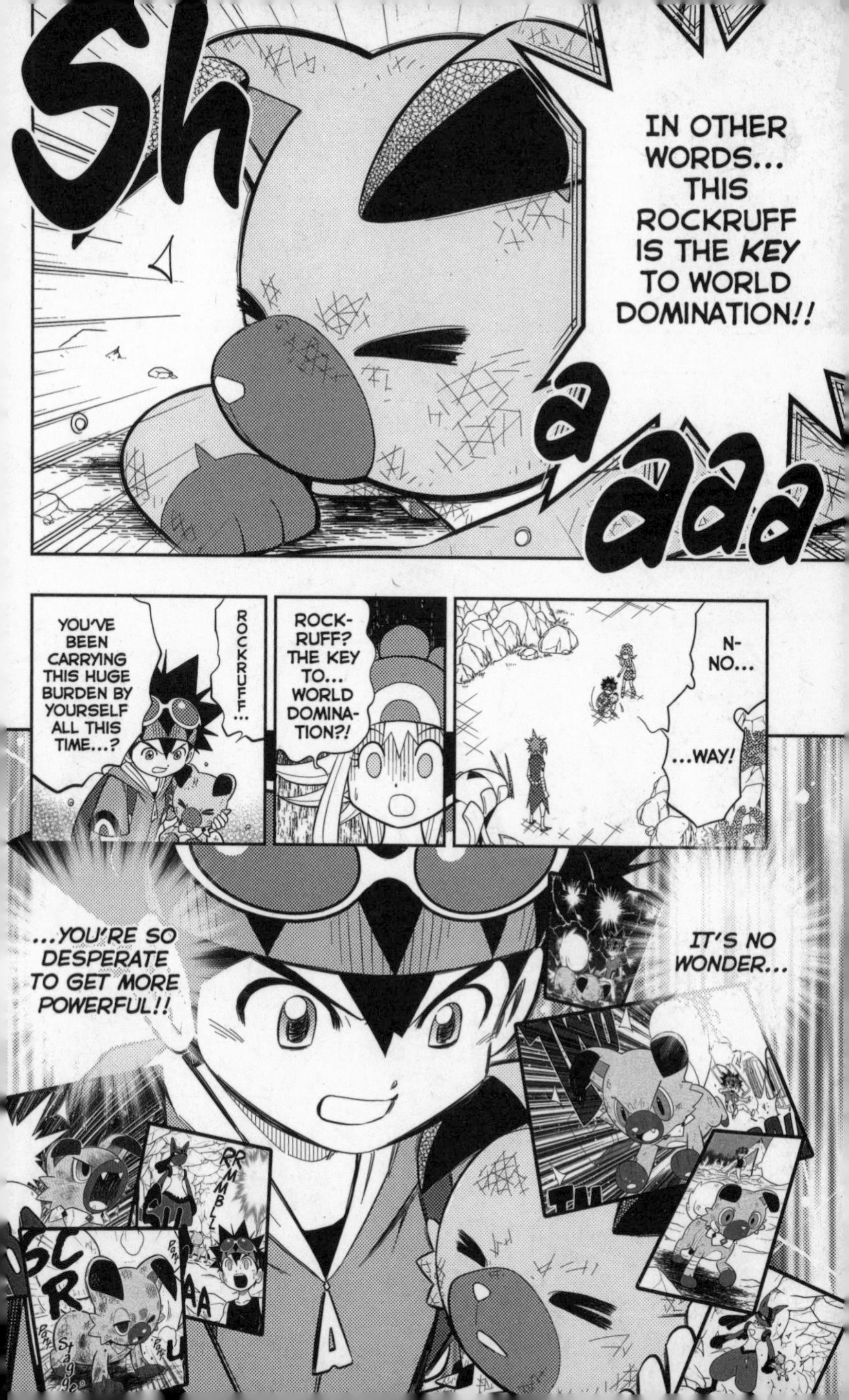

IN OTHER WORDS... THIS ROCKRUFF IS THE KEY TO WORLD DOMINATION!!
Shaaaaa
N-NO... ...WAY!
ROCK-RUFF? THE KEY TO... WORLD DOMINA-TION?!
ROCKRUFF...
YOU'VE BEEN CARRYING THIS HUGE BURDEN BY YOURSELF ALL THIS TIME...?
IT'S NO WONDER...
...YOU'RE SO DESPERATE TO GET MORE POWERFUL!!
RRMMBL
SCR

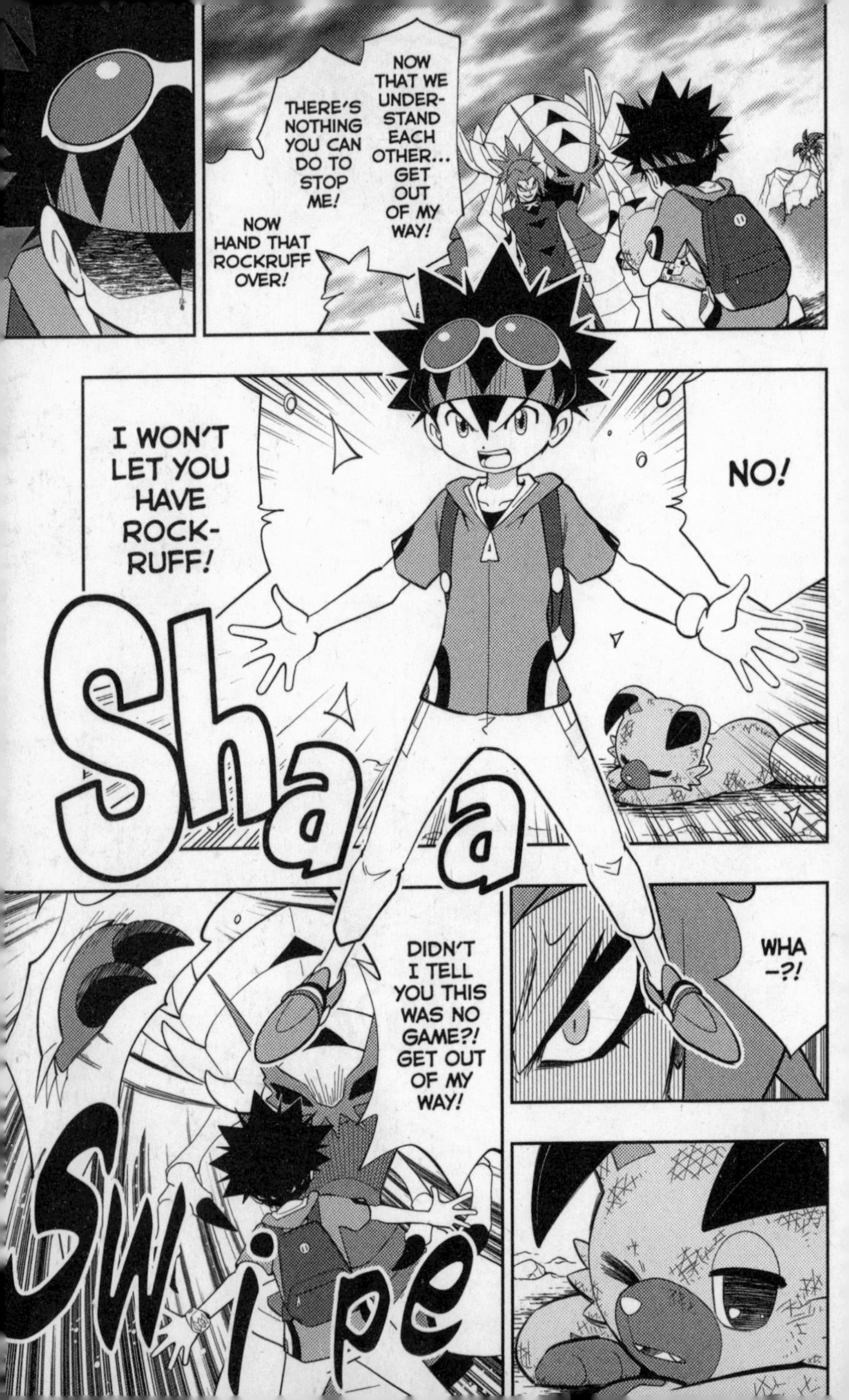
NOW THAT WE UNDER-STAND EACH OTHER... GET OUT OF MY WAY!
THERE'S NOTHING YOU CAN DO TO STOP ME!
NOW HAND THAT ROCKRUFF OVER!
NO!
I WON'T LET YOU HAVE ROCK-RUFF!
Shaa
WHA—?!
DIDN'T I TELL YOU THIS WAS NO GAME?! GET OUT OF MY WAY!
Swipe

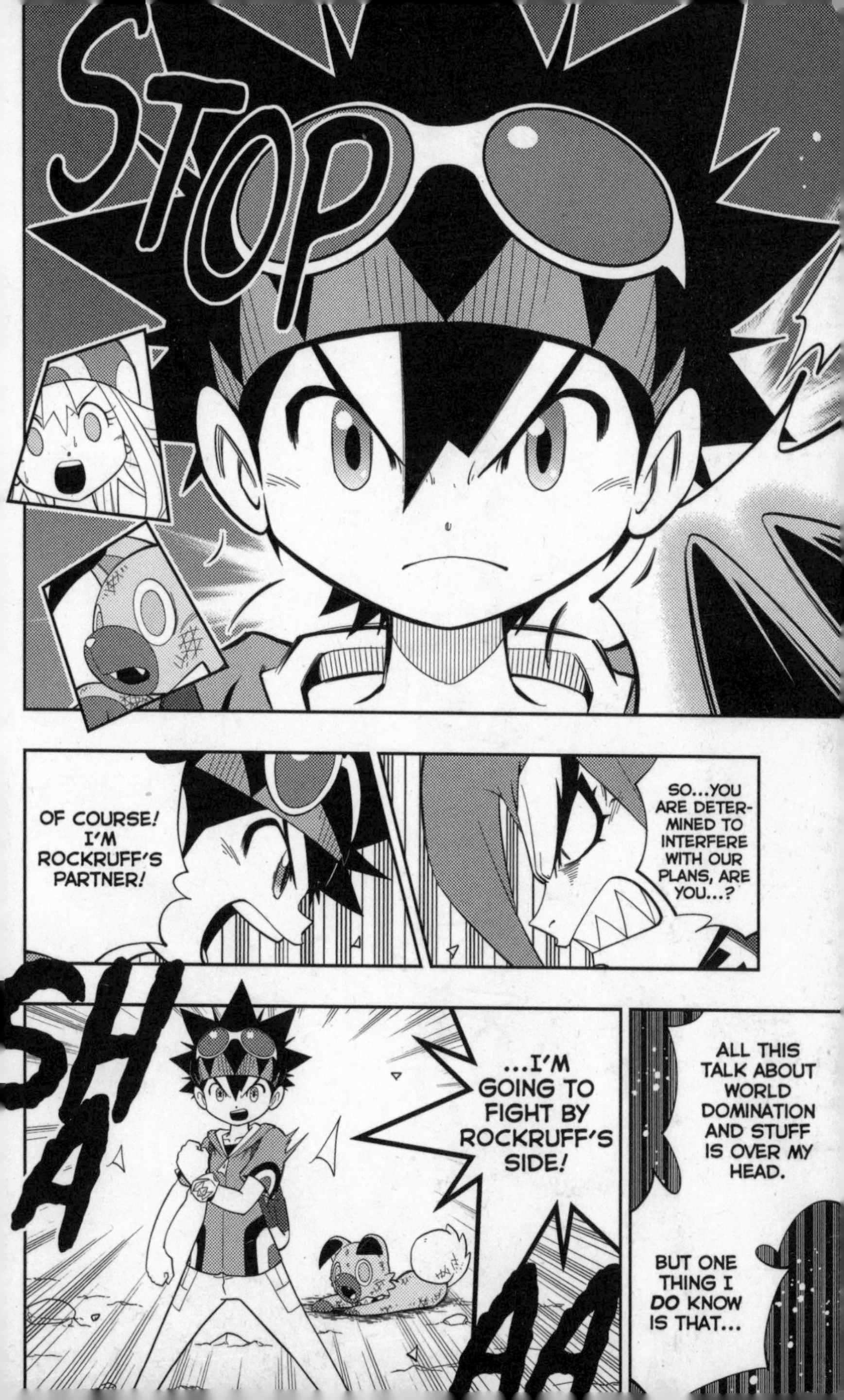
STOP
SO...YOU ARE DETERMINED TO INTERFERE WITH OUR PLANS, ARE YOU...?
OF COURSE! I'M ROCKRUFF'S PARTNER!
ALL THIS TALK ABOUT WORLD DOMINATION AND STUFF IS OVER MY HEAD.
BUT ONE THING I *DO* KNOW IS THAT...
...I'M GOING TO FIGHT BY ROCKRUFF'S SIDE!
SHAAA

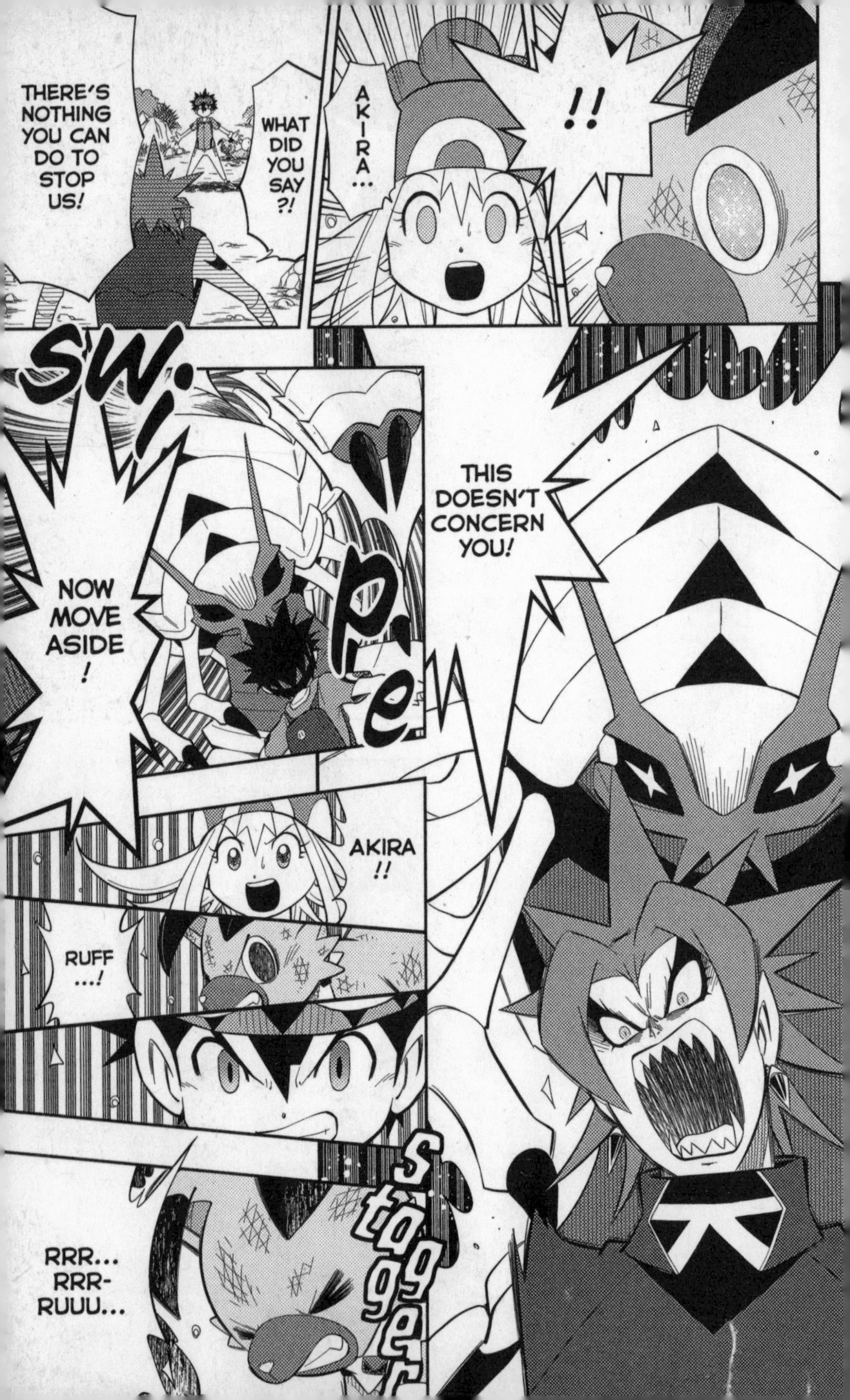
!!
AKIRA...
WHAT DID YOU SAY?!
THERE'S NOTHING YOU CAN DO TO STOP US!
THIS DOESN'T CONCERN YOU!
SWIPE
NOW MOVE ASIDE!
AKIRA!!
RUFF...!
stagger
RRR... RRR-RUUU...

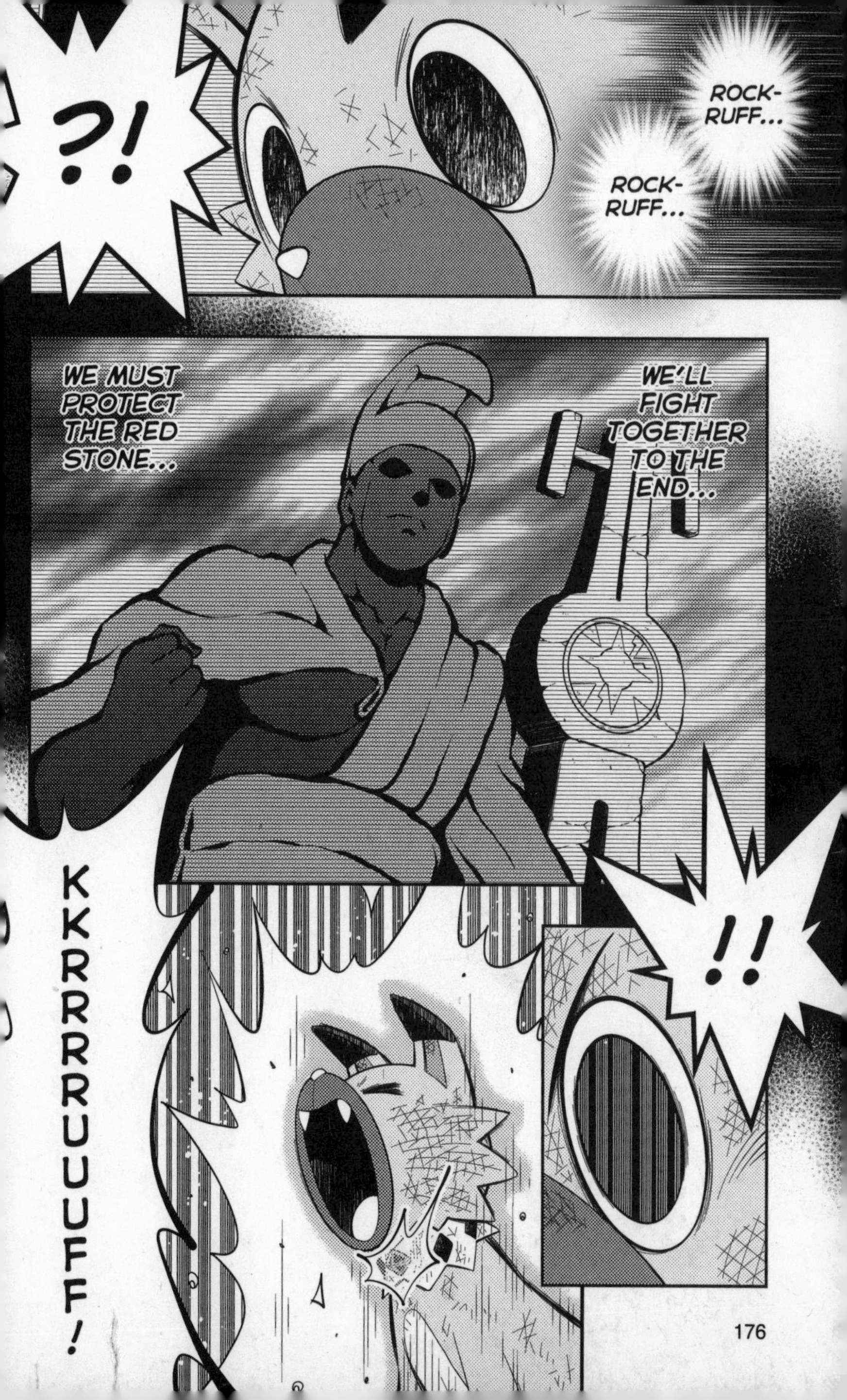
ROCK-RUFF...
ROCK-RUFF...
?!
WE'LL FIGHT TOGETHER TO THE END...
WE MUST PROTECT THE RED STONE...
!!
KKRRRRUUUFF!

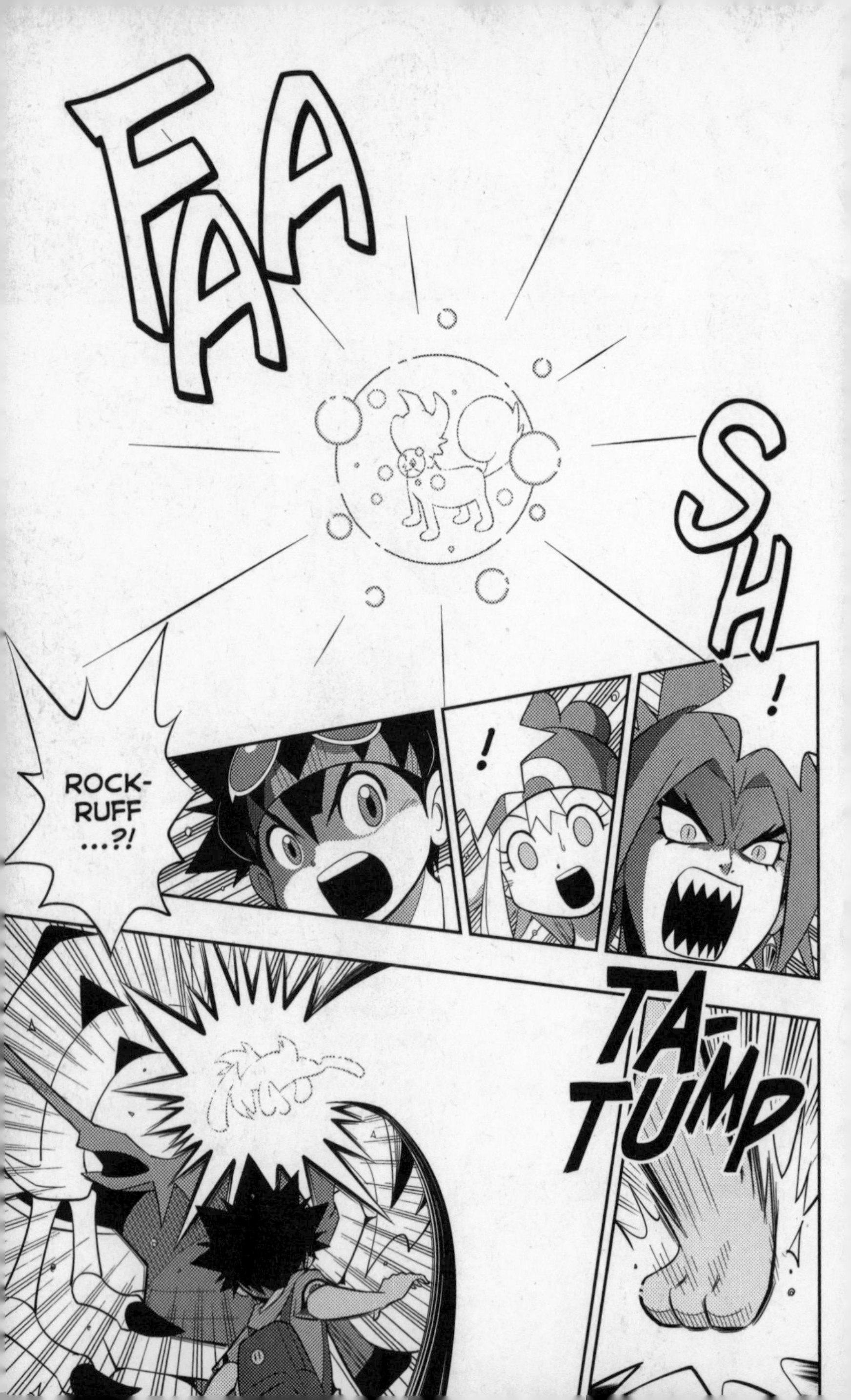
FAA
SH
!
!
ROCK-RUFF ...?!
TA-TUMP

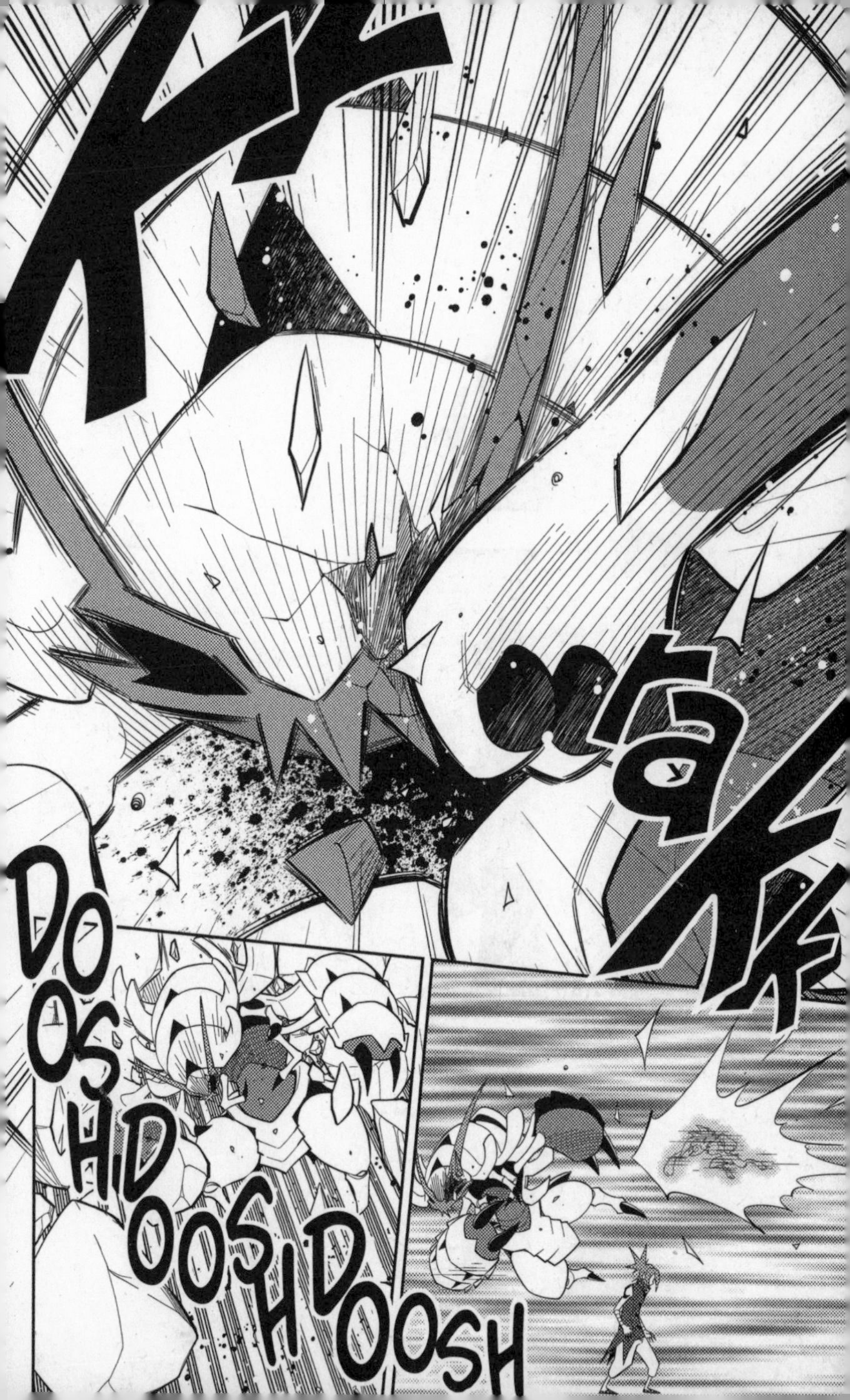
CRACK
DOOSH
DOOSH
DOOSH

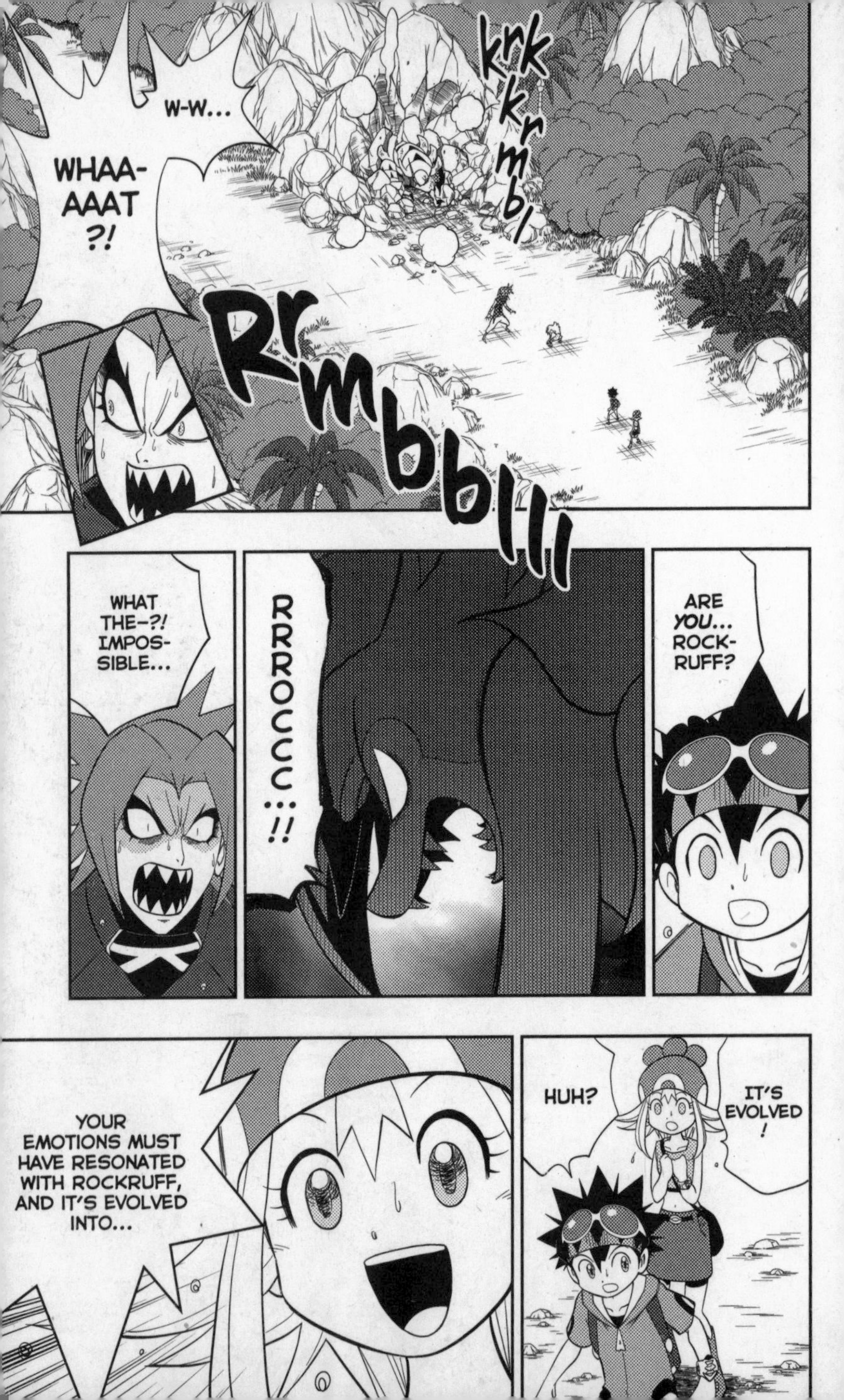
krk krmbl
W-W...
WHAAA-AAAT?!
Rrmbblll
ARE YOU... ROCK-RUFF?
RRROCCC...!!
WHAT THE-?! IMPOSSIBLE...
IT'S EVOLVED!
HUH?
YOUR EMOTIONS MUST HAVE RESONATED WITH ROCKRUFF, AND IT'S EVOLVED INTO...

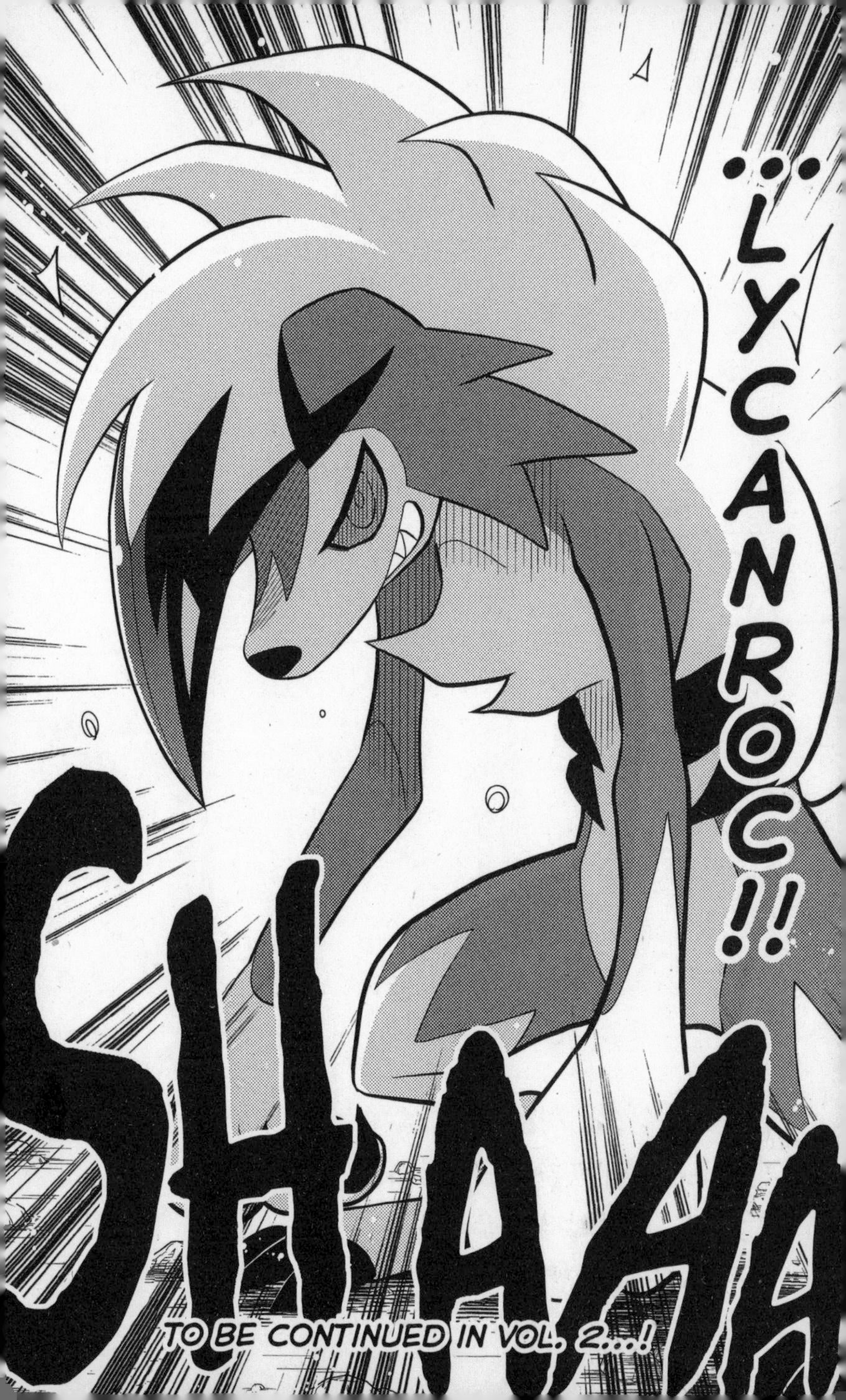
..LYCANROC!!
SHAAA
TO BE CONTINUED IN VOL. 2...!

Turn the page to read the preview that announced this story!

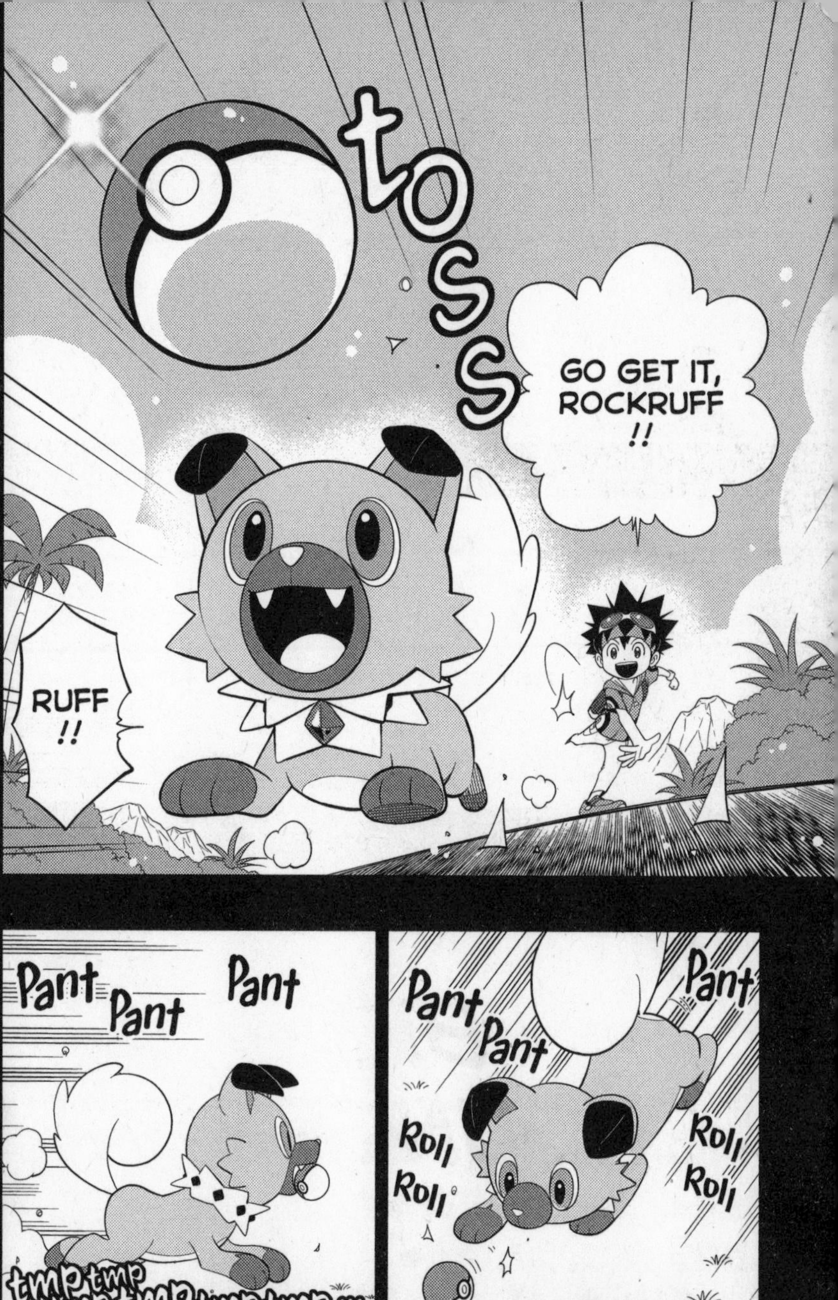
toss
GO GET IT, ROCKRUFF !!
RUFF !!
Pant Pant Pant
Roll Roll
Roll Roll
Pant Pant Pant
tmp tmp tmp tmp tmp tmp...

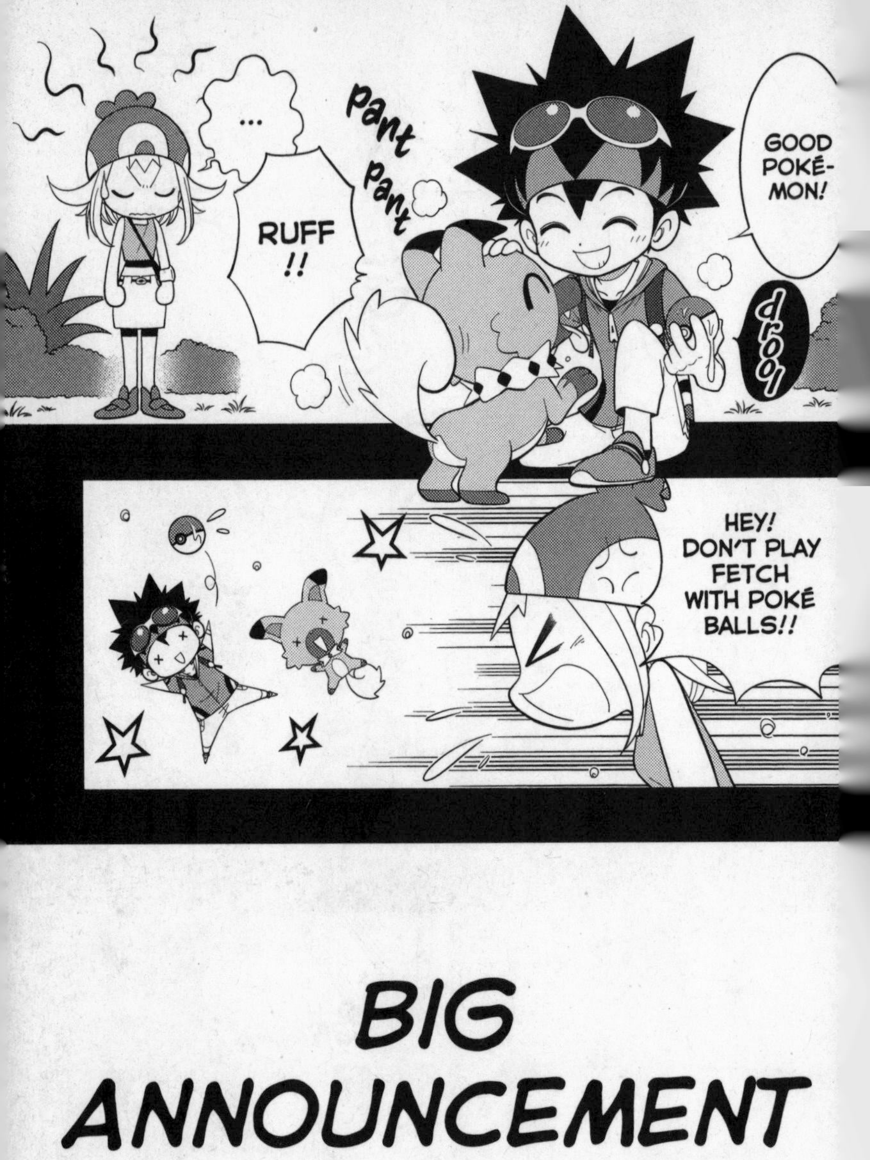
GOOD POKÉ-MON!
drool
pant pant
RUFF!!
...
HEY! DON'T PLAY FETCH WITH POKÉ BALLS!!

BIG ANNOUNCEMENT!

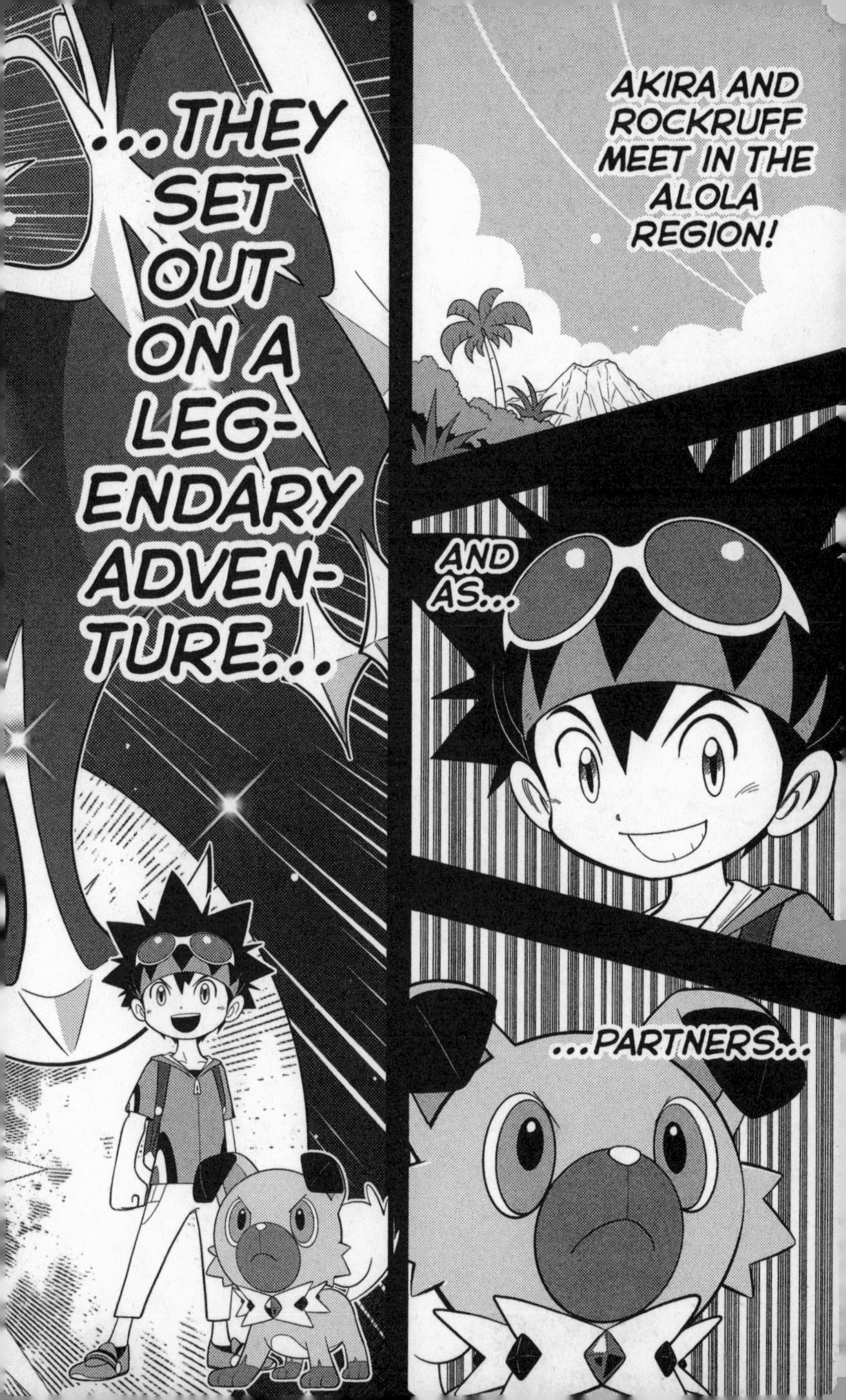
AKIRA AND ROCKRUFF MEET IN THE ALOLA REGION!
AND AS...
...PARTNERS...
...THEY SET OUT ON A LEGENDARY ADVENTURE...

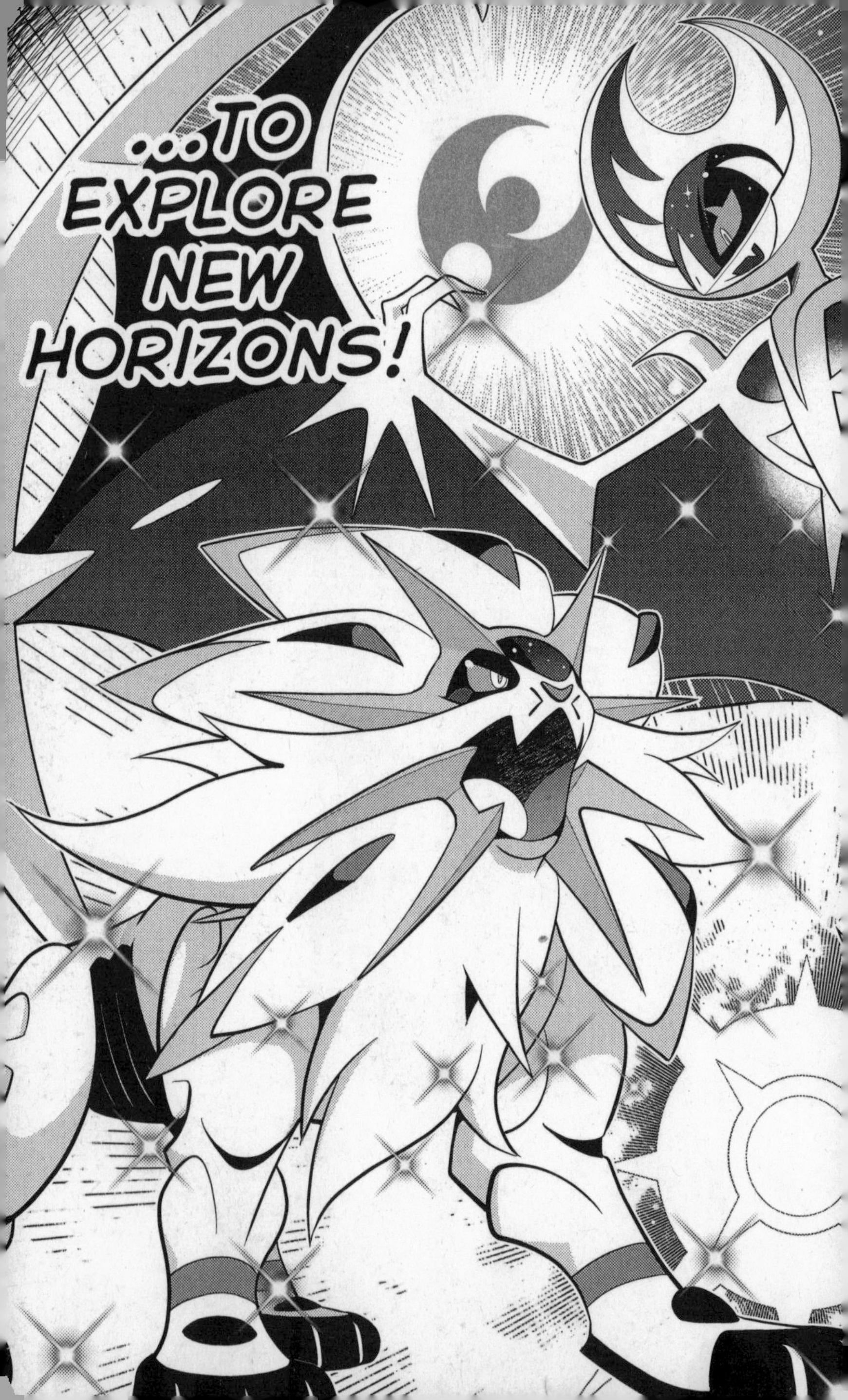
...TO EXPLORE NEW HORIZONS!

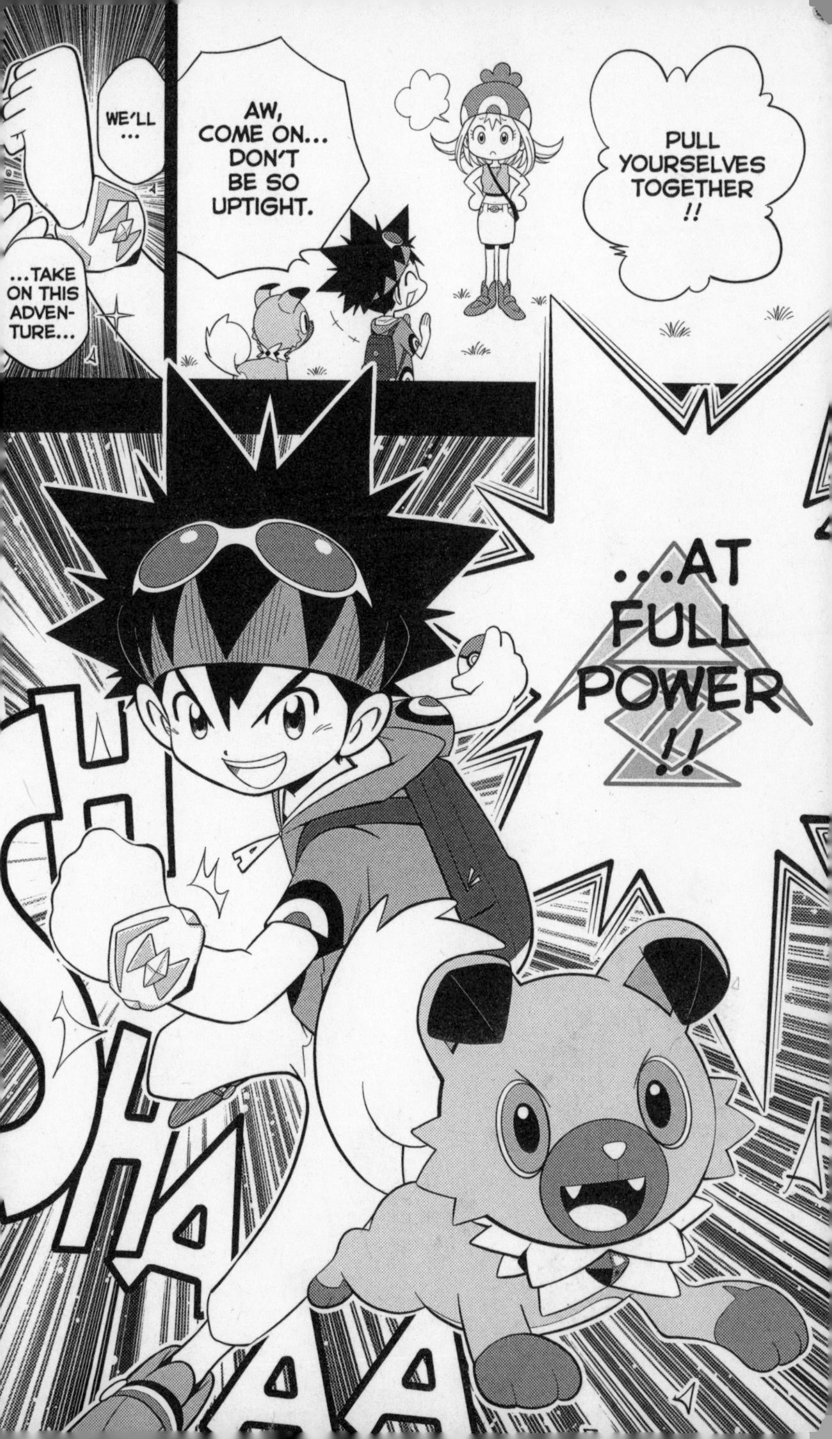
PULL YOURSELVES TOGETHER!!
AW, COME ON... DON'T BE SO UPTIGHT.
WE'LL...
...TAKE ON THIS ADVEN-TURE...
...AT FULL POWER!!

Tenya Yabuno

The horizon is where the sun and moon rise.
Now it's time for you to head for the horizon
to have a new adventure with your
favorite Pokémon!

Born in Tokyo, Tenya Yabuno made his manga
debut in 1990 with his one-shot manga story
Jonetsu no Clipper. He received the 34th Kodansha
Manga Award and 57th Shogakukan Manga Award
with *Inazuma Eleven* in *CoroCoro Comics*. His
other works are *Ultra Eleven* and
Botch Waiwai Misaki E.